Keri Arthur recently won the *Romantic Times* Career Achievement Award for Urban Fantasy and has been nominated in the Best Contemporary Paranormal category of the *Romantic Times* Reviewers' Choice Awards. She's a dessert and function cook by trade, and lives with her daughter in Melbourne, Australia.

Visit her website at www.keriarthur.com

Moon Sworn

KERI ARTHUR

piatkus

PIATKUS

First published in the US in 2010 by Bantam Dell
A division of Random House Inc., New York
First published in Great Britain as a paperback original in 2010 by Piatkus

A CIP catalogue record for this book
is available from the British Library.

ISBN 978-0-7499-4227-4

Printed in the UK by CPI Mackays, Chatham ME5 8TD

Papers used by Piatkus are natural, renewable and
recyclable products sourced from well-managed forests and certified
in accordance with the rules of the Forest Stewardship Council.

Mixed Sources
Product group from well-managed
forests and other controlled sources
www.fsc.org Cert no. SGS-COC-004081
© 1996 Forest Stewardship Council

Piatkus
An imprint of
Little, Brown Book Group
100 Victoria Embankment
London EC4Y 0DY

An Hachette UK Company
www.hachette.co.uk

www.piatkus.co.uk

Acknowledgments

I'd like to thank everyone at Bantam who helped produce this book—especially my editor, Anne; her assistant, David; all the line and copy editors who make sense of my Aussie English; and finally the cover artist, Juliana Kolesova.

I'd also like to add a special thanks to my lovely agent, Miriam, and to my mates—Robyn, Mel, Chris, Freya, and Carolyn. Thanks for listening to my whinges and for providing good advice when I need it.

Moon
Sworn

Chapter 1

*H*ow do you say good-bye to a friend?

How do you say sorry I wasn't there for you, that I wasn't strong enough, that I should have shot the bastard when I first had the chance? How can you say those things when he's no longer around to hear the words?

And how can you get over the grief when his body is little more than memories on the wind and his soul long gone from this life?

You couldn't. *I* couldn't.

So I just stood there on the edge of the precipice, surrounded by the dark beauty of the Grampian Mountains and buffeted by a wind that seemed to echo with wild hoofbeats.

These weren't the mountains Kade had been born in, but they were the ones that he had chosen in death.

His ashes had been scattered here three months ago, the funeral attended by his mares, his children, and his coworkers from the Directorate.

By everyone except me.

I'd been caught in a battle of my own, hovering between this world and the next, torn between the desire to die and the reluctance to simply give up.

In the end I'd chosen life over death, but it wasn't my twin who'd pulled me from the brink, nor was it the vampire who held my heart. My savior had come in the form of a blond-haired little girl with bright violet eyes that saw too much.

But there'd been no savior for Kade.

There should have been, but I'd failed him.

I closed my eyes and flung my arms wide, letting the wind rock my body. Part of me was tempted to just let go, to fall forward into the chasm that stretched out below me. To smash my body on the rocks and let my spirit roam across this vast wildness. To be free, as my friend was now free.

Because with Kade dead, my soul mate—Kye— dead, and most of my dreams little more than ashes, death still sometimes seemed like a mighty enticing option.

But there were people in my life who deserved better. And Kade would certainly want more from me than that.

Tears tracked down my cheeks. I breathed deep, drawing in the freshness of the early-morning air, tasting the flavors within it and half searching for the one scent that would never, ever, be there again.

He was gone forever. I could accept that. But I could never escape the guilt of it.

I bent and picked up the bottle of wine I'd brought with me. It was a Brown Brothers Riesling—one of his favorites, not mine. After popping the cork, I took a drink, then raised the bottle to the dawn skies, the tears pouring down my face.

"May I one day earn your forgiveness, my friend." My voice was barely audible, but it seemed to echo across the mountains. "And may you find peace, happiness, and many willing mares in the fertile meadows of afterlife."

With that, I poured out the wine, letting it stream away on the wind. When the bottle was empty, I tossed it over the edge, watching it fall until the shadows claimed it. I never heard it smash against the rocks. Perhaps the ghostly fingers of a bay-colored man caught it long before it could.

I took another deep, shuddering breath, then swiped at the tears on my cheeks and added, "Good-bye, Kade. I hope we can meet again on the other side. And I hope I'm a smarter friend then than I am now."

The sun chose that moment to break over the top of the mountains, streaming golden fingers of light across the shadows and almost instantly warming the chill from the air and my skin.

If it was a sign from Kade, then it was appreciated.

I dried the last of my tears, blew a kiss to the sunrise, then turned and walked back down the path to my car. My phone—which I'd left sitting on the front seat along with my handbag—was flashing. Which meant there'd been a call for me while I was up at the cliff edge.

I dropped into the driver's seat and reached for the phone, then hesitated. I knew without looking that the call would be from Jack. He excelled at that sort of timing—always catching me when I least expected or wanted it. Besides, everyone else in my life knew that I was up here saying my good-byes, and they wouldn't have interrupted me for anything less than a disaster. And if it *was* a disaster, there were better ways to contact me than using a phone. Hell, Quinn could have just found me telepathically. The link between us had grown a lot stronger since Kye's death.

Kye.

The thought of him had my stomach twisting. I closed my eyes and pushed away the guilt and the anger and the pain that always rose at the mere flicker of memory. I'd killed my soul mate. Willingly. And now I had to live with the consequences.

Even if part of me still just wanted to curl up and die.

I glanced down at the phone again. It was tempting to ignore Jack's call, but I couldn't. I'd chosen to live—and whether I liked it or not, the Directorate was a part of my life.

I flicked a switch on the phone and brought up the call data. It was definitely Jack. I'd told him two days ago that I was ready to go back to work, but now that the time was here, I wasn't so sure.

Truth be told, I didn't *want* to pick up a gun again. I didn't want to have to shoot anybody again—especially after what had happened with Kade and Kye. I feared the hesitation that had led to Kade's death. But most of all, I feared that I *wouldn't* hesitate. That I'd become the unthinking killer that Jack wanted me to be, simply because of the fear that I'd lose someone else if I didn't.

I'd spent a long time fighting Jack's desire to make me a guardian. When I'd finally become one, the fight had twisted, becoming a battle against his plans and my own nature. I didn't *want* to be the killer my brother was. As much as I loved him—as much as I didn't want to live without him—Rhoan's occasional ruthlessness scared the hell out of me.

Kade had once said that everyone hesitates, but he'd been wrong. My brother never did, and neither did the other guardians. Just me.

And that hesitation had cost me Kade.

I felt trapped, caged between the boulders of fate, my own nature, and fear. As much as I wanted to walk away from the Directorate, I couldn't. The drug given to me so long ago was still running rampant in my bloodstream, and the changes to my body were continuing. The scientists monitoring me were *almost* positive that, unlike the other recipients of the drug, I wouldn't gain the ability to take on multiple shifter forms—meaning I was stuck with the alternate shape of a goddamn seagull—but my clairvoyant skills were still growing, still changing. No one was sure where it would stop, and until it all settled down, I was stuck with the choice of the Directorate or the military.

And it was always better to stick to the devil you knew.

I drew in a shuddering breath, then hit the phone's call button. Jack answered second ring.

"You wanted me, boss?"

"Yeah, I did." He hesitated. "Are you okay? You still sound tired."

"I'm fine." But I rubbed a hand across my eyes and half wished that I'd lied. He'd given me the perfect out, and we both knew it. But I really *did* have to get on with my life—even the bits of it I was no longer so sure about. "What's happening?"

"We've got what looks like a ritual killing. If you're feeling up to it, I'd like you to go over there and see if there's a soul hanging about."

"Sure. Send me the address and I'll head straight there." I hesitated. "It'll take me at least an hour, though. I'm up at the Grampians."

He didn't ask me why. He knew it was Kade's final resting place, and he also knew I'd missed his funeral. "That's fine. Cole and his men are only just heading to the scene themselves. I'll send the report and the address to your onboard."

"Thanks, boss."

He grunted and hung up. I threw the phone on the passenger seat, then started the car and swung out of the parking lot. The computer beeped as I turned onto the Grampians Road and headed for the Western Highway. I pressed the screen, getting the address and transferring it across to the nav computer. I didn't bother looking at the report—I preferred getting my impressions from Cole and my own observations. I'd read it later, once I'd seen the crime scene for myself.

The body had been discovered in Melton, a suburb on the very outskirts of Melbourne. It had a reputation for being a rough area, but as I drove through the streets heading for Navan Park, it looked no worse than any other suburb. But maybe this section of Melton was the so-called better area. Every suburb had them.

I drove along Coburns Road until I saw the Directorate van parked at the side. I stopped behind it but didn't immediately get out.

Because my hands were shaking.

I can do this, I thought. I just didn't want to.

There was a difference. A *big* difference.

So why did it still feel like fear?

I took a deep, calming breath, shoved aside the insane desire to drive away, and opened the door, climbing out. Dawn had given way to a crisp, cool morning, but the sky was almost cloudless and the promise of warmth rode the air, caressing my skin.

The scent of blood was also rich in the air.

I locked the car and made my way through the park gates, following the path up the slight incline until the blood smell pulled me onto the grass and toward the group of gum trees that dominated the skyline. The grass crunched under my feet, evidence of how little rain we'd had of late, and the sound carried across the silence.

A figure appeared on the hilltop above and gave me a brief wave before disappearing again. The sharp glint of silvery hair told me it was Cole, and while I might not have missed coming to bloody crime scenes, I *had* missed Cole and his men.

I crested the hill and paused to survey the scene below. The body lay to the left of the trees, half ringed by scrubby-looking bushes that would have offered the killer little in the way of protection. Several yards beyond the trees was a lake in which ducks and toy boats floated. Kids ran around the edges of the water, oblivious to the cops stationed nearby.

I watched one little girl laugh as she chased a red ball that was rolling along the ground. With her blond pigtails and pale skin, she reminded me of Risa, Dia's daughter and the little girl who'd saved my life. She'd begun calling me Aunt Riley, and in my worst nightmares, I sometimes thought that this was as close as I was ever going to get to having a child of my own.

Because of my own inability to carry children, and because my soul mate was dead. The picket fence dream was dead. At least, the version of it that had carried me through childhood was.

I blinked back the sting of tears and forced my gaze back to the body, trying to concentrate on the business of catching a killer. The victim was naked, his flesh sallow and sagging—the body of an old man, not a young one. There were no obvious wounds from what I could see, but Cole was kneeling beside him and obstructing my view of his upper body.

I drew in the air, tasting death and blood and something else I couldn't quite name. I frowned as I moved down the hill. Strong emotions could stain the air, and hate was one of one of the strongest, but this didn't quite taste like that. It was edgier, darker. Harsher.

If I had to guess, I'd say it tasted more like vengeance than hate. And the killer had to be feeling it in spades for it to linger in the air like this.

Cole glanced up as I approached, a smile crinkling the corners of his bright blue eyes. "Nice to see you back on the job, Riley."

"I'd love to say it's nice to be back," I said, shoving my hands into my pockets so he couldn't see them shaking, "but that would be a lie." I pointed with my chin to the body. "What have we got?"

My gaze went past him as I asked the question, and the method of our victim's demise became starkly obvious. Someone had strangled him—with barbed wire. His neck was a raw and bloody mess, the wire so deeply embedded that in places it simply couldn't be seen. That took strength—more than most humans had.

But why would a nonhuman want to strangle a human with wire? Hell, most nonhumans could achieve the same result one-handed.

Unless, of course, our killer didn't only want death, but pain as well.

Which would certainly account for the bitter taste of vengeance in the air.

I knew about vengeance. Kye's death had been an act of vengeance as much as it had been a requirement of my job. He'd been a killer—a ruthless, cold-blooded murderer. And yet he'd made my wolf soul sing, and she still ached for him.

Would probably always ache for him.

Cole offered me a box of gloves, forcing me to take a hand out of my pocket. If he noticed the shaking, he didn't say anything.

"As you can see, he's been strangled," he said. "He's probably been dead for about five hours, and there's no sign of a struggle."

"Meaning he was probably drugged beforehand." I couldn't imagine anyone *not* fighting such a death. Which *didn't* mean he wasn't conscious or feeling every brutal bit of it.

"Or," Cole said grimly, "that he was killed somewhere else and dumped here. There's very little blood on the ground."

I snapped on a pair of gloves then walked around to the opposite side of the body, squatting near the victim's neck. The bits of wire that weren't embedded or bloody shone brightly in the growing sunshine. "The wire looks new."

"Yeah. And we've got very little chance of tracing it back to the source."

Not when barbed wire was still a staple fencing material for most farms—and Melton, despite being a suburb of Melbourne, was surrounded by farms of one kind or another. I touched the victim's chin lightly, turning his head away from me so that I could see the back of his neck. The wire appeared just as deeply embedded at the back as it was the front. I wouldn't mind betting it had severed vertebrae.

"Who discovered the body?"

"Anonymous phone call." I raised my eyebrows at that, and he grinned. "Line trace said the call came from 12 Valley View Road. That's the white brick house above the lake."

I twisted around and looked at the row of neatly kept houses that lined the park. The curtains twitched in 12 Valley View, indicating we were being watched.

"Have the police interviewed the owner?"

"The police weren't called first. We were."

I frowned. "That's a little unusual, isn't it?"

He reached forward and plucked a bloody thread from one of the wires, putting it in a plastic bag before saying "Not when you're reporting that the killer is a red-faced demon."

That raised my eyebrows. "Really?"

"Seriously." His gaze met mine. "My normal response would be to suggest the witness's alcohol intake might have been a little high, but Dusty found cloven hoofprints. Which supports the whole demon thing."

A laugh escaped, then I realized he was being serious. "But demons don't have cloven hooves."

"That we know of. But there's no saying there isn't a branch out there that has."

"I guess that's true." I shifted, my gaze sweeping the park. Neither Dusty nor Dobbs was in sight, and the morning was filled with the sound of children's laughter. It was a happy noise that seemed so out of place given the brutality that lay at our feet—although we'd certainly seen far worse over the years. And done worse. Like shooting a soul mate. I bit my lip for a moment, using one sort of pain to control another, then added, "Anything else worth knowing?"

"Nothing obvious at the moment. I'll send you the report as soon as it's done."

"Thanks." I rose and pulled off the gloves.

And that's when I felt it—the rush of power, the chill of death. There was a soul here.

I scanned the park again, trying to pinpoint the soul's location. There was nothing obvious—no wispy, insubstantial form, no obvious focal point for the energy that was washing across my skin.

"Have we got an ID on the victim yet?" I asked softly.

I felt rather than saw the sharpening of interest from Cole. "His name is Wayne Johnson. He was released from prison a week ago."

"His crime?"

"Murder. I requested the trial records, but they haven't been sent through yet. He served twenty-five years."

Then it had to be a *nasty* crime, because the average sentence wasn't usually that long—unless you were a nonhuman, and then the sentence was death.

"I'm betting he strangled his victim." It would certainly explain the method of his demise as well as the bitter taste in the air.

"I agree," Cole said, "and it would certainly be worth finding out who he killed, and where the victim's relatives were during the early hours of the morning. You never know; it might turn out to be an easily solved case for a change."

I snorted at the improbability of *that* and turned, my gaze moving to the strand of trees behind us. There in the softening shadows drifted a fragile wisp no bigger than a handkerchief.

The soul.

I walked toward it. My ability to communicate with the dead was still growing, and most souls could now gain shape and talk quite coherently. Of course, it was *my* strength they were drawing on to materialize, and it had reached the point where the mere act of talking to the spirit world could leave me weak both in body *and* mind. But it was a weakness I was willing to endure if it meant catching a break and solving a crime.

Not that *this* soul was drawing much energy at the moment. He might be here, but I had a feeling he was of two minds about speaking.

The closer I got to him, the colder it got, until it felt like fingers of ice were creeping into my bones. No one could really explain why these souls brought the chill of the underworld with them, but the general consensus was that it had something to do with them being in between—neither here nor in heaven or hell. Or wherever else it was that souls went to.

As I stepped into the ring of trees, his soul retreated, and fear swirled through the ice of the afterworld. I stopped.

"Why are you lingering here, Wayne Johnson, if not to speak?"

The wispiness that was the soul seemed to pause and then the energy flowing from me surged, the suddenness of it making me gasp.

Why? His voice was guttural, harsh, as it flowed through my mind. *Why did* this *happen? I paid for my crime. They should have left me alone. It's not fair that I should pay twice.*

I couldn't argue the validity of that without knowing who and how he'd killed. I'd learned over the years there were some crimes that deserved nothing less than death, but whether this man's did wasn't the point. "I'm here to find your killer, Mr. Johnson. But to do that, you need to talk to me."

For a moment he didn't answer, but the chill continued to grow until my fingers and nose ached with the fierceness of it. Energy continued to flow out of me, building in the air, giving him the strength to speak.

I didn't really see him, he admitted after a moment. *He was wearing a mask.*

"Are you sure it was a mask?"

Yeah. I saw the elastic around his head, like. He snorted, and the sound reverberated sharply inside my head. *And he was wearing these weird things around his feet that made him run funny.*

Cloven-shaped heels for his shoes, perhaps? But why would someone adopt such a disguise when it was only more likely to catch the attention of anyone who might be watching?

"Why didn't you fight him, Mr. Johnson?"

I couldn't. He sprayed something into my face. The next thing I know, I'm up in these trees with a wire around my neck and the bastard is choking me.

Weakness began to pull at my muscles, and that meant I'd better hurry before he drained me too far. That was the one big fear I had—that these souls would drag me into the shadowy depths with them if I wasn't careful. And that dark part inside of me whispered that it might be easier, that eternal darkness was better than eternal pain.

But I couldn't do that to my brother or to Quinn. No matter how tempting it might seem.

Besides, Jack kept reassuring me that it wasn't likely to happen, even if no one really knew how far this skill would develop, let alone what dangers might be involved.

"So, Mr. Johnson, he approached you from the front rather than behind?"

Yeah, how else would I see him? He was slender and small, like, but he obviously packed a hell of a lot of muscle. He killed me in minutes flat.

Another clue that we were dealing with a nonhuman killer. "Is there anything else you can tell me, Mr. Johnson? Anything that would help us track him down quickly?"

He didn't answer immediately, but the energy flowing away from me seemed to sharpen. A tremor ran through my muscles and my knees suddenly felt weak.

Well, there was the car—

"Car? What type of car?" I interrupted quickly. "Did you see the plate number?"

The energy in the air sharpened yet again, making the small hairs along the nape of my neck and along my arms stand on end. The trembling in my muscles grew stronger, and I really didn't know how much longer I could hold out. Or if I wanted to hold out. I pressed a hand against a nearby tree trunk and tried to stay upright. Tried to fight the growing urge to go with the flow and let oblivion take me.

It was a Toyota Land Cruiser. Really battered, grayish in color. He paused. *I only saw a little of the plate. The first three letters were BUK.*

It was better than nothing, and would certainly narrow down the field. "Is there anything else you noticed?"

No. His voice was softer, but that was more than likely a result of the fatigue gnawing at my body. *I didn't deserve to die like this.*

I thought it likely he *did* but didn't voice the opinion, saying instead, "Go in peace, Mr. Johnson."

I don't want—

He might not want to, but I broke off the contact and sank down to my knees, my breath wheezing out of my lungs and every muscle quivering.

The chill of his presence still hung in the air, but I ignored it, concentrating on breathing, on getting some strength back.

Footsteps approached from behind, and a familiar, spicy scent wrapped around me. "Here," Cole said, shoving a thermos and a cup in front of me. "We decided we needed to keep a supply of the strong stuff handy in case you needed it."

"I think I love you."

"Too late," he replied, amusement in his voice. "My love is already taken."

"Overlooked again." I tried to say it lightly, but tiredness got the better of me and it came out somewhat harshly.

I grabbed the metal flask from him, unwinding the top and pouring the steaming liquid into the plastic cup. The aroma hit my nostrils and I sighed in pleasure. It wasn't hazelnut, but it smelled just fine.

"Did you get anything from our victim?" Cole asked.

I took a sip of coffee and felt the warmth of it begin to chase away the chill of afterlife. "He said his killer was disguised as a demon."

"Well, none of us actually thought we were dealing with a real demon." Cole's voice was amused. "I wouldn't imagine they'd need to use barbed wire, for a start."

Certainly the demons I'd met wouldn't, that was for sure. "He also gave me a partial plate number and a description of the car the attacker was driving."

"Did he say where the murder occurred?" Cole squatted down beside me and handed over a Mintie. It wasn't a burger or even chocolate, but a chewy mint was better than no food at all.

"Here in these trees." I paused to unwrap the mint, popping it in my mouth before replying. "He said his attacker sprayed something in his face that froze him, so you'd better do a full toxicology."

"Like I don't always." He touched my shoulder lightly. "Are you sure you haven't come back too soon? Because you're not looking too good at the moment."

I met his concerned gaze, managing a small smile. "Meaning there were occasions in the past when I actually *did* look good?"

He grinned, and the warmth of it flowed over me,

chasing away the chill faster than the coffee. "I will admit to thinking, every now and again, that you looked great."

"He confesses this now, when he's finally found a girl who will put up with him?" I shook my head in mock despair. "We could have had so much fun."

"I don't think I have the stamina to handle someone like you." He pushed to his feet. "And you very neatly avoided answering the question."

"Not too neatly if you noticed."

He shook his head, his expression concerned. "You need to take it easy, Riley. This job isn't worth dying for, no matter what Jack says."

Again, the frustration surfaced. "Jack doesn't want me dead. I'm of no use to him that way."

"But he will keep pushing until you begin to think you might be better off dead." He reached into his pocket and tossed me another Mintie. "Sooner or later, you're going to have to set boundaries."

"Which is easier said than done." I squinted up at him. "I don't see you saying no too often."

"My situation is not the same as yours."

"No. You haven't been injected with drugs that are changing the very chemistry of your body."

"That's irrelevant, and you know it."

It wasn't, because it was the one reason I couldn't walk away from the Directorate and Jack.

"I'm just saying that you need to be careful." He hesitated, then added, "Jack may be a good boss, but he doesn't run the Directorate. His sister does. And trust me, she's a hard bitch who won't hesitate to suck you dry and then spit you out."

Curiosity stirred, and I raised my eyebrows. As far as I knew, no one had ever met the elusive director Madeline Hunter—none of us plebs, anyway—although they did speak of her in the administration halls with varying degrees of trepidation. "You've met Director Hunter? What is she like?"

"She's everything Jack isn't, and she doesn't care who she has to use—or use up—to get the job done."

The bitterness in his voice raised my eyebrows. "So you've crossed swords with her?"

"Not me personally, but someone I know." He glanced away, his expression grim. "He died because of her, because she and the Directorate kept pushing. I'd hate to see the same happen to you, Riley."

The anger in his voice was very clear, and yet here he was, working for the very people he seemed to hate. "It won't."

"Good."

The short, sharp way he said that made me realize he wasn't about to go into details, no matter how much I might want them. So I wasn't surprised when he changed the subject.

"Did the victim have any idea why the murderer dragged him into full view?"

"No, but the most obvious answer is that he wanted Johnson's body found." I shrugged. "Someone who runs around dressed as a demon obviously isn't dealing with a full deck of cards."

"And that," he said heavily, "is the most sensible thing I've heard all day."

I laughed and rose. I finished the coffee in one swift gulp that burned my throat, then handed him the plastic cup. "You'll let me know if you find anything?"

"Nope," he said, his eyes twinkling as he slapped the cup back on top of the thermos. "I'm going to keep it all to myself."

"Heard that about you."

He smiled and walked away, and I headed down the hill to interview the woman who'd reported the murder.

As it turned out, she wasn't much help. She seemed to be the local busybody, but she was elderly with failing eyesight, and she was *convinced* she'd seen a real demon, not someone dressed up as one. Weirdly, the idea seemed to thrill rather than scare her.

When I got back to my car, I switched on the onboard and typed in the partial plate number, requesting a search for gray Toyotas with those letters. It'd probably turn up hundreds of possibilities, but at least that would give us somewhere to start.

Then I swung the car around and headed for home. I was about halfway there when I realized I was being followed.

Chapter 2

I studied the red Mazda through the rearview mirror. It was just far enough back that I half wondered if I was being paranoid. After all, we were on a freeway, all heading in the same direction, and mostly going the same speed. Well, except for the young idiots in their pimped-out, overly powerful V8s, trying to prove how tough they were by going over the limit.

It wasn't even as if the red car were shadowing all my movements. I moved out to overtake a slower car and red remained where he was, neither increasing nor decreasing his speed.

Imagination, I thought. Or a bad case of nerves.

Except . . . the back of my neck prickled uneasily and I couldn't stop checking out the car. It remained in my sight, remained the same distance away, and it just *felt* wrong.

Well, I wasn't about to ignore my instincts. The last time I'd done that, a friend had died.

Of course, Kade's death was a whole lot more involved than just a case of me ignoring my instincts. And besides, this uneasiness stemmed as much from the warning that Kye had given me before I'd killed him.

A warning that said that Blake—the wolf who'd murdered my grandfather to take over the leadership of the Jenson pack, and a man whom I'd threatened and seriously humiliated almost a year ago—hadn't finished with me yet.

That even now, he was planning his vengeance.

Yet more fucking vengeance.

Just what my already broken world needed.

But by the same token, if Blake wanted vengeance, he knew where we lived. He didn't have to shadow my movements, just hit me where I felt the safest.

Still . . .

I touched my ear lightly, switching on the voice part of the com-link. "Hello, anyone there?"

"Well, well," a sultry and altogether too familiar voice said, "isn't it lovely to hear your dulcet tones again."

I couldn't help smiling. Sal and I would never be friends, but we'd moved from barbed insults to droll comments, and from dislike to companionable trust. She was also damn good at her job—my old job—and had saved my ass on more than one occasion.

"You say that with such conviction that I almost

believe you," I replied, voice dry. "Want to do me a favor?"

"Oh, I live for such moments."

In other words, she was bored shitless and could use something to do. Either that or she was on her lunch break. And like most vampires working for the Directorate in a capacity other than as a guardian, she tended to restrict her feeding to the times she was off duty, which left her with spare time during breaks. Me, I'd be heading out to shop, but as a vamp, Sal didn't have that option.

"You want to pinpoint my location with the satellites and grab the plate number of the red Mazda three cars back?"

"And why would we be doing this?"

I could hear keys tapping, so she was setting the satellites into motion even as she questioned me. "Because I think it's following me."

"Did you pick him up before or after your visit to the crime scene?"

"After. I couldn't say if he was tailing me from the moment I left the park or not, though." I really hadn't been paying that much attention—although I wasn't about to admit that to Sal. She'd only tell Jack, and he'd probably blast me for not showing good guardian form.

As if I ever had.

"While the satellite is lining up," I added, "have you had any luck with the search I requested?"

"There's one hundred and fifty cars so far with a plate starting with BUK." Her voice was dry. "At least

twenty-three of those are Toyotas. It's a proverbial needle in a haystack right now."

But it was a haystack that Jack would still want
searched. "It might be worth cross-checking whether
any of those Toyotas belong to the family of whoever
Johnson murdered."

"You think it's a vengeance kill?"

"It sure as hell smelled like it."

"Well, all I can say is the bastard probably deserved
it. They don't slap you in jail for that long without
good reason." She paused, then added, "Okay, I have a
fix. I'll trace the plate, if you like."

"I like."

I flicked another glance in the rearview, then
changed lanes again. The red Mazda didn't move, remaining obstinately in its own lane. But the distance
between us neither increased nor decreased.

"The car belongs to one Irene Gardener, who lives in
Melton." Sal paused. "She's a little old lady of seventy-
five, and there are no reports of it being stolen or anything."

"Meaning I'm being alarmist over nothing."

"Well, unless she's a seventy-five-year-old who's
taken up following people, then I'd have to say yes."
She paused. "Then again, she might not know the car
is even missing yet. Might be worth trying to shake the
Mazda, just to see what happens."

I couldn't help grinning. "And if I crash, I can always say you told me to do it."

She snorted. "This conversation is not being
recorded, and I will deny it ever happened."

"Right. Thanks, Sal."

I flicked off the com-link and cruised along the freeway for several minutes, doing nothing other than watching the traffic and the annoying red car behind me.

Then a long semi-trailer came into view. Perfect, I thought, and pulled out into the other lane, keeping my speed even as I passed the truck. A glance in the mirror showed that the Mazda remained where it was. I pulled in front of the truck, then hit the gas. The big car surged forward, the speedometer rising. I didn't slow as the traffic increased, weaving in and out with a precision that would have surprised anyone who knew my driving record. The Western Ring Road overpass came into view. Ignoring the lights, I swung onto the on ramp and roared up into the traffic, using the emergency lane for several minutes before cutting into a gap between a truck and a cab. A quick glance in the mirror didn't reveal a familiar red shadow, but I cut across to the Boundary Road exit anyway, only slowing once I'd swung left—tires squealing—onto Fairbairn Road.

No red car.

I was safe.

I blew out a relieved breath and was surprised to discover that my hands were shaking again. I flexed my fingers against the steering wheel and wondered briefly if Kye's warning was nothing more than a way to get at me from the grave. He might not have thought he'd die—especially at my hands—but he knew enough about my relationship with Blake to understand just what his warning would do to me.

Maybe he thought he could use it to get closer to me.

To drag me into his life. He'd suggested that, at the end, before he'd killed Kade and forced me to take the shot I'd been avoiding.

We were both killers, after all. I *could* do what he did, what Rhoan did. I'd proven that amply enough over my years as a guardian . . .

No, I thought, shoving the thought away viciously. I was *not* like him. I *wouldn't* be like him.

And yet . . . it was a possibility. If I stayed in this job, kept hunting down killers, I would continue to harden. It was inevitable.

Maybe that's why my hands were shaking. It wasn't so much the ghost of a threat but rather the fear of the future. A future without my wolf soul mate.

I closed my eyes briefly. This was ridiculous. I needed to stop thinking like that, because I *wasn't* alone. I still had Quinn. My soul might have been reduced to ashes, but I still had my heart.

I continued toward home, parking several doors down from our apartment building and locking the car as I headed back up the street. The rich smell of baking bread wafted around me, making my stomach rumble and reminding me that I hadn't yet had breakfast. I spun on my heel and headed back to the bakery, which was run by the same family that owned the pizza place next door. I'm sure Rhoan, Liander, and I kept the two places in business.

A bell rang as I pushed open the door and Frances—the cheery, matronly woman who was the chief baker—came out of the back room, wiping floured hands on a towel.

"Riley," she said, a wide smile creasing her lined features, "You're up early this morning."

"I had to work early." I stopped in front of the display case and eyed the mouthwatering treats indecisively. The trouble was, they were all so damn good, and if it wasn't for my werewolf genes, I'd probably be the size of a house.

"You should tell your boss these hours are no good for your beautiful face. It's far too cold these mornings."

I smiled. Frances had a thing about cold air causing rosacea, and often lectured me about not wearing a hat and scarf.

"Unfortunately, killers don't really give a fig about how the cold affects my face."

"That is very inconsiderate of them," she said, snapping on some silicone gloves. "Now, what can I get for you this morning? The chocolate croissants are particularly good."

"Then I'd better get a dozen." If she was recommending them, then they had to be.

She gave me a happy smile and bagged the croissants. I handed over the cash, then headed back to our apartment. As I pushed open the front door, a familiar flash of red caught my eye. I spun around, spotting taillights disappearing down a side street, but couldn't see the make of the car. I frowned, wondering if I was getting so paranoid about the possible threat Blake represented that I was now imagining that *every* red car on the damn road posed a danger.

I shook my head and munched on one of the warm

chocolatey treats as I climbed the stairs to our apartment.

Rhoan was waiting with the door open by the time I got there. "I smell chocolate croissants."

I took another one out, then handed him the bag. He took a deep whiff and sighed in pleasure. "There's nothing that smells nicer in the morning."

"Actually, I can think of one or two things that do."

The absence of one of those scents—my vampire lover Quinn—suggested he was either at work or out pounding the pavement again in an effort to get fit. Or fitter, as the case was. I squeezed past Rhoan and was instantly assaulted by the rich aroma of percolating coffee. I flared my nostrils. Hazelnut. Quinn must have put it on before he'd gone for a run. Rhoan would have put the Kona on, because that was Liander's favorite.

I headed for the kitchen, adding over my shoulder, "I thought you were supposed to be undercover this week."

"I was, but it went pear-shaped." He shrugged and shut the door behind us. "An old school friend of mine walked into the bar and recognized me. And of course, the damn suspect happened to be listening in via the close-circuit system at the time and fled."

"Well, he obviously wasn't innocent, then."

"No. There's a kill order out on him, but given he's a bird-shifter, he could have well and truly flown the coop by now."

It wouldn't help him in the long run. Kill orders were issued Australia wide. Sooner or later, the Directorate would get its man.

Liander wandered out of the bedroom he shared with Rhoan, bleary-eyed and looking more than a little worse for wear. I raised my eyebrows. "Big night last night, I'm gathering?"

"Yeah." He rubbed a hand through his tousled silver hair, messing it up even more. "Got that special effects contract I was talking about, and we celebrated big."

"Congrats." I pulled mugs out of the cupboard then went to the fridge to get the milk. "But I hope you realize you can't be out boozing all night when we become parents?"

Liander leaned a shoulder against the door frame and gave me the biggest smile imaginable. "That has such a good sound, doesn't it? Us as parents. Who'd have thought?"

Certainly not me—not with Liander as the father, anyway. I'd known for a while that my own vampire genes and the drugs forced on me by a mad former lover had made me incapable of bearing children, but there'd always been that slither of hope that at least *part* of the dream would be achievable. That I would still find a way to have children with the man I loved.

That hope was gone, buried along with Kye.

But with Liander and Rhoan's relationship stabilizing and deepening, they'd both developed a hankering to become dads. Liander's sister had volunteered to become a surrogate, and I'd had eggs frozen before my body had totally betrayed me—and my eggs were as close as my twin was ever going to get to having children of his own, since he'd gone sterile long before me.

Of course, Liander had dreams of a big family, with

at least a dozen little Jenson-Moores running around. I wasn't so sure I could handle *that* many kids, as much as I'd always dreamed of a big family myself. And the sudden reluctance might have something to do with little Risa—who'd been the sweetest thing going—suddenly hitting the terrible twos and becoming a demon child.

"You'd better hope she has twins, because after seven of her own, she may not want to go through the whole process again for us."

Liander snorted. "Trust me, Emalee loves being pregnant. She's already said she's up for a second round of surrogacy."

She might be saying that now, but she hadn't yet gone full term and made it through the birth. None of us knew what effect the drugs I had been given might have had on my eggs. Or whether those changes would affect Emalee herself. This could still go horribly wrong, as so many other things in my life had. Which was why the doctors were monitoring Emalee carefully.

But I kept my doubts and fears to myself, not wanting to dampen Liander's infectious happiness.

"Oh, that reminds me," Liander added, accepting his coffee with a smile. "Emalee has her first ultrasound on Thursday. She wants to know if we're all coming."

"Too bloody right," Rhoan said, handing Liander a croissant before squeezing past him to grab his coffee. He glanced at me. "I've already told Jack we aren't available that afternoon, no matter what happens or how many crazies appear."

I raised my eyebrows. "But you were supposed to be undercover. How were you going to get around that?"

"Given that's no longer a problem, it doesn't really matter, does it?" He gave me a grin, then took another croissant out of the bag. "I'm betting we have a boy—mainly because I don't think the world could stand two Riley Jensons."

I snorted softly. "Better another me than another *you*."

"It can't be the image of either of you, because thankfully it will have my genes in the mix. Which ultimately means it will at least be sensible," Liander commented. "And I don't care if it's a he or she, as long as it's healthy."

"Amen to that." I leaned past him to grab a croissant for myself, then spotted Quinn coming through the door. "Hey, handsome. About time you got home."

He gave me a grin and snagged one of the towels from the clean laundry basket that was perpetually sitting in the living room. A fine sheen of sweat clung to his face and darkened his blue T-shirt, molding it to his lean, muscular body. Hollywood would have everyone believe that vampires had no need for bodily functions, but that was nonsense. They might not eat the same way as the rest of us did, but they still had to drink to survive, and what went in had to come out in one form or another. And while they didn't sweat *that* much, it happened.

Quinn had recently added long-distance running to

his fitness regime. He was getting fit for the baby, apparently—which said a whole lot more about his anticipation of the impending birth than my staid old vampire's often blasé attitude would have us believe.

Liander shifted to give him room to pass, then flared his nostrils. "You know, it's damned unfair that he smells so good after running fifty kilometers."

"It was only twenty-five today," Quinn corrected, then grabbed my hand and tugged me into his arms, kissing me quickly but thoroughly. "Because I have an appointment with a real estate agent at nine."

"You're determined to get us all out of this apartment, aren't you?" Rhoan said.

"Neither Liander nor I is used to living in a hovel, and we need some breathing space. And babies do tend to bring their own mountains of mess. We'll all end up feeling trapped before you know it."

"It isn't *that* bad," Rhoan protested.

"I agree," I said, a grin twitching my lips. "There's actually plenty of space. You just need to clean it up better."

"It's not Liander and me that make the mess, so why should we be the ones cleaning?" he retorted dryly, then kissed my nose. "I'll hire a housekeeper once we move, though I think she'll face an impossible task."

He had *that* right. I wrapped my arms loosely around his waist and breathed in the scent of him. Liander was right—he smelled delicious even when he was sweating. "So, where's this latest house situated?"

"It's not a house. It's a three-story brick warehouse in Abbotsford, situated right next to the banks of the

Yarra River, with Dickinson Reserve and Studley Parks on the other side. Each couple could have one floor, and the general living area could be in the middle. It even has a fenced parking lot that can be converted into a safe playground for little werewolves to play."

"Sounds ideal," Rhoan commented. "Between that and Riley's land in Macedon, we have the perfect mix of city pad and country retreat."

"Let's make sure the place actually matches the real estate blurb before we start making plans," Quinn said, then reached past me to grab a mug, his damp body pressing against mine and fueling the already-stirring embers of desire.

But with it came an odd wave of reassurance. Not everything in my life had gone so horribly wrong. Quinn was here, still standing by my side through all the tears and the heartbreak and the more than occasional bad mood.

He loved me and he wouldn't go away—he'd told me that so often in the last few months that it had almost become a joke between us.

He was also damn hard to kill, because he wasn't just a vampire but an Aedh—a being who could became shadow and mist, and for whom there were few physical threats. Which didn't mean he couldn't be killed—he certainly could when in flesh form—but he was harder to kill than your average vampire, and for that, I was mighty grateful. I'd lost my soul mate. I didn't think I could live through losing my heart's desire, as well.

I pressed myself a little harder against him and said, "So, you want company in the shower?"

"That's another reason to get another apartment," he said, dark eyes sparkling as he glanced at me. God, I could lose myself forever in those depths. "The shower in this place is far too small for couples."

"Squishy is fun," Liander said. "You just have to use a little imagination."

"Oh, trust me, Riley has enough imagination for the two of us." Quinn's voice held a dry edge, but the smile teasing his lips just about melted my bones. "That doesn't make it any more comfortable, however."

"You forget, he's a sedate old vampire," I said, my grin growing, but nowhere near as much as the pleasure blooming deep inside as his fingers came to rest on my hip. "And you know what old people are like when it comes to their comforts."

One dark eyebrow rose, and the depths of his eyes sparkled with warmth and love. "So I'm sedate and old, am I?"

He moved quickly, his body a blur, and before I knew it, I was being thrown up and over his shoulder. Luckily for me, he swung around so my head didn't smash against the fridge door. But with my nose buried in the middle of his back and his scent filling each breath, some of this morning's sadness washed away.

I had this.

I had him.

Life wasn't so bad, no matter what had happened.

"I think," he added heavily, "the pup needs another lesson on being polite to her elders."

"You know she doesn't like to learn," Liander commented. "She's stubborn like that."

"Hey, I bought you breakfast," I protested. "You should have the decency to forgo the insults—at least for now."

"The croissants are gone, so I'm officially free to insult." Liander moved aside to let Quinn through, and I took a swipe at him as we passed—which he avoided with a laugh.

As the kitchen floor became the living room carpet, I said, "I thought you had a very important meeting with the real estate people?"

"Letting real estate people know you're eager for a property is never a good idea," Quinn said easily. "They'll wait."

"Well, good." Although I wished he'd tip me the right way up. Having my nose stuck in his back was far from unpleasant, but being upside down and bounced around like a sack of potatoes as he strode toward the bathroom wasn't much fun.

"If you wanted to be right way up," he said, obviously following my thoughts, "you wouldn't have made snarky remarks about my age."

"And *I* would have thought that one of the four oldest vampires in the country would have learned to take insults by now."

"He has, except when it's more fun to do otherwise. Prepare to be ravished by your ancient but extremely fit lover, my dear."

"Oh, I'm prepared." More than prepared, really.

But of course, my cell phone chose that moment to

ring. I was tempted to ignore it, but the ring tone said it was Jack, and he never phoned just to chat.

Quinn put me down without being asked. With a frustrated sigh, I pulled the phone out of my pocket and answered it. "Hi, Jack."

Quinn kissed the top of my head, then continued on into the bathroom. I leaned against the door frame and watched—frustration growing—as he turned on the shower taps then stripped off his sweaty running clothes, revealing the long, lean lines of his body.

Lovely was the first word that came to mind. He reminded me of an athlete—not a bodybuilder or a runner, but sitting comfortably in between the two. His was a body to run your fingers over time and again. As I had—each time delighting in the silky smoothness of his skin and the play of muscle beneath it. And I *really* wanted to be doing it again this morning.

Damn Jack and his timing.

"Riley, are you even listening to me?" Jack said, sounding a little exasperated.

I briefly thought about lying, but I knew from past experience he'd ask me to recite back his words—and then get even madder when I couldn't. "Sorry, momentarily distracted."

"I won't ask by what, because I probably wouldn't want to know." His voice was dry. "We found the Toyota the victim's soul mentioned. It was abandoned in Keilor. Apparently the owner didn't even know it was missing. A sharp-eyed citizen reported two men leaving the vehicle."

"Two? Our soul only mentioned one."

"He might have only seen one, but that doesn't mean there wasn't someone else there."

True, but I'd also only smelled the one. Or had the smell of vengeance been so thick and ripe that it had overwhelmed all other scents?

"Has Cole had a chance to check it out yet?"

"Dusty's there now. He's found a partial print that didn't match the one the police have listed in their database for the owner."

Meaning the owner had a record. "And do you have a matching listing for the print?"

"Yep. It belongs to one Hank Surrey, a vamp who turned fifty-five years ago."

I watched as Quinn stepped into the shower and closed the glass door. The fierce desire to just hang up, strip, and step in beside him swept through me. I swallowed and tried to quell the trembling in my limbs, but it took all the control I had *not* to follow that urge.

"Have we got a recent address listed for him?" Even as I asked the question, I had my fingers crossed that we didn't.

But fate, as usual, wasn't giving me even the tiniest of breaks.

"We have him in Mt. Martha, although the last check on his location was done almost a year ago."

Mt. Martha was a well-to-do suburb down on the peninsula that catered primarily to families. It wasn't the sort of place where you usually found vamps— young or old. They tended to stick closer to the city, where feeding was a whole lot easier—especially with the advent of the blood whore clubs.

I said as much to Jack.

"Well, they have a cracking little golf course down there," he said, "and they've installed night lights for those of us who can't beat the little white ball through the grass during the day."

My eyebrows rose. Jack was a golfer. Who'd have thought? "I wouldn't think a vamp who resorts to stealing cars would be too interested in golf or clubs." Unless he intended to *steal* the golf clubs.

"Hey, everyone has to have a hobby. I'll send his address through to your onboard."

In other words, leave immediately. I blew out a frustrated breath, then said, "Heading out now."

"Report in if you find him," Jack said, then hung up.

I shoved the phone back into my pocket and wasted a few minutes watching the soap trail down the wet planes of Quinn's back.

"I have to go," I said, mentally shaking away the images of what I'd rather be doing. "I'm not sure when I'll be back."

I wanted to go in and kiss him good-bye, but I wasn't sure if I could handle that sort of closeness and still walk away.

"Call me when you finish," he said, turning around and blowing me a kiss. Obviously, he was still following my thoughts. "We'll grab either lunch or dinner, depending on the time."

"It's a deal."

And I walked out while I still had some resolve left.

* * *

J glanced into the rearview mirror as I pulled onto the Citylink tollway and my pulse leapt. Several cars behind me was a red car. Same make, same model as the one that had been following me only hours before.

I watched it for several minutes, wondering again if I was merely imagining it. I mean, everyone knew that red cars traveled in packs—see one, and you see at least three.

And red was an *extremely* popular color.

But the same red Mazda sitting three cars behind me twice in as many hours? That was a little bit too much of a coincidence.

I switched on the com-link and said, "Sal, I think I'm being followed by that little old lady again."

She laughed. "You've obviously pissed off said little old lady. Which wouldn't be hard, given you do the whole pissing-people-off thing so well."

"Except I haven't been near any little old ladies of late. You want to see whether this one is missing her car yet or not?"

"On it now." Silence fell, and I kept half an eye on the annoying red Mazda. It retained the distance between us, sitting right on the edge of keeping me in sight and losing me altogether.

"Okay," Sal said. "The little old lady has been contacted and is mighty annoyed that I woke her so early. She reckons her nephew has borrowed the car for the week."

"Have we got a license photo and address for the nephew?"

"Requesting that now, as well as doing a search through the data banks. I'll send anything I get through to your onboard."

"Send me the photo immediately. I'm going to try and corner my follower."

"Will do." She hesitated, and in the background I heard Jack muttering something. "The boss says be careful, and don't delay too long in getting out to our suspect's place."

I wanted to ask why the hell it mattered when the vamp had turned only fifty-five years ago and wouldn't be going anywhere until the sun went down. Vamps had to be at least several hundred years old before they could start tolerating the touch of the sun. Hell, Jack was over eight hundred years old, and even he could only go out in the early hours of the morning and the late evening.

But I knew why he wanted me there ASAP. Our suspect would be easier to catch, easier to handle, now. This was Jack's version of mollycoddling me.

So I simply said, "I'll be in touch."

Jack's voice rolled through the background again, then Sal said, "He says to keep the com-link open so we can hear what is going on, but we both know that won't happen."

I grinned but did as requested, although I *did* cut their ability to talk to me. I didn't need Jack or Sal buzzing in my ear if things got nasty.

I continued to drive along Citylink. The computer beeped, indicating it was receiving information. I touched the screen. The image that appeared had red hair and bright blue eyes, and he was young—probably no more than nineteen or twenty. It had to be the least threatening image I'd ever seen, but I'd learned over the years never to judge a book by its cover. For all I knew, this innocent-looking kid could be the underworld's best hit man. With that face, no one would ever suspect him.

When the High Street exit ramp came into view, I moved over to the left lane, then took the ramp. Several cars back, my red follower did the same.

It was looking less like imagination every minute.

The lights turned green as I approached, and I followed the traffic around to the left. A parking lot came into view, so I swung into that, parked the car in front of the trees, then quickly jumped out, locking the car before shifting into my seagull form.

The red Mazda came into view just as I walked under the car to keep out of sight.

It slowed but didn't stop. I couldn't see the driver thanks to the fact that I was under the car, but I didn't dare come out, because I had no idea how much my follower knew about me.

When the car had moved far enough away, I walked out from beneath the car and took to the air, surging upward swiftly and easily—something I'd have sworn wouldn't have been possible when I'd first started learning to fly.

The red car crawled along the curb until there was a break in the traffic, then did a quick U-turn and parked in the lot on the opposite side of the street to the one I was parked in.

I landed on the outstretched limb of a scrawny gum and walked along its length to get a better view of the Mazda's driver.

It wasn't the granny's nephew. The driver was a swarthy-looking man who was all teeth and nose. His shoulders were thickset and his arms were the size of tree trunks. He didn't look like a wolf, because we tend to be slender, and I couldn't really see Blake using a non–pack member against me. He wouldn't risk that sort of exposure with people he couldn't trust absolutely—or put the fear of God into.

Of course, he *had* used Kye to guard his son, but at least Kye had been a wolf. He'd also been the very best killer that money could buy.

Except that he wasn't the best, because I'd killed him.

So did that make me the best?

No, I thought. *No!*

I forced the darkness away and tried to concentrate on the here and now. Whatever this man was, he could never be called the best. He couldn't even tail someone properly.

But maybe that was the whole point.

I watched the driver for several minutes. When it became obvious that he had no intention of going anywhere until I did, I fluttered down to the road and strutted up to his car. He didn't even look my way.

I shifted back to my human form, keeping low as I waited to see if he picked up my presence. But there was no movement from inside the car and no sting of tension or excitement in the air—either of which would have indicated he was aware that *something* was close, if not me.

Which meant either he was too intent on his target to hold an awareness of his surroundings—which would make him a very bad tracker—or he was something other than a wolf.

Either way, he was about to regret his decision to follow a guardian.

Chapter 3

I silently counted to three then surged to my feet and ripped open the door, almost pulling it off its hinges in the process. The man jerked sideways, his fist swinging in reaction. He was fast, but not wolf fast, and while his scent wasn't human, I didn't think he was entirely nonhuman, either.

I avoided his blow, grabbed a fistful of shirt, and hauled him out of the car. He came out swinging, making me duck and weave as I thrust him back against the rear door.

He grunted but otherwise showed little reaction to the force of my push. He really *was* a man-mountain, his stocky, muscular body matching his thick shoulders and boulder-like arms. But I was a wolf *and* a vampire. He had no hope against me.

I held him pinned with one hand, then caught one

swinging fist in the other. The smack of flesh against flesh sounded like a gunshot.

Even this close to him, I couldn't tell if he was human or not. He didn't seem to have any particular scent, which made me wonder if he was using a scent neutralizer—though I'd never heard of one that actually erased the markers of your species.

"Enough," I said, squeezing his fingers. Even though my hand wasn't large enough to entirely cover his, I could still cause some serious damage if I wanted to. And he was smart enough to realize it.

"What fucking right have you got to haul me out of the car like that?"

"Scum who are spotted trailing guardians don't have any rights. Why are you doing it, and who's paying you?"

"I have no idea what you're talking about. I was just sitting there drinking my coffee."

My gaze flicked briefly to the inside of his car. He did indeed have a travel mug sitting in the center console, but I seriously doubted the rest of his story. There was too much tension emanating from his body for an innocent man.

"We have two options here," I said, squeezing his hand a little harder. I could smell the sweat on him so I knew it had to be hurting, but there was no sign of fear or pain on his face or in his eyes. A tough man, through and through. "I can beat you to a pulp and then get my answers, or you can simply give me the answers I want and walk away without broken bones."

He considered it for several heartbeats, then said, "How do I know you're a fucking guardian?"

I shifted my grip slightly and pulled out my badge, showed it to him, then put it away again. "Now, why are you following me?"

"Because that's what I'm being paid to do."

"By whom?"

He shrugged. "I'm just a contractor."

Meaning there was some sort an underworld job agency hiring out thugs? I'm not sure why I was surprised, given all that I'd seen over the last few years, but for some reason I was.

"So give me your boss's name and we'll call it quits."

He snorted, spraying fine particles of snot over my hand. Charming. "Get real. He'll kill me if I did that."

"And I'll kill you if you don't."

I wouldn't—and couldn't if he *was* human, thanks to the law—but it never hurt to make the threat. Both the general public and the criminals we hunted know so little about what guardians can and can't do that making threats was often the easiest way of getting results.

"Fuck." He shifted his stance a little, and I tensed, half expecting him to try and kick me. But he didn't. "Okay. I'm not getting paid enough to mess with the likes of you."

"So he didn't tell you I was a guardian?" I reached out telepathically and lightly connected with his thoughts—not enough for him to sense me but more than enough to tell truth from lies.

"No." His voice was hostile, indicating he wasn't too happy with his boss right now.

"And the plate number didn't make you realize?" I mean, the Directorate, like all government departments, had their own plates. It would have been a little hard to miss the fact that he wasn't following an ordinary car.

"Well, yeah, but you could have been an office worker for all I knew. I didn't know we had female guardians who weren't vamps."

Few people did—mainly because I was the only one. "So, the name of your boss?"

"Henry. Henry Bottchelli."

"And Bottchelli didn't tell you why he wanted me followed?"

"Nope. Just that I had to follow you for the next couple of days, providing regular updates about your location."

That bit of news sent a chill down my spine. "Did he say why he wanted this information?"

"Nope. I'm paid to do a job, not ask questions."

And I was thinking it was more a case of "the less he knew, the less he could blab." "Is Bottchelli his real name?"

"Yeah." He hesitated. "As far as I know."

"How do I find him?"

He moved again, and the quick desire to lash out ran through his thoughts. He dismissed it, but not easily. I squeezed his hand harder, making him concentrate on me and the pain rather than the escape he was contemplating.

"I've only got a cell number. He contacts me with the job, and I contact him when the job is done."

Meaning whoever the boss was, he was extremely cautious. Which sounded very much like Blake.

"When did he contact you about this job?"

"Yesterday morning."

"How did you find me in Melton?"

"Cell phone scanner. Heard them call you to the murder, so I just waited out of sight."

Meaning I'd have to change my number, pronto. "Give me the number you use to contact your boss."

Again he hesitated. And this time, the need to retaliate surged into action and he lashed out with a booted foot. I jumped away from the blow, but the tip of his steel-capped boots skimmed my shin with enough force behind it to make pain shimmer up my leg. But I didn't let go of him and my sudden movement unbalanced him, pulling him away from the car. His free arm flailed as he tried to regain his balance, but I released his other hand and gave him an additional shove.

He landed heavily on his hands and knees. I planted a heel on his back and forced him into the dirt.

"Now, shall we try that again?" I said, voice cold. "Or shall I drive this stiletto right through your spine?"

"Bitch," he muttered—though his thoughts were a whole lot more colorful and creative.

"Phone number," I said, barely resisting the impulse to smile. Only to have the impulse die almost as suddenly as it had risen.

What had happened to the reluctance to do this job?

What had happened to the fear that I could one day take it too far?

But I didn't ease the pressure of my heel on his back. I might fear what I was becoming, but I feared whatever Blake had planned more.

He gave me the phone number. I shoved it into my memory banks, then said, "And your name?"

"Rudy White."

His thoughts said he was telling the truth. They also told me where he lived, so I could find him again if I needed to.

"Well, Rudy, I suggest very strongly that you give up trailing, because you're not very good at it." I stepped away and he scrambled to his feet with surprising dexterity for such a big man. "And if I spot you following me again, I'll throw your ass in jail and throw away the key."

"You can't do that—"

"I can do anything I want with scum like you. Remember that the next time you take on a job that involves Directorate personnel."

He scowled but didn't say anything.

"Now get into the car and drive away," I added.

He obeyed. I waited until he'd left the parking lot, then pressed the com-link button and said, "You heard all that?"

"Yep," Sal said, "Jack's already applied for a new cell number for you. We should have it within an hour or so. The phone number White gave us is listed as belonging to a Frank Wise. Who, according to our records, was beheaded several months ago in a robbery gone wrong."

Interesting. "What about Bottchelli?"

"He's another man with no official records of any kind."

I might not have any proof, but I'd bet my very last dollar that Blake was the man behind both identities. "Meaning he has unofficial ones?"

"Actually, no. But his name has been linked to a number of armed robberies, including several that ended up with fatalities."

Not a bad effort for a man who apparently didn't exist. "Meaning we haven't got as much as a license picture or an address for him?"

"No. Jack's just given the go-ahead to break into the phone records of both men to see if we can find any connecting numbers. That'll give us a starting place."

Which meant Jack was taking this situation seriously, because even he could get into considerable trouble for doing that without approval from the higher-ups. Not that *that* had ever stopped any of us before. "Let me know what you get. I'm heading over to the vamp's place now."

"Right."

I crossed the road and headed back to my car. Once there, I got rid of my bra, which had—as usual—been shredded by the shift into seagull form. One of these days, I thought, flinging it onto the backseat, the Directorate were going to have to pay me for the cost of replacements, because bras were costing me a small fortune. And while Quinn might have bags of money, and had offered more than once to provide for me, I refused to be looked after like that. I might want to spend the rest of my life with him, but I wanted to pay my own way whenever possible.

I got back onto the freeway and made my way down to Mount Martha. The vampire suspect lived in the middle of an estate situated between the Nepean and Moorooduc highways, and certainly didn't have any of the sea views that the area was famous for. The house itself was a standard brick veneer—the type of house that could be seen in dozens of different estates all over Melbourne. But the gardens were well kept, the grass cut, and there was a average-looking station wagon parked in the carport. I wondered if the neighbors were even aware that they had a vampire living amongst them.

I parked several houses down from the suspect's, then climbed out and walked back. The curtains were all drawn in the front of the house, and even the glass near the front door was covered. Which was no surprise, given the owner was a vampire.

I walked through the carport and headed for the front steps. From inside the house came the sound of voices overlaid by music, meaning our vamp was up and watching the TV. I recognized the ad. I pressed the doorbell and resisted the urge to peer through the windows via the gap in the curtains. When there was no immediate response, I pressed it again, leaning on it a little longer this time.

There were no answering footsteps, but my skin crawled with awareness, and several seconds later, a wary voice said, "Yes?"

"Mr. Surrey?"

"Who wants to know?"

Was it my imagination, or had a whole heap of tension just crept into that quiet, wary voice?

"Riley Jenson, from the Director—"

I didn't even finish my sentence before he was running. I swore and spun, bolting for the backyard. I leapt the picket fence dividing the two yards one-handed and ran around the back of the house, looking for the rear door. I'm not entirely sure why he'd run this way, because if he was a vamp, then he wasn't coming out in this sunshine anytime soon without doing himself serious damage.

The back door was locked. I swore again and thrust a shoulder against it, smashing it open. As the door hit plaster, punching a hole in the wall, I ran through the laundry, following the thick scent of vampire.

It led me to a bedroom.

And to a bolt hole.

I swore yet again then knelt down beside it, peering cautiously into the hole. It was a tunnel, and little more than two feet in diameter, barely enough for a man of any decent size to navigate. It dropped about eight feet down through the concrete and into the earth, widening out just enough to turn, then it disappeared sideways into the earth. The hole barely looked big enough to crawl through.

It could be a trap. I could drop down into that hole and find myself staked or shot. But the sour smell of vampire was retreating, and really, anyone who'd bolted at the first mention of the Directorate didn't really seem the type who'd stand by ready to kill.

I took a deep breath, then gripped the rim of the bolt hole and dropped down into it. No stake surged out of the darkness. The vamp was on the run, not hanging about to get rid of unwanted visitors.

With the scent of rich earth thick in my nostrils, I squatted down and had a look at the side tunnel. It appeared even smaller from this angle than it had from up above, and I really didn't think my shoulders would fit through it all that well. Which meant that either he was smaller than I was, or he also had an alternate shape.

Like a rat, I thought. This certainly seemed the sort of standby escape a rat-shifter would have.

I shifted shape, then in wolf form squeezed into the hole, following the scent of vampire. But even as a wolf, my body was too large, and little rivulets of earth cascaded down every time I brushed the sides or the ceiling. I found myself fervently hoping the vamp had known what he was doing when he'd dug this bolt hole, because right now, it felt like the whole thing was going to collapse on top of me.

Of course, it would have been better if I'd chosen my seagull form over my wolf, but if something jumped out at me, my wolf had a better chance of fighting back. The seagull was useless for that sort of stuff.

The tunnel stretched on. My paws made little sound on the soft ground, but my panting seemed to echo loudly. I had no real sense of direction, since the darkness and the heavy feel of the earth seemed to blind my other senses.

Then my nose caught a change in the flow of air. It was sharper, cooler, smelling less of earth and more of oil and car exhaust. And those smells were accompanied by the sound of a car starting up.

The bastard had not only an escape tunnel but an escape vehicle.

Which didn't mean he was guilty of the crime I'd come here to question him about, because lots of vampires had either safe rooms or escape hatches built into their homes. But the fact that he'd used his certainly wasn't pleading his innocence.

The wolf couldn't move any faster without running the risk of making the tunnel collapse around me, which meant it was time to shift shape.

In seagull form, I exploded out of the tunnel, sweeping upward on silvery-gray wings. Only to find myself in a garage, staring at the back of a fast-disappearing van.

It was a white Ford transit—one of those big square vehicles with no side or rear windows, and tinted front windows. The perfect vehicle for vampires, in other words.

Surrey drove at breakneck pace onto the Nepean and headed back toward Frankston, weaving through the traffic like a madman and running most of the lights. He slowed down as he neared central Frankston, moving off the Nepean and onto a series of side streets, until he reached an industrial area. Finally the van slowed as it approached a line of basic, gray-painted warehouses. The heavy steel door of the warehouse in the middle began to roll up, and the van pulled inside. I swooped in after him and flew up into the ceiling, perching on one of the rafters as the van came to a halt and Surrey climbed out.

He looked like a man in a panic. Sweat beaded his face, and the scent of fear was so intense I was aware of it even in seagull form.

He paced the length of the van several times, running his hands through his thin hair and generally looking like a man possessed, then stopped and dug his phone out of his pocket.

"Come on, come *on,*" he muttered, his voice crackling with anxiety.

Whoever he was calling didn't answer. "Fuck," he said, then spun, throwing the phone at the wall. It hit with force, smashing into a hundred different plastic and metal bits before it even hit the floor.

I wondered if Cole and his team would be able to pull information out of them. It probably depended on whether the main chip had survived the impact.

He swore again and stalked toward a small office tucked into the far corner. I leapt off my perch and flew down to the van, shifting shape as I neared the ground, landing lightly and silently at the rear of the vehicle.

Surrey remained in the office. He might have been a vampire, but he obviously was in such a state of panic that he hadn't yet registered my presence.

I crept forward and peered in through the driver's window. There were guns on the front seat, which meant Surrey himself was more than likely armed.

I wasn't. All my weapons were locked securely in my car.

I slid my fingers under the door handle and flicked it upward as carefully as I could. The resulting *click* was soft, but it still seemed to echo across the silence as sharply as a gunshot.

"Who's there?" Surrey demanded.

I reached in, grabbed one of the guns, then said, "Riley Jenson from the Directorate, Mr. Surrey. Put down any weapons you're holding and come out of the office with your hands up."

He didn't reply, but the tension and fear riding the air seemed to ramp up several degrees. I glanced down to check whether the gun was loaded, then flicked off the safety and wrapped a finger around the trigger.

I didn't want to shoot him, but I didn't want to take any chances, either.

"Come out of the office," I repeated, when there was no sign of movement from within the small room.

"What do you want with me?" His voice was edged with panic.

I'd dealt with many vampires over my years as a liaison and a guardian, and I'd never come across one who was so afraid. Which suggested he at least had *some* involvement with the murder.

"I just need to talk to you," I said.

"What about?"

"About a murder that happened in Melton." As I spoke, I reached out telepathically, feeling for his thoughts. If I could break through his shields and get to his mind, I could not only freeze him but find out once and for all whether he was actually guilty of this morning's murder.

Only what I hit wasn't the buzz of shield but rather blankness. This vamp was mind-blind, just like my brother. Which meant no one, no matter how powerful, could read or control him telepathically.

I cursed silently. So much for trying to do it the easy way.

"I don't know anything about no murder." And yet the anxiety staining the air ramped up several more notches, belying his words.

"Then you've got nothing to worry about." I scanned the warehouse quickly. There was a whole lot of space between me and the office, and while there were no windows looking out in this direction, he didn't really need them. He was a vamp. Not only did he have infrared vision at his disposal, but he'd hear my heartbeat and feel the rush of blood through my veins. "Just come out and talk to me, Mr. Surrey."

He didn't answer. I blinked and switched to infrared myself. Vampires tended not to have a lot of body heat, although they were far from cold—especially the older ones, like Quinn. Surrey was a deep, dark-red blur huddled in the corner of the office.

What the hell did he think he was doing? There was no escape from that room—and if he'd had another bolt hole, he would have used it by now. So why was huddled there like a cornered rat?

Was he waiting for someone?

It was certainly possible. He'd had ample time to phone for reinforcements while driving.

I swept my gaze through the shadows again. There was a door at the rear of the building, but even from here I could see the padlock. Meaning the only way in or out was the still-open roller door. I backed around the van, keeping my eyes on the office and my senses attuned to the open door behind me. When I reached the driver's side, I reached in and pressed the remote. The door began to rattle closed.

"What are you doing?" Surrey all but yelled. "Why are you closing the door?"

"I'm just making sure no one can sneak up on me, Mr. Surrey." I edged around the car door and made my way to the van's snub nose. My gun was still aimed at the office, but I doubted he was coming out. More than likely, I'd have to go in and get him. "There's no reason to panic."

"You're going to kill me, aren't you?" His voice was becoming shriller. "That's why you closed the door, isn't it?"

My gaze switched from the deep-red blur that was Surrey to the office door. It would only take me a heart-beat to get there, but once there, I was a sitting duck. Surrey might be panicking, but he was still a vamp and still had reflexes as fast as mine. Was I willing to bet my life on the fact that his panic would make his aim less perfect? The answer to that was a categorical *no*. "Mr. Surrey, I just want to talk to you. If you have nothing at all to do with the crime, you won't get into any trouble."

"You're lying. I can taste it!"

"Mr. Surrey, please calm down. I promise—"

I didn't get the rest of the sentence out. Surrey finally moved, launching himself through the doorway and firing his weapon in one swift, deft movement.

Chapter 4

The shot reverberated through the emptiness. I threw myself sideways, felt the sting of metal past my cheek, and fired my own gun. I hit the concrete with enough force to bruise, but ignored the shock reverberating through my muscles and rolled into a kneeling position, the gun held at the ready.

I needn't have bothered.

My shot had flown true, hitting Surrey in the middle of his forehead. Not even a vampire can survive having his brains splattered out of the back of his head.

Nausea rose. I closed my eyes and fought back the bitter taste of bile in my throat. Justified or not, I'd let instinct take over and had fired to kill rather than wound.

I don't want to do this anymore. The thought came thick and fast, its force so strong it made me shake.

But the truth was, I would. Time and time again. I would do what I had to do, until the killer took me over.

Because I had no other choice, no other option.

Kye had offered an option, some stupid, silly part of me whispered. It might have even been a way out.

But it was a way out that would have involved more killing. He'd been a hunter, just like me, only he'd *enjoyed* it. He wouldn't have changed even if I'd asked.

But I hadn't asked. I'd killed him instead.

Tears stung my eyes, but I savagely blinked them away. Feeling sorry for myself wasn't going to help.

I took a deep, somewhat shuddery breath, swiped a hand at the blood dribbling down my cheek, then flicked the safety back on the weapon and pushed to my feet.

Surrey might be dead, but I could still get my answers—if his soul was a little more cooperative than his flesh had been, that was.

I walked across to the office doorway and squatted beside his body. In death, he looked small and harmless, his body so thin it was almost wasted. His face was gaunt, his nose and cheeks sharp and prominent, and his skin had that pale, translucent look of a vampire who wasn't feeding enough. The thick scent of the blood and brains that were leaking from his head made my nose twitch, but it was the smells riding underneath that caught my interest. Because underneath the reek of vampire was the tantalizing, nebulous aroma of werewolf.

Sometime in the last few hours, he'd been in close

contact with one of us. And if Surrey *had* been in the van Johnson's soul had mentioned, then he'd just given us our first clue as to who his partner in crime was.

I rested my arms on my knees and waited. For some odd reason, humans seemed to believe that vampires had no souls. Maybe because, for most vampires, the turning process *did* involve the death of their human forms as their bodies evolved into vampire—and for humans, death generally meant the soul moved on. But whatever the reason, it wasn't true. Although right now, it seemed Surrey's soul was a little afraid to come out and speak to me.

I shuffled back a fraction, hoping that by giving him a little more space, he'd feel a little less jumpy.

I'd never met a soul that was scared of me before. Confused and frightened by what had happened to them, yes, but not actually afraid.

It took a few minutes, but gradually the chill of death began to infuse the air. Wispy strands of smoke began to rise from his body, the tendrils gathering several feet above his flesh until they'd formed a ghostly, almost humanlike figure that had no features. He didn't swirl as so many other souls did, but I felt the sharp tug of him sucking at my energy.

You lied, he said, his voice far clearer, stronger, than was usual for the dead. But maybe that was merely a result of the freshness of his demise. Usually I didn't arrive on the scene until at least an hour afterward.

"Anyone who shoots at a guardian needs to be prepared. We don't often miss." Although I could have, if I'd just taken a moment to think rather than react. It would have been better to interrogate his live body rather than his dead one.

But I didn't kill anyone, he said. His anger and fear swirled around me, through me, in a bitter, vengeful cloud.

It was the same bitterness I'd tasted in the park.

"If you didn't kill Johnson, then why were your prints found in the van? And why was your scent at the murder scene?"

He just sat there, a pulsing cloud of conflicting emotions. And he didn't seem more inclined to talk in this form than he had when flesh.

"If you want to move on and find peace, you'd better talk to me, Mr. Surrey."

I had no idea if it actually worked that way, but I was betting he didn't, either.

He stirred, sending a tendril of smoke swirling outward from his main form. The energy flowing from my body increased sharply, and pain stabbed through me. Obviously, I needed more recovery time between souls.

The bastard deserved what he got, he spat. *He killed my family. Tortured them.*

"He went to prison for his crimes—"

Hah, Surrey retorted. *Twenty-five years for my wife and her daughter. Does that seem fair to you?*

"That's not—"

Yeah, yeah, you bastards all stick together. Well, I don't regret my actions. He deserved it. I can move on in peace now, knowing he can't do that to anyone else.

"But you didn't actually do anything, did you, Mr.

Surrey?" It was a guess on my part, but a pretty certain one. Surrey might be a vampire, but he didn't seem to have the balls for torture. Sure, he'd had no compunction about shooting at me, but I think that was more fear and panic than courage.

His sullenness swirled around me. The pain of him sucking at my strength was growing, as was the dull ache behind my left eye.

No, he said eventually. *I hired someone.*

"Tell me who."

I never knew his name and he never got out of that stupid costume he was wearing.

"The demon costume?"

His smoky form moved, which I took as assent. Maybe he'd forgotten he no longer had flesh.

"How did you get in contact with him, then?"

There was an ad in the paper.

I blinked. Contract killers were now taking out ads? "What sort of ad?"

A problem-solved ad. I contacted them, told them about Johnson, and they said they could help me.

By sending around a hit man? Interesting. "Was it their idea or yours to accompany the killer?"

Mine. I wanted to see the bastard die, wanted to feel it. Wanted him to know just how it felt to spend the last minutes of your life in such pain and fear.

Which was why the scent of vengeance had been so thick and bitter.

"Which paper did you see the ad in?" Dizziness swirled through me as I spoke, and I dropped a hand to the concrete to steady myself. But the weakness was growing. I'd need to end this soon.

The local paper, Surrey said. *It runs every week.*

"And there's nothing else you can tell me about the man you hired? How did you pay him?"

Cash up front. His smoky form began to swirl and his anger sharpened. *I can feel you growing weaker, guardian. Perhaps you should join me in—*

I didn't wait for him to finish, just chopped down on the link between us, cutting him off. The abruptness of it sat me back on my butt, but it had an even more resounding effect on him.

He screamed.

It was a high-pitched sound of agony and frustration combined, and the tendrils that had formed his body shattered, flying like broken glass in a hundred different directions.

Then he was gone.

I swallowed heavily and hoped like hell I hadn't destroyed his soul as easily as I'd shot him.

For several heartbeats I sat there on the cold concrete staring at his body, but the trembling in my limbs got worse, not better, until it felt like I was shaking from the tip of my toes to the end of my hair. I wrapped my arms around my knees and tried to get a grip, but it didn't seem to help. Coldness swept me—a coldness that had nothing to do with souls and everything to do with death.

And not just this death, but all deaths. The ones in the past and the ones in the future. The ones that had stained my soul and the ones that would.

I can't do this any longer.

I didn't *want* to do this any longer.

But short of death, I couldn't see a way out. I needed someone to talk to, someone who would understand . . .

I'm here. Like a cool, calming breeze, Quinn's thoughts poured into mine, instantly stemming the rising tide of panic. *Talk to me.*

I couldn't. The words wouldn't form. I just wanted him here in the flesh, wanted him to wrap his arms around me and tell me it would be all right. That in the end, fate's fickle finger would start pointing at someone else, and my life would become sane again.

His warmth and love flooded down the link, battering away the doubts, the fear.

My thoughts unfroze. Panic subsided.

Sorry, I said eventually. *I didn't mean to disturb you like that.*

Sweetheart, you can disturb me anytime, anywhere, for any reason. He paused, and I felt the wash of his concern. *What happened?*

I killed a suspect.

Not without reason.

No.

Then you were doing your job—nothing more, nothing less.

I know, but—

Stop beating yourself up, Riley. His voice came, soft but firm. *The only person you need to worry about at the moment is yourself. I can take care of everything else— even if that means getting you away from the Directorate.*

I smiled. It was very nice being loved by this man.

But was I ready for him to go to war for me? Because that's what it would take to get me away from the Directorate. Jack was a great boss and a fair vampire, but he was still a Directorate man and he'd worked for a long time to get me where I was today. He wouldn't release me easily.

And while I didn't think Jack would resort to violence to keep me—especially against a vampire who was older and stronger—Jack wasn't the sum of the Directorate. His sister was—and she was both older and stronger than Quinn. I had no idea just what she was capable of.

I wasn't about to risk putting Quinn in harm's way. I'd already lost my soul mate. I wasn't about to lose my heart, as well.

But there was also the larger problem of the drug in my system. Quinn might own pharmaceutical companies, but they weren't set up to monitor me like the Directorate was. Until we knew the direction of those changes, I was basically stuck.

Riley, he said softly, *if you want out, I'll make it happen.*

I know. And that's what worried me. *But it's not that simple.*

It can be.

I rubbed a hand across my eyes. Maybe it could. Maybe if I gave up fear and simply trusted, it would all fall in place.

But I couldn't. Not yet.

Not when everything was still so raw and fresh.

I think I just need time, I said softly. *Time to understand what I really want.*

Time to gain the courage to go after it.

Maybe you also need to talk to someone who has been through what you've been through, he said. *How long has it been since you've talked to Ben?*

Once upon a time, he would have seen Ben as a threat, but after everything we'd been through of late, I think Quinn finally understood just how secure he was in my world. It didn't matter if the moon heat drove me into the arms of another—it hadn't anytime recently, and certainly never with Ben—because for a wolf, sex was a physical thing, a need as deep and driving as Quinn's need for blood, and it did not affect the heart or mind. The possessive, controlling part of him had finally given way to understanding.

In return, I gave him my all. Or as much of me as there was left to give.

I talk to Ben all the time. And he *did* understand, because he'd lost his soul mate and had come out the other end.

But maybe that was also the problem. He'd coped. I really wasn't.

I think you need to go talk to him again. Quinn paused. *You need to talk to someone.*

I closed my eyes. The pain behind that statement was easy to hear. *I'm sorry, love. I don't mean—*

I know. He cut me off gently. *And I know I told you in the past that I didn't want to know about you and Kye. But you need to release the pain of it, Riley, or it's going to eat you up and destroy you.*

I know. I took a deep, shuddery breath. *I'll arrange another meeting with Ben.*

And after that, maybe, finally, I could find a way to talk to Quinn. To open up about the pain and the hurt that still festered inside.

Though he sensed that hurt. He was too attuned to me now not to.

I need to report the kill to Jack, I said eventually. *Whether we'll meet for lunch or dinner very much depends on what he wants me to do next.*

I'm here at the office all day, so just call when you're ready.

I will. I paused, then added softly, *Love you.*

He smiled. It came down the link between us like sunshine through rain, all warm and glittery.

And you are my world, and everything that means anything to me, he replied. *Remember that, when the demons start getting the better of you.*

Tears stung my eyes and I blinked them away. I must have done *something* right if fate had left this man in my life.

I sent him a mental kiss, then closed down the link between us. My gaze fell on Surrey and, with another sigh, I dug my phone out of my pocket. Humans often got surprised that things like phones could come through the change with us. To be honest, I really couldn't explain it myself. But the things we wore—on our bodies and in our pockets—were looked after by the magic, in much the same way as our clothes were. The things we carried—like handbags— weren't. Where it all actually went when we were in our alternate shapes I had no idea—and, really, I preferred *not* to know.

I hit the record button, ignored the fact that my hands were still shaking, and propped the phone in position.

"The victim's name is Hank Surrey," I said, moving around to the other side of his body so I wouldn't obstruct the recording. "One shot was fired to the middle of his forehead, resulting in a clean kill."

I didn't bother adding that I'd fired in self-defense. It wasn't really relevant in this case, and Jack didn't care anyway.

I reached into Surrey's pockets and began pulling items out. Under normal circumstances, it wouldn't be me doing this but Cole. But given that Surrey wasn't actually responsible for the killing, we needed to find some answers fast.

Or rather, *I* needed to find the answers fast.

"Handkerchief and three-fifty in coins found in left front pocket of jeans." I dumped those back, then moved to the right side. "Wallet found in right side pocket."

It contained about forty dollars in cash, several credit and key cards, and several bits of folded-up newspaper. I repeated this for the phone's benefit, then drew out the paper and unfolded them. Both were newspaper clippings, and both were relatively small but explosive in their own way.

The first was a short article that had obviously been in his wallet for many years. The ink was all but faded and the paper so thin it was coming apart along the well-worn crease lines. It spoke about the brutal murder of a woman and her child in a park playground in Eltham, and it was little more than a couple of lines long. But that was enough to hint at the brutality of the event.

Surrey's wife and adopted child, obviously.

No wonder the air had been thick with the scent of vengeance. Surrey had been holding on to his anger for a very long time indeed.

The other bit of paper was the ad he'd spoken about, and it simply said *all personal problems solved,* and gave a contact number. It was a land line rather than a cell phone, and in this day and age that was unusual.

I repeated it for the benefit of the recording, then continued searching, but there was little else of interest. Moving the search to the van produced the same result. I stopped the recording, then sent it to the Directorate and rang Jack.

"Riley," he said. "We've just installed a scrambler program onto your cell phone, so hopefully that'll stop the scanners from picking up any information until we get a new number. What's happened?"

"I cornered Surrey and he wasn't happy,"

"Meaning he's dead." It wasn't a question, and in so many different ways that was disturbing. The worst being the fact that Jack had no doubt that I would shoot to kill, and *that* certainty was the one thing I'd wanted to avoid.

I desperately wanted him to have doubts. *Needed* him to have doubts, for my own peace of mind if nothing else.

"Surrey's soul rose and I questioned him. It appears he hired a hit man through an ad in the local paper. The clipping was in his wallet—"

"You recorded your search?" he interrupted. "Cole's very particular about that."

And I'd been told off enough times by him to do it automatically nowadays. "It's already on its way to you, though you might want to warn him he'll also find my prints in the van. I now need to trace the phone number I found." I reached for the ad and read out the number. "I might as well go investigate it if we can pin down a location."

"Hang on." He plonked the phone down, then murmured something to whoever was in the main office with him. Papers shuffled, then he came back online. "The labs just came back with the latest test results."

My stomach twisted, then sank. The tests had become such a regular part of my life of late that I barely even thought or asked about them. But if he was mentioning it, it could only mean the genetic markers had moved. I licked suddenly dry lips and said, "And?"

"And it appears your DNA is shifting toward vampire."

I frowned. "That really isn't unexpected."

Especially given Rhoan was already more vampire in his genetic makeup. It was always a possibility that eventually I'd head down that path, even without the DNA-altering drugs that Talon had given me.

"To some extent, it's not," Jack agreed. "But they're not the changes we were, to some extent, expecting."

Why was I not surprised? I rubbed a hand wearily across my eyes and said, "So what's happening?"

"We're not exactly sure." For a minute, he sounded almost as weary as I did. But then, me becoming more vampire-like seriously cocked up his plans for a day division. "We've compared your results to Rhoan's. His have been stable for years—and yours are not comparing favorably."

"Meaning whatever is happening, it's not making me like Rhoan?" Which in some ways was a good thing, because Rhoan had to drink blood during the full moon, and that was something I was desperate to avoid. I hated the taste of blood, even when it came after the thrill of chasing and catching rabbits.

If Jack was right, it seemed I *was* going to avoid the whole blood-taking thing—but at what cost?

What exactly was that damn drug turning me into?

"Given our success rate at predicting where these changes will go, I think it'll be safer if we upped the monitoring."

And wasn't *that* what I wanted to hear. The tests might not bother me as much as they used to, but there were some months where I could sympathize with pin cushions. "Are we talking weekly?"

"At least."

Crap. "It's not going to alter anything, Jack. It's not going to help."

"It's better that we track the changes rather than find out the hard way, Riley."

I guess so.

"Okay," he added, "we have the address. We'll send it through to your onboard."

Which I was nowhere near. And suddenly part of me didn't want to go anywhere near it. I drew in a shaky breath and blew it out slowly. It didn't help calm the nerves or the aching desire to just flee. "I'll head there now, then go for lunch."

"Keep the com-link on, Riley."

He hung up. I shoved the phone into my pocket, then pushed to my feet. The smell of blood stung the air, metallic and cloying. I briefly wondered if that smell would ever call to me. Just because my DNA seemed to be veering away from that aspect of vampirism didn't mean it couldn't veer back.

I turned resolutely on my heel and walked away. I couldn't change what was happening to me, and I wasn't about to spend time dwelling on it. I had enough troubles on my plate; I didn't need anything extra.

It didn't take me long to fly back to my car, but three shape-shifts into seagull form in as many hours had totally shredded my top. I grabbed a T-shirt out of the trunk and dragged that on before jumping into the car and driving over to the address Jack had sent me.

It turned out to be a less-than-impressive-looking concrete apartment building in the back streets of St. Kilda. I found a parking spot several buildings down, then climbed out of my car and strolled back slowly. The apartment that was linked to the phone was situated on the fourth floor, which in this case was the top floor. I studied the windows but couldn't pick which one was our target. They all had the same limp-hanging curtains, the only difference being the color. Some were blue, some were pink. All were sun-faded and somewhat grimy looking.

The building didn't appear to have any sort of security system installed up front—which, given the somewhat rundown appearance of the place, wasn't really surprising. The door was painted a gay red, but the paint was peeling and the wood pockmarked with holes. The air coming out of the place was a rich mix of sweaty humanity, cheap perfume, and sex.

Which suggested it was probably a brothel. And while brothels had been legal for more than a few years, I wasn't sure they were supposed to be situated in this section of St. Kilda. As a general rule, they had to be away from main living areas, but it wasn't unknown for councilors to be bribed to look the other way.

I glanced through the doorway as I walked by and saw a rather large and muscular-looking guard sitting in the hallway. Which maybe explained why there was no outside security, but it still seemed like overkill. This area was well policed, and, as far as I knew, there hadn't been any trouble here for months.

But maybe he wasn't just here to guard the ladies. Maybe he was also a sentinel for the room upstairs. The one that held a rare land line.

I kept walking until I'd gotten around the corner, then once again shifted shape, hoping like hell the T-shirt held up better than the blouse. I was running out of spare clothes.

I flew up to the rooftop and landed on the filthy tiles. I didn't immediately change back to human form, but instead strutted around like any regular gull as I checked it for security features.

And I discovered a *ton* of them.

Cameras, heat sensors, and sound monitors—everything that *hadn't* been in evidence downstairs, and all of which seemed a little over the top for what looked like a low-end brothel.

I strolled on, looking for some way to get in. There was a door, but it didn't have a handle on this side. Which meant it was more than likely padlocked on the inside. And while I could no doubt break in, someone was bound to hear or see me with all the security. Right now, it seemed a damn good idea to avoid detection—at least until I knew just what, exactly, all this was protecting.

Which meant finding another way in.

I leapt skyward again, flying for a bit before swooping down the side of the building. A third-floor window was open, so I circled around and landed on the sill. From inside came the sound of a bed squeaking and the grunts of a man. The smell of sex and sweat was so heavily ingrained that even in this form I could smell it.

I ignored it, hopped from the sill to the floor, then looked around for security. There didn't appear to be anything here—no cameras, and no monitoring devices of any kind that I could see, except for a discreetly placed button wired to the end of the bed. To be used if customers got nasty, no doubt.

The couple were in the lone bed. The man was obese

and sweating heavily, the woman slender and dark skinned. She was chewing gum in time to the man's movements.

I shook my head. I could never really understand the human necessity to pay for sex—mainly because I couldn't understand what joy there was in only one partner having a good time.

But then, I was a werewolf, and sex was something to rejoice and celebrate. Maybe you needed to be human to understand the concept of paying for sex.

Unfortunately, the door was closed. I padded across the threadbare carpet to check it out anyway, but in seagull form, I was never going to open it. I swore internally, then moved under the only other bit of furniture in the room—a somewhat bedraggled-looking chaise longue.

Thankfully, the sex didn't last all that long. The man came, the woman looked at her watch, then hit him lightly on the back. "Time's up."

Her voice was gravelly and uneven. I wondered if it was natural or caused by too many cigarettes. The man grunted and climbed off her, his body wobbling in all the wrong places. He threw the condom in the trash, then dressed and walked out of the room—and slammed the door shut behind him.

The woman reached for a packet of cigarettes on the scrappy-looking dressing table beside the bed, popped one out, then lit up. She sucked in a deep breath and blew out several rings, then turned her head and looked straight in my direction.

"Who the fuck are you, then?"

Chapter 5

I hesitated for a heartbeat, then strolled out. She might have spotted me, but she hadn't yet started screaming for help. That was something, I guess.

I didn't change shape immediately, though. There was always an off chance she just liked talking to seagulls, so I pecked at something disgusting on the carpet and tried to act birdlike.

"I like the attempt," she said, casually drawing on the cigarette again, "but I'm sensitive to weres and shifters, and I felt you out on the sill. Shift shape and talk to me, or I'll scream for help. And I'm figuring you don't want that if you're sneaking in through windows."

Given little other choice, I shifted shape, then sat on the chaise longue. My T-shirt hadn't fared much better than the other shirt, forcing me to tie the ends together to stop my breasts from falling out.

"What are you?" she asked, her gaze sweeping me critically. "You can obviously take on bird form, but you feel like a wolf."

"That's because I am."

She raised an eyebrow. "Lucky. So, why are you here?"

"That depends on how fast you want to run downstairs and report my presence to the guard."

"Ah. Well." She sat up and swung her legs around. She was naked, but as uncaring as a wolf. Which was unusual for someone who smelled human, but I guess in her line of business, you'd lose your modesty early. "I earn fifty bucks for twenty minutes in this dump. Pay me that, and my lips are sealed."

I heard nothing but truth in her words and her mind. So I reached into my pocket, retrieved my wallet, and pulled out fifty bucks. But I flipped the note away as she reached for it. "I want honest answers. And I can tell truth from lies."

"Deal. Though I may not know what you want."

"Fair enough." I let her have the cash. "What can you tell me about apartment 404?"

She raised a well-plucked eyebrow. "Only that it's off limits for us ladies."

"But that hasn't stopped you from being curious, has it?"

She smiled. "No." She paused to take a drag on her cigarette. "There's two men who head up there regularly.

One is a werewolf, the other is a shifter of some kind. A bird, I think, from his scent."

"Can you give me descriptions?"

She shrugged. "They're men. Leaner and fitter than the bozos I service, but still men. The wolf has brown hair and brown eyes, the other is a blondie with green eyes."

"And how do they walk?"

She smiled. "Like men you wouldn't want to tangle with. Are you a cop?"

"Guardian."

"Meaning things just might get interesting around here."

"That depends on what, exactly, is in that room."

"Well, I can tell you they walk upstairs with nothing and come back down with notes. And a phone rings up there a lot."

"You've never heard voices up there, or seen anyone else enter the room?"

"Nope. And the rest of the rooms are storage, from what I've heard."

"What about security?"

"Camera on the stairs going up. Probably an electronic lock, too, because I've heard the beeps. Other than that, I can't say."

I was betting the camera was an infrared. Given all the technology on the roof, it would be pretty pointless putting anything else in.

"Who watches the camera? The guard in the hall?"

"I doubt it. Frankie is asleep more often than not."

I raised an eyebrow, amusement playing around my

lips. "So he's a visual deterrent more than a physical one?"

"Basically. Although I wouldn't want to get him annoyed—he's got muscles on his muscles."

Which didn't mean a thing if you didn't know how to use them. "There's no other security anywhere?"

"Not that I've seen, but that doesn't mean there isn't."

"What about backup systems?"

"Other than Frankie, I don't think there are any." She shrugged. "The power grid is pretty stable here, so I don't suppose they think it's necessary."

And *that* at least gave us a way in. "What about the owner?"

"T.J.? He only comes here once a week to pay wages. Vonnie handles the day-to-day stuff."

"She got a last name?"

"None of us have last names," she drawled. "Not unless you pay more."

Not a chance when we could search through the business registrars. "Do you know if the windows upstairs are locked?"

She shook her head. "But half the catches in this dump don't work, so I wouldn't be surprised if the same applies upstairs." She contemplated me for a minute, then added, "The windows are too heavy for your bird form, and the sill would be a hell of a balancing act for your human one."

"That's never stopped me before."

"Heard that about you lot." She glanced at her watch. "I'm expected downstairs in ten minutes for my next customer. Unless you've got any more questions, I need to get cleaned up."

I rose. "What time do those men usually come to check the upstairs room?"

"They're due this afternoon. They usually get here about two." She smiled. "For another fifty bucks, I'll leave the window and the door open in case you need it."

"You're a shark in disguise," I said, nevertheless getting my wallet back out.

"A girl has to live," she drawled.

I guess she did. And while the conditions here weren't top notch, at least there *was* security, and she wasn't on the street. That had to be a good thing.

"I'll try not to disturb you when I come back in."

She snorted. "Did I look as if I'd mind being disturbed?"

I grinned. "Thanks for your help."

"Cass," she said. "My name is Cass."

"Thanks, Cass."

She nodded, then opened the dresser drawer, grabbing a little tin and tucking the cash inside. I shifted shape and in seagull form flew out the window, circling the building and checking out the different top-floor windows before heading for the side street. I changed shape, adjusted my clothes, then walked back to my car. But I didn't get in, grabbing my cell phone out of my pocket instead. I pressed Quinn's number and waited impatiently for him to answer.

"Well, hello," he drawled, the gentle Irish lilt in his voice sounding oh-so sexy. "I wasn't expecting to hear from you so soon."

"I've been visiting a brothel," I said, imagining his expression and smiling at the image.

"And I'm sure there's a perfectly good reason for it," he said, "even though I can't really think of one."

"It had a phone."

"Most of them do."

I laughed. "This phone is the contact number for a bunch of hit men for hire."

"Interesting." His voice was dry. "So why are you calling me?"

"Because I need food and sex, and not necessarily in that order. I figured you might be interested in sating one or both of those desires."

"You figured right. Where would you like said sating to occur?"

"Somewhere not too fancy. I need to be back at the brothel by one-thirty, so I haven't got time to go home and change. And several shape-shifts has shredded the last spare T-shirt I have in the car."

"Which is a look I quite enjoy," he said. "I take it you're close to the city?"

"St. Kilda."

"Excellent. There's a small spa in Acland Street that does a great lunch and spa treatment regimen. I'll send you the address and meet you there in twenty minutes."

"But I don't want—"

"Riley, trust me."

"Okay," I grumbled. "But you know how bitchy I can get when my hungers aren't satisfied."

He laughed. The warm sound flowed through me like a caress. "Trust me, love, I aim to satisfy us both."

"Well, good." I glanced at my watch. "I'll see you in twenty."

"You will."

He hung up, and I rang Jack. "Boss," I said, the minute he answered, "that land line is located on the top floor of a brothel, and the whole floor is bristling with electronic security."

"Meaning they're hiding something," he said. "Can you break in, or do you want some professional help?"

"Well, I'm thinking that electronic security usually needs electricity to work, so would it be possible to arrange a little blackout in the area around two?"

"It'll take out the entire block, but yeah, it can be done." He paused. "We ran a trace on the number. The phone is listed as belonging to the brothel. The owner of said brothel is one T. J. Hart. We're trying to track down an address for him."

That raised my eyebrows. "It isn't on the business registration?"

"It's a post office box."

I frowned. "I didn't think it was legal to do that. I thought it had to be a street address."

"Normally, it does."

Meaning T.J. either knew someone or had paid someone. Which meant he had money or connections that weren't obvious from the condition of his business.

"He has no license or police record," Jack continued. "The tax office has his address listed as Fitzroy, but the house was razed for apartments earlier this year."

Meaning he could be missing or simply didn't want to be found. I made a mental note to check with Cass this afternoon, then said, "Is it possible to put a tap on the phone?"

"It's in the pipeline, so make sure you leave no trace of your presence."

Which meant scent, if we were dealing with another were. I frowned and glanced at my watch, wondering if I could get to Liander's workshop and back to St. Kilda in twenty minutes. I knew he kept scent-erasing soap there, simply because he often redid my look for undercover operations, and scent erasure was a vital part of that. I might be pushing it time-wise, but it had to be done.

"There are two men who regularly collect the messages," I said. "I'll try to get pics of them today, and send them through."

"Good. And we don't think this is a one-off. There's a report coming out of Sydney about a brutal murder that bears striking similarities to our case."

"Meaning the victim was a recently released, long-term prisoner?"

"Yeah. We're trying to get full details at the moment."

"It might also be worth working up a list of recently released or about-to-be-released long-term inmates." If this was the beginning of a murder spree, such a list might help us save some lives.

"We're onto that, too," Jack commented. "We've already located two possibilities—two men were released from Perth penitentiary three weeks ago. One has since relocated to his hometown in Dunedan—which is in the middle of Western Australia—and the other went to Brisbane."

"I gather you've contacted the Directorate divisions in Brisbane and Perth, and warned them there might be trouble?"

"Yes. And I've also sent requests to *all* Directorate divisions to provide us with information on any crimes of a similar nature. We expect to get some hits. An organization this well protected probably won't be targeting just criminals."

Not if they were advertising in local newspapers. "This must be a new operation, though. Otherwise, we'd surely have heard of them before now."

"Not necessarily. If they've kept their operations interstate until now, there would have been no reason for us to be notified. Each division is basically autonomous."

Yet they'd all come from the one source— Melbourne—and I was betting Director Hunter kept a close eye on the other divisions. The Directorate was her baby, after all.

"I'm going to lunch now, boss, but I'll be back at the brothel by one-thirty."

"Okay, but I want you to return to the Directorate after that. You need to write up the report for the murder and the shooting incident."

I wrinkled my nose. I hated paperwork at the best of times. And, I thought, with a wash of sadness, there was now no Kade to sweet-talk into helping me.

"Will do," I said, and hung up. My phone beeped notification of an incoming message. It was the address

Quinn had promised. I opened the car door and fired up the onboard computer, switching it to navigation and typing in the address. It turned out I could probably walk there in less than five minutes.

I turned off the computer and locked the car, then once again shifted shape. With all this flying, my arms were starting to get a little tired, but there wasn't anything I could do about it. There was no way on this Earth I was going to drive to Liander's workshop and then back to St. Kilda in the twenty minutes I had. Not with traffic the way it was.

Of course, the skies had traffic of a different kind, and between avoiding the flocks of seagulls and pigeons—which always went somewhat crazy when I neared them—and the strengthening wind, I was a few minutes late getting back to the Acland Street spa.

I pulled my outfit together the best I could, then strolled through the old bluestone gateway that was the main entrance to the spa. The good thing about being in St. Kilda was that no one really took any notice of what you were wearing—or almost wearing. The strange and outlandish were common around here, and not even the receptionist batted an eyelid as I strolled into the foyer.

"How may I help you?" Her voice was deep and rich, and oddly in tune with the opulent foyer.

"Riley Jenson. I'm here to meet Mr. O'Conor." Though I kept my voice soft, it seemed to echo in the lush stillness of the place.

"Ah, yes," she said, and pressed a button.

I heard no bell, but two seconds later, a thin brown

woman appeared out of a side door and gave me a welcoming smile. "Ms. Jenson," she said, "if you'll just follow me, Mr. O'Conor is waiting."

Her words swirled through me, oddly reminding me of the people who *weren't* waiting. Kade. Kye. The bitter darkness rose, but I shoved it back ruthlessly. I had a man who loved me—and whom I loved—waiting for me. It was enough.

No, that dark part whispered. *It isn't.*

I ignored it and continued to follow the woman.

We went through a different door, and the smell of chlorinated water began to dominate. But underneath that ran tantalizing wisps of vanilla, orange, and spices.

"This is the spa treatment area," the woman said, obviously doing the guided tour. "The message therapy rooms are in the other wing. If you'd like a treatment after your spa, we can arrange that easily." Her gaze skated down to my hands. "The two-hour hand and foot ritual is very relaxing."

I followed her gaze. My nails weren't *that* bad. Well, okay, the polish was chipped and my nails a little rough, but they didn't deserve the sort of look *she* was giving them.

"I'll keep that in mind," I said mildly, although I was betting this place was *way* out of my price range.

She nodded, then knocked on the last door before opening it. "Mr. O'Conor, Ms. Jenson has arrived."

"Thanks, Sasha."

Sasha nodded, then closed the door behind me. I raised an eyebrow at Quinn. "You're on a first-name basis?"

He smiled, his dark eyes twinkling. "Is that jealousy I hear?"

"Depends on why you're on first-name terms."

He laughed and walked around the bubbling pool that dominated the room. His feet were bare, and each step slapped softly against the dark marble floors, the sound oddly in tune with the water. The walls behind him were a warm brown and the fittings on the spa gold. Basically, the whole room screamed opulence. But even so, there was nothing in the room as sumptuous as the vampire who walked toward me. Not even the delicious scent of ham and fresh breads rising from the buffet tucked into the corner behind me could tempt my gaze away from him.

My nostrils flared, drawing in the rich aroma of him as he drew closer, then he took me in his arms and kissed me. Not sweetly, not softly, but with all the hunger of a man in need. I wrapped my arms around his neck and returned the kiss in kind, and for many minutes there was nothing but this kiss and this man and the need that rose like a bonfire between us.

He finally pulled back, his eyes aglow with desire. "To answer your question," he said, "a friend of mine couldn't raise enough financing to open this place, so I invested. I know the staff because I'm a silent partner."

"So that's why you could get this room on such short notice."

"I'm certainly not above abusing my position if the need arises."

My gaze swept across his clothed body, coming to

rest on his groin. "And it certainly looks to me like the need has arisen."

"It has. Shall we retire to the water?"

"I thought you'd never ask."

I shucked off my clothes, then watched Quinn do the same. Once naked, he took my hand then helped me step into the tub. The water smelled faintly of chlorine, but it wasn't overpowering, and the bubbly warmth quickly worked its magic on my body, making me feel more relaxed than I had in ages.

I sank down into it with a sigh of pleasure. "This was a good idea."

"It was, wasn't it?" He floated over to me, a teasing smile on his lips and heat in his eyes. "But I thought you'd come here to have more basic needs sated . . . "

"Maybe the water is enough," I teased, entwining my legs around his body and drawing him closer. The spicy, luscious odor of him, rich with the scent of desire, swam around me, enhancing my need.

I smiled and pressed myself against him, enjoying his warmth and his closeness.

"Meaning I shouldn't kiss you senseless?" he murmured.

His lips were so close I could almost taste them. Almost. It was like being offered chocolate but not being able to eat it. And it made me want him even more fiercely.

"Meaning," I replied, the quaver in my voice all desire, "you should only kiss me if you really, really want to."

"Oh, wanting has never been a problem when it comes to you," he murmured.

His hand slid around my waist, his fingers pressing heat into my spine as he pulled me even closer to his warm, hard body.

The kiss was heat and desire and love all entwined into one luscious package, and it said everything there was to say without words.

Then his lips moved on, exploring, teasing. My throat, my shoulders, my breasts. I returned the attention in kind, nipping and exploring the hard planes of his body, until the rich smell of lust razed the air and my whole body burned for him.

When his cock slipped slowly but deeply inside, I moaned in pleasure. Then he began to move, and all I could do was move with him, savoring and enjoying the sensations flowing through me. Enjoying the completeness—a completeness that was heart and mind as well as body. And yet an awareness lurked in the deep, dark recesses of me, a hunger that could never be satisfied now that Kye was gone.

But as long as I had this, as long as I had Quinn, I could find a way to survive.

He took his time, stroking deeply as he licked and nipped and kissed. But the little waves of water began to flow away from our bodies with ever-increasing speed as our movements became more and more urgent. The sweet pressure began to build low in my stomach, fanning through the rest of me in waves as rapid as those that surrounded us, becoming a molten force that made me tremble, twitch, groan.

His breathing became harsh, his tempo more urgent. His fierceness pushed me into a place where only sensation existed, and then he pushed me beyond it.

He came with me, his teeth entering my neck at the same time, sharpening and prolonging the orgasm, until my body was trembling with exhaustion and utter satisfaction.

For several minutes afterward we didn't move, just allowed the warm bubbly water to caress our skins. Then he stirred and gave me a sweet, gentle kiss.

"I suppose I should now let you tend to the second of your needs."

I draped my arms loosely around his neck. "I don't think I have the energy to move right now."

"Well, we can't have you starving to death. I like my women with meat on their bones, thank you very much."

With that, he slipped his hands under my body and lifted me up. I laughed in delight and kissed his cheek. "So, if I was as naturally skinny as most werewolves, you wouldn't love me?"

"Oh, I'd still love you," he said, dark eyes twinkling as he climbed out of the tub. "I'd just always be trying to fatten you up. But as luck would have it, my girl normally has luscious curves. I just want them back."

With a smile teasing my lips, I began to kiss and nip his neck and earlobe. "That could cost you, you know," I murmured. "Because I have quite an appetite."

"Oh, I think I'm more than capable of catering to your appetites."

And over the next hour or so, he did indeed prove more than capable.

*I*t was almost one forty-five by the time I got back to the brothel. I flew up to a rooftop on the opposite side of the road, then shifted shape and found a position behind a billboard that provided shadowy cover yet allowed me to see what was going on down the street.

For the next fifteen minutes, nothing happened. Several clients came out, but none went in. Maybe midafternoon was a slow time.

At two—right on time—the lights in all the nearby buildings went out. And there wasn't a bad guy in sight. I cursed softly and briefly wondered if Cass had played me. But I'd felt no lie in her words or in her thoughts, so either she was better than a vampire at concealing lies, or the two men hadn't turned up for other reasons.

Which would be just my luck.

I continued to wait, silently hoping Jack could keep the power grid down for long enough.

At two-ten, a battered-looking brown station wagon cruised by slowly. It turned around at the end of the street then came back, pulling into a parking spot several doorways down from the brothel. Two men got out—one brown haired, the other blond.

Cass hadn't lied.

I took out my phone and began taking pictures. The blond moved toward the brothel, but the brown-haired

guy remained near the car, his gaze sweeping the surrounding buildings. Though I knew he wasn't likely to
spot me in the shadows of the billboard, I still drew them
closer around me. Better safe than sorry—especially
when you had red hair.

When I looked back over the building's edge, the
blond was just disappearing into the brothel and the
wolf was leaning against the back of the car, his arms
and feet crossed, the picture of casualness. Only his
ever-alert expression and the tension evident in his
body suggested otherwise. I took a final picture to
make sure I got the plate number, then carefully moved
backward. Once I'd pocketed my phone, I shifted
shape again and circled around the block, coming at
the brothel from the rear.

On closer inspection, the broken window I'd noticed
earlier would barely provide enough room for a spar-
row to get through, let alone a seagull.

I swore—which came out as a harsh squawk—then
shifted shape. My T-shirt—or what was left of it—fell
from my shoulders, and my jeans were looking decidedly worse for wear. I swore again as the wind swirled
around me, freezing my skin and buffeting my body.
The windowsills in this old building might have been
deeper than usual, but that didn't mean they were any
less precarious. I teetered for several seconds, trying to
gain balance. Trying to ignore the old fears that rose in
a rush every time I looked at the drop below me. Such
fears were totally ridiculous, because my seagull shape
now meant drops of *any* length no longer had the

power to hurt me, but I guess some fears were just too ingrained to be easily erased.

I checked the window for wires and sensors, but couldn't see any, so I dug my fingernails under the sill and lifted it upward. Cass had been right about the locks—this one basically fell apart as the window slid open. I slipped inside, dropping to the floor softly, my senses alert for anything and anyone.

The first thing I spotted was the camera in the far corner, but it was pointed at the other wall and wasn't moving. Temporarily cutting the power had worked—at least in this case. I just had to hope they didn't have backups on the other systems.

The air was stale and smelled faintly of urine—but whether it was human or animal in origin, I couldn't say. Although the little pellets littering the floor suggested at least one possum had taken up residence. I wondered how they'd gotten in without triggering the security system. Obviously, the little buggers were smarter than me. The room itself held little else but empty shelving units that were thick with dust and webs. I shut the window—just in case the power came back on at the wrong time—then padded forward, avoiding loose-looking floorboards and possum poop as much as possible.

Once at the door, I wrapped my fingers around the handle but didn't immediately open it. Instead, I switched my vision to infrared. A quick sweep of the rooms beyond the door revealed life in a room near the front of the building. That had to be the blond shifter—and given he was supposed to be a bird of some kind, it was worth the risk of stepping out. The wolf might have smelled me, but birds generally didn't have great olfactory senses. And these rooms, like the ones below, weren't very bright, which meant the shadows lay thick in the corners. With any luck, I could hide in those shadows.

I twisted the handle and opened the door, but just as I did, the shifter moved, his body heat showing him stepping through the doorway. I froze, half in and half out of the room, hoping the shadows were enough to conceal me.

He glanced my way, then stopped, and his sense of alertness increased twofold. He drew his gun and pressed a button on his lapel.

"Greg, we have an open door on one of the storerooms. I'm going to check it out."

Meaning he hadn't spotted me *yet,* but if I didn't do something real quick, he would. The shadows weren't strong enough to hold up under any sort of close scrutiny. Not when it was daylight, anyway.

But rather than step back, I hit him telepathically, slipping into his mind as silently and as efficiently as any vampire. I wrapped ghostly fingers around his control centers, stopping his movements and washing any awareness that something was wrong from his mind.

Then, knowing I didn't have much time before his partner started getting suspicious, I rummaged quickly through his thoughts. His name was James Cutter, and both he and the wolf worked for the Melbourne division of an organization known as Revanche. Cutter didn't know who owned or ran the organization, but the man they reported to was one Dillion Pavane. I searched for more information, but he didn't really have much. There were no offices located in Melbourne, as far as this man knew. They always met in bars, and never the same bars. He was paid in cash—another rarity in this day and age. He was also sick of the courier duties—which involved checking the various phones situated throughout the suburbs—and eager to make his first kill.

Meaning whoever was behind this organization didn't trust *any*body.

I grabbed my phone and quickly typed in all the locations of the other phones, then placed the image of a closed door and a conviction that nothing was out of place other than a smashed window in his mind. With that done, I turned him around and released him.

For the barest of seconds, he paused, as if wondering what the hell he was doing, then the suggestions I'd put in his mind took hold, and he touched his lapel communicator again. "There's a smashed window in back storeroom number three," he said. "Nothing to worry about."

He paused, listening to the comment from the other end, then added, "How the fuck do I know how the door opened? Maybe the catch is broken, like everything else in this dump. The main thing is, no one can get in or out, except those damn possums."

Again he paused, then added, "Yeah, I erased the tape after I took the notes. Don't fucking worry."

He turned and walked away. I waited until the door slammed, then glanced down at the handle in my hand

and snapped it off. When the men came back, they'd be expecting a broken door lock, so I'd better provide it.

As I turned around, the power came back on, cutting off any chance of investigating the other rooms. I just couldn't risk it when the whine of the camera beginning to rotate filled the dusty silence. And who knew what other security measures were in place that I hadn't yet spotted. Jack would be less than impressed if I inadvertently let them know we were onto them.

I quickly closed the door then shifted shape—half wondering as I did so whether I was going to have *any* remnants of clothing left by the time I got back to the car.

The camera had already begun its rotation back toward the door, and was almost at the window. If I didn't go now, they'd see the window, realize it wasn't actually smashed as the shifter had said, and start to wonder why he'd lied. And if they had a decent enough telepath on their team, he'd probably uncover traces of my presence in the shifter's mind.

I couldn't take that chance.

I jumped forward, flapping my wings as hard as I could, aiming for the tiny hole in the middle of the glass. At the last moment, I closed my eyes and tucked my wings together, bracing for the impact. I hit with speed, shattering the glass and spraying it outward. Which might make them wonder how, exactly, the glass had broken, but I couldn't help that. The jagged edges of glass scoured my side, tearing past feathers and into skin. Then I was out in the open air and tumbling downward. Panic rose just for a moment, then I spread my wings and began to fly, swooping past several rooftops as I curved around to the front of the building. I perched on the nearest rooftop, briefly shifting to my wolf shape and back again to stop the bleeding, then took to wing again.

The men were in the car, driving away. I followed them for a couple of streets, then swung around and flew into Cass's window. I needed to question her a little more about her boss.

She was with another man, but the door was open as she'd promised. Given that I didn't particularly want to watch her in action again, I sauntered through the door to have a look around. The hallway beyond was long and shadowy, and there were four doors leading off it. One was closed, but the other three were open and the rooms empty. I walked to the stairway and looked up. The camera sat above the landing, and was indeed an infrared.

It seemed a lot of trouble to go to for what was basically little more than a phone depot, but then I hadn't explored the other rooms, so who knew what was in those?

I suspected it wouldn't be much. Even though it had been Surrey's soul that had given us the lead, Surrey himself would probably have done so had he lived— even if he'd done it unwillingly, via a telepathic raid. We would have found this place—and this phone— one way or another, and I very much suspected they'd be ready for such an event.

I went back to the room. Cass's client was just finishing up, so I waited until he left, then shifted to my human shape.

"Couple of nasty-looking wounds you have there," Cass drawled, swinging her legs around and sitting up on the bed.

"Glass will do that," I said. "I don't suppose you know where T. J. Hart lives, do you?"

She raised an eyebrow, amusement glimmering in her eyes. "It's not listed on the business registration?"

"Apparently not." I plopped down on the chaise longue and tried to ignore the stale scents rising from it. "I'll give you another thirty for the information, because that's all I've got."

She considered me for a moment, then said, "How much trouble is T.J. in? Because as much as the clients suck, this is a reasonably secure and clean place to work."

I hesitated. "It depends on whether he's merely renting the room or actively involved in what is going on."

"Well, I know he raised a hell of a fuss about the shit they put on the roof, so I suspect his only involvement is a pocket-level one." She held out a hand. "Payment first. You look the trustworthy type, but I've been fooled before."

I dug out my wallet and handed over the last of my cash.

She tucked the cash into her tin, then gave me a smile. "T.J. lives down the road in Elwood. He likes to be near his investments."

She grabbed a scrap of paper and wrote down the address before handing it to me.

I shoved the scrap into my pocket. "So he has more than one brothel?"

"Yeah. The other one is in Caulfield. It's a little more upmarket. I used to work there when I was younger." She shrugged, like age and demotion weren't really a problem.

"Can I ask why you're still in the business? I mean, you seem pretty savvy, and I suspect you could get a job doing something else easily."

"I trained as a personal assistant and I'm a damned good one, so there's no doubt that I could. But the money here is good, I can set my own hours, and medical is included." She shrugged again. "Another year or so, and I'll probably open my own—"

She paused and cocked her head sideways. "T.J.'s just walked into the building."

"He's a shifter?"

She nodded, amusement playing around her lips. "Unfortunately for him, his alternate form is less than exciting. He's a hare."

I laughed. I couldn't help it. "A hare?"

"Yeah. It does explain his penchant for the sex business, though." She paused again, then frowned. "Those men are back. The bird-shifter—"

The rest of her sentence was cut off by two short, sharp gunshots.

Chapter 6

As screams erupted from the floors below, I glanced at Cass and whispered urgently, "Get under the bed and *don't* come out until I say so."

As she scrambled to obey, I headed for the door. There was a blue silk dressing gown hanging from a hook near the door, so I grabbed that and put it on—more to blend in than to cover my partial nakedness. Then I pressed my back to the door frame and switched on the com-link.

"Jack, we have shots fired at the brothel. Something's gone wrong."

"Did they spot you coming in or out?"

"I'd say no except for the fact that they're back here and shooting. Maybe there were some security systems that weren't taken out by the power outage."

"And maybe they got wind of us tracking down Surrey and are now erasing all possible leads back to them. And that would mean the phone number Surrey knew, and possibly anyone who knows its location."

"That's pretty cold-blooded."

"And so are your targets."

He probably had that right. I took a quick glance around the corner. Shadows and sunshine vied for prominence in the hallway. The door down the end of the hall was still closed, but as I looked, a bolt slammed home. The occupants had obviously heard the shots— not that a bolt would stop a determined shifter. I glanced over my shoulder to ensure Cass couldn't be seen, then edged out into the hallway.

There were people running up the stairs and others running for the rear of the building. The air was thick with the smell of fear and blood, but at least the screaming had stopped. But although there were no more gunshots, those men were still down there. I could smell the wolf, as he could no doubt smell me. Hopefully, he'd just think I was working here. It might be unusual for a wolf to work in a brothel, but it wasn't unheard of.

They were obviously going after their main target first, and that *had* to be the owner, the man who'd rented them the room. Anyone else they'd take care of when and if they had the time.

I reached the banister and took a quick glance down. Two half-dressed women were fleeing up the stairs, and several yards behind them ran a man wearing a lot of gold jewelry. Behind them all, one flight down, was the blond bird-shifter with the gun. His movements were calm, assured. Maybe he knew there was no way out up here—other than jumping out a window. And if anyone who didn't have wings attempted *that* from this height . . . Well, he'd probably save himself some bullets.

I reached out telepathically, intending to slip into his mind and stop him, only to hit an electronic wall. The bastard was wearing a nanowire. And a strong one, if the recoil of energy was any indication. I *could* break it, but it would take time and, more important, leave me open for attack from the wolf. I couldn't psychically attack two men simultaneously, even if I was one of the Directorate's strongest telepaths.

I stepped back into the shadows and waited. The two women ran past, smelling of sweat and fear and sex. They didn't even see me, just ran toward Cass's room. Then the man appeared. He was small and wiry, with big ears and a twitchy nose—currently dripping sweat. My inner wolf snarled—she liked *hunting* rabbits, not saving them.

I grabbed him with one hand and hauled him over the banister, then clamped my other hand over his mouth, cutting off his yelp before it could leave his throat.

"Riley Jenson, Directorate," I whispered, my lips so close to his ear I could almost taste the blood from a bullet wound on his neck. My wolf soul ached to rip and tear into the flesh she so often hunted up in the hills of Macedon, but the vampire wasn't having anything to do with his foul stench. And that in itself was a reason to celebrate, given the sudden swing in my DNA toward vampire.

"If you want to live," I added, "get under that bed and stay there."

He, like Cass, scrambled to obey. Jack said into my ear, "Riley, we need them alive if it's possible."

"Boss," I murmured, hoping like hell the wolf was far enough away not to hear me, "I've only been away for a few months. I'm not *that* rusty."

Nor was I that much of a killer. I hoped.

"Do you need assistance?" he added.

I hesitated. Assistance meant calling in either Rhoan or Iktar, and the reality was, there'd be no chance of either of them getting here before the action was over—even if they were in the city. And I doubted my brother was. "No. I'm fine."

"Okay. I've ordered the cleanup team to your location. They'll be there in twelve."

I didn't answer. I couldn't. The bird-shifter was now far too close, his scent tainting the air with its sharpness.

The sound of a gunshot ripped across the tense semi-silence, and I half jumped. But the shot had not been aimed at me. It hadn't even been fired by the shifter on the stairs. It had come from the ground floor, from either the wolf or whoever was left alive down there.

A heartbeat later, the screaming began again. I flexed my fingers, fighting the urge to help those women. I might be a guardian, I might have the advantage of speed and power, but the reality was it was still two against one, and both of them were armed.

And Jack would be pissed if I got myself killed after everything else that had happened over the last few months.

The shifter's steps were barely audible over the sounds of panic and sobbing. I briefly wondered whether Frankie—the brothel guard who'd apparently had muscles on his muscles—had been the first victim, or whether he was still down there trying to do his job, then stilled the thought as a blond head stepped onto the landing and turned.

I didn't give him the chance to see me. I simply launched straight at him, one hand grabbing for the arm that held the gun. I hit him waist-high and we went down hard, his body cushioning mine. He reacted as any trained fighter would—with power and quickness. His fist pounded into my side so hard it felt like concrete, and it was all I could do to hang on to the arm that held the gun. He hit me again, and something inside me cracked. I swore and flicked an elbow upward, smashing it under his chin and driving his bottom jaw up into his top. On a human, such a blow would have broken his jaw, but this man was not human, and we were bred tougher. He spat out some bloody teeth and grabbed me one-handed, rolling me around so that he was on top.

"Let go of the gun, my pretty," he said, his breath like dead meat, "or I'll be forced to break something else."

"Try it, and I'll break *you*."

He chuckled and raised his fist. I bucked my body, lifting him off me far enough to get one leg underneath him. Before he could release his weapon, he came down, balls first, onto my knee. Air exploded from his lungs and he went an odd shade of puce.

I ripped the gun from his grasp, smashed the butt of it over his head to knock him out, then dumped him off me.

Only to hear another set of footsteps coming up the stairs.

Crap.

I jumped to my feet, grabbed the shifter's arms, and dragged him into the nearest bedroom. I dumped him near the bed then threw off the mattress, hoping like hell the squeaking I'd heard earlier was an indication that these beds had those cheap metal springs. And for once, fate gave me a break.

I grabbed the nearest spring, ripped enough wire free to give me a decent length of metal, then shoved the shifter on his side. After hauling his arms around his back, I tied them together with the wire, wrapping it around and around his limbs, right up to his shoulders. Of course, it wouldn't hold him if he shifted shape, so for good measure, I smashed the gun butt down onto his elbow. The crack of breaking bone made me wince, but a shifter free and unable to fly was better than nothing. I tied the rest of the wire off the best I could, then stepped over him and headed for the door.

The footsteps on the stairs had stopped. I flared my nostrils, searching for the scent of the wolf. He was close, but not close enough. And he was more than likely as aware of my presence here as I was of his.

I had two choices: Wait him out, or go down after him.

I was leaning toward the first option when the gunshots and the screaming started again. Not just any screams, but ones that transformed into wet, gurgling sounds, only to be silenced by another gunshot.

He was shooting to maim before he killed them. Trying to lure me out with the pain of the women.

It worked.

I took a deep breath, then ran as fast as I could for the stairs. I grabbed the banister one-handed and flung myself over it, dropping down the stairwell onto the second to last step and landing half crouched. I saw the wolf immediately. Saw the gun pointed straight at my head. I threw myself sideways, smashing several balusters as I tumbled out into the third-floor hallway. The bullet meant for my head thudded into my shoulder, and pain erupted.

The bastard was using *silver*.

I'd been shot *far* too many times by the wretched stuff, and my flesh reacted instantly. Fierce, aching fire flared down my arm, stealing sensation, stealing strength, before I could even blink.

If I didn't take him down soon, I wouldn't be able to.

But the minute I moved, he'd shoot me again. And with the silver already in my shoulder, I just didn't have the speed behind me anymore. Not even my vampire blood could save me from the effects of it.

So instead of moving, I remained where I was, shuddering and shaking and sweating. It wasn't an act.

The pain was intense, and growing sharper. But my fingers—the ones on my right hand, the hand I could still feel—were wrapped around a sturdy piece of broken baluster. It wasn't much of a weapon, but it didn't need to be when you had the strength of a vampire behind you.

Although if he didn't move soon, the silver might snatch *that* from me, as well.

For several seconds, nothing happened. He remained where he was, motionless and silent, except for the slow, steady rhythm of his breathing. But I could feel his tension, could smell his readiness to act should I even twitch.

Finally, he stepped forward. One step, then two. Soon the sharp aroma of male wolf filled every breath, and it was all I could do not to twist and plunge the stake into his flesh. He wasn't anywhere near close enough for that.

So I waited as the fire in my shoulder flared even brighter and the numbness began to creep across the rest of my body.

He toed my back, then retreated quickly. I didn't react. He tried again, harder this time. I moaned—a sound that was real and heartfelt because he'd hit the broken bone. He chortled softly, then stepped over me.

I lashed upward with a booted foot, striking him hard in the nuts. As he stumbled and dropped, I twisted upright, driving the balustrade into his upper arm, forcing it through flesh and muscle and then into his side, pinning his arm to his body. He screamed, his fingers jerking reflexively and releasing the gun. I twisted, knocking him off his feet, then jumped to mine, staggering forward for the weapon.

"Jack," I panted, as I wrapped my fingers around the gun. I swung around and smashed it across the wolf's face. He went down and didn't move. "Get someone here quickly. I've been shot by silver and I'm fading fast."

He swore. "The men?"

"Out of action for the moment." My back hit the wall and I slumped down its length, my rump hitting the floor hard enough to send a wave of pain through me. For a moment, I saw red. Sweat broke out across my forehead and stung my eyes. I blinked fiercely and tried to concentrate on the wolf. He might be unconscious right now, but if the bastard woke and so much as twitched in my direction, I'd shoot him. And right now, with the silver burning in my flesh, I didn't really care if I killed him or not.

"The team is four and a half minutes away," Jack said. "Hang in there, Riley."

I wasn't going to make four minutes. I doubted I'd even make two. The burning was getting worse and my hand was beginning to shake so hard I'd be in danger of shooting myself if I actually fired the weapon.

"Cass," I yelled, my voice hoarse and scratchy. "I need help here."

There was no immediate response, and I can't really say I blamed her.

"Cass," I screamed. "The men are down, Directorate reinforcements are almost here, and I've been shot. I really, *really* need your help."

"They're three minutes away," Jack said into my ear.

Really? I thought, a little dazedly. Cole was really pushing the speed limits.

The numbness was beginning to creep up my neck. Breathing was getting harder. Oh god. I couldn't die— I didn't *want* to die. Not like this.

Strength flooded me—a strength that was love and warmth and everything that was still right with my world. It battered the numbness away from my neck, allowing me to breathe a little easier. It didn't erase it— it couldn't erase it—just subverted it, sending it down toward my legs rather than into my chest and throat. It bought me time, and I needed that desperately.

You will not die, Riley, Quinn said. *I won't allow it. Keep breathing. Keep fighting. I'm on my way.*

No, I thought weakly. *Don't. I'll be fine.*

And even as I said it, I knew he'd ignore me. And part of me was mighty glad of that fact.

After a few more precious seconds, footsteps echoed on the stairs, heading down.

"Riley?" Cass's voice was tentative, as if she were ready to flee given the slightest provocation.

"Here," I croaked.

Her head appeared in my line of sight, but it was fuzzy. Or maybe it was just my eyesight that was fuzzy. Her gaze widened when she saw me, and her face went white.

"Oh god," she said, one hand over her mouth.

"Yeah," I said. "He was using silver bullets. I need you to take it out."

"Two minutes," Jack intoned. "Hang on."

Cass drew in a shuddering breath and said "I can't—"

"You can," I interrupted harshly. "You *must*."

I put the gun down on the floor. My hand was shaking far too hard now for it to be safe.

She made a distressed sound low in her throat, then took another breath. "I'll get Marla. She's better at—"

"No. You need to do it. *Now*."

"But I haven't got any tools—"

"You have hands, Cass. Just hook a finger into the wound and dig it out."

"Oh, *fuck*." But she dropped down beside me and a hand touched my shoulder. Her fingers were shaking almost as much as mine.

Find something to bite down onto, Quinn suggested. *It'll help.*

I groped for some wood then shoved it in my mouth as she took another deep breath. "Okay."

That was all the warning I got. She plunged her finger into the wound and a scream wrenched its way up my throat. Everything went red and the sweat on my brow became a river.

Cass was crying and shaking, but she didn't stop. Blood spilled from the wound and pain seemed to consume my world. It was all I could do to stay conscious. Heaven help the lot of us if one of those men became aware enough to attack now.

Then the bullet moved. Sideways, not upward. Not out. White-hot fingers of pain rolled through me, and I bit down on the wood so hard splinters drove into my tongue.

Cass swore bitterly and drove her finger a little deeper. The bullet moved again, but this time it came up, making a slight popping sound as it came free of my flesh.

The relief was almost instantaneous. I leaned my head back against the wall for several heartbeats, drawing in great gulps of air, feeling the fire wash away and hoping like hell the numbness did, as well.

"Thank you," I said eventually, and opened my eyes. Her eyes were puffy, her nose pinched and red, and she was as pale as possible for a dark-skinned woman. "You just saved my life."

"And you saved T.J.'s and ours. A fair swap, I think."

"Yeah." I raised a still-shaky hand and wiped the sweat from my eyes. "But I think he shot some of the girls and the man-mountain guarding the stairs."

More tears spilled from her eyes. She scrubbed at them hastily, then spun around at the sound of footsteps, her fear ramping up several notches.

"Riley?" Cole's voice, harsh and urgent.

We were safe.

I could let go.

Once I'd shifted shape to stop the bleeding and heal my broken rib, that's exactly what I did.

When I came to, it was to find myself in warm, familiar arms. They were wrapped around me, holding me steady, pressing me against a body that was hard and strong.

"Hmmm," I murmured, snuggling in a bit deeper. "This is how a girl should wake from every night-mare."

Quinn kissed the top of my head, his lips light but warm. "I don't mind the 'holding you while you wake' bit, but let's avoid the whole 'getting shot by silver' part in the future, shall we?"

"Love to." I opened my eyes and blinked at the un-expected harshness of the light. We were obviously no longer inside the shadowy confines of the brothel. "The problem is the bad guys. They seem intent on using the stuff."

"Well, you'll just have to learn to avoid them better."

I snorted softly and sat a little. Quinn's arms slipped from my waist to my hips, but he didn't let me go. Maybe he was afraid I'd fall flat on my face. And given the tremor that invaded my muscles when I moved, he was more than likely right. "The trouble with avoiding bad guys is the fact that it's my job to bring them down."

"Then maybe we need to change your job."

I glanced at him and saw the seriousness in his ex-pression, the little lines of tension and worry around his eyes. I raised a hand and caressed the strong, beautiful planes of his face. "Maybe."

He smiled and kissed my fingertips. "The wolf still enjoys the hunt. When she doesn't, let me know."

"I will." I leaned forward and kissed him, slowly and sweetly.

The ringing of the phone interrupted us. "That will be your brother again," Quinn said dryly. "He wouldn't believe me when I said you were okay the first dozen times."

"Such sarcasm from the man who came running to my side. Against my wishes, I might add."

He shrugged and handed me his cell phone. "I'm more connected to you now than he is—and if it had been really bad, then I could save you only by being beside you."

"Really? How?" I said, then pressed the answer button and added, "Rhoan, I'm fine. Really."

"So Quinn said, but I needed to hear it for myself. What the hell happened, Riley? I was getting all sorts of weird sensations."

"I got shot with silver." I flexed my left hand as I said it. I had full motion back, but there was a definite lack of sensation coming from my fingertips. What was it about my left limb that bad guys seemed to hate? First I'd lost a finger, then I'd lost a chunk of skin, and now it looked like I might lose sensation. That would totally suck—but I guess if it was going to happen, then better my left hand than my right, given I was right-handed.

"Well, that explains the burning and numbness that hit me. You okay?"

"I'm alive, and I can move. That's always a bonus after being shot." I didn't mention the continuing numbness. There was nothing anyone could do about it, so why bother?

"Totally true." He paused, and I heard murmuring in the background. "Liander said he'd do roast lamb for dinner tonight. He thinks you need the treat."

"Tell him I'll love him forever if he does."

Rhoan snorted. "God, you can be so easily bought."

"Totally. I'll see you tonight, bro."

"You should be coming straight home after such a close call, not lingering at work."

But he wouldn't have come straight home, and we both knew it. "I have a job to do, Rhoan, and it's not finished yet."

He grumbled something I couldn't quite catch, then said, "Yeah, yeah, see you tonight."

I grinned as I hung up, then handed the phone back to Quinn. He pocketed it, then gently brushed the still-sweaty strands of hair away from my forehead. His fingers were unusually cool against my skin, and I frowned. "Why aren't you as warm as usual?"

He raised a eyebrow. "I am. You, however, feel like you're burning up."

"Oh." Maybe it was an aftereffect of the silver. Or the fact that we were sitting here in the warm sunshine. Although, it wasn't even sunny enough to drive Quinn inside.

But that didn't mean it wasn't hot enough for someone whose vampire genes were coming to the fore . . .

I thrust the thought aside, not wanting to dwell on such possibilities right now. My skin might be warm but it wasn't frying, so I saw no point in worrying about it yet. "How long was I out?"

My gaze moved to the building on the other side of the road. There were several ambulances out front, as well as Cole and the coroner's cars. In fact, the entire street was blocked. I could see the cops diverting traffic.

"Less than ten minutes," he replied. "Just enough to get you out of there and find somewhere to sit, really."

That somewhere was the bus stop. Just as well the bleeding had stopped. "We would have been more comfortable in your car."

"We would have, but my car wasn't here at the time. I travel faster out of it."

I looked at him, seeing again the little lines around his eyes and suddenly realizing they were from fatigue rather than worry. "That's why your skin is cooler. You used your Aedh form."

As an Aedh, he could become smoke and travel places the vampire couldn't go—not even a very old one. He could ride the wind and survive attacks few other vampires could. But like any ability, it had its drawbacks. In the case of his Aedh powers, it left him weak. The more he used it, the weaker he got.

"I also fed you energy," he said, and shrugged. "I'll be fine in a few hours."

"Good." I paused, then added, "You said before you could save me only by being beside me—what did you mean by that?"

"The Aedh are blood cousins of the Reapers. They are the dark to our light. We are the gatekeepers and they are the guides, but our powers are similar." He hesitated, his gaze sweeping mine, as if what he were admitting somehow alarmed him. "I could have—if I'd wished—stopped your soul from rising from your flesh and kept it bound until we removed the silver and had you breathing again."

I stared at him. Was I ever going to fully know all

the facets of this man? Was I ever going to truly know just what he was capable of?

And did it matter?

The answer to that question was a decided *no*. I loved him, no matter what he was, no matter what he could do.

"That is as scary as hell."

"And the reason why there are so few of the Aedh around. Humans kill what they fear, and the Aedh can be killed as easily as any man if caught in human form."

The key being catching them in human form. A harder task than it seemed, given they could turn to smoke in the blink of an eye. "So if you could do all this, why didn't you drag me from unconsciousness when I was in hospital after Kye died? I mean, Death—or the Reaper, or whoever the hell that shadowy cloak figure waiting for me was—could have snatched me at any time. Why didn't you just pull me awake?"

"Because I can't, just as the Reapers can't." He hesitated. "Or in their cases, won't. The soul has to make the choice to leave the body before either of us can act."

Well, I guess *that* was a comforting thought.

Across the road, two ambulance officers appeared, with a stretcher between them. On it was a woman and, even from here, I could hear the ragged sound of her breathing. But she lived, and I guess that was something.

But I couldn't help wondering just how many others

had died. Suddenly, I *had* to know. Besides, I needed to thank Cass, and make sure she was okay.

I blew out a breath and forced myself to get off his lap. He let me go but kept one hand close, and it was just as well because the street suddenly decided to do a drunken dance around me.

"Damn," I said, grabbing at his arm for support. "The silver has really drained me."

"You need to go home—"

"I will," I interrupted, "but after I talk to Cole."

"That's fine." He slipped his hand under my elbow. "We'll just go talk to him together. And then I'll drive you home."

"I thought you didn't come in your car?"

"I didn't." He gave me an amused glance as he escorted me across the street. "But it's not far away, either. And I'm quite capable of driving yours."

"You can't leave your car, because the local street kids will either redecorate or steal it. And I'm not leaving mine for the same reason." I patted his hand. "If you're that worried about me, you can follow me home."

He didn't say anything, but he didn't need to. I could feel his annoyance through the link between us. And that wasn't surprising, given right now I felt as weak as a kitten, but it would pass soon enough.

We walked up the steps and into the building. The smell of blood, sex, and fear mingled with the scent of antiseptic, creating a cloying mix that stuck in my throat and made me cough. I dug out my badge and flashed it toward the crime scene recorder set up just above the doorway, then stepped over the blanketed figure lying between the main entrance and the waiting area. Frankie had obviously been one of the first killed. And if the bulge evident on the side of his hip was anything to go by, he hadn't even fully drawn his weapon before he'd been shot.

There were two more bodies in the waiting area, one woman and one man. Both had taken a shot to the head at close range. I moved through into the next room, and found Cole squatting beside yet another woman.

"Gunshot to the chest," he said unnecessarily. He glanced up, his expression as angry as I'd ever seen it. "It's times like this I'm glad the Directorate has kill orders. The bastards who did this deserve death."

But only after Jack had extracted the information he needed. "How many dead?"

"Seven. The guard by the door, two in the front room, this poor lass, and three others who were running for the back door."

Meaning T.J. and the women I'd told to stay hidden had survived. That was something. "Did you round up the brothel owner? He was here, as well, and he's the one they were after."

"He's scampered, but we'll track him down easily enough."

If we didn't, then the organization behind all this would. If T.J. had any sense, he'd come to that same conclusion and turn himself in. Even so, I reached into my pocket and drew out the scrap of paper Cass had given me earlier. "Here is his address. You might as well add it to your report, because I need to rest before I write up mine."

He nodded and slipped the piece of paper into an evidence bag. I glanced around at the sound of footsteps, and watched another two ambulance officers walk a stretcher past. This time, the person on it was in a bag. I hadn't saved them all. I couldn't have saved them all, and yet some small part of me regretted that. Quinn slipped his hand into mine, gently entwining our fingers and squeezing lightly. Comforting without saying a word.

My gaze returned to Cole. "Have you seen a woman named Cass?"

"Yeah. She went to the hospital with one of the women. Why?"

"Because she saved my life and I just wanted to thank her again."

"Then she's someone I need to thank, as well," Quinn said. "She saved me from having to bring back the dead."

Cole raised an eyebrow, expression suggesting he was unsure whether Quinn was joking or not. I didn't bother enlightening him but simply said, "Did Jack tell you about the top floor? It's bristling with security equipment guarding a phone and God knows what else."

He nodded. "Dusty's up there now, hacking into the system. It shouldn't take him long to get in. Do you want to be advised when we do?"

I hesitated, then shook my head. "I'll just read the

report. I really need to go home, grab a shower, then rest."

His gaze swept me, and his voice was wry as he said, "Oh, I don't know. Bloodstained blue silk looks quite fetching on you."

And if I didn't watch it, that would be all my life contained. Bloodstains. On my skin, in my soul. I forced a smiled then walked away, Quinn by my side.

I raised a hand to cut the glare of the sun as we walked out of the building, pausing on the front step as I looked down the street. My car was still parked where I'd left it.

I squinted down to the other end of the street but couldn't see Quinn's car. "Where's your car parked?"

"A few streets over. I abandoned it when I felt you slipping too fast." He bent to kiss me, his lips still cool on mine. "I'll be right behind you within a minute."

"It's not like I'm going to pass out while I'm driving," I said. "I'm really not *that* weak."

He smiled, and lightly touched my nose. "You lie, Riley Jenson, but I appreciate the effort."

With that, he turned and walked away. I watched him for several seconds, enjoying the lithe, economical way he moved, then turned and headed for my car.

Within minutes I'd joined the steady flow of traffic heading for the city. Quinn's black Porsche was three cars behind me.

We were on Queens Road, cruising past Albert Park, when I saw the truck. It was on the other side of the road and driving way too fast, its movements erratic, swiping the cars that were trying to get out of its way and sending them spinning into others.

I edged over into the other lane, hoping that would keep me out of harm's way. After surviving a silver bullet, the last thing I wanted was to be mown down by a goddamn truck.

I couldn't see any cops behind the truck, but they surely couldn't be too far away. The driver was obviously high on either drugs or alcohol, and someone would have reported him by now.

He drew closer, but the sheer height of the cab and the darkened windows made it almost impossible to see the driver. He was little more than a dark shadow, and for some reason, the small hairs on the back of my neck rose.

Which was ridiculous.

He was just another idiot in the grip of some form of substance abuse or this was his idea of fun driving. I'd seen plenty like him before, and I had no doubt I'd see plenty in the future.

And yet something suddenly felt *wrong*.

I watched him draw closer, my fingers tense on the wheel. The truck swerved away from my side of the road and, for an instant, I felt safe.

But I'd barely relaxed my grip when the truck's tires squealed and the huge grille suddenly filled my vision. I cursed and ripped the wheel sideways as I hit the gas pedal. The car half spun as it surged forward and the truck hit the rear, smashing me into a lamppost. The impact flung me about violently and the side airbags popped, catching my head before it could hit the window. Metal crumpled as the passenger side of the car bent around the post.

We'd barely come to a standstill when another car hit us head-on. It tore my car away from the pole and sent it skidding backward, the windshield shattering under the impact and spraying me with glass. For a moment I couldn't see anything, my vision filled with white bags and the steam erupting from my engine. I eased up on the gas pedal, but it didn't make a damn bit of difference. I reached forward and turned the key, shutting the engine off. Moisture ran down the side of my face as I moved, stinging my eyes. I swiped at it irritably, and my fingers came away bloody. I hadn't even felt a bump to the head.

Over the groaning of metal and the hiss of escaping steam came the deep-throated growl of the truck's engine. The driver was still moving, still finding targets. And Quinn's car had been three behind mine.

Fear surged and for a moment I couldn't even breathe. Then I grabbed the handle and flung the door open. In my haste to get out I forgot the seat belt and it snapped tight, almost choking me.

I cursed, undid the thing, then climbed out. The road was awash with wrecked vehicles and dazed people getting out of cars. Ahead, the truck had found another victim. A black car had been turned onto its side, and the truck was hitting it again and again, rolling it over and over. There was blood on the windshield, and the back half of the car was crumpled almost beyond recognition. No one could survive such a mess . . .

Suddenly, what I was seeing hit.

That black car belong to Quinn.

"No!" The scream was wrenched from my throat. I flung myself past the door and ran down the road. I couldn't lose him as well. Not like this. Not in some stupid, senseless act of violence . . .

Something sharp hit my arm and I stumbled, whacking against the road hard, skinning my hands and knees in the process and grunting in pain.

I swiped at the thing in my arm and realized it was a dart. A goddamn hunting dart. "What the fuck?"

I reached for it, but my vision was suddenly blurry. The dart became two, then three, then all of them danced away. I swore and tried to get to my feet, tried to keep running, to get to Quinn and to stop the truck, but my legs wouldn't obey me.

The world was spinning; my mind was spinning. Everything was going around and around, until I just wanted to throw up.

"Well, what have we got here?" The voice was rich and somewhat arrogant. It was also far too familiar.

Blake.

The Alpha of the red pack. The man who'd made my childhood hell. The wolf who'd sworn revenge for the humiliation I'd dished out to him not so long ago.

Kye had warned me Blake was planning his vengeance, and yet despite that, I just hadn't expected he'd act *this* soon.

He moved toward me, his bulk filling my vision and his gait oddly erratic. Like something was wrong with one of his legs and he couldn't put much weight on it.

"You'd better hope you haven't killed the man in that black car," I croaked, blinking desperately to gain some clarity in my vision.

God, I just wanted to close them. To rest.

I jerked them open instead. There were fading bruises and almost-healed scratches all over his face, an indication he'd been in some sort of accident recently.

Shame he didn't die in it, my inner wolf snarled. *It would have saved me the trouble.*

Though I couldn't help wondering what had happened—and whether it had been an accident, or someone's attempt at retribution.

"Oh, he's dead, have no doubt of that," Blake said. "The car doesn't even resemble a vehicle anymore."

Fear leapt into my throat, my heart. I didn't want to believe him, but I couldn't feel Quinn. Not in my mind, not in my heart.

He couldn't be dead.

He *couldn't*.

Boots invaded my vision. Shiny brown boots. I swiped a hand across my eyes and forced my head up. Past the boots and the medical uniform, until Blake's blunt features swam into view. His silver eyes glinted with pleasure and his expression was victorious.

"I *will* kill you, Blake." Though the words were shouted inside my head, they came out as little more than a croak. "And if I don't, the Directorate will."

"Oh, the Directorate can only legally kill me if I kill you. And I don't actually intend to *kill* you. That would be too easy. The person I intend to kill will be someone else entirely."

Which made absolutely no sense. I licked my lips. The sick fear churning my gut seemed to be sweeping through the rest of me, sapping my energy. My arms and legs were quivering with the effort of holding me upright, and it was all I could do to not collapse.

"Don't you dare go near Rhoan," I spat, "or I'll fucking erase you and every one of your goddamn sons from this earth."

"Oh, I have no intention of killing him. Him being unable to find or save his sister will be punishment enough." He gave me another sharklike smile. "And you, my dear wolf, won't even remember who you care for, let alone who I am. Hell, you're not even going to remember who *you* are. I bid you farewell, Riley Jenson. I hope you enjoy the week you have remaining— but I very much doubt you will."

And with that, my world went black.

Chapter 7

Waking was an abrupt and ugly process. Sensations flooded my mind, overwhelming and confusing and, most of all, painful.

My body burned, my skin burned, my head burned. Everything hurt. My back, my legs, my arms, my face. Even my goddamn brain.

It felt like someone had strung me up and used me as a punching bag. A bag that now lay abandoned and forgotten.

I lay on my back, and the surface beneath me was sandy and hot. It stuck to my skin, grinding like sandpaper, itching and hurting all at the same time.

The air was also heated, and ripe with flavors that were strange and oddly exciting. There was a vastness to the air, an emptiness, as if I were lying somewhere that held nothing and nobody except me and the burning earth.

I tried to open my eyes and discovered I couldn't. I frowned and lifted a hand. My arm felt heavy, tired. My fingertips, when I brushed my face, felt nothing, although the lack of sensation did not apply to the hand as a whole. Frown deepening, I switched hands. Felt the dry stickiness caking my eyes.

Blood.

There was blood on my face.

Why was there blood on my face?

I didn't know, and that scared me far more than the burning in my body and brain.

I rubbed the blood away and forced my eyelids open. The sky above me was blue. A deep rich blue from which the sun burned brightly.

That's why my skin burned. I *was* getting burned.

I twisted my head, looking for cover. The land stretched out before me, filled with sandy red hills and scrubby-looking plants. It seemed totally empty of any other sort of life.

How the *hell* did I get here?

I didn't know. I really didn't *know*.

Fear swirled, briefly catching in my throat and making it hard to breathe. I forced it away. I could worry about the hows and whys later. Right now, I needed to find myself some shade or I wasn't going to survive much longer.

And I didn't want to die. I'd followed that path once before, and though it had been tempting, in the end it had not been for me.

I frowned at the thought, not really understanding it and too damn worried about the here and now to chase it.

I forced myself upright. If I thought my body had been aching before, then that one action proved just how wrong I'd been. God, it *hurt*. Fiercely. Brutally. Tears stung my eyes and fell down my cheeks, mingling with a warmer liquid that seemed to be running down the side of my face.

More blood.

And not just on my face.

My torso was a mass of bruises and cuts. There was an ugly, half-healed wound on my shoulder, abrasions scattered across my skin, a massive yellowing bruise stretching from under my breast down to my hip, and my knees were cut and scabby.

Had someone used me as a punching bag? Right now, it sure as hell felt like it. But if they *had,* how had I ended up here, in the middle of goddamn nowhere?

I didn't know. Not *anything*. The ache in my brain seemed to be all-consuming, and nothing was getting past it. Nothing except pain and the need to find shelter before the sun burned me to a crisp.

I lightly hugged my knees with my arms and stared at the landscape around me. Hill after red hill. Few trees, no houses, no cars, and certainly no people.

There weren't even footprints in the earth. How I'd gotten here was anyone's guess. Hell, I might have been dropped from the sky for all I knew. But sitting here wondering how I'd gotten into this situation rather than doing something about it wasn't going to stop my skin from getting redder.

I braced my hands against the warm, sandy soil and pushed upright. Every part of me protested the movement, and I ached with a ferocity I wouldn't have thought possible. Sweat broke out anew across my forehead, and my breath hissed past gritted teeth. But I forced my sore knees to lock and made it upright.

Just.

I stood there, wavering, for several seconds. Or maybe it was the landscape around me that was wavering. I couldn't have said for certain.

Taking another swipe at the sweat and blood dribbling down the side of my face, I resolutely focused my gaze on a lone gum tree and headed toward it.

Luckily for me, the soles of my feet were fairly tough—in fact, I think they were the only bits of me that weren't aching—and the heated earth, sharp stones, and barbed scrubby bushes didn't do much to hinder my progress.

It took about an hour to finally reach the shade. The sun seemed to be hotter even though it was clearly late afternoon, but the minute the dappled light of the tree caressed my skin, the relief from the burning was almost instantaneous. I sighed and, for a moment, closed my eyes, fighting the urge to sit down, to rest.

If I sat, I might not get up. It would be easy to die in a place like this.

I don't intend to kill you, whispered a voice through the fog and the pain clouding my brain. *That would be too easy.*

I knew that voice, but I couldn't name it. Couldn't bring to mind an image of the man who spoke the words. Didn't know why he would want to put me in such a place, in such danger.

Why would someone want to dump me in the middle of nowhere? I was just . . .

What was I? *Who* the hell was I?

I didn't know. Reach as I might, no information was getting through the fog.

Anger rose, and I swore softly, frustrated by the lack of memories and understanding.

Someone *had* put me here, that much was obvious. I couldn't have gotten here any other way, unless I could fly.

The thought made me pause.

Could I fly?

I frowned, uncertain. It seemed right, and yet wrong. Like it was something I could do even if it wasn't something I was born to, wasn't something that was a part of my soul.

But what was my soul?

Hunter, hunter, sleek red hunter. The chant ran gently through my subconscious and memories surfaced—me, being chased by a boy with wild red hair and bright gray eyes. A boy who sang the child's chant moments before he slipped from human to wolf form and pounced.

Wolf.

I was a werewolf.

The relief I felt at that realization was incredible. It flowed through me sweetly, giving me an odd sort of strength. If I could remember that, then I would remember everything else with time.

Besides, a wolf could easily survive in wild places like this. She could find food and water that I, the humanoid, would never spot. She also had a thick red coat to protect her skin from the sun. I needed that protection—needed it badly.

I closed my eyes and called for the wolf within. But instead of power, what rose was another wash of pain. It was thick and fierce and hit like a punch to the gut, leaving me winded and shaking.

The wolf was there. I could feel her, fierce and angry. But she couldn't answer. There was some sort of barrier between us, something that was stopping her, and I had no idea what that something was.

I screamed then, and it was a thick and angry sound filled with frustration and pain.

Damn it, what the hell was going on?

How could someone stop the wolf? She was a part of me, part what I was. How could that be stopped?

I hope you enjoy the week you have remaining, that arrogant voice had said. *But I very much doubt you will.*

Fear surged again, its taste so bitter that I almost gagged. A week. I had a week, if that voice was to be believed. A week to discover who I was, where I was, and what the hell was going on.

It suddenly didn't seem like a whole lot of time.

I swung my fist savagely, hitting the tree trunk and sending bark flying. Pain rippled up my arm, joining the various other aches that ebbed and flowed across my body. I swore again, this time at my own stupidity, and shook my bloody hand. Hitting the tree wasn't going to achieve anything.

I glanced up at the sun again. I couldn't go out in that. My skin was already red and tender, and it felt like I was burning from the outside in, meaning the sunburn had gone fairly deep. Shape-shifting would have solved that problem, but that was—for whatever reason—out the question. I'd have to wait out the heat and travel at night.

Meaning, whether I liked it or not, I was stuck here until sunset. I crossed my legs and plopped down on the sandy soil. After a while, I closed my eyes and breathed deeply, trying to rest, trying to ignore the aches and the internal fires and the confusion.

I didn't succeed.

Time passed slowly, but eventually dusk cast its bloody ribbons across the sky and the heat began to fade. I rose stiffly to my feet and sniffed the air, searching for something, anything, that might give me a direction.

Nothing but crisp, clean emptiness.

I blew out a breath, saw the evening star beginning to twinkle in the sky, and headed that way. It was as good a direction as any.

Dusk continued to blaze across the sky, vivid and beautiful, but eventually gave way to night. The stars came out, dominating the sky, brighter than I could ever remember seeing them. Not that *that* was saying much, because it wasn't like I could remember a whole lot.

I kicked up a puff of soil with my toes, watching the

dust float away on the breeze. Was I meant to die out here? That arrogant voice had said he wasn't going to kill me, but maybe he'd simply meant he wasn't going to do it himself. Maybe this was his method of revenge—trapping me out here, in the middle of nowhere, with no resources and no one to call on. Not even my wolf.

In the distance, crickets droned. Or maybe they were locusts, because they were certainly making a whole lot more noise.

And they were on the move, getting closer, getting louder.

Too loud, in fact, to be either crickets or locusts. I stopped and frowned up at the sky. Saw the lights— lights that were moving, circling. A *plane*.

"Hey!" I ran forward, waving my arms frantically. "Hey, I'm here."

It was night, the landscape was vast, and the chances of their seeing me were next to none, but that didn't stop me from screaming like a maniac or trying to catch their attention.

Light shot out from the plane, spearing the hill above me. I ran toward it, saw it dart sideways, and dove frantically for that patch of bright salvation. I hit the turf hard, rolled to my knees, and looked up, squinting against the harshness of the light.

"Help!" I screamed again. "I need help!"

For a moment there was no response, then the light flicked off and the plane banked away.

"No!" The word was wrenched from my throat. I punched the ground in frustration, my vision suddenly blurred with tears. Damn it, they couldn't leave. They couldn't . . .

They weren't.

The plane was descending, not leaving. I scrambled to my feet and ran down the hill toward it.

The plane taxied to a halt and the small rear door opened. A red-haired man scrambled out and ran toward me. That fleeting image of the boy who'd chased me rose again, and something inside me leapt for joy. But as my gaze fell on his face, my steps slowed. That face wasn't the face I remembered. Wasn't the face I was expecting.

For a start, it was a whole lot *younger*.

He didn't seem to notice my sudden hesitation, just reached me and swept me into a hug that was fierce and strong.

"Jesus, Hanna," he said, his voice hoarse. "I thought you were dead."

Hanna. I rolled the name around internally, but for some reason, it didn't sit right. "Obviously, I'm not."

He laughed—a rich warm sound—and stepped back, holding me at arm's length. His bright gray eyes—so familiar, so alien—searched mine. "You look like shit."

"Not surprising, given that's how I feel." I stepped back, away from his touch. "Who the hell are you?"

Surprise rippled across his features. "What do you mean, who the hell am I? Who do you think I am?"

"If I knew that, I wouldn't be asking the question." I crossed my arms and stared at him. He was a little taller than me, and broader in the shoulders. His face was rough-hewn but oddly handsome, and his scent said he was a wolf. From the red pack, if his longish hair was anything to go by.

Part of me felt like I should have known him, but the other part, the instinctive part, said he was a stranger.

"Hanna, you know who I am." He reached for my hand, but I avoided his touch. Surprise ran through his eyes. Surprise and concern. "You really don't, do you?"

I didn't bother answering. Just waited.

"For fuck's sake, what's happened to you?" He scrubbed a hand across his face. "I'm Evin. Your brother."

My *brother*.

No, I thought, staring at him. He *wasn't* my brother. Not the brother I wanted, not the brother I was expecting.

God, this was all so damn confusing.

"How do I know you're telling the truth?"

Frustration and hurt rippled through his expression. If he was acting, then he was damn good.

Why would I think he was acting?

I didn't know. I just didn't *know*.

It was becoming somewhat of a theme for me.

"I can't prove it here, obviously. I didn't bother collecting our life history when I came looking for you." But he reached into his pocket and pulled out his wallet, flipping it open to show me his license. His name was indeed Evin. Evin London. He flipped it closed before I could catch the address, and said, "Happy?"

No, I thought. But simply said, "So, you knew I was out here?"

It came out almost as an accusation, and he raised his eyebrows. "I didn't know for certain. But when we found your car—"

"My car?" I couldn't remember a car. No surprise there, either.

"Yeah. By the look of it, you'd hit a kangaroo hard enough to roll the car. It's a total bloody mess. I had to hire another one."

But I *didn't* hit a roo, I'd hit a truck. Or rather, it had hit me.

Or was that just more mixed memories?

"What the hell did you do with your clothes? They weren't in the car," he said.

I shrugged, not knowing and not caring. "Where did you find my car?"

"About an hour out of Dunedan. The local cops have already hauled it back into town."

Which was not helpful, given I had no idea what or where Dunedan was. "And where are we now?

"About a hundred miles southeast of that point."

Which was a hell of a long way to walk in the time I'd apparently been missing. "Then how did I get here?"

His gaze ran down my battered body. "Looking at the mess your feet are in, the answer is pretty obvious. And you've got a nice sunburn going."

He peeled off his shirt and handed it to me. His body was well toned, but it wasn't the body of someone who trained regularly. For some reason, that struck me as odd. I put on his shirt on and did up the buttons. It was long enough to cover my butt, which was probably a good thing if I was going back to civilization. Humans tended to get antsy about nakedness.

"Now, let's get you to—"

"No hospital," I interrupted. "I hate hospitals."

His eyebrows raised even further. "Dunedan hasn't got a hospital. Can't you remember *anything*?"

"No. Not who you are, not who I am, not where I am." I paused. "Why can't I shift shape?"

He frowned. "I have no idea. You could before the accident."

I had a sudden vision of a truck grille and a black car that rolled over and over and over, until it resembled nothing more than mashed metal. Felt the panic and fear rising, until it closed my throat and I was all but gasping for air. But it wasn't a truck I'd hit. It had been a roo. It had been flesh, not metal, that had caused this damage.

But not the damage to the other car, the black car. God, what had happened . . . ?

Again the thought faded, but the terror remained, thick and agonizing.

"Hanna, snap out of it." The voice was sharp, filled with concern, briefly sounding so warm and familiar that tears stung my eyes.

I wanted, *so* wanted, whoever that voice reminded me of, but for all I knew, that person was standing right beside me, grabbing my arm and desperately trying to comfort me. Maybe it was just my memories that were faulty, that were wanting something or someone who might not even be real.

No, no, no, that inner voice whispered. *Something is wrong. Something is very wrong.*

I had to trust that instinct. I certainly couldn't trust anything or anyone else right now. Maybe not even that man who said he was my brother.

But until I knew more about me—and more about what was going on—I just had to play along. It was either that or return to the emptiness and the heat of the red sands, and that path could lead only to death.

"I'm okay," I said, taking several deep breaths in an attempt to calm the turmoil still raging inside. "Really, I'm okay."

"Yeah." He didn't sound convinced, and he didn't let go of my arm. In fact, he looked like he expected me to keel over at any minute. "Why don't we just get you back home, and I'll call in the doc to have a look at you."

He guided me toward the plane, his grip on my arm gentle and firm.

"I thought you said Dunedan didn't have a hospital."

"It doesn't, but it has a doctor. Has to. It's a tourist town."

I guess so. I grabbed the guide rail and climbed the steep steps into the plane. There were only two seats in the back. I took the one away from the window and wasn't entirely sure why I felt safer doing that.

"Nice to see you in one piece, little lady," the pilot

said, handing me a bottle of water. He was a rough-looking man with a bulbous nose and scraggly gray beard. "The laddie here was extremely worried about you."

I glanced up at the laddie in question and raised an eyebrow. He took the hint and said, "Hanna, this is Frank. He runs the local pub and owns the plane."

I held out my hand. "Hello, Frank. Thanks for coming out to rescue me."

He laughed, flashing teeth that were yellow-stained and crooked. His hand wrapped around mine briefly, his grip firm and strong. "Wouldn't be neighborly to let our newcomers get themselves lost the first few days they hit town, now would it?"

"I guess not."

I began to sip the water and it was the sweetest thing I'd tasted in a long while. Which wasn't saying much given the state of my memories.

Evin drew the steps inside the plane then closed the door and sat down in the remaining seat. As the plane's propellers roared to life, he said, "We arrived in town a day ago. Your accident was reported this morning."

Which didn't really explain the state of the various wounds on my body. I might be a wolf, but I was one who apparently couldn't change, so why were there so many half-healed wounds on my body? The one on my shoulder looked bad, and it surely should have taken more than a day to heal without a shape change. "What was I doing alone in the car in the middle of nowhere?"

And why couldn't I remember hitting a roo?

He shrugged. "You said you wanted to be alone for a while and went for a drive."

"An odd thing to do if we'd only just arrived in town, wasn't it?"

His sudden grin crinkled the corners of his eyes and warmed his bright eyes. "We'd been cooped up together for ten days in that car. We may get on like a house on fire, but ten days is a *long* time. So no, it wasn't surprising."

"Why were we traveling?"

His smile faded. He studied me for several seconds, his expression serious and eyes suddenly sad. "You don't remember?"

Something caught in my throat, and I had an image of that truck again, and that crumpled black car, rolling over and over. I licked suddenly dry lips and said, "Remember what?"

He took a deep breath and blew it out slowly. "Maybe it's better if you remember in your own time."

"Remember *what*?"

I grabbed his arm, my fingers tightening reflexively. He winced and, for a moment, seemed surprised by my strength. Which struck me as odd, given he was my brother and should have known what I was. What *he* was.

He scrubbed a hand over his face. "Jesus, Hanna, I don't know if it's the right time—"

"*Tell* me," I demanded. "What don't I remember? Why are we here?"

"He's dead," he said abruptly, but with sympathy in

his expression. "Your soul mate is dead. Hit by a truck and crushed."

I stared at him. Just stared at him, as the words rolled around and around in my brain. *My soul mate is dead.*

Yes, I thought. *Yes.* The emptiness was there, deep inside. It felt true and right. I closed my eyes, again saw that truck, that black car, and felt the rising pain—a pain so deep it felt like my heart was being torn apart. He was *dead.* The man who couldn't be killed was *dead.*

Tears stung my eyes and suddenly I was sobbing and shaking uncontrollably. Evin took me in his arms and held me tight as the plane roared into the night.

*W*e landed on an airfield that was little more than a strip of dust beside a ramshackle collection of aging buildings. By that time, I was numb. The tears had stopped and there was nothing left except emptiness and an odd sort of disconnect.

I stared out the window, taking in the scenery. There was little enough to be seen. Not because it was night, but because there was nothing there. No tower, no guide lights, and certainly no terminal. Frank taxied around to one of the few large buildings in the immediate area, then killed the propellers and twisted around to face us. "If you're feeling like a drink later, lassie, the first one is on me. Sounds as if you could do with one."

I forced a smile. "Thanks. I just might take you up on that."

"Do." He flung open his door and climbed out, quickly disappearing inside the old hangar.

Evin opened the back door and lowered the steps, climbing down before turning around and offering a hand to me.

I paused on the top step and looked around. There were buildings and houses in the distance, their lights twinkling like stars, but I'd been expecting a city and Dunedan obviously wasn't anywhere near that large. The air itself was rich and clean, and smelled ever so faintly of the ocean.

This place, like the man waiting at the bottom of the steps, was unknown to me.

"You coming?" Evin said.

I placed my hand in his and let him help me down, but he didn't release me, keeping hold as we walked around the back of the building. An old blue Toyota four-wheel drive was parked at the far end, and it looked as beaten as I felt. Obviously, we couldn't afford to hire anything better.

Evin opened the passenger door, waited until I climbed in, then slammed it shut and walked around to the driver's side.

"Why did we come to Dunedan?" I said, as he reversed the car and pointed it in the direction of the buildings.

He glanced at me. "Because you wanted to get away from everything. Friends, family, everything."

Well, I'd obviously succeeded, because I couldn't remember anything. And how much more "away" could you get? "But why here?"

He shrugged. "You took a pin and poked it in a map. This was the nearest town to that pin, and here we are."

"Why did you come with me?"

He smiled. "Because, sister, we do everything together. Besides, Mom would have had a fit if I'd let you come out alone in your condition."

Mom. It was a word that raised a surprising amount of emotion—and not all of it was good. Yet I couldn't even picture her face. "What do you mean, my condition?"

He hesitated. "You survived your soul mate's death, but you were being treated for severe depression. Which was why I was looking for you so frantically. I thought you might have gone off your tablets and tried to kill yourself again."

I frowned. His words had the ring of truth, and yet, there were lies there, too. Or was I merely seeing problems where there were none? I rubbed my forehead wearily, and wished the aching would stop. I'm sure it would all make so much more sense if it just didn't hurt so much.

"Meaning I've already tried to kill myself?"

He grimaced. "That wound on your shoulder is from a gunshot. You only missed because I managed to grab the gun in time."

Liar, liar, pants on fire . . .

And yet, the wound *was* a gunshot wound. Maybe

he was telling the truth. Maybe it was my internal voice that was lying.

"How did I get hold of a gun?"

He snorted. "We're licensed security officers, so guns aren't a problem."

I didn't *feel* like a security officer. I felt like I was something more. Not a cop, but something along those lines. Someone who dealt with life and death on a daily basis.

Which I guess a security officer could do, if we were in the business of guarding people rather than possessions.

I looked out the window, watching the emptiness go by, feeling its echo deep inside. "I can't remember any of this."

His gaze swept me again—something I felt rather than saw. "Well, you've obviously received several nasty blows to the head, so that's probably why. Give it time."

Time. For some reason, that was something that seemed in very short supply.

A week, that voice had said.

What would happen after that?

I didn't know, and I didn't intend to hang around long enough to find out. Whatever this was, whatever was going on, I needed to sort it out well before then.

I shifted my focus to the approaching town. It didn't look huge, but it seemed quite pretty. The main street was about half a mile long, with grand old buildings clustered on either side of the road and the blue of the moonlit ocean visible down at the far end. Cars were angle-parked along the street, and people strolled about casually—some in beach gear, some not. Trees and wide verandas provided shade from the elements, as did the white umbrellas that sat above the tables in the outside restaurant areas. Hanging pots filled with flowers and creeping vines dangled from the ornate light posts that lined the street, and the nongardener in me wondered how the hell they managed to keep them alive in the heat.

"Where are we staying?"

"Bayview Villas. We have a two-bedroom unit right on the beach."

"Sounds nice."

"It is." He swung into a side street and the buildings gave way to old but pretty houses. We passed several more streets then swung right. The sea suddenly seemed a whole lot closer, the sound of waves crashing against the shoreline sharper.

He swung left, into a driveway, and stopped. The building was white concrete, but had the same wide verandas that the older buildings did. It also had a big blue-and-white sign out the front that said POLICE.

I raised my eyebrows and looked at him. "Why are we here?"

He undid his seat belt and climbed out. "Because I reported your accident and the fact you were missing, and now need to unreport you, before they arrange another search party for tomorrow. You coming?"

I shrugged but climbed out and followed him into

the station. The inside reception area was cool and dark. A woman behind the desk glanced up as we entered and gave us both a warm smile.

"Evin," she said, standing up. She was tall and thinnish in build, with sandy-colored hair and sunburned cheeks. "You've found her."

Her scent said she was a werewolf, and if the hunger in her eyes was anything to go by, then she was very interested in Evin, but he didn't seem to notice or care. And *that* oddly seemed right.

"Yeah," he said, stopping several feet away from the desk and studying her with an almost amused expression. "Is Harris about?"

"No, he's been called out."

"Well, could you let him know I've found her? If he wants me to make a report, then he knows where to find us."

"I will." She paused, then added, "Are you going to the pub later on?"

"Sorry, love, I don't drink. But that doesn't mean I won't be there later." He gave her a wink, then swung me around and headed out.

"You do *so* drink," I said, when we were out the door. "Why didn't you tell her the truth?"

"What, that I'm moon-sworn and unavailable? Why spoil her day?"

Shock rippled through me and I stopped, ripping my arm from his grasp. "When did you go through the moon ceremony?"

Something flitted through his eyes, and I had a vague suspicion he'd just said something he shouldn't have. But why would he want to keep something like that a secret?

Why was I so damn suspicious of *everything*?

"You can't remember anything right now, so is it really surprising you don't remember the ceremony?" he said awkwardly.

"So I was there?"

"Yeah." He grabbed my arm again and walked me—quite forcibly—toward the car. "Now, let's get home, get you cleaned up, and then call the doc."

Let's not, I thought, and pulled my arm from his grasp again before stepping back. Damn it, he was my *brother*. Surely to God I could trust him? But I didn't, and I didn't know why, and it was just so frustrating that I wanted to scream. I drew in a breath to try and calm the sudden, angry shaking, and that's when I smelled it.

Blood.

There was blood on the wind.

A lot of it.

Which could only mean that someone nearby was dead.

Chapter 8

I swung around to follow the scent and side-stepped Evin's attempt to grab my arm. "Can't you smell that?"

"It's blood. So what?" He fell in beside me, his expression none to happy.

"It's *human* blood," I corrected. "Someone's dead. Or about to be."

"Hanna, we're not cops. This is *not* our business."

"Well, I'm making it *mine*." I frowned up at him. "What if we walk away and the victim could still have been saved?"

He tried grabbing my arm again, but I slapped his hand away. He growled in frustration and said, "This is *not* smart—"

"Damn it, Evin, if I can save someone, I will. I'm more than a little fed up with the other option."

Confusion flicked through his expression, which I suppose was understandable, given I wasn't entirely sure what I was talking about, either.

I followed my nose into a side street that was little more than dust, and past several houses. Ahead lay a grassed paddock. A small dam filled with muddy-looking water dominated the middle of the paddock and, beyond it, there was a stand of scrubby-looking wattle trees and shrubs. The blood scent was coming from that direction.

Evin's steps slowed. "Hanna, we really *should* get the cops."

"Then do it." I walked on.

He muttered something under his breath and dragged his phone out of his pocket, but continued to follow me nonetheless.

"Cathie?" he said, his voice seeming to echo across the overheated air. "It's Evin again. Look, we've scented blood in the paddocks behind the station. You might want to get either Harris or Mike out here."

I tuned him out, my gaze sweeping the ground. There wasn't any sign of a fight that I could see, and no indication of either recent tire tracks or footprints. Of course, there was also no reason that there *should* be. Just because this was the most logical way for pedestrians to come if they were heading for the few houses dotted beyond this paddock didn't mean whoever was lying either dead or near dead in those trees *had* actually walked this way.

I passed the dam and switched my gaze to the trees. The scent of blood was so strong my nose twitched, but

I couldn't yet see a body. But blood dribbled down the trunk of one of the nearest wattles, gleaming wetly in the moonlight.

Evin's footsteps faltered. "Jesus, Hanna—"

I frowned and glanced around at him. His face had gone white. "What the hell is wrong with you? Anyone would think you've never seen a body before."

He glanced at me sharply, "Which sounds like you *have*."

"It's an everyday part of our goddamn job." My confusion was growing. Why was what I was saying and half remembering so at odds with how he was reacting?

Who was the disconnected one here?

"It's not an everyday part of *my* fucking job." He scrubbed a hand through his hair. Gold gleamed thickly amongst the red. "Look, Cathie says we should avoid disturbing the area too much. Harris is on his way."

"I have no intention of disturbing the crime scene." And no intention of simply standing back here waiting for the cops to arrive, either.

I kept walking. Evin sighed, and it was a sound of frustration if I'd ever heard one. Which I probably had.

The air underneath the trees was a riot of aromas. First and strongest was the metallic stench of blood, but under that ran a mix of vanilla from the yellow blossom puffs and the aromatic resinous smell of the smaller wattle shrubs scattered between the bigger trees.

And below even those, the scent so faint part of me

thought I might have been imagining it, was the taste of anger. Of vengeance.

This murder had been planned, not accidental, if that scent was anything to go by.

I scanned the ground again. There were footprints here. Weird prints that resembled cloven hooves rather than anything human. Maybe our victim had been attacked by a goat.

The body lay in a small clearing in the middle of the trees. He was big-boned and rough-looking, his skin pale and flaccid, as if he neither saw much sunshine nor did much to look after himself. His head was bald, but thick black hair matted his chest, trailed down his stomach and . . . my gaze stalled at his groin.

His genitals were gone. Penis, balls, and all, just gone. Hacked out of his flesh, leaving only a raw, gaping wound that still oozed blood—an indication this death hadn't happened very long ago.

"Oh, *shit*." Evin's voice was hushed, as if he feared disturbing ghosts.

"Someone *really* didn't like the way this man used his tool." I said it lightly, trying for humor but obviously not succeeding if Evin's expression was anything to go by.

"How can you joke about something like this?" He motioned toward the body with a hand that appeared to be shaking. "Someone cut this man's *nuts* off!"

"And maybe they had a damn good reason." It was absently said. There was something here, something I couldn't quite catch or explain . . .

"And there'd better be a damn good reason for you

two being here." The voice was deep and authoritative, and not one that I knew. "Especially when Cathie's already warned you to stay away from the crime scene."

"Tell me about it," Evin muttered, then added, "Hanna thought we'd better check, just in case there was someone here who needed medical help."

"Hanna?" The other man's gaze seemed to rest on me. I could feel the weight of his annoyance. "Isn't she the sister that went missing?"

"Yeah. We just got back. I asked Cathie to let you know."

"Well, she didn't." He stepped up beside me, surrounding me with his scent—warm spices and musky wolf. "You really need to step away."

"And you really need to know that there's something else here."

"What?"

I glanced at him then. He was several inches taller than me, with dark hair and well-defined, handsome features. His shoulders were broad, his body lithe—the build of an athlete, not a bodybuilder. Something within me leapt and my gaze jerked up to his face, searching for a reason for the tug of familiarity. He was wearing dark glasses, so I couldn't see if his eyes were as dark as his hair. But part of me wanted them to be— expected them to be.

Except that he was a werewolf.

That bit didn't fit with what I was expecting.

I tore my gaze away from his and motioned toward the body. "There's something else here. An odd sort of energy."

It was thick and strong, and it felt like fingers of ice caressing my flesh, cooling the heat of sunburn, sucking at my strength.

It was also something I'd felt before, back in the times I couldn't remember. I had no fear of it, even when the slivers of pain began to stab at my brain—a pain that was scarily similar to the pain that occurred when I'd tried to shift shape.

Something had obviously gone *seriously* wrong when I'd hit whatever it was I'd hit.

"I can't feel—"

I grabbed Harris's arm, stopping him. His muscles tensed under my fingertips, but he didn't pull away. I pointed with my other hand. "There."

"What?" His voice was patient, as if he were dealing with a crazy person. And who knew, maybe he was.

Except that I could *see* it. A faint wisp of white hovering just above the victim's head.

"A soul."

"A *soul*? Lady—"

"Damn it, it's *there*. Just because you can't see it doesn't mean it doesn't exist."

"Yeah, right. Evin, I think you'd better—"

"Sorry, Hanna," Evin said, and before I could react, something hit me over the head and the world went black.

I woke to darkness. I lay there for several seconds, staring upward but not really registering that there was a ceiling above me rather than sky and stars.

Then memory hit and I jerked upright. Only to wince in pain as my head protested the movement. I raised a hand and felt a bump the size of an egg on the side of my head. *Evin*. The bastard didn't *have* to hit me so hard.

I swung my legs off the bed. A dozen different aches awoke, and my skin felt like it was glowing. Obviously, the werewolf quick-healing thing wasn't working too well on my sunburn.

I was still wearing Evin's shirt, and his scent hung on the air. How could my own brother smell so familiar and yet so strange? It was weird, and I really didn't think it had anything to do with the lack of memory. It was something that went deeper.

Everything that was happening went far deeper than a lack of memory—of that I was sure. I just had to try to figure out the what and whys without raising anyone's suspicions in the process. I don't know why, but I had a bad feeling *that* would not be a good idea just yet.

There were voices in one of the rooms beyond mine, and it took me several minutes to realize it was probably the TV. I couldn't hear Evin moving about, but I could smell coffee, and my stomach rumbled a reminder that I hadn't had anything to eat or drink in a while.

I scrubbed a hand across my face. I felt grimy and achy, and I desperately needed a shower, food, and coffee. But more than anything, I needed to understand what was going on.

And first on that list was remembering *me*.

I rose and walked across to the mirror attached to

thē small dressing table. My reflection was thin and
sunburned. My face was pleasant enough, and there
was a sense of familiarity about it—though why this
surprised me, I'm not entirely sure. I mean, it was *my*
face. What did I expect? Surgical changes?

My hair was the same red-gold as Evin's and cut into
a short, elfin style. *That* felt different. I touched it
lightly, feeling oddly bereft. It should have been longer.
Had been longer.

There were fading bruises and cuts over my cheeks
and above my eyes, and one earlobe looked as if someone had taken a knife to it. Weirdly enough, that apparently didn't prevent me from wearing earrings.
They were overly large stud earrings with a blue stone
in the center, and really ugly. I tried to take them off,
but the damn things seemed to be attached to my flesh
and would not be budged.

I frowned and undid the shirt instead. The bruises
over my torso were as bad as they'd felt, and the gunshot wound looked puckered and red. It wasn't in-
fected, but it had been. If I'd been able to change before
the accident with the roo, why hadn't that healed?
Surely I would have taken steps to heal my own flesh?

But then, if I'd been depressed, maybe not.

Maybe not remembering anything was a good thing,
not bad.

I stepped back, then caught sight of the wallet sitting
on the bedside table. I opened it up and dragged out the
driver's license tucked into the one of the side pockets.
The picture was crappy—as they always were—but
the face on the license matched the face in the mirror.

And the name listed was Hanna London. I was who Evin said I was.

Even if I didn't *feel* like a Hanna.

I shoved the wallet back onto the dresser and headed out the door to find Evin.

It turned out the villa apartment wasn't very big. There was a second bedroom next to mine and, next to that, an average-looking bathroom. The main room was one big space comprised of a kitchen, a dining area, and a TV area. The furnishings were a basic, durable pine, and the curtains and cushions consisted of an almost garish blue and yellow flower print. There wasn't much in the way of decorations, but I guess you didn't need them when one wall was glass, and the vista beyond was all white sand and blue ocean. Even at night, it was a sight to behold.

Evin was sitting at the table under the small front veranda reading a newspaper. I followed my nose to the coffee machine, made myself a drink, then grabbed an apple and headed outside to join him.

He looked up as I sat down, and there was a decided wariness in his gray eyes. "How are you feeling?"

"I'd be great if some uncaring bastard hadn't cracked my head open earlier tonight." I took a sip of coffee and winced at the sharp, bitter taste. Definitely *not* to my liking, but it was hot and strong and better than nothing.

"Hanna, you were acting rather weird—"

"You'd be weird if you could see souls, too." I glanced at him over the rim of my mug. "Why don't you know about that?"

"Maybe because it was never mentioned?" He shrugged. "We may spend a lot of time together, dearest sister, but we don't tell each other every single thing that goes on in our lives."

But we do . . . Or at least, I thought we did. I bit into my apple, enjoying the juicy sweetness, then said, "So what secrets are you hiding from me? Aside from the fact you're apparently moon-sworn."

"That's not a secret. You just can't remember it." He picked up his cup, and I saw with surprise it was tea rather than coffee.

When did my brother start drinking *tea*?

"How long are we staying here? And how long was I out?"

He raised his eyebrows. "What, sick of the place already?"

Wary was more like it, but I didn't say that. I simply shrugged. He folded the paper and put it on the table. "You slept through the entire day. And we paid for seven days, and we won't get a refund if we leave early. Neither of us can afford to lose that sort of money, so we're stuck here until then."

So I'd wasted a day. An entire day.

"And after the seven days are up?" I couldn't help tensing as I said that, because the words of that stranger still echoed in my mind.

"After that, who knows?"

If he was a part of whatever was going on, why wouldn't he know? There again, if he did know and this *was* a plot rather than the imaginings of a sick mind, why would he tell me?

I munched on the apple and watched him watching me. It felt weird, like we were strangers rather than brother and sister.

"What happened to the doctor you were going to call?" I tossed the apple core into the tussock grass lining the veranda. The birds and the ants could feast on what remained.

"This town has only one doctor, and he doubles as a coroner when there's a murder. So, we're no longer his first priority." He hesitated, then said, "You better keep taking your tablets until we talk to him."

I raised an eyebrow. "They were for depression and I don't feel depressed."

He tapped his fingers on the table, a soft drumming that for some reason annoyed me. "Maybe you don't feel depressed, but you've lost your spark, Hanna. And you've already tried suicide once. So forgive me if I'm blunt here, but you'll fucking take your tablets even if I have to force them down your throat, because I do not want to lose anyone here."

The emotion in his voice, particularly when he said that last bit, had tears prickling my eyes. It was the truth—the honest truth—in a sea of lies.

I took a deep breath and blew it out slowly. "Okay, I'll take the tablets. Where are they?"

"In the bathroom." He leaned back. "I think I'll go to the pub for a meal. You interested?"

I snorted softly. "Like this? Thanks, but no. I think I'll stay here and have a bath."

"Cool." He glanced at his watch. "I'll be back in a couple of hours."

I shrugged. "Don't hurry on my account. Enjoy yourself."

"Like that's—" He caught the words, and shrugged. "I'll bring back some beer, if you like."

I nodded, wondering what the hell he'd been about to say, and why he'd checked it. I finished my coffee as he disappeared into the darkness, then I stood and made my way into the bathroom.

There was a pill bottle sitting on the ledge underneath the mirror. I picked it up and read the label— these were definitely my tablets, and they were dated several weeks ago. I frowned and tipped one out into my hand. They were large and brown—more like something you'd feed a horse. I contemplated the tablet in my hand for several seconds, then clenched my fingers around it.

I couldn't take it. I just *couldn't*.

I dropped it into the shower and crushed it underneath my heel, then turned on the taps, stripping off the shirt before stepping inside.

I kept the water cool because of my sunburned skin, but it still felt like bliss. For several minutes I did nothing more than stand there, letting the water sluice off me, washing away the worst of the blood and dirt even as the chill began to seep into my body and ease the fires burning there.

After I'd washed hair and skin, I turned off the taps, grabbed a towel, and stepped out to dry myself. Then I swung around and headed for my bedroom. There was a suitcase at the foot of the bed. The clothes in it were a mix of old and new—some of them smelled of me, but most didn't.

I grabbed a pair of faded denims and a low-cut T-shirt but didn't worry about a bra—the strap would have rubbed the half-healed wound.

Once dressed, I glanced at the time. Evin had been gone for twenty minutes. That left me an hour and forty minutes to do my investigations.

I grabbed my wallet and the apartment keys then headed out. The night was still crisp and a little on the cool side. The sigh of the waves washing up the shore mingled with the distant sound of laughter and music. All the nearby villas were silent—maybe everyone had gone into town. From the little I'd seen of this place earlier, there probably wasn't much else to do.

Once clear of both the villa area and the nearby caravan park, I broke into a run, cupping my breasts with my hands to compensate for my lack of a bra. The rubber soles of my shoes made little sound on the dusty road, but the little puffs of dirt that rose with each step meant I'd be noticed if there was actually anyone about to notice. But even though there were one or two houses that had their lights and TVs on, no one seemed to be paying any attention to what was going on in the street.

Interestingly, the air closer to town was thick with the musk of wolf. There were a *lot* of us here, and it made me wonder if Dunedan was a werewolf community. It was certainly remote enough—although it was unusual for such a community to also be a tourist destination.

I swung into a street just before the police station and headed for the paddock from the other side. There were fewer houses here, meaning less chance of being seen.

I slowed once I hit the grass. The thick scent of blood had faded—not surprising, given twenty-four hours had passed.

Yellow-and-black police tape fluttered in the slight breeze and I wondered if the body would be transferred elsewhere for the postmortem. If Dunedan was so small that the local doctor acted as coroner in an emergency, then I doubted they'd have a proper morgue. In fact, even the cops might have to call in specialists. They surely wouldn't have had to cope with many murder investigations in a community this size.

I ducked under the tape and stopped just inside the trees. I didn't want to disturb the murder scene any more than necessary and, besides, I really didn't need to go close to where the victim had died to feel his soul.

I could feel it from here.

I couldn't actually see him, but that really didn't matter. He was here. The thick chill said as much, as did the energy flowing from me, building in the air, giving him strength and sapping mine.

I had no idea of his name, so I simply said, "Why do you linger?"

Why was I murdered? I came here to start a new life, not have it ended.

His words were angry and his fury filled me, roaring through my body like a wave. But his statement sent a sliver of alarm through me. I'd heard a similar complaint once before . . .

But where?

"What is your name?"

As I asked the question, awareness washed over me. I was no longer alone in the strand of trees—and the thick scent of warm spices mingled with sweat said it was Harris. I internally cursed my luck, and hoped like hell he let me finish questioning the dead man's soul.

Marcus. Marcus Landsbury.

Which wasn't a name that seemed even remotely familiar.

"How did you end up in this field, Marcus?"

I don't know. One moment I was walking home, the next I'm here, unable to move or talk, and some bastard is cutting my tackle off.

"So you saw him?"

No. He was wearing some sort of costume.

A sense of déjà vu ran though me. I'd heard this before, even if I couldn't remember where.

"What sort of costume?"

A red devil mask. It had horns. He hesitated. *I swear he had cloven hooves, as well.*

Again that sense of familiarity. "Is there anything else you can tell me about him? Was he big? Small? Fat or thin?"

He was on the small side, but strong—really strong. He had to be, didn't he, because I'm not exactly small. He had broad shoulders and big arms, though. Moved efficiently, like it was a job, nothing more.

Meaning it could have been a professional hit. Especially given they'd probably used some form of immobilizer to take him down so quickly. Things like that weren't available over the counter—though easily enough gotten on the black market.

And just how would I know something like that?

I rubbed my left temple wearily. Energy continued to flow away from me, and the pain slithering through my brain was increasing. "And what did you do, Marcus, that warranted being slaughtered in such a fashion?"

I've done my time. It doesn't matter. The words were angry, ricocheting around my head as sharp as nails.

I winced, blinking back tears. "It obviously matters to someone, Marcus, or you wouldn't have been killed in the manner you were."

He was sucking at my energy like a man possessed, and my knees were threatening to buckle under the strain. I tried locking them, but knew I'd have to end this soon, answers or not.

It shouldn't matter. Damn it, it was a long time ago!

Well, someone obviously hadn't forgotten. "Tell me what you did."

Why? What fucking good does it do now?

"I guess that depends on whether you want to stay here haunting this scrawny patch of trees, or move on."

The energy was draining at a faster rate now, and my head was beginning to ache fiercely. My knees suddenly unlocked, and I hit the dirt.

I braced myself with one hand as Marcus said, *I raped several women.*

"Define 'women.' " Because the brutality of his murder suggested there was more than rape involved—especially if he'd been put away for a while. The sad fact was, courts and judges didn't treat rape as seriously as they should.

Anger swirled, thick and sharp. The stabbing pain got worse, and suddenly I was struggling to breathe.

Okay, it was girls. Sixteen-year-olds. We held them for several days and did them over proper, like.

We. The word caught in my brain, but before I could question him more, my brain overloaded and all I felt was pain. Sheer, bloody, agonizing pain. I hugged myself for several seconds, rocking back and forth, then realized he was still there, still draining me.

"Go," I whispered. "Find whatever peace you damn well can."

He went. Not happily, not easily, but he went, and the draining stopped. "Harris," I said to the man standing quietly behind me. "If you don't want the crime scene contaminated any further, you might want to help me out of here. I'm about to throw up."

Arms grabbed me, lifting me as easily as a kitten. Or a pup, as the case might be. We'd barely made it out of the trees when my gorge rose, and I struggled out of his grip and staggered away before losing the little I had in my stomach.

God, I felt *awful*. If I'd let Marcus drain me for much longer, it could have been fatal—though with the way my brain was feeling, it had come damn close anyway.

"Here," Harris said, handing me a half-empty water bottle. "Rinse your mouth out with this."

I accepted it gratefully, rinsing away the bitter taste then spitting it out. I repeated the action and felt a little better, though my head still ached like a bitch and my muscles were trembling.

I forced myself to stand upright and handed him back the water. He was dressed in blue sweatpants and a gray tank top that clung to his body and emphasized his lean strength, and his dark hair was damp and curling up at the ends. But his eyes were blue—a blue the color of the ocean that surrounded Dunedan—not black.

Why was I expecting black? Who did he remind me of? Suddenly that question seemed vital, and yet I just couldn't answer it.

Why, why, why?

He shoved the small water bottle back into its pocket on the side of his pants, then said, his expression grim, "Tell me why I shouldn't arrest you for entering a restricted area?"

"Well, if you'd had a man stationed here like you were supposed to, it wouldn't have been a problem, would it?"

He didn't look amused. "People around these parts respect the law. They know—"

"As *I* know." I rubbed my head wearily. I really didn't feel like a lecture right now. "But people around these parts probably can't talk to souls, either. I *can*. But it has to be done shortly after the death, otherwise they get too weak to talk."

And if I could remember stuff like that, then why couldn't I remember the important stuff? It was like someone had systematically gone through my mind and erased random bits of information. Some of the big stuff, some of the small, leaving total chaos behind.

Harris stared at me for several seconds, his expression unchanged. It was hard to know whether he believed me or not.

"I think you and I need to sit down and have a serious talk."

"As long as it's somewhere with decent coffee and something to eat. Otherwise I'm likely to pass out on you."

He raised an eyebrow, but all he said was "I know just the place. You need a hand?"

"Yeah, I think I might."

He wrapped an arm around my waist, half holding me up as we moved forward. It felt like daggers were merrily stabbing at my brain, and my muscles felt incredibly shaky. Did this always happen when I talked to souls?

Something within said no. This was something new—a fresh twist on an old problem.

We didn't head toward the police station as I'd half expected, but rather toward a little white weatherboard house on the far edge of the paddock.

"My home." Harris opened the old wrought iron gate and led me up the garden path. Not literally, I hoped. "We can talk here unofficially, then move across to the station if I feel it's necessary."

He opened the door one-handed—obviously, being

the town cop meant never having to lock it—then helped me inside.

The hallway was long and wide, with various doorways leading off it. The walls were painted a warm off-white and decorated with brilliant photos of the sea and surrounding countryside that gave the place a bright and homey feel. The floors were timber and well worn, creaking slightly as he led me down to the end of the hall. The room beyond was a huge kitchen.

"Have a seat," he said, motioning me toward the old oak table and chairs. "What sort of coffee do you want?"

"Hazelnut." I said it automatically, and wished again that the important things would pop back as easily.

"I meant decaf or regular." There was amusement in his voice. "We country folks don't go for those fancy mixes."

"Regular. And trust me, not many city folks are into hazelnut, either."

I pulled out a chair and watched him make the coffee. He moved with an economy that spoke of both grace and understated power. It was nice to watch.

He pulled some bread and sandwich fillings out of the fridge and dumped them on the table, then grabbed the coffees and some knives, and brought them over.

"Help yourself," he said, handing me my coffee before sitting down opposite.

I raised an eyebrow. "No plates?"

"The table's clean and it saves washing up."

I snorted softly. A man after my own heart. I grabbed the bread, slapped on some butter, then added several thick slices of beef and cheese. It was the best thing I'd tasted in ages.

"So," he said, once I'd demolished the first sandwich and made inroads on the second. "Have long have you been able to see souls?"

I shrugged. "I can't say, simply because I can't remember."

"Really?" There was disbelief in his voice again.

"Really," I echoed, trying to control the sweep of irritation. "I can't actually remember anything before my accident. I didn't even know my name until Evin told me."

His gaze rose to my head. "That sort of memory loss is extremely unusual. And I can't see a wound that would indicate extreme trauma."

And yet Evin had said there *was*.

"No." I finished the second sandwich and wrapped my hands around the mug of coffee. "Bits and pieces are slowly coming back, but nothing major. It's frustrating."

"I bet." He took a drink of his coffee, then said, "So this soul talked to you?"

"It did. You were there early enough to hear my end of the conversation, though."

He nodded. "How did you know his name was Marcus?"

"He told me. Marcus Landsbury. He was apparently jailed for a long period for the rape and torture of a couple of teenage girls." I paused. "But I guess you know all that."

"I do," he said. "And I suspect his crime had a lot to do with the method of his demise."

You didn't have to be a cop to figure *that* out. "Yeah. Only he said he didn't do the crime alone, and if his partner is also in town, you'd better find him. He's probably next on the list."

"His partner hasn't been sighted in town, nor have we had any notification that he's coming." Harris studied me for a moment. "What makes you think his partner is next? This might just be a random murder."

He didn't believe that any more than I did. I shrugged and said, "I have a feeling I've seen something like this before."

"Back in the past you can't remember?"

Again the suggestion that it was a little too convenient—not that I could really blame him for thinking that. I took another sip of coffee and didn't bother answering.

He smiled, but it didn't reach the blue of his eyes. "What else did he say?"

"That the man who attacked him used some form of immobilizing spray that made it impossible to scream, and that he was wearing a costume. A red devil costume complete with cloven hooves."

"So you saw the tracks?"

"Yes. And I've seen them before."

"Where? Wait, you can't remember, right?"

I lowered my cup and stared him straight in the eye. "Either boot me out or arrest me if you don't believe me, but don't sit there making snide remarks. I'm trying to be helpful."

"I'll reserve judgment on that." He reached forward and snagged a slice of beef, munching on it as he studied me. "Tranquilizers can act that quickly, but I've never heard of a spray capable of the same thing."

"Well, they're out there." I grabbed another piece of bread and rolled it around a bit of cheese. "What's happening with the autopsy?"

"It'll get done," he said mildly. "I'm more interested in you and your brother."

I raised an eyebrow. "Why?"

"Because there are several strange things about the pair of you."

A smile teased my lips. "You're not the first person to say that."

He didn't look amused and I resisted the urge to sigh.

"I did some investigating when you were reported missing," he said. "The owners of the Bayview can't remember seeing you when your brother registered, and no one in town saw you wandering about before you went missing—although they can remember Evin coming in to buy groceries or to use the phone in the pub."

I shrugged. "Evin said I'd been depressed. Maybe I was just keeping to myself."

"Maybe," he agreed. "But it's quite a coincidence, don't you think, that not even an hour after you've been found, a mutilated body turns up? A body that you and your brother just happen to come across?"

I leaned back in my chair and stared at him. "Do you really think I'd be stupid enough to murder someone like that, then hang around not only to report it, but hand you a whole series of clues?"

He raised his eyebrows, his gaze assessing. "Why not? There's plenty of documented evidence about murderers getting their jollies by pretending to be witnesses."

I slammed my hands down the table and tried to control the anger that whipped through me. He was only doing his job, I knew that, but damn it, I was trying to *help*. "That man was attacked while I was out in the desert. Check with Frank as to where and when I was found if you don't believe me or Evin. In the meantime, why don't you run a check for similar crimes? Because this *has* happened somewhere before, I'm sure of it. And while you're there, run a check on me. That way you'll know whether I'm dangerous or not."

"Oh, I have no doubt you're dangerous, lady," he said softly, his blue eyes glinting. "The question is, are you a murderer or merely a fruitcake?"

Chapter 9

*M*urderer. The word seemed to echo around my aching brain with a resonance that was both familiar and frightening.

Was I a murderer?

No, something inside said. Then, frighteningly, *yes*.

I grabbed my coffee with a hand that was shaking, and wasn't entirely sure whether it was due to the weakness still washing through my body or that whispered revelation. I finished the coffee in one quick gulp that scalded my throat, then pushed to my feet. The room spun violently, and it was only my grip on the table that kept me upright.

"Am I under arrest?" I said, through gritted teeth.

"Not yet." He leaned back in his chair and continued to study me through slightly narrowed eyes. "But you and your brother should consider yourselves to be persons of interest."

"If you do the damn check, you'll discover we shouldn't be." I spun and headed for the front door.

A chair scraped backward, then footsteps followed me up the hall. "One more question," he said, as I flung open the front door.

"What?" I said it without looking back or even stopping.

"There's very little blood on your car and the damage—though extensive—doesn't look recent. Also, if you hit the roo hard enough to roll the car several times, why isn't its body anywhere in the immediate vicinity?"

Interesting observations, both of them. "Can I see the car?"

"No. And don't leave town, Hanna." He said it softly, but his words seemed to echo across the night as I retreated down the street.

I was a suspect.

And the worst of it was, even *I* wasn't so sure that I shouldn't be. Everything was so screwed up—both this situation and my mind—that right now, anything seemed possible.

I hit the main street and turned to head back to the villa, then paused.

Harris had said that Evin used the phone in the pub. Why would he do that when there was a perfectly usable phone at the villa?

With curiosity stirring, I spun around and headed for the pub. It was easy enough to find. All you had to do was follow the noise. Music and laughter ran riot through the air, and the aromas of wolves, beer, sweat, and humanity overlapped one another—a mix that was both enticing and repellant.

The building reminded me of something you'd see in an old Western. It might have been constructed out of red brick rather than wood, but it was two stories, with wide verandas on both levels and old-fashioned swinging doors.

Obviously, no one was worried about security in this place. But then, if this *was* a werewolf town, it'd be a brave soul that tried to steal anything.

I pushed through the doors and stepped into the main bar. The place was packed, and it was hard to see the bar let alone Evin or a phone.

I looked around for a moment, then approached a group of women standing to the left of the doorway. Three were wolves, the other two human.

"Excuse me," I said, catching the eye of the tallest woman. She had dark skin, dark hair, and a somewhat broad nose, and she reminded me a little of Harris, except that her eyes were a warm brown. "Can you tell me if there's a public phone here?" I had to raise my voice to be heard above the din.

"At the back," she shouted, pointing with her glass.

I waved her a thanks and headed that way. Everyone was so tightly packed it was difficult to get past anyone without actually touching them, and while the experience wasn't exactly unpleasant, it wasn't really exciting, either. Which was weird. I mean, I was a female werewolf without a mate, and this bar was full of males in the prime—and not so prime—of their lives. Once upon a time, I would have been dancing and flirting, and generally having a good time as I squished past them all. But my soul mate was dead and it felt like a chore. Like something I had to put up with, then escape.

No, that little voice inside whispered, *it's not that. Ben lost his soul mate, and he still desires. He can still enjoy sex and the company of others.*

I didn't even *bother* trying to recall who Ben was. My memories were obviously going to take their own sweet time returning.

I eventually found the phones at the rear of the room near the two bathrooms, but Evin wasn't there. Maybe he'd made his call and was somewhere else in this cauldron of humanity and wolves. I couldn't smell him, but that wasn't really surprising given the sheer number of male wolves in the room.

I found a spare chair in the corner and stepped up, looking out over the sea of dark heads in an attempt to find a red-gold one. There were several blonds and the occasional brown, but no redheads. Maybe he'd gone back to the villa.

I stepped down and pushed my way back through the crowd. But I was barely halfway across the room when I ran nose first into a rather solid-looking chest. It felt like I was hitting a brick wall.

"Ouch," I said, rubbing my nose as I stepped back and looked up. And up. Christ, he had to be at least six and a half feet tall.

His skin, like that of many of the wolves in the

room, was dark, and his face was flat and broad of nose. His mouth was small and pinched looking, and his eyes . . .

Something within me shivered.

His eyes were brown, but there was little warmth in them, little humanity.

"Little lady, you just spilled my drink."

"Sorry." Then I glanced at his hands and realized he wasn't even holding a glass. My gaze shot up to his again. There was something snakelike about his smile. "Would you mind moving out of my way?"

There were several men behind him, watching the two of us and smiling in anticipation. I had a feeling that this—whatever *this* was—was a game they'd played often.

"I'm afraid I can't move until I get a kiss in replacement for my drink." He reached for my waist, but I slapped his hand away.

Something flickered in his eyes. He didn't like being rejected. Well, tough.

"Move," I said. "Or I will *make* you move."

He laughed and glanced over his shoulder. "Hear that? You think I should be scared?"

"Please," I said, with the barest hint of a growl running through my voice. "Just move."

He grabbed me, moving so fast I didn't have time to stop him, and dragged me against his body. He smelled of old sweat and rotting grass. Not a pleasant combination.

"Kiss me," he said, as the men behind him began to egg him on, "and then you can go. Just one little kiss."

"Over my dead body."

"It would be my pleasure," he whispered, and swooped.

I shifted my face so that the kiss landed on my cheek rather than my lips then reached back, grabbing his fingers and yanking them backward as hard as I could. Bone snapped and he hissed in pain. But pleasure flicked through his eyes and his excitement surged around me, thick and hungry.

He got off on pain. Great.

So I gave him something else to get happy about, and kneed him in the nuts as hard as I could. And apparently I was stronger than I knew, because he went down like a ton of bricks. His friends—charmers that they were—jumped out of the way rather than trying to help him.

"I did ask you nicely to move," I said, then looked up as the crowd parted and footsteps approached, to meet the gaze of an unhappy-looking Harris. The man obviously had a nose for trouble.

He looked from me to the man-mountain writhing on the floor, and I swear a slight smile touched his lips. But when his gaze met mine again, his expression was all dour and businesslike.

"I guess I should have also warned you to stay out of trouble," he said, voice heavy.

I held up my hands. "Hey, he grabbed me and wouldn't let go, even though I did ask nicely."

He glanced down at the man unconscious on the floor, then motioned to the two men who'd let their friend fall. "Get him out of here."

They scrambled to obey, dragging their unconscious friend out the door. It was interesting to note that no one seemed too worried about the fact that he'd been felled by a stranger.

Harris's gaze came back to me. There was little emotion to be seen in the blue of his eyes, and once again it reminded me of someone else. I wished I could remember who.

"I think you'd better come with me." His gravelly voice was firm, and it was obvious he wouldn't take no for an answer.

Of course, part of me wanted to say just that, but it wasn't exactly the wisest course of action when I had no idea what the hell was going on. So I blew out a frustrated breath and followed him out of the bar. At least I didn't have to fight my way through—the crowd parted for Harris as easily as the sea for Moses.

"I'll escort you home," he said, once we were out the door. "Just to ensure you don't get yourself into any more trouble."

"I can handle myself." I rubbed my arms lightly. The night air seemed a lot cooler now than it had when I'd entered the bar. Maybe my sunburn was finally starting to heal.

"You probably can, but Denny doesn't like being taken down by *anyone,* let alone by a woman." His blue gaze met mine, assessing, calculating. A wolf undecided whether I was friend or foe. It was mutual. "Watch yourself, because he's likely to seek retribution."

I raised my eyebrows. "So warn him off."

"I will. But it won't make a blind bit of difference. And until he actually tries something, I can't do anything."

"If he tries to get back at me, he'll regret it."

He didn't smile. Didn't frown. Didn't really react in any way at all, in fact. It made me wonder at the reasons for the tight control.

"His dad is the pack second," he said evenly. "He's well connected, so watch how you react."

Don't damage him too much, in other words. I smiled grimly and shoved my hands into the pockets of my jeans. "So what pack runs this town?"

"West. Remy West is the leader, although you won't often see him in town. He dislikes tourists."

That raised my eyebrows. "Then why open the town for tourism? If these lands are pack owned, you have the legal right to restrict entry."

He snorted softly. "Not if the land has some significant natural feature. In such cases, the government insists it be available for all."

"And Dunedan has a significant natural feature other than red dust, heat, and ocean?"

Amusement briefly twitched his lips and lent his stern features a surprising amount of warmth. "We have what is known as a fringing reef, which means the coral starts right at the water's edge. It's rare, and therefore significant."

"I'm guessing the pack makes a whole lot of money from that significant feature."

"We all live rather comfortably," he agreed.

I studied him for a moment, then said, "You don't look like the rest of the pack. Why's that?"

He slanted me a sideways glance. "You don't mind getting personal, do you?"

I shrugged. "When you can't remember anything of importance, you quickly learn to ask questions, personal or not."

He was silent for a moment, but his gaze roamed across the darkness and there was an alertness about him that suggested he was ready for trouble. If that trouble was Denny, then he could relax. Werewolf or not, I didn't think he'd be capable of walking for a day or so. I really *had* hit him hard.

"My mother came from a different pack, hence the blue eyes and lighter skin."

"And I'm guessing the pack never let you forget that you weren't entirely one of them."

His gaze flicked to me. "What makes you think that?"

"Because I know what it feels like to be unwanted by the pack."

"That's an odd statement," he said, "given your brother has been heard to say that his upbringing was happy."

I shrugged. "That doesn't mean mine was."

"Indeed." But again, I got the impression he just didn't believe me.

The caravan park came into view. Few lights were on and the caravans were little more than hulking shapes in the darkness. The perfect place for an ambush, except the cool air was free of any scent. The only people out in this darkness were Harris and myself.

"I can make it the rest of the way by myself," I said. "You don't need to baby-sit me."

"I'm protecting my packmates, not you." It was said as flatly as he said everything else, but this time, the teasing hint of amusement touching his lips also reached his eyes.

I smiled. "Good night, Officer Harris. I daresay I'll be seeing you around."

"Not in any official capacity, I hope."

I raised my eyebrows. "Does that mean you're open to unofficial approaches?"

"No. It simply means stay out of trouble."

"I'm not sure I'm capable of doing that." And the truth of that statement echoed right through my very being.

Trouble and I were old mates. Of that I was sure.

"Good night, Hanna," he said, then turned and loped off into the darkness. I watched him disappear, then headed past the caravans and to the villa.

Evin was sitting on the sofa drinking a beer, his bare feet up on the coffee table. "There's more in the fridge," he said, as I entered the room and closed the glass sliding door.

"Thanks, but I'm more a champagne person." And why wouldn't my own brother know that? I dropped down on the other sofa and crossed my legs. "So tell me about our pack."

He raised a pale eyebrow. "Why? You'll remember it soon enough."

"Maybe. Maybe not." I hesitated, then added, "You had a happy childhood?"

"Why?"

"Because I feel like I didn't. When you mentioned Mom before, I had this very weird feeling." I hesitated. "And yet if you were happy, why wasn't I?"

He suddenly looked uncomfortable. "Well, you did have the tendency to get into trouble. Some of the stories about you and—"

He stopped dead and confusion crossed his face.

"Me and who?" I asked.

"I don't know." He shrugged, and took a long drink of beer.

And again I wondered if he was telling the truth. He seemed to be, but that didn't mean he actually was.

Was I always this damn suspicious of my own brother? Because I *did* believe he was my brother— even if he wasn't the one I remembered or wanted— but there was little else coming out of his mouth that appeared to be the truth.

"Tell me about our family, then."

"There's really not much point when you'll remember soon enough."

It was said with just a touch of impatience, and I raised my eyebrows. "There's no harm in humoring me, is there?"

"I honestly don't know. I guess not."

Which, as comments went, was odd. There seemed to be a lot of that going around.

He took another long drink of beer, then crushed the can and lobbed it toward the trash. "We're a fairly large family unit for our pack. Mom met Dad fairly late, but she made up for it. Beside me, there's a younger brother and a set of twins. Two girls."

Sisters. I had *sisters*. Something twisted in my stomach and an odd sense of sadness and regret rose.

"What are their names?"

"Our brother is Raynham, and was named after my mother. The twins are Jobie and Nelia." He glanced at me. "I'm guessing by your expression you don't remember them."

"No." *How can you remember someone when you've never even met them?* The question rose out of the mire of my mind, clear and strong. "What are they like?"

He smiled. "Raynham is the studious type. He likes his books and computers. Nel is the adventurous one. She's stubborn and strong, and has a nose for trouble. A smaller version of you, basically."

"And Jobie?"

"A homebody. She's already saying that when she grows up, she wants nothing more than a soul mate and babies. Lots of babies."

Which is what I want. And something I'll never achieve. Not without someone having them for me, anyway. I rubbed my head wearily and wondered if the ache was ever going to fade enough to bring back memories and understanding. Or was this pain, and the fleeting, annoyingly incomplete memories, all I was ever going to get?

Then I frowned as the rest of his words hit. When she grows up? "Just how old are they?"

"Raynham's seven. The twins are five."

Shock rippled through me. I was more than twenty years older than any of them. No wonder I didn't know them—I'd left the pack long before they'd even been born.

My gaze swept Evin. Even *he* looked younger than me. "How old are you?"

He hesitated. "Twenty-four."

And that just seemed *so* wrong I wanted to be sick. My brother *shouldn't* be that young. He just shouldn't.

But it also made him far older than our other siblings. So why didn't I know him? He might be younger, but he was old enough to have been around during my time with the pack. Surely to God I couldn't have forgotten my own brother—not to the extent that he seemed a complete and utter stranger.

"You mentioned Raynham being named after our mother, but you haven't mentioned our father. Why do I have a feeling that I have no father?"

"Maybe because you told him before you left that, as far as you were concerned, he ceased to exist." His gaze met mine rather than sliding away, but I nevertheless sensed the lie.

I didn't have a dad. Not a dad that had played a part in my upbringing, anyway. My dad had died long before I was born.

Part of me wanted to grab Evin and shake him, make him tell me the truth. But I couldn't. I had an odd sense that the web that had been woven around me was elaborately constructed, and while Evin might be a part of it, he wasn't a controlling part. He was just a player, like me. Hell, for all I knew, he might be as trapped in this mess as I was. Until I knew where all these lies led, I had to remain as I was—confused, angry, and maybe even a little frightened.

Of course, it was also possible that I *was* crazy. That there was no plot against me, and that my depression over my soul mate's death was slipping into neurosis.

No, that inner voice said. *No!*

Evin rose abruptly. "I'm off to bed. You'd best be getting some sleep, too."

"Probably." Except that I wasn't sleepy. "But I think I'll watch TV for a little bit."

He shrugged, gave me a sketchy wave goodnight, then disappeared into his bedroom. I leaned across to the sofa and grabbed the remote, idly flipping channels and trying to find something decent on. The news and the shopping channel were about as interesting as it got.

I threw the remote back on the sofa, then got up and made myself a cup of coffee.

What I needed, I thought, as I wrapped my fingers around the mug and leaned back against the counter, was a laptop. With it, I could do some investigating of my own. At the very least, I could do a search for that other murder I was half remembering and uncover whether it was real or just a figment of my twisted imagination.

There wasn't anything resembling a laptop in the main living room, and I couldn't remember seeing one in my bedroom. But Evin might have one. It was worth asking, anyway.

"Hey, bro," I said, not bothering to raise my voice.

He'd hear me if he was awake, and given he'd only just gone to bed, I doubted he'd be asleep yet.

"What?" he said, sounding less than pleased.

"Have you got a laptop with you?"

"Why?"

That definitely sounded like something my brother would say. "Because I want to do a search for a killing similar to the one we found today."

"Why don't you just let the police do their fucking job and drop the matter?"

Because keeping my mind busy keeps the pain and the anguish at bay, that little voice said. But I couldn't—wouldn't—admit something like that to Evin.

"Because I'm curious, that's why. I just want to know if there was another killing elsewhere, or whether I'm simply imagining it."

"What does it matter if there was?" Footsteps echoed lightly. He might be arguing, but he was getting up, which meant he did indeed have a laptop.

"It doesn't matter, but it will solve my curiosity."

"You know the old saying about curiosity and the cat," he said, as he entered the living area with the laptop tucked under one arm.

"Then it's just as well I'm a werewolf, isn't it?"

He snorted softly. "And I'm guessing that if I didn't have a laptop, you'd just go out and find yourself one."

I grinned. "You're learning, little brother."

"I certainly am," he muttered, and handed me the computer. "Promise me you'll drop the matter if you don't find anything."

"If I don't find anything, I will."

"And if you do find something, talk to Harris. Let him handle it."

"I'll talk to Harris." Whether I let him handle it without sticking my nose in it was another thing entirely.

Evin grunted and half turned away, then paused. "Why is this so important to you?"

"I don't know," I said, honestly enough. "It just feels like unfinished business, for some reason."

He shook his head. "Hanna, we work security for the pack. We roam boundaries and keep rabble off pack lands. Murder, in any way, shape, or form, does not enter our realm of experience."

I worked for the pack? That seemed so damn unlikely that laughter bubbled up inside of me. It didn't escape, but only because of an extreme effort of will.

"Look, I may have simply read about it in the newspaper. If that's the case, then Harris will be more than aware of the connection, and I can let it slide."

"Then that's what I'm hoping for. We're here to relax and recuperate, not chase after ghosts and get caught up in murder investigations."

"So tomorrow I'll relax."

He snorted again—but this time it was a sound of disbelief. "I'm beginning to think that's not in your nature."

I had a vague suspicion he was right. "Night, little brother."

He half waved as he headed back to his bedroom. I fired up the laptop as I walked across to the sofa and sat down, then waited for it to pick up the Internet connection. When Google finally appeared on the screen, I typed in "murder" and "red-horned devil" in the search area.

And discovered there were apparently hundreds of murders committed by red-horned devils the world over. I refined the search area, hitting the Australia-only button, and reduced the number of murders down to only a couple. One in Brisbane and two in Sydney.

I clicked the links and checked out the newspaper articles related to both murders. Of the two Sydney murders, one was a woman who'd been found hanged in the closet of her home, and the other a man who been wood-chipped. Apparently, both methods of murders reflected crimes they'd spent time in prison for. The Brisbane murder was a little different, in that the woman never spent time behind bars. She was the victim of a hit-and-run—the very crime she'd been acquitted of several months previously.

None of the murders was the one that sat like a bad smell at the back of my mind. I leaned back against the sofa and frowned at the computer.

There were definitely similarities in all three crimes, and I had no doubt that there was a connection between them all. But what about my crime? Why wasn't that in the news?

Maybe I needed to refine the search more. By state, for instance—only my memory failed to come up with where I lived. I shoved the laptop on the sofa beside me, then jumped up and walked to the bedroom. I grabbed my wallet and dragged out my license, this time actually taking the time to look at the address.

Cona Creek, Queensland.

Not a place that sounded or felt right.

I tucked the license back into the wallet then headed back to the laptop. A search for Cona Creek revealed very little about the place—even Google maps didn't show a whole lot, with the satellite pics revealing little more than dirt and trees. Although I suppose if it was pack land, then there may not be a town, as such. Many packs preferred the scattered approached to communal living rather than the clustered development favored by humans and packs like the one that owned Dunedan.

None of which helped me get any closer to uncovering the who and what behind the murder that was lurking in the recesses of memory.

I tried variations of the search but still came up empty-handed. Maybe a kill order had been placed on the story—but why would they do that when the other stories were already out there?

Once again, I just didn't know.

It was a fucking frustrating sensation.

I gave up and turned off the computer. Maybe what I needed was sleep. With any sort of luck, tomorrow would bring new ideas and fresh memories.

*S*omeone was knocking heavily. *Bam, bam, bam* it went, relentless and loud. It took me a few minutes to realize the noise was outside my head rather than inside, and I opened a bleary eye.

I was still in that small, uninspiring villa bedroom. The nightmare gremlins hadn't decided to transport me back to my real life, wherever and whatever that was.

"What?" I said, then winced. Speaking seemed to aggravate the daggers in my head. Apparently, I still had my headache, too.

"Harris is here to see you, Hanna. You need to get up."

"What time is it?" I glared blearily at the clock on the bedside table, but the little numbers weren't making a whole lot of sense.

"It's nearly midday. Get dressed. I'll have a coffee waiting."

"Right." I flung off the blanket and sat up. The room spun violently around me, and my stomach reacted to the sensation by leaping up my throat. God, I felt *awful,* and I had no idea why. It wasn't as if I'd taken whatever the damn tablet was that Evin had kept insisting I take.

But maybe *that* was the problem. Maybe this general feeling of crappiness was a result of coming down off whatever the drug was.

I swallowed heavily and pushed carefully to my feet. A glimpse out the window revealed bright sunshine and blue skies, so I grabbed a tank top and a pair of shorts, and padded out barefoot.

Harris was sitting on a stool at the kitchen counter, sipping coffee and eating toast.

"Nice to see you've made yourself at home," I said, looking around for Evin but not seeing him. I did see another coffee cup and two bits of buttered toast waiting on the counter, so I sat down on the stool next to Harris and slid the coffee toward me. "Where's my brother gone?"

"Into town to grab the paper." Harris looked at me, amusement touching the corners of his blue eyes. It changed his features from merely handsome to extraordinary. "He did mutter something about needing the break from baby-sitting."

I was tempted to snort, but it would have hurt my head. I took a sip of coffee, wished it wasn't so damn bitter, and said, somewhat gingerly, "So why are you here? Not to give my brother a break from the baby-sitting duties, I take it."

"No." The amusement fell away from his face. "I made a few inquiries, and it appears you are indeed Hanna London, a border guard and troublemaker from the Cona Creek London pack."

"You almost sound disappointed."

"It isn't often my instincts are wrong." He shrugged. "I spoke to Tyson London and he backed up everything Evin has said."

Tyson. Something within me shivered at the sound of that name, so obviously it had once meant something to me. Something unpleasant.

"Did you run any other checks?"

He raised his eyebrows. "The word of a pack leader isn't enough?"

"Pack leaders aren't infallible, you know. They lie and scheme as much as the rest of us."

"You really haven't got a very high opinion of pack alphas, have you?"

"Apparently not." I pulled the toast toward me and picked up a piece. "Does this mean I'm no longer a suspect in the crime?"

"No, it simply means you're not lying about who you are. The whole crime thing is another issue entirely."

And if he was drinking our coffee and eating toast, then I very much doubted he was here in any official capacity. He seemed the type to be a stickler for rules—written *and* unwritten—and regular cops didn't usually sit at a suspect's kitchen counter eating their toast and drinking their coffee, because any evidence gathered that way would be inadmissible in court.

Which didn't mean he wasn't fishing.

"Has the autopsy happened yet?"

He took another drink then shook his head. "These things take a time in this part of the world. I did, however, read about similar crimes in Sydney and Brisbane."

I nodded. "They're revenge crimes, just like this one. Which suggests there's a fairly big organization behind it. There has to be, given they've hit people in four places now."

He raised his eyebrows. "Four?"

"I Googled the murders last night. None of them matched the information my—admittedly faulty—memory is providing."

"Then how would you even know about it if you didn't read about it, either online or in the newspapers?"

"I don't know." I finished the rest of the toast, then wiped the crumbs off my hands. "Have you sent an information request to the Directorate? This would be their sort of gig."

"Marcus Landsbury was human, and he was killed by someone wearing a devil mask. That isn't Directorate territory."

"It is when the person wearing the mask isn't human."

The last hint of friendliness dropped from his gaze. "What makes you say that? There was no scent other than Landsbury's at the crime scene."

"And you didn't find that odd? You're a wolf. You should have been able to smell the killer given how fresh the kill was."

He didn't say anything to that, so I continued. "Besides, Landsbury said his killer was small but he moved him easily. That in itself signals nonhuman involvement, because most humans simply couldn't have lifted a man his size with any sort of ease."

"But neither of those is the reason you think there's nonhuman involvement, is it?"

"No." I hesitated. "I really do have no idea where half this stuff is coming from, but I didn't kill Landsbury."

"If I was accusing you of anything, we'd be down at the police station, not sitting here drinking coffee."

Which didn't mean he thought I was innocent. "Look, I keep getting this feeling that I was involved in investigating a similar case. Whether that was as someone who has a talent for talking to souls, or in a more official capacity, I can't say."

"If this other crime exists, then there'd at least be a record of it somewhere in the system—"

"Not if it's a Directorate case."

"True. But if it *was* a Directorate case, my sending in an official query about a possible copycat would have prompted a response. So far, it hasn't."

"The query would be red-flagged. How fast they get back to you depends on what other cases they have ongoing." I hesitated. "It also might depend on which Directorate office picks it up."

"It'll go direct to Perth. That's our closest main office."

"Meaning if an Australia-wide alert hasn't yet gone out, then it'll be classed as low priority. You may not hear anything back for a few days."

Curiosity stirred through his expression. "You seem to know a lot about the Directorate for someone who works as a pack border guard."

"That's the thing," I said, crossing my arms and leaning against the countertop. "I really don't think I'm a border guard."

"Meaning your brother is lying?"

"No." I blew out a breath. "Maybe. I don't know."

"*If* Evin is lying, that means your pack leader is, also. And that's one pretty big fabrication." His gaze slid down my body then rose to meet mine again. I had absolutely no idea what was going on behind those blue eyes. "I'd have to ask, why would they bother?"

His words stung, though I don't think he meant them to. "That's what I need to find out. If this is all part of a fabrication, then why me, and why here?"

"Well, Dunedan *is* the middle of nowhere. If you wanted to get someone away from everything and everyone, then this is a pretty good start."

I took another sip of coffee and briefly wondered if they sold other brands in the local store. This one, whatever it was, sucked. Although Harris didn't seem to mind it.

"Dunedan is also wolf owned. For some reason, that strikes me as odd. If my memory loss is due to the machinations of others rather than an accident, then why not erase the memory of being a wolf?"

"Because you may erase the memory, but you can never erase the fact. A wolf—regardless of whether they remember what they are or not— will be affected on the onset of the full moon and will still change shape on the actual night."

"True." I took another drink, then winced and shoved the disgusting stuff from me. It was making my headache worse, not better. "But what if the whole object of the fabrication was to destroy and terrify? What if it was an act of vengeance designed solely for that purpose?"

"Then I'd have to say, that person has some pretty powerful enemies." He studied me intently. "Do you have enemies that powerful?"

I snorted softly. "Are you really expecting an answer to that given the state of my memory?"

A smile tugged at the corners of his mouth. "I guess not."

"Good." My own smile faded. "It makes the whole situation even more frustrating, though. And there's no guarantee I'll *ever* remember everything."

"I doubt it's possible to erase someone's memory so completely. At least, not when that someone is as strong-minded as you seem to be."

I smiled at the jibe. "I think I've been called strong-minded—and worse—a few times in my life."

"Why am I not surprised?"

I laughed. "The thing is, it *is* possible to erase someone's memory. It is possible to give that person a completely new identity and life."

He raised his eyebrows. "You've witnessed this?"

"No." I hesitated. "Yes." I threw up my hands in confusion.

"Either way," he said, "if all this *is* planned, then it means that either the erasing wasn't entirely successful, or it was meant to be half-assed, to add to your frustration."

I hope you enjoy the week you have remaining, that arrogant voice had said, *but I very much doubt you will.*

"You could be right," I said gloomily.

"I usually am." He finished his coffee and pushed the cup away. "Tell you what—I'll do a more general search on your identity. I'll search police, tax, and government records, and see if I can find anything untoward that will help clear up this situation one way or another."

"That would be great." At least then I might know

whether this was a plot or merely the imaginations of a very sick mind. Mine, specifically. "But do me a favor?"

"That depends on the favor."

"Don't tell my brother."

"Don't tell your brother what?" Evin said behind us.

Chapter 10

I somehow managed not to jump, and twisted around on the stool. He was standing in the doorway, a newspaper in one hand and what smelled like fresh croissants in the other. My stomach rumbled happily at the thought.

"That she's been helping me with my inquiries," Harris said smoothly, face as expressionless as they came.

"I didn't want you to worry," I added. "Especially given you didn't want me to get involved in the first place."

Evin grunted and stepped inside the unit. "I'm pretty sure Harris is more than capable of investigating a murder without your assistance."

Especially given he still half thought I might be involved. But before I could say anything, Harris said, "She saw the soul. I didn't."

Evin walked around the counter and dumped the newspaper and the bagged croissants on the counter. "And you believe her?"

"There are stranger things in this world than the ability to see souls," Harris said evenly. Which didn't really answer Evin's question. He rose and glanced at me. "I'll be in touch."

"Thanks." I watched him walk out, admiring the low-key, animal feel of it and wondering again who the hell he reminded me of.

Evin pushed the bag of freshly baked treats toward me. "I got chocolate chip and blueberry. Take your pick."

I reached in and grabbed a chocolate chip one, taking a bite and almost melting in pleasure. But my gaze rose to meet my brother's. "So why don't you believe I can see souls?"

"I didn't say that—"

"You implied it," I countered. "So explain."

He hesitated. "It's not a gift that runs in the pack. Telepathy, yes, but not this whole soul-seeing thing."

Clairvoyance runs in the pack, the internal voice said, *Soul seeing was just a twisted version of that.* "Telepathy? We're telepathic as a pack?"

"Mostly. Not everyone gets the skill, of course. Some flip the other way and are mind-blind." He shrugged. "Our siblings are mind-blind, and so are you."

I was? Again, that statement just felt wrong. And yet, I'd been picking up nothing telepathically from anyone in this town, and surely if I was telepathic, I should have been able to. Of course, there was the whole daggers-in-the-brain factor. Maybe I wouldn't be able to do *anything* until that eased off.

So why could I see that soul? Why would the pain affect one talent and not the other?

Maybe they didn't know about the other talents, that perceptive little voice inside me whispered.

Of course, I had no fucking clue just who "they" were. Or whether they were nothing more than an overstressed imagination.

But I was really doubting that imagination had *anything* to do with all this. It was real, and it was happening, and I needed to find out why.

"Well," I said lightly, "that sucks big hairy ones, doesn't it?"

He laughed and dragged a croissant out of the bag. Blueberry, if the color of the juices that oozed out of it were any indication. "So, what are we going to do today?"

I shrugged. I knew what I wanted to do—a little more crime scene investigation—but I wouldn't be able to if Evin was going to stick like glue to my side. "I don't know. Maybe a little swimming, a little sunning, and a whole lot of eating."

"Sounds like a plan. It's already getting warm out there."

"Then I'd best go change into a suit." I grabbed another croissant—this time blueberry—and munched on it happily as I headed into my bedroom to change.

The rest of the morning passed peacefully enough. I

swam, I sat on the sand and soaked up the sunshine—or at least I did until my skin began showing signs of severe sunburn again. Why was it suddenly so damn sensitive? I shifted to the shade of the trees, drank coffee, and read the newspaper. There was no mention of Landsbury's murder anywhere, although the paper catered to Western Australia as a whole, not just this town. And given the vastness of WA, maybe the murder of a rapist wasn't considered newsworthy enough.

Or maybe an embargo had been placed on it.

Lunch came and went, and it was midafternoon when Evin decided he was going to have a little siesta. I glanced at my watch and waited fifteen minutes to insure he was well asleep, then wrote him a note telling him I was going to buy some decent coffee. I slathered on some sunscreen, then grabbed my wallet, hat, and sunglasses, and headed out.

The air was unbearably hot and the sun beat down almost relentlessly. I could feel its heat caressing my skin, but this time, it didn't feel like it was burning as deep. Obviously, sunscreen and I were going to become firm friends while I was in this part of the world.

There were plenty of people out and about in the caravan park, though most of them were sticking to the shade of the big old gum trees. There were a few kids splashing about in the crystal blue water, but most were—like me—slathered with sunscreen and wearing hats. All of them smelled human. It wasn't until I reached the main town that the scent of wolf became stronger.

I headed down the side street again and walked

toward the stand of trees. There was a young, bored-looking uniformed officer standing under the shade of one of them, and I smiled. Harris had obviously taken my jibe about protecting the crime scene seriously.

Of course, this also meant that I couldn't nose around like I wanted to. I gave the young officer another smile as I walked by the trees, and continued on until the grass gave way to the tufted wild grass. I turned around and studied the houses surrounding the paddock. I couldn't imagine Landsbury living in the immediate area—not with the police station and Harris's house so close, but he'd have to live somewhere near the paddock because otherwise someone would have noticed him being carried. Although for all I knew, someone had. Harris wasn't about to tell me stuff like that.

The houses behind Harris's—the ones closer to the pub—were all pretty, well-looked-after places. Which didn't seem the sort of place someone like Landsbury would be living in, so that left the area to the left of the park. It was more isolated, more rundown. The perfect area for a criminal wanting to get away from his past.

I spun on my heel and headed left. The cop was still watching me but, even from this distance, it didn't "feel" suspicious. More an "I'm bored and there's a leggy redhead wondering around in a bathing suit" type of feel.

Interested, but not aroused.

It struck me then that since I'd woken up in the desert, nothing remotely resembling desire or lust had hit me. Which was odd, because I was a werewolf and sex was an important part of our makeup. But the urge just wasn't there.

It couldn't be *just* the soul-mate factor. Losing a soul mate might rob a werewolf of happiness and their life companion—and sometimes even their life—but it didn't erase the need for sex. It couldn't. That was in-grained in us and, when a soul mate died, the restric-tion of having sex only with them was lifted.

But maybe they'd stolen *that* the same time as they'd taken my memories, I thought glumly.

I headed past the last of the houses lining the pad-dock, then turned left into what was little more than a dusty side track. The houses lining either side of this track were even more decayed than they'd seemed from a distance, with most needing major structural work as well as a good lick of paint. The sea air obvi-ously played havoc with timber surfaces. There were ten houses in all, and I walked past each of them slowly, drawing in the scents and trying to uncover anything that vaguely resembled Landsbury's stench.

I found it in the last house on the street. I paused and took off a shoe, shaking imaginary sand out of it as I studied the building. It wasn't much to look at, but the windows were unbroken and the curtains appeared to be newish. There was a dead bolt on the front door and padlocks on the side gate, and both were new.

Awareness surged at that moment—someone was coming toward me. Not Harris; someone else. I put my shoe back on and kept walking. A big, dark-skinned man was approaching, and he didn't look happy.

"Well, I'm guessing you'd be Hanna London." His

voice was gravelly, and filled with a sense of familiarity that seemed out of place, given he was a stranger.

"That's what my driver's license tells me," I said somewhat flippantly. "Who are you?"

"Mike West, the other cop stationed in this shit hole we call a town. Harris told me that you might wander down this way."

He stopped, waiting for me to get closer. His scent washed across the air—an odd combination of smoke and dirt.

"I didn't realize it was illegal to walk around this section of town."

He turned around and fell in step beside me. "It's not—except when the person doing the wandering has already been warned away from a crime scene twice and was seen there yet again only a few moments ago."

So the young officer didn't only ogle. Good for him. "I didn't go anywhere near the taped-off area. I just walked through the field."

"A technicality, as we both know. Consider this a final warning. If we find you near that field again, we'll arrest you."

I raised my eyebrows. "On what charge?"

"Obstructing an investigation." He glanced at me. His eyes were brown—like almost everyone else in the West pack—but his seemed to hold his emotions clear and sharp. What I saw was resentment, unhappiness, and just a touch of anticipation.

And it was that last one that struck me as odd, because while it wasn't sexual in nature, it did seem to center on me.

"I can hardly obstruct an investigation when there's not a lot of investigation happening."

"That's because we have to wait for the big-city cops to come down and do it. We apparently haven't got the right expertise or knowledge for that sort of stuff."

Though there was no edge in his voice or expression, his derision rode the air, bitter and sharp. Mike West wanted more than what his job was offering. But then, was that really surprising? Most folks who became cops did so because they wanted to help others, or they wanted to catch criminals and make a difference.

And if the emotions I was sensing in Mike West were anything to go by, being a cop in a small town in the middle of nowhere wasn't achieving either of those two aims.

"So the autopsy results haven't come back yet, either?"

He slanted me a glance. "Like I'm going to tell you that. Harris would have my head."

"He doesn't have to know."

Mike snorted. "Harris knows *everything*. The man has an instinct for it. Makes me wonder why he decided to transfer to a dead-end place like this."

"Well, he is from the West pack—"

"He had a stellar career as a detective in Sydney, but he suddenly ups and runs back here?" Mike shook his head. "The man is mad."

"Or he just missed home turf."

"Yeah, there's a whole lot to miss in this hellhole."

I squinted up at him. "If you hate it so much, why not transfer?"

"I've applied, trust me."

"Then why aren't you getting anywhere?"

"Because it's hard to fill positions in shit holes, and they're reluctant to transfer people out of them."

"So what are you doing about it, besides bitching?"

He laughed. It was a sound as bitter as the emotions that were still swirling around me. "Putting out feelers. Pulling in favors." He shrugged. "Stuff like that."

The snarky part of me wondered just how many favors a cop in nowhereville could actually pull in. Not a lot, one would have thought.

We hit the main street and I turned right, heading back to the store to grab the coffee I'd told Evin I was coming out to get. Mike followed.

"You don't have to baby-sit me," I commented. "I won't go back to your precious crime scene."

Now, going back to the *house*—that was another matter entirely. And one he hadn't actually warned me away from. Of course, if I got caught breaking into said house, it could land me in a whole lot *more* trouble.

So shadow and don't get caught, that little voice inside whispered.

Which made about as much sense as pigs flying, but even so, my pulse raced at the thought. Vampires shadowed, and I wasn't a vampire.

Was I?

No, I thought, squinting up at the sun. If I was a vamp, I'd be toast by now. Yet if there was vampire blood in me, it would explain the surprising sensitivity to the sun.

"When you start heading back to the villa, I'll head

back to the station," Mike commented. "Until then, consider me a thorn in your side."

"There's obviously very little to do in this town if you can waste time baby-sitting me."

"That's what I've been bitching about, remember?" He snorted softly. "The most exciting things to have happened in this town are your appearance and the damn murder."

I raised my eyebrows as I squinted up at him. "How is my appearance exciting?"

"Well, you got lost, didn't you? Gave us something to do for a day. It's a shame Evin had to find you so quickly."

Had to? That was an odd way of putting it. I climbed the steps and walked into the supermarket. "Well, I'm sorry that we cut your fun short, but I'm damn glad he found me when he did."

"I guess you would be."

There wasn't a whole lot of choice in the coffee department, so I grabbed some Kona and headed for the cash register. Mike followed—a thorn in my side, indeed. As I dragged out my wallet and paid the woman, I squinted up at him and said, "How come he was the only one in the plane?"

"His choice." Mike shrugged. "The logical search area was fanning out from where your car was crashed, not hundreds of miles south."

So how did he find me if he wasn't my twin? Something in my stomach fluttered at that thought, but no matter what I did, I couldn't catch the tail of it and make it something more. Make it a memory.

The woman gave me my change and a smile, and I headed out the door. "So why did he hire the plane?"

And where did he find the money if we were supposedly so broke we couldn't afford to go home and therefore waste the money we'd paid for the villa?

"It's the quickest and easiest way to cover a large amount of ground." He glanced down at me. "Why does this even matter? You were rescued—that's the main issue, isn't it?"

No, it wasn't, but I wasn't about to say that. For some odd reason, I trusted Harris, but I didn't trust his sidekick. There was something about him that tickled my instincts and said *wrong*.

"I guess it is." I forced a smile. "Now, I'd better get this coffee home before my rescuer gets too grumpy."

Mike stopped on the supermarket landing and leaned against one of the veranda supports. "Don't detour past the crime scene," he reminded me.

"Trust me, I won't."

And I didn't. But he watched me walk down the long street, his gaze a weight I could feel between the shoulder blades. Mike West didn't trust me, but that was all right, because I didn't trust him, either.

Not one little bit.

*D*arkness was coming. The colorful flags of dusk took forever to fade, as did the last remnants of daylight. We took pizza out of the freezer rather than ordering in and drank the fresh coffee—which tasted a whole lot better than the muck Evin had been giving me beforehand, but it still wasn't fantastic. But then, Kona was Liander's favorite, not mine.

Liander.

I waited, but no image or information came to match the name. I flexed my fingers against the mug, knowing frustration wasn't going to help, then took another sip. It didn't improve with a second taste, but it was at least drinkable.

Maybe the almost constant, headachy pain in my head wasn't so much caused by blows to my head but rather withdrawal from decent coffee.

After the dishes were washed, Evin glanced at his watch and said, "Well, I'm off to the pub for a beer. You want to come?"

I hesitated, glancing at the sky. "I think I'll go for a walk along the beach instead. I need to stretch my legs."

"Just don't get lost again. I can't afford to hire the plane a second time."

"I wouldn't have thought we could afford it the first time."

He hesitated. "We couldn't. Mom transferred some money to my account. I'll pay her back once I'm working again."

I nodded, and didn't believe a word of it. "I'll see you in an hour or so."

"You will." He shoved his hands in his pockets and walked out.

I waited five minutes, then jumped to my feet, grabbed my purse, and ran out. I didn't bother locking up. There wasn't anything in the villa that mattered to me—everything that mattered was locked behind the hazy pain that still resisted any attempt to ease it.

Evin was taking the main road into town. I raced along the beach, keeping to the shadows and out of sight as much as possible.

When the town center came into view, I cut through a back lane, pausing long enough to check that Evin hadn't actually come onto the main street yet, then dashed across the road to the pub.

It was as crowded and as noisy as the night before. And, like before, it smelled sharply of wolf and humans. This time, though, the scent of desire was more noticeable on the air.

The moon was rising toward fullness—another week and it would be here, so how did a town like this cope with so many humans around? From what I'd seen, it didn't appear to have the wolf-only clubs that most of the major cities did—clubs that protected wolves as much as they did humans. So were the werewolves of Dunedan more circumspect with their sexual drives, or did they simply retreat for the four or five days necessary to ride out the moon heat and subsequent shape change?

And why was *I* not feeling the force of it? Why wasn't the moon heat beginning to stir through my blood? I was a wolf, wasn't I?

Yes and no, that annoying deep-down voice said. Which was, as usual, no help at all.

I made my way through the crowd, then ducked into the bathroom. It was close enough to the phone that, with any sort of luck, he wouldn't scent me and I just might be able to hear at least some of his conversation.

He arrived a few minutes later. The toilets were at an angle to the phone, so I had a good view of the number pad. He picked up the handset and dialed 0356—but before I could see the rest of the numbers, some stupid woman stepped between me and the phone and flung out a hand to push open the bathroom door. I jumped back, grabbed some paper towels from the dispenser, and pretended to dry my hands. The woman took forever to pee, so by the time I got back to spying, Evin was already talking.

"Are you all right?" His voice cracked as he said it.

As the person on the other end of the phone answered, he closed his eyes and leaned his forehead against the wall. After a few minutes, he said, "I know, I know, but there's nothing we can do about it. We do what we have to, love. Hopefully this won't go on too long."

He fell silent. Then, "I don't know what will happen. You're in contact with him more than me—ask him."

Several moments of silence, then his hands suddenly clenched against the phone. "Damn you, that wasn't—"

Whoever was on the other end of the phone must have cut him off, because he didn't say anything for several minutes. Finally, he all but spat "Fine" and slammed the handset back onto the receiver.

I ducked back as he swung around, listening to the sound of his footsteps retreating and wondering what the hell was going on. Whatever it was, my brother wasn't happy. Maybe my earlier guess that he was as much trapped in this as I was wasn't so far off the mark.

But as much as I wanted to go after him and confront him about what I'd overheard, I couldn't. There were still too many things that I didn't know—and I doubted he would tell me anything yet. He wasn't really desperate enough—or, rather, the situation *itself* wasn't desperate enough yet.

But that might change as the full moon drew closer. Evin had let slip that he was moon-sworn—and if he was stuck out here with me, then that obviously meant that he and his partner were separated. A wolf who didn't have sex during the moon heat was heading for trouble—and while the moon bond killed the desire for anyone other than your partner, it didn't actually kill the need for sex. Both Evin and his partner would be forced to take others if they remained separated.

And that was a terrible situation for a moon-sworn wolf to be forced into.

He would get more desperate as the full moon drew closer—and maybe then I could get the information I needed out of him. Especially if his nightly phone calls continued to go as badly as tonight's apparently had.

Of course, I was also in the same boat. I might not feel any real desire at the moment, but if I didn't indulge, then the blood lust would hit me just as surely as it would hit Evin. And I'd been down that path once before—

The bathroom door slammed open and I barely

jumped out of the way. "Oh, sorry," a young woman said, giving me a wide and friendly smile.

"No problem," I replied, as I slipped out the door. I grabbed the chair I'd used as a vantage point the previous night and stood up on it. Evin was at the bar, staring down at the pint of beer he was nursing. If his dark and gloomy expression was anything to go by, he was intending to stay there for quite a while.

Which gave me the opportunity for a little housebreaking.

I made my way through the crowded bar, keeping to the back of the room as much as possible. Once out on the street, I headed for the beach rather than walking down the main street, not wanting to risk running into either Harris or Mike. They'd be looking out for me—I'd bet on it.

When I neared the beginning of the caravan park, I stepped over the little rope fence and loped through the shadows, keeping my footsteps light.

As I neared the road on the far side I slowed, senses alert, listening to the sounds riding the air and searching for any indication that someone was near.

Aside from a couple trying to calm a screaming kid in the nearest caravan, the night was reasonably still.

I raced across the road, jumped the fence, and ducked into the trees. I kept to their cover as I made my way toward the older part of town. When it was no longer possible to stay within their comforting shadows, I paused, my gaze scanning the houses. I couldn't see Harris, or anyone else for that matter. There were people in the house next to the victim's—I could hear the rattle of dishes and the occasional snatch of conversation. But other than that, the area could have been abandoned.

I blew out a breath, then shoved my hands into my pockets and strolled forward. No one jumped out from the cover of the nearby houses to confront me. The place really *was* as deserted as it appeared.

I jumped over the front gate rather than risking it squeaking, then padded around to the back of the house. The yard held little more than bare earth. Apparently, Landsbury hadn't been big on gardening.

I reached the back door and discovered crime scene tape across it. Obviously, Harris *wasn't* waiting for the boys in the big city, no matter what his sidekick might think. I carefully plucked one edge of the tape free so I could restick it later, then studied the lock. It wasn't a dead bolt—just an ordinary key lock. I punched the sweet spot and the door sprang open.

The house was hot and smelled stale. Stale and rotten. Although given the heat over the last couple of days, if Landsbury had left a bag of garbage sitting out, it'd probably be fermenting by now.

The first room was a small laundry. I stepped inside cautiously, senses alert for any sign of movement. Tiny claws skittered across wooden floors in the room beyond the laundry—mice rather than rats. I shut the back door, then moved into what turned out to be the kitchen. The rotten smell was more intense here, reminding me of meat left out of the fridge for too long. I tried breathing through my mouth rather than my nose, but it didn't seem to help. I could still taste the decay at the back of my mouth.

The kitchen wasn't large, consisting of little more than a basic cooking area and a small two-seater table. There were empty beer bottles on the table and scattered around the counter, but the sink was clear and there were clean dishes draining in the rack. The meat I could smell was still sitting in a pack on the stove. Maybe Landsbury had taken it out of the freezer in preparation for the night's meal. Almost every surface had fingerprint dust over it.

There wasn't much in the way of drawers, but I went through them anyway, using the clean tea towel sitting next to the dish drainer to open each one. I ran the risk of wiping off the fingerprint dust, but whoever was being sent from Perth to investigate the killing would probably do a complete reprint of the house anyway. The last thing I needed with Harris so suspicious of me was my prints being found in the victim's house.

I didn't find anything more useful than a stack of unpaid utility bills, so I headed into the hallway. Four doors led off it—one a bathroom, two bedrooms, and the third a living room. I headed into the living room and found it surprisingly clean. There was dust, but then, there was dust in my apartment back home, too . . .

The thought had me stopping in surprise, but once again it didn't lead anywhere. I cursed softly and continued looking around.

Two chairs and a TV dominated the room. In between the chairs stood a coffee table, and on it were several days' worth of newspapers. The top paper was a racing form for Belmont Park in Western Australia, and several screwed-up tickets were sitting nearby. Landsbury obviously liked to bet. There was little else of interest in the room, so I moved into the bedroom. His bed was unmade, but the sheets looked clean and the room was tidy. I'm not entirely sure why I expected Landsbury to be untidy or dirty—maybe it was just the foulness of his crime.

A small beside table sat to the left of the bed, so I walked around and, using the tea towel once again, opened the drawers. The first drawer held nothing but underwear and socks, but in the second I found gold— a notebook.

I lifted it out and carefully began to flick through. My stomach turned as I read—each page was headed by the name of a girl and various details about her: approximate age, description, habits.

Landsbury had been building up to another crime spree, if this was anything to go by.

Which meant the bastard had certainly gotten what he deserved.

There were ten girls in all, and it made me wonder if the one of their fathers had uncovered Landsbury's unhealthy little obsession. It would certainly explain the method of his murder.

Yet that didn't explain the whole red-horned devil. That *wasn't* a coincidence, and I doubted it was a copy-cat. Besides the fact that it didn't feel right, if Harris hadn't known about the other murders, why would anyone else?

I flicked through the remainder of the notebook, but

there was nothing else in it. I put it back, slid the drawer closed, and stood up.

As I swung around to head out, I heard the footstep. It was whisper soft, barely stirring the air, but it was there. I flared my nostrils, trying to smell who it was, but the air was rich with the scent of decay and it over-rode everything else.

I moved quickly but quietly to the side of the dresser, squeezing in between it and the wall and squatting down in an effort to be less noticeable. Even though the bedroom curtains were open, the moon hadn't risen fully yet and the darkness lay fairly thick in the room. I had to hope it would be enough to conceal me.

There were no more footsteps, but the hairs on the back of my neck rose with the awareness of another. I still couldn't smell him—or her—but he was close.

A shadow appeared in the doorway and I recog-nized his outline immediately. Harris.

The damn man was a bloodhound. For an instant, he looked straight at me, but there was no sign of recognition, no indication he actually realized I was there, and I frowned. Maybe the darkness and shadows were deeper than I figured.

I stayed where I was, watching him, hoping against hope he'd continue to not see me, not smell me, and would just give up and walk away.

I really should have known fate had other plans.

"I know you're here somewhere, Hanna. Come out."

I didn't move. He could have been bluffing.

"Come out, and we'll discuss your reasons for being

here. If you don't, I will throw your ass in jail and bury the key."

If it had been Mike making that offer, I would have stayed where I was. But it was Harris and, for some reason, I trusted him.

I rose to my feet and stepped out of the shadows. His gaze swung around and I saw the barest flicker of surprise.

"How the fuck did you do that?"

I frowned. "Do what?"

"You weren't *there*. There was nothing but shadow in that corner." He stared at me. "Only vampires do stuff like that."

"I'm not a vampire." But again that ripple of doubt ran through me. I might not be a vampire, but did that blood run through me?

Yes, that inner voice said. *Yes.*

It was coming back. Slowly but surely, it was coming back.

"I know that." There was a sharpness in his voice that suggested annoyance, even if it didn't show in his expression. "And yet you obviously just shadowed."

"Look, I've been nothing but honest with you. I don't know who and what I am. I don't know what I can and can't do. I'm trying to uncover all that and, the minute I do, I'll let you in on the secret." I paused, my gaze searching his and once again seeing little. "How come you keep tracking me down? Have you got some sort of weird ability to sense trouble before it starts?"

"Something like that," he said, voice short. "So tell

me, just how is breaking into a crime scene going to help you recover your memories?"

I gave him a thin smile. "As I've repeatedly said, Landsbury's murder reminds me of another. If I uncover his killer, maybe I'll shake loose some more clues as to how and why I was involved in investigating that other murder. And that, in turn, just might lead to a revelation about identity."

He stared at me for a minute, then said, "Did you find anything?"

I hesitated but decided I'd better be honest. If he *did* have some sort of psychic gift, lying would only get me in deeper trouble. And right now, I needed someone on my side.

An odd thought, given that Evin was supposedly my brother.

"There's a notebook in the bottom drawer that lists some rather chilling details about ten local girls."

The only reaction Harris had was a slight flaring of the nostrils. Yet I could feel his anger—a rush of heat that briefly seared the air.

"You placed it back exactly as you found it."

"Of course, but why—" I stopped, studying him. "You're using it as bait."

"Yes. We don't know whether his partner is in town under an alias, but if he *is,* then it's possible he'll know about the notebook and attempt to recover it."

"Good plan, except that I doubt the partner had anything to do with Landsbury's murder."

"No, but if we can flush him out, we can get him out of harm's way."

Meaning Harris *did* think it was a revenge killing. "So you think someone in this town might have realized what Landsbury was up to?"

His expression was noncommittal. "If someone *had,* they would have gone to Remy."

I frowned. "Why not you? You're the cop, not the pack leader."

"I'm here for the benefit of the tourists. State law dictates we have fully trained police officers in charge when a pack town is open to humans."

"Then you have no control over the wolf population? How does that work?"

"In town, I have the say and the power to control pack members when necessary. Beyond town, it falls to pack rule."

Which was the basic setup of most packs. "But this murder happened in Dunedan itself, so why would they go to Remy rather than you?"

His smile was slightly bitter. "Because I am not well liked in this town."

I raised my eyebrows. "But they respect you. I saw that in the pub the other night."

He snorted softly. "They respect my previous achievements. They respect my fairness. They do not respect *me*."

"Because you're not a full-blood West-pack wolf."

"Yes. Packs tend to be very insular, and outsiders are not welcomed easily."

"That must have made your mother's life hell."

"It did. But my father was pack second, so no one

said anything openly. My peers, however, showed no such restraint."

"Then why did you come back here?"

"Because I could no longer stay in Sydney."

"Why not?"

He raised an eyebrow. "Are you always this up front?"

"I think so. And if people refuse to answer, I find out other ways."

He grunted. "Why does that not surprise me?"

I restrained my grin. "Look, you're obviously a damn good cop with amazing instincts, and Mike said you had a stellar career in Sydney. So why come back here?"

He considered me for a moment, then said, "Two reasons. The first being the fact that my soul mate— who was also a cop—was killed in the line of duty."

And coming here was one hell of a good way to get away from every reminder of her. Part of me understood that, but at the same time, I didn't. Running from a situation never solved anything.

I didn't offer Harris the usual lines of sympathy, nor did I tell him that I was in the same position. His expression suggested neither comment would be welcome. And *that* I could totally understand. There was nothing—certainly no words—that could ever ease such a pain. It had to come from inside. From the desire to move on.

Do you want to move on? that voice whispered. *Are you ready?*

Yes. But again, the vision of the black car rolling over

and over hit. *But only if there's something—someone—to move on with.*

I swallowed heavily and said, "And the second?"

"My mom was dying and had no one to look after her."

"What about your dad?"

"He died several years before. Heart attack."

Which was damn unusual for a wolf. He couldn't have been very fit.

He made a sharp sweeping movement with his hand. "Did you find anything else here?"

Meaning, obviously, that *that* line of questioning was *over.* "No."

"And I'm gathering you've left no fingerprints behind?" He didn't wait for my answer, simply added, "We've been ordered to preserve the scene, not investigate. The murder boys are due in tomorrow."

If his expression was anything to go by, he was hoping Landsbury's partner would make his appearance sooner rather than later. Which meant he'd been watching the house, even if I hadn't seen him.

"They're going to be less than happy about the print dust everywhere."

And it was odd that Homicide was taking over. Usually they worked *with* the local detectives, not above them. But maybe it *was* simply a case of the local boys being seen as not having the expertise—despite Harris's time in Sydney.

"That happened before we were ordered away." He shrugged, but there was a glimmer of amusement in his eyes. Harris wasn't about to give up his case for anyone, and that was something I could totally understand. And respect.

"What about the coroner's report? Was there anything interesting in the toxicology report?"

"Yeah. A drug known as DH208. Apparently it's a military-only drug that's designed to almost instantly freeze the central nervous system of humans and non-humans alike." His gaze met mine again. "You were right."

"Which doesn't mean I applied the stuff."

He smiled. "I wasn't actually thinking that."

"So you no longer think I murdered him?"

"I never did. But it's a cop's job to be suspicious of everyone and everything. Especially when coincidences keep pointing a particular way."

"Which just goes to prove you can't trust coincidences."

"I don't. But here you are, the biggest of them all." He tilted his head a little, studying me through slightly narrowed eyes. "Why is that, do you think?"

"What? Why am I here, or why are these murders happening while I'm here?"

"Both."

"I think the murder thing is simply bad timing, but I guess whoever is behind the mess surrounding me wasn't to know that I was investigating the very same crime or that it would actually happen here. As to the other . . . to be honest, I don't know. Evin said we'd only be here for a week. After that, he wasn't sure."

"If he was a part of the scheme, wouldn't he be aware of whatever plans there are?"

"Only if he's a willing participant. I have a feeling he's not." I hesitated. "Which reminds me—I have another favor to ask."

He simply raised his eyebrows, so I continued.

"As you've already mentioned, Evin goes to the pub to make a phone call every night. I caught part of the number last night—the first four digits are 0356. Is there any chance of getting a printout of the calls made on that phone and tracking down the full number?"

"You don't want a lot, do you?" He frowned and rubbed a hand across his stubbly chin. "I know someone who might be able to do it on the sly."

I frowned. "Why not request it officially?"

"What reason would I give? If there *is* a bigger plot behind your memory loss and sudden appearance here, don't you think they'd have set up checks? A request for information on that particular phone might just send an alert to the very people you're trying to uncover."

My heart warmed at his statement. He *believed* me. He might have emphasized the "is," but the belief was there in his eyes, if not his words.

"That might be a good thing. It might just lead to them making a mistake and exposing their identity."

"Or killing you outright. There'd have to be someone else other than Evin on watch here."

"I guess." I might be able to defend myself, but there was no defense against a long-range bullet. And while I kept hearing that voice telling me he didn't want me dead just yet, that he wanted me to suffer, that didn't mean I wouldn't end up dead if things started going wrong before my seven days were up. After all, I was a long way from home.

Home.

God, I ached for it—ached for the people who I couldn't remember but who I was suddenly certain made home *home*—so badly the word stuck in my throat and made breathing suddenly difficult. I might not remember where home was exactly, but I *so* wanted to see Rhoan and Liander and . . .

Someone else, someone who was my heart if not my soul.

Someone who was in that battered, bloody, black car. Someone I'd already been told was dead.

No, something inside me screamed. *No!*

I rubbed my forehead wearily and battled to keep that scream inside. At least *some* information was slowly leaking back. I had two more names now: Rhoan and Liander. They were a part of me—not just a part of my life. I felt that with every fiber.

Which meant one of them, at least, was my brother.

Rhoan, that little voice whispered. *My brother, my twin.*

I took a deep, somewhat shuddery breath and released it slowly. I was tempted to ask Harris to do a search for him, but instinct said not to. Harris was right—whoever was behind this plot had planned it thoroughly. If Rhoan *was* my brother, then any official search for him might just raise alarms. Hell, even if I found his phone number, just ringing him might lead to more drastic action. Like his death.

That voice had said that he wanted me to suffer. And what better way was there to achieve that than to wipe my memories, take me away from everything and everyone I loved, then slowly allow those memories to come back—only to have each and every one I cared about murdered the moment I contacted them?

It would be his style. Whoever "he" was.

But first things first. I needed to find my brother's location, either through Google or the old-fashioned way, via the White Pages—and at least looking through a phone book would leave nothing to trace.

I could decide what my next step should be once I'd found him.

"You're looking rather lost in your thoughts," Harris commented, and the sudden sound of his voice made me jump. I'd totally forgotten he was there for a moment. "Care to share?"

"Just remembering some names." I shrugged. "Their relationship to me, however, remains tantalizingly lost in the fog."

He grunted, and I wasn't entirely sure he believed me. "You ready to leave?"

I raised an eyebrow. "I have a choice?"

Again a slight smile tugged his lips. "No, you do not." He waved a hand toward the doorway. "After you, Hanna London."

I opened my mouth to tell him that wasn't my name, then snapped it closed. My name was there, I could feel it, but it just wouldn't reveal itself.

Patience, I reminded myself.

Only I had a suspicion patience was the one thing I *didn't* have a lot of.

I made my way through the house and out the back. Harris closed and locked the door behind us, then turned around and said, "I won't find you inside again, will I?"

I smiled, but my reply was cut off by the sudden sound of screaming.

Screaming that was male and filled with fear.

Screaming that was cut off almost as quickly as it had begun.

Chapter 11

"Stay here," Harris said, barely even looking at me as he ran off.

I snorted softly. Like I was really going to obey *that* order when I hadn't obeyed any of his others so far.

I took off after him, our footsteps ringing sharply across the darkness. The wind remained free from the scent of blood, but the taste of fear was growing sharper.

We rounded the last of the buildings and turned in to the paddock area where Landsbury had been attacked and killed. The young policeman was still at his post, but he was staring at the emptiness beyond the hills. He looked relieved when he saw Harris.

"Sir," he said, voice a little strained, "there's some sort of kerfuffle out in the Northern Ranges."

"Did you see anything or anyone, Benny?" Harris asked.

"No, sir. Just heard the screaming."

Harris nodded and ran on. I followed close on his heels. We raced out of the paddock area into a sandier, wilder area, sprinting up a hill. Harris paused at the top, and I stopped beside him, my nostrils flaring to catch any hint of blood or vengeance or any other scent that didn't belong. None of those rode the wind, but the smell of fear was thicker.

"There," Harris said, pointing sharply to the left.

I followed the line of his finger. Several hilltops away, metal gleamed briefly but brightly in the moonlight. Someone had raised a knife, but whether that someone was male or female was anyone's guess, because—thanks to the hill—all we could see was the hand and the knife.

"This time, stay *here*," Harris said, and plunged down the slope. He shifted shape as he ran, flowing from human to brown wolf with a fluidity and grace that was breathtaking to see.

I plunged after him and reached for my own wolf. I could feel her, feel her eagerness, deep within my soul, but there was still some sort of barrier between us. Pain flared so bright and hard inside my brain that I stumbled and had to flail my arms to keep my balance.

Tears stung my eyes and frustration burned through my body. Whoever had done this to me would pay. Big time.

I ran on, my feet flying over the sandy soil, oddly keeping up with Harris even though he was in wolf form and could move with greater ease over the ground. Maybe there really was vampire in me.

The scent of blood began to stain the air. We were too late—far too late—to save the life of whoever it was who'd screamed. But we still had a chance to catch the killer.

We ran up another hill, plunged down the far side. From beyond the next hill came a brief flash that lit up the night. It looked for all the world like someone was taking a photo.

But only a sicko would take photos of their handiwork—although given these murders seemed to be based on vengeance, maybe it *wasn't* the work of a sick mind, but rather someone taking snaps for whoever was behind this particular murder. Not everyone could attend the murder scene like Hank Surrey had . . .

I filed the name away and continued running. As we reached the top of the hill, the scent of blood and death and fear sharpened, filling the night air with its taint. Just below us, spread-eagled and naked, was a man. Like Landsbury, he had a gaping, bloody wound where his penis and balls used to be.

We ran down the hill, Harris shifting back to human form as he did so. His shirt was ripped across the back, but his clothes seemed to hold together a whole lot better than mine ever did. Of course, Harris wasn't the type to wear flimsy lace. I was, and I paid the price for it when I shifted. It was annoying that I could remember that, and not more important things.

"No scent of the killer," he said as he stopped near the body.

"He's probably using a scent-nulling soap." I said it absently, my gaze scanning the night, looking for something, anything, that might give some clue as to where our murderer had gone. He can't have just disappeared—unless, of course, we were dealing with a vampire, then yeah, he could. Or at least, he could disappear to the human eye.

But *not* to nonhumans. Not to the eye of someone who had vampire blood in them. I blinked, switching from one type of vision to another.

After a moment, I became aware of Harris looking at me.

"What?" I said, not bothering to meet his gaze. We needed to find the whereabouts of our killer fast if we were to have any hope of catching him.

"You really do come out with some of the most amazing facts."

"I know some pretty amazing people." In the distance, I spotted a hint of red. It was vague, and darkish, nothing solid, more insubstantial, and oddly pulsing. *Body heat.* Only it wasn't the heat of a human body—it wasn't bright enough. Our quarry was a vampire.

"There," I said, pointing. "He's damn fast."

Harris had barely looked at where I was pointing before he was running. He flowed again from one form into another, his tongue lolling out and eyes bright. Every wolf enjoys a good chase, and the murderer was certainly giving us that.

But we were holding our own. Slowly but surely, we were catching him.

Another sound rode across the night—a soft *whump, whump*. It took me a moment to realize what it was.

"Helicopter, closing in fast." It was a rather useless statement given Harris was in wolf form and would hear it better than I could. So I added, "If we don't stop him, he'll disappear as quickly as the other killers have."

Harris responded with an increase of speed, until it seemed our feet were flying over the red sands. The heated blur of our quarry was closer, but so, too, were the sounds of the helicopter. It had no lights on to give away its position. The only way we knew it was near was by the ever-increasing volume of the rotor blades.

Then it became visible, swooping in from the skies like a big, pot-bellied bird. And we were nowhere near close enough to stop the vampire from climbing aboard.

The bastard was going to get away.

Fuck, fuck, *fuck!*

Harris shifted shape again, his speed slowing a little in human form but still running damn fast. Energy began to stir around me. Initially it was little more than a gentle caress that raised the hairs along my arms, but all too quickly it became a tornado, stinging and tearing at my skin.

And its focal point was Harris.

He didn't say anything, his gaze on the helicopter. It was close to the ground now, its blades stirring huge clouds of dust, making the invisible visible. Our vampire murderer was a man—a rather slender man, not big like Landsbury had stated. As a vampire, he didn't need to be.

Harris flung out his right arm, his fingertips flaring, as if he were throwing something. That maelstrom of power flew across the night, slapping into the copter with the force of a storm.

But it was a very precise storm. The helicopter wasn't flung about like a leaf but rather slapped down sideways. The rotor blades chopped into the soil, throwing huge chunks of dirt and grass into the air as it crumpled into the earth. Bits and pieces of metal went spinning away into the night, and sparks rose like eager fireflies. The vampire didn't hang about to see what had happened. He simply turned and ran in a completely different direction.

"Grab the pilot," I said to Harris. "I'll go after the vamp."

He didn't argue, though I guess by rights he should have. Maybe he realized that I wasn't going to be deterred, no matter what he said. Or maybe he simply couldn't see the vamp—though given his unexpected talent of kinesis, who knew what other little goodies he kept up his sleeve?

I swerved to the right, kicking up dust as I ran after the vamp. I had no idea where he thought he was going, but I knew from experience there wasn't much out here in the way of shelter. All I really had to do was keep him in sight and let him run until the sun came up.

Of course, crisping him in sunlight wasn't going to get the answers we needed.

So I reached for all the speed I had and flew across the sands. It was almost as if I was flying: like I was a bird, swooping low over the red soil . . .

Power swept through me, over me, and suddenly I *was* a bird.

A seagull, in fact.

A weird mix of surprise and relief swept through me. Surprise because I really hadn't been expecting it, and relief because not all my skills had been placed beyond my reach.

He didn't know about the alternate shape, that inner voice whispered. *He couldn't prevent what he didn't know.*

Which still left me wondering how the hell anyone could prevent a shifter from shifting.

I shoved the thought aside and swooped upward, gaining height. Maybe if the vamp thought we'd given up he'd slow down—and make it easier for me to drop down on top of him.

But it soon became obvious he *did* have a second escape option. From high above, I could see lights beginning to twinkle in the distance. It looked like some sort of farmhouse, and it had various outbuildings. What were the odds that at least one of those buildings had a vamp-ready car waiting to go?

Or worse yet, help?

I might not have been chasing him for very long or very far, but I'd already run out of time. I swooped downward, folding my wings and flattening out my body to streamline it as much as possible. As I got closer,

I shifted shape, moving back to human form. He sensed me then, but spun around rather than looking up.

I rolled in the air and hit him feetfirst, smashing him down into the soil and landing half on top of him. The sheer speed behind my dive had me stumbling forward, fighting to keep my balance. Behind me, the vampire snarled—a sound filled with pain and anger.

I swung around and saw the vamp shake his head, sending blood and snot flying, then he pushed to his hands and knees. I didn't give him the chance to rise fully. I didn't even give him the chance to see me. I just twisted around and lashed out with my foot. My heel smashed into the side of his face and the force of the blow knocked him sideways, sending him flying back.

He struggled again to rise, but this time I threw myself at him, hitting him with all the force I could muster. His head snapped back, and he slumped to the ground.

I pushed off his back then hauled him over. He might be out cold, but I was not about to bet that he'd stay that way. I tore the sleeve off my shirt and used it as a gag, prying open his mouth and shoving the knot into it as extra insurance against a bite. He wouldn't be happy once he woke, but right then, I couldn't care less.

With that done, I hauled him up and over my shoulder, letting him flop like a bag of grain over my back. If he happened to wake up, he'd be in pain.

Part of me hoped he *did* wake. Both Landsbury and tonight's victim might have deserved the death they'd received, but that didn't make their killer worthy of fair treatment.

Harsh, one part of me whispered.

At least he's not dead, another retorted.

All of which made me wonder if half the reason for the gaps in my memory was a desire *not* to remember exactly what I'd been or done in the past.

I turned around and trudged back toward Harris and the shattered helicopter. It might not have been far, but by the time I arrived, I was hot, sweaty, and tired. The vamp wasn't big, but that didn't mean he was light.

Surprisingly, there was no one else there yet. Harris obviously hadn't called in help. The helicopter rested on its side like some forgotten child's toy and the pilot lay beside it, trussed securely with wire that had obviously been ripped out of the copter. He was bloody and bruised, and looked rather the worse for wear. He was also unconscious.

Harris was leaning into the fallen helicopter, pulling out bits of papers and scanning them, but swung around as I approached. Relief touched his features as he dropped the paperwork and walked across to me, grabbing the vamp by the waist and hauling him off my back. I sighed in relief and rubbed my aching shoulder, watching Harris dump the vamp on the ground beside the pilot.

"How come you haven't called for assistance?" I asked.

"Because," he said, swinging around to face me, "I tried ringing Mike but he's not answering his phone. And if you're right about there being a plot surrounding you, then I don't think it's wise to let too many other people know that you helped me bring down a vamp."

I frowned. "The young officer saw me running with you, and the vamp certainly knows I brought him down. I wouldn't think either is going to keep my presence a secret."

"Did the vamp actually see you?"

I frowned. "No. Why?"

"Because you were shadowing when we were racing up here. Benny wouldn't have seen you, and he wasn't close enough to scent you. So if the vamp never actually saw you clearly, then we don't have a problem."

I'd had no idea that I was shadowing. Obviously, whatever had been done to my mind had somehow switched my "other" skills from conscious to automatic. "The vamp never bothered looking around to see who was chasing him, and I never gave him the opportunity once I brought him down."

"Good," Harris said. "Then leave, and make sure no one sees you. Loop back the long way if you have to. I'll take care of these two."

"Will the cells at the station be strong enough to hold the vamp?"

He smiled. "They're strong enough to hold werewolves. They'll hold a vamp."

I wasn't so sure, and maybe my expression said as much because Harris added, "But we have several pairs of titanium handcuffs. We'll use those on the bugger, just to be sure."

I nodded. "The Directorate will want to interview him."

"That's only *if* the Perth office considers our problem interesting enough to come down here. We still haven't had any communication from them."

"You might not. They might just show up on your doorstep tomorrow." I hesitated. "There's also the problem of the vamp's telepathy—"

"We have nanowires," he cut in. "This place may be in the middle of nowhere, but I've ensured we're equipped to deal with anyone *and* anything."

"And I'm betting all the fancy equipment came out of pack funds, not government." State governments Australia-wide were still struggling to supply the bulk of their city forces with nanowires, so it was doubtful they'd be wasting them on places like Dunedan, where vamps were likely to be few and far between.

Harris's gaze narrowed a little. "You know altogether *too* much about the workings of the police and the Directorate. If you're one or the other, and have gone missing, it's a wonder there's not an all-state alert out."

I shrugged. "Maybe there is. Driver's licenses can be faked, you know."

"Yours is in the system."

"That doesn't make it any more real."

"True, but the picture *is* of you, and that alone should have raised interest." He glanced at his watch. "You'd better leave, or I'll be dealing with questions as to why I waited so long to call this in."

"Then consider me gone."

I spun on my heel and loped away, taking the long way back to our villa. The place was dark and the TV was off. I frowned. It seemed unlikely that Evin would still be at the pub, or that he'd gone to bed. It was far too early. I unlocked the sliding door and slid it open.

"Evin?" I said without actually stepping inside.

No answer came, but an odd, tingly awareness ran across my skin.

Something felt *wrong*.

I flared my nostrils, drawing in the air, searching for scents that didn't belong. There were two—pine and smoke, combined within the musk of male. The scent of a stranger.

Someone had been here.

I blinked, switching to infrared as my gaze swept the darkness. There was no hint of body heat within the villa. Whoever had been here was long gone. I reached across to the light and switched it on—not the brightest thing in the world to do given I was still in infrared mode. I blinked away tears and returned to normal vision.

Nothing seemed to have been touched. The room wasn't destroyed and everything was sitting where we'd left it. I stepped inside, locked the door behind me, then walked into Evin's bedroom. Again, nothing appeared to have been moved, although he didn't seem to have much in the way of personal items. Not even a picture of the woman he was sworn to.

I walked out of his room and into my own. Again, nothing appeared to have been disturbed.

I frowned and wondered if the scent simply belonged to a cleaner. Except—why would they come at night? Didn't hotel cleaners usually work during the day, when most guests were out and about?

No, there had to be another reason for that scent being here.

I spun around and walked back out to the kitchen. And that's when I saw the note stuck to the fridge.

I tore it free of the magnet and opened it. The writing was strong and dark, the words ugly.

You owe me, it said. *Meet me at the Whale Station ruins by eleven, or you won't see your brother alive again. And don't bother calling the cops—he'll be shark food long before anyone gets there.*

Anger surged, but I wasn't entirely sure who I was more angry at—them for doing this, or myself for not realizing they might pull a stunt like this.

But then, despite Harris's warning—or maybe because of it—I'd expected Denny to come after *me*. Attacking Evin was the coward's way out.

Meaning he wouldn't be waiting for me alone. He'd have friends to back him up. His sort always did.

I was tempted to crumple the note up and toss it in the bin, but I resisted the temptation. The note was evidence, and I had a feeling I'd need that—especially given that Denny was the son of the pack's second. It would be his word against mine without this note, and his father's status in the pack *would* matter, even if it wasn't supposed to.

So I went through the kitchen cupboards until I found some plastic wrap, then covered the note with it, trying to touch the paper as little as possible so there'd be less chance of smudging whatever prints might be

on it. Then I shoved it inside my jeans pocket. I wasn't
about to leave it here. They'd already proven locked
doors didn't stop them, and I wouldn't put it past them
to have someone waiting for me to leave so they could
come back in and grab the note.

So where the hell was the old whaling station?

Frowning, I walked around the kitchen counter and
grabbed the information booklet that was sitting near
the phone. After flicking through several pages, I
found it. It was, according to the map, at least a two-
and-a-half-hour drive. I glanced over my shoulder to
the clock. It was almost nine—I'd never make it if I
drove. But then, I had other options—options Denny
and his friends *couldn't* know about.

So why would they bother giving me a time limit
they knew I couldn't make? Unless the whole point
was to panic me so that I'd simply rush there without
thought or aid?

After all, if they *did* have someone watching the
house, they'd know when I left and could estimate my
arrival. Which meant I'd have to at least make a show
of being panicked, just in case.

I blew out a breath, then walked back to the kitchen
and opened the drawers. There wasn't much in the
way of weapons—a set of old steak knives was about
the extent of it. But they were better than nothing, so I
shoved one down each sock.

I went back into my bedroom to change from my
warm and sturdy shirt to something a little more
flimsy, then grabbed my coat, found the car keys, and
raced out, making a pretense of fumbling the locks.

I didn't see anyone, didn't scent anyone, yet I had a feeling they were out there all the same. The back of my neck crawled with the sensation of being watched.

I jumped into the car, started it up, then spun it around and fishtailed down the drive. I kept my foot flattened, racing through town and out into the dark hills. By the time I was a good ten or twenty miles out, it was obvious I wasn't being tailed, so I slowed down and starting looking for someplace to hide the car.

There weren't a whole lot of options in this land of endlessly rolling sand hills, so I simply drove off the road, then up and over the nearest hill. The tracks in the soil would give me away if anyone bothered looking hard enough, but hopefully they wouldn't be.

I climbed out, locked the car, then closed my eyes and imagined the seagull shape. For a heartbeat, pain flared, but unlike when I tried reaching for the wolf, it was a distant, insubstantial thing that didn't hold the strength to prevent the change.

Power surged, sweeping around me, through me, changing and molding my body, forcing the limbs of a human down into those of a gull. And the mere act of changing when I actually wanted to felt so good that part of me raged again against those who had contained my wolf. Then the anger was swept away, because I was leaping skyward.

I followed the long dusty road north, seeing nothing, hearing nothing, except the roar of the surf far below me. This part of Australia was a wild and empty place.

Eventually, a warm light began to flicker through

the darkness. I swooped toward it, and the light became a campfire burning brightly near the shoreline. Meaning no one was likely to notice a curious seagull.

There were three men sitting near the fire. Their laughter rode across the night, filled with anticipation. One of those men was Denny, but the other two I didn't recognize.

I dipped a wing and swung around to the left. There was another man standing behind a rusting hulk of machinery, and a fifth on the opposite side of the camp, squatting next to a huge metal tank. Inside the tank lay Evin. He was trussed up tight and wasn't moving. Despite my fears about his involvement in whatever was happening to me, I found myself hoping he was okay. That he was merely tied and sleeping rather than unconscious.

Or, worse still, dead.

I swooped upward again and swung back to the campfire. Five men. Even for me, those were pretty tough odds. If I was to have any hope in this fight, I'd need to even the numbers out a little.

I swung around again and headed for the man near the machinery, landing on one of the metal struts then waddling toward him. I was downwind of him, so any sound was being carried away rather than toward him, and he didn't pay me any attention. His gaze continually swept the night and his posture was alert, tense, but he had a beer in one hand, and the smell of alcohol was sharp enough that I was aware of it even in bird form.

Which meant, I hoped, that his reflexes would be crap.

I took to the air again and flew across to the next rusting hulk, where I landed and quickly changed back to human form. My flimsy shirt had all but shredded, and a good bit of breast was on show.

With any luck it would be enough to distract the men, because the firelight would eliminate any possibility of shadowing.

Although—ideally—I'd like to take *this* guard out without being seen.

I turned around and padded down to the end of the rusting tank. With my back pressed against the still-warm metal, I peered around the corner. The guard hadn't moved.

I wrapped the shadows around me and dashed across the short distance between us. As I neared him, he spun around, his nostrils flaring as he scanned the night. He could obviously scent me, but he couldn't see me. I gave him no time to react, simply hit him hard and fast—chopping him across the throat then kneeing him in the balls—and he went down like a ton of bricks. I let him slump to the ground, trusting the sand to dampen the sound of his fall, but I caught his beer can before it could clatter against the metal.

After looking around to ensure that no one had seen anything, I grabbed his arms and dragged him into a sitting position, propping him against one of the machine's struts. I put his beer beside him then stepped back. If the others glanced this way, they might think he was just sitting down. Which was good. But I needed to ensure he couldn't actually get back up.

I bit my bottom lip and scanned the rusting hulk,

seeing nothing useful in the way of rope or wire. So I spun and walked back to the tank. Again, there wasn't anything I could use, but several yards away from the tank sat the semirotten wooden remains of an old shed of some kind, and inside, the snaking remains of the building's wiring. I ripped several yards free then retraced my steps back to the guard.

I tore off his shirt, used that to gag him, then trussed him up.

One down, four to go.

I shifted shape and took to the sky again, flying back to the guard on the other side of the encampment. He was still squatting next to the tank, but he was within view of the campfire, so if I took him out his fellows were likely to notice he was missing.

I circled around for several minutes, wondering what the hell I was going to do—whether I should just take him out and bring the odds down to a more manageable level, or whether I should continue to pick them off one by one. After all, they were all drinking, and they'd surely have to wander off for a pee sooner or later.

I swooped around for yet another pass and spotted their cars. They were parked halfway between the whaling station and the dusty road, off the track leading to the station but not hidden.

I flew toward them. There was no guard here, but the one watching Evin would have been able to see them if he stood up.

It was a mistake—and one that just might work in my favor.

I landed behind a blue pickup and shifted shape, keeping as low as I could as I regained human form. If I could incapacitate two of the cars, distract the guard, then get Evin out in the third vehicle, I might not have to fight the other men at all.

It was a lot of "ifs" but I really had nothing to lose by trying—nothing except all the bruises I'd get if I did have to fight them.

I checked which of the cars had keys in the ignition, and discovered both the blue pickup and the white Toyota did. The pickup had a bigger engine, but the Toyota looked newer and was a four-wheel drive. In the end, I decided on speed over versatility and reached through the open window, grabbing the keys and slipping them into my pocket. The other set of keys I tossed as far away as I could.

Then I reached down and withdrew a knife from one of my socks and crept across to the Toyota. One of the trucks had an air compressor on board, so merely letting out the air wasn't going to work. The tires were thick and new, and it quickly became evident that no matter how strong I was, a little steak knife just didn't have the strength to do little more than scratch the rubber. It might damage an ordinary car tire, but not to these.

I crept over to the next truck. Luck was with me this time—the back tire was almost bald. I picked out what looked to be the thinnest spot and punched the knife into the middle. After twisting it around to ensure a largish hole, I pulled the knife out. Air began to hiss, sounding overly loud in the hushed darkness. I crept around to the other side of the car and peered around. The guard hadn't moved. In fact, he wasn't even looking in this direction.

I took out the second rear tire, then wrapped the shadows around me and rose. I still needed to immobilize the other car. If the steak knife wasn't strong enough, maybe there was something in the back of the pickups. After all, men the world over seemed to carry all sorts of tools in their cars.

It turned out these men were no different—there was an unlocked tool kit in the back of the pickup, and inside I found a solid-looking screwdriver. It mightn't have a point, but when you were a dhampire, you didn't need one.

I paused and smiled at the thought. One more piece of the puzzle that was me.

Whatever *had* been done to my mind, it obviously wasn't holding. I wondered if that were deliberate, or whether it was just luck.

Although fate didn't often throw luck my way.

I shoved the screwdriver into both the back tires, listened for the hiss of escaping air, then placed the screwdriver back into its box.

And noticed the flashlight sitting nearby.

Perfect. Just perfect.

I grabbed it and retreated, running into the darkness and looping right back around the encampment until I reached the hills on the far side.

Once there, I turned on the flashlight and climbed to the top of the hill, pointing the light straight at the campfire, so that the waiting men couldn't fail to see it.

"Well, well, look at that." Denny's harsh voice carried easily over the sand. He rose from the log on which he'd been sitting, and, even from where I was standing, I could see the triumphant twist of his lips. "Our quarry has arrived, boys."

They laughed—a harsh, drunken sound. They were stupid to drink so much, but I guess they didn't know what they were dealing with.

"Where's Evin?" I asked. I didn't actually want him moved, but even in their alcohol-fueled state, they might think it odd if I didn't at least inquire about him.

"He's safe," Denny assured me. "Come down and see for yourself."

"I think I prefer to remain where I am for now."

"Come down, or we'll slice your brother's pretty face open."

I contemplated them for a moment, seeing their jubilation, smelling their anticipation, then said, "You know what? The drive out here has given me a lot of time to think."

"Now, that ain't a good thing, little lady—"

"Yeah, it is," I said. "I was stupid to come out here without help, so I might just go back and get some."

"You do that, and he's fish food."

"But I have the note threatening just that. Hurt him, and you'll be prime suspects."

And with that, I turned and ran in the opposite direction. For several seconds, there was no reaction, and I inwardly cursed. Damn it, they needed to come after me. It was our only chance of getting out of there without a fight.

Then I heard cursing, and Denny shouting orders, and I smiled. They'd taken the bait. And they were too drunk to realize one of their number was missing.

My feet flew across the sand, moving so fast I was barely leaving tracks. I raced up the next hill, then plunged down. But at the halfway point, I stopped and shoved the base of the flashlight into the sand, so that the bright beam cut skyward. Then I shifted shape, flying as hard and as fast as I could back to where Evin was.

Denny and his two friends had split up, Denny taking the direct route while the others approached from either angle. They were nowhere near as fast as I'd been, but then I suspected that had more to do with the alcohol in their systems than the fact I was half vampire.

They'd barely reached the first hill. It would take them another five minutes, at least, to discover the abandoned flashlight.

It wasn't much time, but it would have to do.

I flew across the campfire and straight at the man guarding Evin. He looked up as I approached, and I saw the awareness flash across his face. He wasn't as drunk as the others, and he'd recognized that I was a shifter. Whether he knew it was me or not didn't matter. As he opened his mouth to shout for the others, I shifted shape and plunged down on top of him.

He had enough sense to dive out of the way, so that my feet hit his back rather than his face, driving him earthward but not knocking him out like I'd hoped. I landed then twisted, lashing out with a heel. He blocked the blow with his arm, the force of it reverberating up my leg, then followed it up with a jab to my face. I dipped a little so that the blow passed over my right shoulder, then punched upward, aiming for his jaw. But again, he saw it coming and swayed backward so that the blow hit air rather than flesh and left me momentarily unbalanced. His fist hit my upper stomach, the force of it pushing me backward as air exploded from my lungs.

He laughed, then raised his voice, half looking away as he said, "Hey, she's over here!"

It was a stupid thing to do.

I kicked his knee as hard as I could. The impact made his leg bow unnaturally and bone shattered, the sound like a gunshot in the darkness. As he howled and started to go down, I clenched my fist and delivered an uppercut to his chin. He dropped to the ground and didn't move.

For a minute, neither did I. Breathing *hurt*. I took shallower breaths but it didn't seem to help. Nor did I have the time to worry about it.

Denny and his friends had been warned, and their shouts filled the night. I needed to grab Evin and make my escape.

I turned and ran for the front of the rusty tank. Evin was still lying where I'd seen him. His hands were tied behind his back, and the rope holding him was thick and strong. The metallic smell of blood rode the air, even though he didn't look like he'd been beaten. One look at the ropes binding him explained why—his wrists were raw and bloody. He'd obviously been trying to work himself free.

I dropped down beside him and touched his face. He jumped and his eyes flew open.

"Jesus, what the hell are you doing here?"

"Rescuing your butt," I said. "Are you injured?"

"They've wrapped silver wire around my neck. It's burning."

Which explained why he hadn't shifted shape to escape the ropes. Still, if his injured wrists and silver burns were the worst of his injuries, then he was damn lucky.

I grabbed the other knife from my boot and sawed the ropes off his bloody wrists, but it took forever, and all the time my awareness of the men was growing. I couldn't risk slicing the ropes off his feet. I should have done them first.

"I haven't got time to undo your feet. We need to get out of here." I stood up, grabbed his raw and bleeding hands, and hauled him upright. "Can you hop?"

"I'd fucking attempt to fly if it was the difference between getting the hell out and staying here." His voice was grim, determined.

"Then let's get the hell out of here."

He leapfrogged forward. I kept one hand on his arm to steady him, but the going seemed painfully slow. My awareness of the other men continued to sharpen; they were closing in on us far too fast. If we didn't get to the third truck soon, they'd be on us.

"We're moving too slow," I said.

"I'm jumping as fast as I fucking can," he practically spat.

"It's still not fast enough. Stop."

He did. I twisted, grabbed his wrist, shoved his arm around my neck, then bent, dragging him over my shoulders and holding his thigh to keep him steady.

"Fuck" was all he said as I ran forward.

We made it to the car. I flung open the passenger door, dropped him onto the seat, shoved his legs inside then shut the door and ran around to the driver's side.

Denny and his men were almost on us. I grabbed the keys out of my pocket, slammed the door closed, hit the lock button with my elbow, then leaned across and locked Evin's door.

And jumped about a mile high as a rock hit the windshield and the glass became a spidery network of cracks.

But I could see the men through them. Could see their vicious expressions. If they got their hands on us now, it wasn't going to be pleasant.

Not that it was actually going to be pleasant before.

"Fucking hell," Evin said. "Get us out of here!"

"I'm trying." I shoved the key in the ignition and fired the big engine up, then released the hand brake and threw the truck into reverse.

It rocketed backward. Another rock hit the windshield, this time punching through and landing with a *thump* on the seat between Evin and me. I twisted the wheel, pointing the truck's nose in the general direction of the road, then changed gears and hit the gas pedal.

As the truck surged forward, something hit the bed behind us. My gaze flicked to the rearview mirror, and I saw one of Denny's friends scrambling into the back. I hauled on the wheel and the big truck turned sharply to the left. The man behind us flew sideways, his shoulder smashing into the side of the truck and his body half flying out.

Yet somehow he managed to maintain his grip and didn't fall all the way out.

Evin twisted around. "Turn the other way."

I kept my foot planted and twisted the wheel in the opposite direction. Our passenger flew across the truck and tumbled out over the side. I glanced at the side mirror, saw him bounce several times in the sandy soil, then roll to a stop. He didn't get up.

I kept accelerating. I couldn't see Denny and his other friend, but I wasn't about to risk slowing down until we were well out of the area.

For a long time, the only sound was the growl of the big engine as we arrowed through the night. I handed Evin the knife and he hacked away the rope binding his legs. He tried undoing the silver wound around his neck, but it was twisted on tight.

I didn't say anything and, eventually, he cleared his throat and said, "I don't suppose you could stop and take the silver away? My skin feels like it's blistering."

I didn't look at him. Didn't slow down.

"That depends."

I could feel his gaze on me—a heat that held no anger, only the hint of confusion. Whatever else Evin might be, I didn't think he was a particularly devious man.

"On what?"

I met his gaze then. Saw his gaze widen, so heaven only knows what he actually saw in my eyes.

"It depends," I said softly, "on whether you tell me what the hell is going on."

Chapter 12

*H*is expression didn't alter, but his fear leapt between us, thick and strong. "I have no idea what you mean."

"I mean," I said harshly, "that I am *not* Hanna London. Someone has erased my memory and abandoned me here, and I want to know why."

"I don't know what you're—"

"You do," I interrupted harshly. "And if you don't answer my questions, I promise you, whatever those men intended to do to you will pale in comparison to what I'll do!"

He stared at me, his expression fierce and yet scared. "Hanna, I'm not sure why you'd think—"

"Who's holding your soul mate hostage, Evin? Who are you really?"

He didn't say anything for several seconds, then he

sighed. It was a defeated, desperate sound. "How long have you known?"

"That you aren't my brother? Almost from the beginning. Initially, I couldn't have told you his name or what he looks like—"

He looked so shocked that I stopped and stared at him. "What?"

"But I *am* your brother."

And he said it so adamantly that I half believed him. But it wasn't true. I knew my brother. Evin *wasn't* him.

"Evin, my brother is my twin—" I paused, letting that word roll around my mind again. My brother, my twin, my life. God, I missed him, even if I couldn't even recall what he looked like right now. "—and that's a connection that goes beyond the physical."

"Connection or not, it doesn't alter fact." He said it with such unwavering certainty that again I found myself questioning my memories.

But they weren't off. His belief *was*.

Which meant maybe a little memory manipulation had been going on. It would certainly explain his unshakable belief that I was his sister.

"This is all going horribly wrong." He rubbed a hand across his eyes, then added softly, "You haven't been taking your tablets, have you? They said it would be a problem if you didn't."

"Who said?" I demanded. "And what were you putting in the coffee?"

He shrugged. "I don't know. I was told to use it and I did. I figured you suspected something was up with the coffee when you went and bought your own, so I stopped."

That explained why the coffee had started tasting slightly better recently—but it still wasn't hazelnut. I hungered for that almost as much as I hungered to see Rhoan and . . . someone else. Someone who looked a whole lot like Harris. Someone who might well be dead. My throat closed over at the thoughts, and I had to force my question out. "And you report to the people behind this every night?"

"Yes." He slumped down in the car seat a little. "Look, in all honesty, I can't really tell you much."

"Then tell me what you do know."

He was silent again, staring out the window, his expression miserable. I almost felt sorry for him.

Almost.

"My real name is Evin Jenson. I'm a border patrol guard for the Glen Helen Jenson pack."

A chill ran through me. I knew that name. Knew that location. I'd grown up there, learned to fight and hate and fear there. *The home of your birth,* that internal voice said. *But not the home of your heart.* "That's in the Northern Territory, isn't it?"

His brow furrowed. "Yeah, but not many people would know that."

"Unless that's where you were born."

He blinked. "You *can't* be from the Glen Helen Jenson pack, because I would have recognized you."

I smiled grimly. One of the problems with implanting a sole memory or belief was the fact you could never account for all the questions that might provoke the wrong sort of answer. Or right one, as it was in this case.

Evin *didn't* know me, despite his belief to the contrary.

"There's a few years' difference between us," I commented. "Which probably meant we would have run in very different circles."

And there were other reasons we might never have met—reasons I couldn't remember right now, thanks to whoever had meddled with my mind.

"But the pack isn't that big and you're my sis—"

"Evin," I said softly, "I'm not. That's a belief someone has planted in your mind."

"What?" He looked at me like I was crazy.

And very possibly, I was. After all, I was just going on instinct here, and it had sometimes led me very far astray.

"Look, someone has seriously messed my memories. It isn't just the tablets. Someone with telepathic abilities has erased—or at least contained—not only the knowledge of who I am, but where I lived, what I did, and who I loved. It's probable that someone has snatched pieces of your memory, too, just to make it easier for you to project the lie."

"You're wrong. I *know* you're wrong." He stared at me for a moment, confusion bright in his eyes, then said, "Even so, I can't have been lying all that well if you've seen through it."

"The whole situation felt wrong, Evin. It wasn't just your lying." Although that didn't help. "Did you ever meet with any of them?"

"No. There was a meeting arranged, but they didn't turn up. Contact after that was always via the phone."

"Then how did you get your instructions about me?"

"Text, mostly."

"So they told you nothing about my real identity?"

He shook his head and rubbed a hand across his face. "This is all so fucked up."

He had that right. "Tell me what you know, and maybe together we can unfuck it."

He snorted. "You and what friggin' army? There's more than one damn person behind all this, I know that much."

"Oh," I said, my voice soft and flat, containing very little in the way of anger and yet all the more deadly because of it, "I don't need an army. I can do plenty of damage on my own. Trust me on *that*."

His gaze was a weight I could feel, but I didn't bother meeting it. He said, in a voice that was soft yet filled with sudden wariness, "Just who the hell are you?"

"That's what I'm trying to find out." I glanced at him briefly. "Whoever did this to me is going to pay, Evin. And while I don't think you're involved more than peripherally, you had better believe that I'm willing to do whatever it takes to get whatever information you have. So talk, or I'll make you."

He believed me. The brief flash of fear across his features was evidence enough of that. "Lyndal—my soul mate—was snatched in Melbourne about a fortnight ago. I was told to go to a warehouse in Richmond and wait for instructions—"

"Melbourne?" I interrupted, once again feeling that sweep of familiarity. I worked there. In Spencer Street, at—somewhere. I bit back a growl of frustration and added, "That's in Victoria, isn't it?"

"Yeah. Lyndal and I were holidaying down there. I went to the warehouse and waited as directed." He stopped, and frowned. "You know, I *did* lose time in that building. Is it possible for someone to tamper with your memories without them even going near you?"

"A trained telepath could stand in front of you and make you blind to their presence," I said. "How much time did you lose?"

"Just a few minutes. I just remember looking at my watch and thinking it was odd."

I nodded. "What happened after that?"

"I went back to our hotel and found a folder waiting in our room. It told me about you—the Hanna London you—and said that I was to be your guard. And if I went to the cops—or spoke to anyone at all about it— then Lyndal was dead meat."

"So they didn't actually give you the instruction about being my brother?"

"No," he said. "Because that bit is true."

I shook my head but didn't argue. He continued to stare at me, then raked his hands through his hair and said angrily, "Fuck. They could have made me do *anything*. I'd never have known."

"They could have, but they didn't. I think they wanted me to be suspicious. Whoever modified my memory has left just enough to make me doubt my reality."

He frowned at me. "But why would they want to do that?"

"To frustrate me, probably. I can remember someone telling me to enjoy what was left of my life—and they obviously meant that I *wouldn't*."

"What was left of your life? What the fuck does that mean?"

"What do you think it means?" We finally hit the bitumen and the truck's tail whipped out sideways as I spun the wheel and flattened my foot. The roar of the big engine filled the night—a deep throbbing sound that oddly felt in tune with the anger within me. "Did you really think that they'd play this game for a couple of weeks then let us all go?"

"Honestly? Yeah, I did." He scrubbed a hand across his chin. "I don't know why, but I did."

That belief *had* to have been implanted, too. Evin might be a trusting soul, but even he couldn't be *that* innocent. Not if he came from the same pack that I did.

"I gather they've been allowing you to talk to Lyndal when you report in every night?"

"Yeah." Fury and desperation swirled through his voice, sharp in the darkness. "They've been given her a rough time."

Which could have meant anything from verbal to physical abuse, but I didn't ask him to clarify because, really, there was no point. There wasn't anything we could do to prevent it right now.

"She's still alive, Evin. Hold on to that."

"But she's *pregnant*."

I briefly closed my eyes against the fury that swept me. They were bastards. Complete and utter bastards.

"I'd rather hold on to the hope of revenge," he added as his gaze met mine. His gray eyes were dark and his expression was pensive. "Will you help me get that?"

"If you help me get mine—and not just by giving me information. I mean tracking these bastards down and stopping them. Whatever it takes."

"Whatever it takes," he murmured, and shivered. "I have a feeling you're far more used to that sort of thing than I am."

"If you're a border guard, then you obviously can fight. That's what I need. I can handle the finer details."

"Of that, I have no doubt."

He touched his neck briefly, then jerked his fingers away. I thought about stopping the truck to undo the wire, but he didn't seem to be in great discomfort and I wanted to get as far away from those men as possible. I really didn't trust them not to have some form of backup plan in the event of things going wrong—like us escaping.

Evin added, "You know, I'm really surprised that they didn't just kill you. It would have been less dangerous for them."

"But not as much fun."

"If this is someone's idea of a good time, then they are seriously warped."

"Yeah, he is," I said, and again heard that smooth,

cultured voice telling me to enjoy the time I had remaining. Damn it, I needed to remember!

Pinpoint pricks of light appeared in the distance. There was a car on the horizon, and it was approaching fast.

Denny's backup plan, perhaps?

"What's the cell phone reception like up here?" I asked, flexing my fingers against the wheel. It didn't do a whole lot to ease the tension suddenly rolling through me.

"It's pretty shitty, actually," he said. "Why?"

I nodded toward the growing light points. "What are the odds of another car being on this particular road at this time of night? The road only goes to the whaling station ruins, and it's not exactly a good time to be viewing them, is it?"

"They had a CB radio in one of the other trucks— I heard them talking on it— but there's no way help would get here *this* soon."

"Unless someone was already nearby. How far does the pack's land boundary extend?"

"I have no idea."

We drove on, watching those twin specks of light grow brighter and brighter. Tension crawled through my limbs, and I was gripping the steering wheel so hard my hands were beginning to cramp. I flexed my fingers and forced myself to relax.

The lights flicked down to low beam as the car drew nearer. I pulled over to the edge of the road, allowing the other car plenty of room. He repeated the action and we passed each other quickly and without incident. I had a brief glimpse of a white face, dark hair, and sharp, arrogant nose and knew, without a doubt, who it was.

"Shit," Evin said. "That was Mike West."

"There was another murder in town tonight," I said, voice grim. "I wonder why he's here and not helping Harris."

"Maybe someone told them about Denny's plans."

"Maybe." But West would have had to have left Dunedan not long after me to get here this soon. And while I had no doubt that someone had been watching our villa, I very much doubted whether they'd have gone running to either Harris or West the minute I'd disappeared.

So why was West out here?

Was this the reason he hadn't been answering Harris's calls?

Maybe I was being suspicious for no reason; maybe he really *did* have a good reason for being here. But whoever was behind my kidnapping *had* to have someone else other than Evin here in Dunedan—and what better backup could there be than one of the town cops?

And it might just explain why Harris had been getting no responses to his queries to the Directorate. West could have easily either not sent them or intercepted them.

I glanced in the rearview mirror, watching his taillights, half expecting him to turn around and chase us. But he didn't, and I wasn't entirely sure whether that was a good thing or bad.

One thing was sure, though—I needed to talk to Harris, and as soon as possible.

I glanced at Evin. "Is there anything else you can tell me?"

"I think they have someone else on the ground here. They seem to know stuff that I haven't mentioned." He hesitated, and glanced at me sharply. "You don't think it could be West, do you?"

I smiled. "Sometimes you're so like me it's almost like you *are* my brother."

"But West is a *cop*."

"A cop who is desperate to get out of this town and into some 'real policing,' as he puts it."

"I don't know—"

"Neither do I," I cut in. "But I sure as hell intend to find out."

"But how?"

"By talking to the man in charge."

"Harris? He works with West. He's not going to believe the worst of a workmate."

"Harris is a good cop. He'll listen, he'll consider the evidence, and he'll make his own decision."

Evin grunted. And it wasn't a convinced-sounding grunt, either. "There *is* one thing they did tell me."

When he didn't go on, I raised an eyebrow and looked at him. "What?"

He hesitated. "It sounds kind of silly, but they told me to make sure you never took the earrings off."

Something inside me twisted. The earrings. I *knew* there was something odd about them. "Did they say why?"

"No." Again he hesitated. "Not exactly. They just said you needed them on so that controlling you was easier."

Controlling me? Or controlling my wolf and other gifts?

I swerved over to the side of the road and stopped the truck. Dust flew around us as the tires skidded on the uneven shoulder. "Open the glove compartment and see if there's a knife in there."

He didn't move. "Get the wire off my neck, Hanna. Fair is fair."

He was right. I motioned him to turn around. He did so, and lifted his hair so I could get to the knot at the back easier. His neck was raw and weeping, and guilt spun through me. I really should have taken it off earlier.

I reached for the wire, but the minute my fingertips touched it, blue sparks erupted. I jerked my hand away and glanced at my fingertips. They were burned.

"What's wrong?" Evin said, voice sharp.

"It would appear I'm extremely sensitive to silver. Wait here."

I climbed out of the cab and into the bed at the back, quickly flipping open the tool box. There was a wire cutter sitting on the top, but that was next to useless— the silver was sitting too tightly against Evin's neck to risk using it. I pushed the tools around and found not only a pair of gloves but also a switchblade. I grabbed them both, then jumped back into the truck.

I pulled on the gloves then cautiously touched the wire. Even through the gloves I could feel the heat of the silver, but it wasn't hot enough to stop me from un-doing the wire.

Evin jerked away the minute the wire was loose enough and quickly rubbed his raw neck. "Fuck, that stuff burns."

I chucked the wire out the door then slammed it shut. "I gather you've never had an encounter with sil-ver before?"

"No. But I take it you have?"

"I've been shot by the stuff so many times I'm now super-sensitive to it." I flicked open the switchblade and studied the point. It was certainly sharp enough to do the job. After a moment, I became aware of Evin's heated stare. "What?"

"Did you even hear what you just said?"

I smiled. "Yes. And no, I can't explain it, beyond the fact that I'm involved on some level with the Direc-torate."

"Then whoever is behind all this is playing a mighty dangerous game. Even *I* know you don't fuck around with Directorate people. Not if you value your life."

"Which is probably why he gave me another iden-tity. Then he could kill me without raising any alarms."

"As I said before, this whole situation is fucked." He gave the knife point a somewhat dubious look. "I take it you want me to take the earrings out of your ears."

"I tried taking them off the first time I had a shower. They wouldn't budge. Cutting them out seems to be my only option."

He took the knife somewhat gingerly. "It'll hurt."

I shrugged. "I'm tough."

"I'm beginning to realize that," he muttered, then motioned me to turn around.

I did so, reaching across with one hand and sweeping the short strands of my hair out of the way. His touch on my ear was light and firm.

"It does feel like they're embedded," he commented. "Don't jerk away when I cut or I might just tear your lobe off."

"I won't."

Cold metal touched my ear, slicing into my flesh. Evin's touch was surprisingly delicate, and the cut didn't hurt all that much. After a few seconds, the blade was gone and his fingers were pulling at my ear. Something dropped onto the seat between us and bounced onto the floor of the truck.

"Other one," Evin said.

I resisted the impulse to reach down and grab whatever had fallen out and twisted around on the seat, so that he could reach my right ear. He repeated the process, but this time, he had to pry the thing out of my ear. It felt like it was being pulled out of my ear canal rather than my lobe, a sensation that had my stomach rising and my head spinning.

"Fuck," I said, jerking away the minute it was free and rubbing my ear fiercely. "That one hurt."

And other than the pain, I didn't really feel any different with the earrings gone. For some reason, I thought I would.

But maybe I needed to do something—like shape-shift—to see if removing them had actually improved my situation. Right now, we didn't have that time.

West would be close to the whaling station by now. We really needed to get moving, just in case he came back. I took the brake off and hit the gas. Dirt and stones sprayed the underneath of the truck as the tires skidded then gripped, and the big truck surged forward once more.

"It looks like a battery," Evin said, examining the earring. "Only it's got a tail."

I held out a hand and he dropped it into my palm. It was small and round, and the silk-fine tail was about two and a half inches long.

Evin reached down and picked up the remains of the other earring. It was also small, but without the tail.

"I have no idea what they are," he said. "Do you?"

I shook my head. "But when I tried to shift shape, I was hit by an intense pain—it felt like my brain was on fire. Maybe this is the reason why."

"How the hell can something *that* small stop a shifter from taking their other shape?"

"Nanotechnology means the smallest devices can be extremely powerful."

"Granted, but that doesn't explain how it manages to stop a shape-shift."

I shrugged. "From what I've read, the electrical activity emanating from the brain increases exponentially when we shift. Maybe the device somehow disrupts that surge and prevents the shift process."

So why hadn't it prevented the seagull shift? I frowned down at the thing in my hand. Maybe it could be programmed. Maybe shifting into different shapes resulted in different energy signatures, and if these things *could* be programmed, then it was here to prevent the wolf shift.

Because he doesn't know about your alternate form, that internal voice whispered. *He doesn't know about your other skills.*

If only I could figure out who *he* was, my life would be a whole lot easier.

I dropped the metal mouse back into Evin's hand. "Keep them safe for me."

He looked surprised but pleased. "I will, trust me."

I did. And not just because he wanted my help to rescue his soul mate. There was no cunning in his gaze, no artifice in his actions. Granted, he may have spent the last few days doing nothing but lying to me, but that wasn't his nature. Wasn't his soul.

Evin was honest. I'd stake my life on it.

And given the situation, I probably was.

"So what's our plan of action?" he asked.

I hesitated. "As I said earlier, I think the first thing we need to do is talk to Harris. What happens after that very much depends on whether he believes us or not."

"If he doesn't, we're stuck. I can't leave Dunedan until I'm told to, because if I don't report in every night, they'll kill Lyndal."

"So they've told you to call from that phone only?"

"Yes. They gave me the location and number, and said if I use any other phone, Lyndal will pay."

"Meaning they're using caller ID—and there are ways around that." *Not* that I could actually recall any of them at the moment. "Is the number you call local or interstate?"

"Interstate. The calls are killing my credit card."

I snorted. "They're making you pay for the calls?"

"And the villa. The bastards aren't exactly free with the cash."

"I guess it's one way to avoid a paper—or credit—trail."

"And if they were planning to kill us at the end of it, I guess it's probably easier to waste my cash than theirs."

"Probably. If Harris can trace the phone number for us, that'll at least give us a starting location." Though I very much doubted the phone number would relate to wherever they were keeping Lyndal. That would be a dumb move, and whoever was behind this wasn't dumb. Arrogant, yes, overconfident, probably, but not dumb.

"We've still got to get her out of there without them suspecting."

"We will."

"I don't think you and I have enough firepower to stop them."

"I don't intend for it to be just you and me."

He glanced at me. "Your brother?"

"If I can remember him, and find him, trust me, we won't need a fucking army."

He didn't say anything to that, but the sliver of fear whisked through the darkness again. Silence fell. I kept the truck thundering through the night, but it was well after one before we got back into Dunedan.

I swung the truck down a side street and drove straight to the police station. I expected the place to be lit up, but it was as dark as a grave.

Trepidation slithered through me. I pulled up by the curb rather than the driveway and threw the gears into neutral.

"He's not there by the look of it," Evin said.

"But he should be. He had two captives that needed to be locked up. One of them was a vamp." And Harris, despite his extraordinary abilities, wasn't used to dealing with vamps. I shouldn't have left him alone.

And yet if I hadn't, Evin might now be dead and I wouldn't be one step closer to much-needed answers.

I peered through the side window, scanning the building's windows and doors. There were no broken windows, no smashed locks or doors. Everything looked in order.

And yet every instinct I had said something was wrong.

"Stay here," I said, reaching for the door handle.

"Hanna—"

"No arguments, Evin," I cut in. "This is what I do. Lock the doors and keep the engine running. If anyone but me or Harris comes out of that place, run for it."

He was staring at me again. "Only guardians hunt vamps. Werewolves aren't—can't—be guardians."

"They can if they possess special talents or mixed blood. I'm a dhampire, Evin. I can do what vampires do, without the drawbacks." And as a werewolf who not only had vampire skills but who could shift into bird form, I certainly fit both those conditions. Even if I couldn't remember it. I climbed out of the cab. "Keep safe. Don't do anything stupid."

"Like come after you?" He snorted. "Sorry, Hanna,

but I didn't willingly sign onto this gig, and I have a pregnant mate to consider. If there's a vamp loose in there, he's all yours."

"Then make sure you stay safe for her."

I closed the door, watched him lock both, then walked around the truck and headed toward the police station. I blinked to switch to infrared and scanned the inside of the building. The body heat of four people shimmered inside, meaning Harris had called in help.

I was barely four steps away from the door when energy brushed across my mind. It was a light, probing touch—inquisitive, and not yet dangerous. My shields were up enough that he couldn't read my thoughts, but I still felt the power surging under the surface of that touch, and it was very strong indeed.

Then I realized what I was doing, what I was feeling. That vamp might be telepathic, but so was *I*. Obviously, removing the earrings *had* worked.

As I reached for the door handle, the vamp hit me telepathically, the blow fierce and hard. I froze in my tracks for the barest of seconds, then threw all the energy I had to my shields, clenching my fists as I battled blow after mental blow.

Damn it, I'd had enough of people messing around with my thoughts! This bastard *wasn't* going to get in.

But he didn't seem to want to quit, either.

Sweat began trickling down my face and, in the pit of my stomach, fear swelled. I had strong shields, and this vamp was pushing me to my limits. What hope did Harris—and whoever else was in there with him—have? They'd only had nanowires to protect them, and against a telepath *this* strong the wires were next to useless.

Then his telepathic attack ceased as suddenly as it had began. I took a deep, somewhat trembling breath and pushed the door open. Darkness greeted me, thick and silent. I flared my nostrils, drawing in the scents. Harris didn't seem to be close, but the other wolf stood in the shadows just behind the door.

He was barely even breathing. I reached out telepathically to assess the state of his mind and hit the electronic buzz of the nanowire. I could break past its protection—I'd done it often enough in the past—but it took time and effort, and I didn't want to risk it with another powerful telepath nearby. He might just use my concentration to get underneath my own shields.

I flexed my fingers, took a deep breath, then dove through the doorway, hitting the floor with my back, rolling neatly to my feet and spinning around.

To find the barrel of a gun pointing straight at my head.

Chapter 13

He didn't hesitate, just pulled the trigger.

I dove out of the way, but as fast as I was, it just wasn't enough. The bullet ripped through the fleshy part of my thigh and wedged somewhere inside. Pain welled, thick and hard.

Not because I'd been shot. Because the bullet was silver.

Fuck.

I hit the ground hard, felt rather than saw his movement, and knew he was already aiming again. I shifted position and swept my good leg around with all the force I could muster. The vamp in control of the cop's mind was too focused on shooting me to notice the blow coming, and I hit the young cop's legs just as he pulled the trigger. The shot aimed at my head hit the ceiling instead and the cop's butt hit the floor so hard air exploded from his lungs and the gun went flying. I didn't give him—or the vamp—time to recover, just lunged forward and smashed my fist against his nose and mouth. Which was a dirty thing to do given the young cop wasn't at fault, but with silver burning in my body, I had no time for niceties.

As he fell to the floor, I pulled myself to my feet, hauled him onto his side so he wouldn't choke on his own blood, then grabbed the gun from where it had fallen and half hobbled, half hopped around the reception desk. The door leading to the back rooms was open, and I could see the blood heat of three others. All of them were in the back area, in what looked like separate rooms. Cells, obviously.

But why would Harris be in a cell?

I wiped away the sweat that was threatening to blur my vision and wished I could get rid of the burning in my leg as easily. It was a burning that could end my life if I didn't get the bullet out of my flesh quickly.

None of the people inside the cells was moving. The vamp was obviously alive and well, but I had no idea about the state of the others.

And there was only one way to find out.

I hobbled around the corner, moving with neither speed nor grace. But every sense I had was alert and the gun was steady, despite the trembling weakness beginning to flare up my leg.

The room immediately beyond was small and little more than a waiting area for the main holding cells. The two areas were divided by a barred steel gateway—

which was currently open—and beyond that were four cells. Only one was open.

I hobbled forward. The vamp was in the first cell. I couldn't actually see him from where I was standing, but I could smell *and* feel him. Not physically but mentally. The wash of power flowed around me like a stream, not aimed at me but at the cop in the other room. He was trying to wake him, trying to make him attack again.

I stopped and peered through the food tray opening. The vamp was sitting on his concrete bed platform and glared my way balefully. He didn't, however, look too concerned.

"Quit the telepathic attacks," I said flatly, "or I'll make you."

"I think I'll take the second option," he said, his expression overconfident, almost jovial. "I can smell your blood and feel your flesh burning, wolf. We both know you won't come into this room right now because you have neither the physical strength nor the speed to beat me. And with the silver in your flesh, you're barely keeping your shields at maximum. All I have to do is wait, and you will be mine."

The bastard was right. Given the fact my leg was already going numb, there was no doubt my shields would weaken as the silver drained more and more of my strength.

But it wasn't like I had no other options and, given the situation, I wasn't afraid to take them. I raised the gun, aimed it through the feeding slot, and shot him.

The bullet smashed through his kneecap, spraying

blood and flesh and bits of bone across the grimy white walls. He screamed and clutched at his leg. My second shot took him high in the shoulder, and the caress of energy dropped to nothing.

"Try to control anyone else, and I'll shoot to kill," I said, and slammed the food tray slot closed. It didn't do much to muffle his screams.

I knew how he felt. I very much felt like screaming myself.

I hobbled on, all but dragging my right leg. Blood was pouring from the wound, but it was the burning—and the numbness that was spreading like tentacles across my flesh—that was the biggest concern.

A quick look in the next cell told me it contained the pilot. He was lying on the concrete bed, but his eyes were open and his expression was an odd mix of defiance and fear.

The third cell held Harris. He was also lying on the bed, but his eyes were closed and the side of his face was battered and bloody.

"Harris?" I said. "You okay?"

He didn't respond, and his breathing was shallow and rapid.

"Harris," I repeated, louder this time. "Wake up."

He jumped, then groaned and somewhat groggily scrubbed a hand across his bruised and beaten features before turning his head toward the door. "What?" he said, the word coming out a little slurred.

"Where are the keys for the cell?"

He blinked rather owlishly. Concussion, I thought. "Why do you want that?"

"Because you're stuck inside of one."

"I am?"

He sat up abruptly, but the movement was too sudden, and he vomited without warning. It splattered across the concrete floor, making me suddenly glad I wasn't standing inside. The smell was bad enough from out here.

I waited impatiently, watching the blood trickle down his cheek, feeling it pour down my leg. My jeans were saturated, and blood was beginning to drip onto the tiled floor.

"Harris, you need to concentrate. Where are the keys?"

"There are none." His words, though still slurred, seemed a little stronger.

"What?" I glanced down at the door and noticed for the first time it had two methods of locking. One was the traditional key lock, the other electronic.

"What's the combination?"

"Four oh eight one. Is the vamp neutralized?"

"For the moment, yes." I pressed the code in and an alarm sounded as the little light flicked from red to green. I twisted the handle and pulled the door open. "Why didn't he attack you rather than Benny?"

"Because I'm mind-blind, and Benny's not." He pushed to his feet and stood there, wobbling for a bit. "How is Benny?

"I'm afraid I busted his nose and probably some teeth." I paused for breath. Damn, my chest felt like it was getting heavier. Fear swelled but I pushed it down.

I would *not* die. Not like this. "He shot me with silver and I really didn't have the time for finesse."

He glanced at me sharply and I saw his gaze widen fractionally. "We'd better call you a doctor."

"Call them if you want, but I can't wait for them to arrive. I'm extremely sensitive to silver, and my leg is already numb. We need to get this bullet out *now*."

"Fuck." He scrubbed a hand across his face, then walked—a little unsteadily—forward. "There's a first aid kit in the reception area. We'll need that."

He wrapped an arm around my waist and half guided, half carried me back down the corridor—though I wasn't entirely sure who was supporting whom.

His nostrils flared as he passed the vamp's cell. "I smell blood."

"As I said, I didn't have the time for finesse." I shrugged, and the movement sent pain rippling. "A vamp with two bullet wounds isn't going to be capable of attacking anyone telepathically for a while."

Harris grunted. It wasn't a happy-sounding grunt, but he didn't actually say anything. Maybe even he could see that tough situations called for tough measures.

Even if they *were* against police rules.

But then, I wasn't police. I was Directorate. The damn vamp was lucky he wasn't dead. I might not want to kill, but all bets were off when the bastards attacked me.

We went through the barred gateway. He paused, briefly releasing me to close the door and punch in a code, then we staggered forward again. Harris guided me through the door then around to the left, behind the reception desk. Benny was where I'd left him.

"How did you manage to get locked in the cell?" I said, as Harris kicked out a chair then dropped me into it.

"I had no idea the vamp was even awake until Benny attacked me. It was lucky that I saw him move at the last moment, because the wrench smashed down the side of my face instead of the top of my skull." He retrieved a large first aid kit from underneath the desk and opened it up. "I saw stars, but I had enough sense left to kick his feet out from underneath him and run for the cells."

I grabbed my wounded leg with both hands and hauled it up onto another chair. The damn thing felt like so much dead flesh and, deep in my stomach, the fear of losing the use of my limb gnawed. But I guess I was lucky it was my leg rather than my shoulder. I'd been shot far too many times in that region now, as the numbness and sensitivity in my fingertips indicated. I might have died instantly, rather than merely suffering.

Harris pulled on a pair of surgical gloves, then grabbed a pair of needle-fine scissors. "Why didn't he simply punch in the code and open the door?"

"Because I have an override locking code that no one else knows. I used it on both the vamp's cell and my own."

He began slicing away the material from the wound. Despite the fact he was being careful, the sharp point of the scissors dug into my flesh several times. Luckily, I felt the movement, not the pain. My flesh was too numb to feel anything right now.

"How did you lock the door from the inside the cell?" The keypad was nowhere near the food tray opening, and unless he was Mr. Elastic, there was no way known he would have been able to reach it.

"There's a time delay on it. You have one minute to close the door before it locks." He dropped the scissors on the chair next to my foot then reached for the long tweezers. His gaze met mine. "This will probably burn like a bitch."

"The wound is numb, so it won't really matter." But my fingers tightened reflexively around the arms of the chair.

"Numb?" His expression deepened to worry. "That happened fast."

"As I said, I'm extremely sensitive."

He grunted and carefully pressed open the sides of the wound with his free hand. Blood poured out over his fingertips and started dripping on the floor. Thanks to the numbness it didn't actually hurt, but something inside of me trembled anyway.

"I can't see a goddamn thing through the blood," he muttered.

He carefully pressed the tweezers into the wound anyway, driving them down into my flesh.

"You're going to have to tell me when I hit the bullet."

He dug deeper and hit it. Only gently, but it felt like he was driving a red-hot poker deeper into my flesh. I just about jumped through the roof, and sweat popped out across my forehead as my breathing became short, sharp gasps.

So much for the wound being numb.

"Meaning I've hit it," he commented. "Hang on hard to something and try not to move."

If I gripped the arms of the chair any tighter, I'd fucking shatter them. And the damn things were *metal*.

The bullet moved again. Heat flashed, white hot, through my muscles and nausea rose thick and fast. I swallowed heavily and closed my eyes, hoping that *not* watching would make me less aware.

It didn't.

I felt every inch of the bullet's journey upward. Felt it when his grip slipped and the bullet fell back into my flesh. Sweat dripped from my forehead and ran in rivers down my back, and bile rose so fast it took all of my control *not* to vomit on his shoes.

Then the heat was gone and Harris was holding up the tweezers with the bloody bullet clamped firmly between its jaws.

"Done," he said. "But you need to change to stop the bleeding."

"Thanks." I rolled out of the chair and reached for the shifting magic, instinctively calling to my wolf rather than the seagull.

There was no hesitation, no pain, this time. Just a surge of power that swept through my body, numbing and reshaping my body, until what stood there was wolf rather than human. I stayed in her form for several seconds, simply enjoying the feel of her, then, somewhat reluctantly, shifted back. The wound was nowhere near healed, but at least the bleeding had stopped.

Harris closed the first aid kit then put the bloody tweezers and scissors into a plastic bag. "What now?"

"Well, the vamp has proven capable of getting past the nanowire and controlling Benny, so our first order of business is to get him contained. And Evin's waiting outside in the car for an all-clear, so we need to bring him in."

He raised an eyebrow. "Why is he outside?"

"Because I knew something was wrong the minute we pulled up. I'm used to dealing with vamps. He's not." I shrugged. "I was simply keeping him safe."

"Given the vamp is injured but telepathically unrestrained, how safe would it be to bring him within range?"

"With the silver out of my leg, I'll be able to protect him."

I said it with more assurance than I felt, but Harris didn't seem to notice. He pushed away from the bench and moved toward the front door.

"I thought you suspected him of being a fake brother and connected to the evil plot surrounding you?"

"He *is* a fake, but he's not willingly connected to the machinations."

"Meaning you've unraveled more clues?"

"I certainly have." And some of them he *wasn't* going to like.

He opened the front door and waved Evin in, then walked across to Benny and squatted down beside him.

He pressed his fingers against the side of his neck, then gave a slight nod. "His pulse is steady, but his nose will be mighty sore when he wakes."

There wasn't much I could say to that, so I didn't say anything.

He glanced around as the door opened and Evin stepped inside. His gaze quickly swept Harris, Benny, and then me, taking in the blood on my pants and around the chair. "What the fuck has been happening?"

"Long story," Harris said. "Grab Benny's feet. We need to get him into a cell."

Evin did as ordered, and the two lifted the young man with ease. "He looks as if he needs a doctor, not a cell."

"He susceptible to vampire suggestion, so he goes into the cell," I said, connecting just enough to his mind to feel if the vampire tried to control him. "And we can't risk a doctor for the very same reason."

"Oh."

For someone who didn't have much to do with either cops or vampires, Evin seemed to be handling it all amazingly calmly. The two men disappeared through the door. A few seconds later, the cell door slammed shut and footsteps echoed as they returned.

"So why are you two here?" Harris asked as he walked into the reception area. Evin followed him out and propped his butt on the reception desk.

"It's not that I don't appreciate the intervention," Harris continued, "but I ordered you to stay away."

"And we know how well ordering me to stay away in the past has worked, don't we?" He rolled his eyes. I smiled and added, "I needed to ask you some questions."

"Then fire away." He strolled across to a percolator and flicked a switch. The rich aroma of brewing coffee soon filled the air, making my taste buds water.

I crossed my arms and said, "How well do you know Mike West?"

He gave me what I could only call a "cop look" and said, voice flat, "Mike West *isn't* involved in any nefarious plot against you."

"Then do you know why he was driving toward the whaling station just over an hour ago?"

Harris shrugged. "Why is that even important?"

I sidestepped the question with another. "Then do you know what Denny and his friends have been up to over the last few hours?"

"No. Not only have I been out of contact with Mike, Denny, and any of his friends, but I was with *you,* chasing a killer and then getting locked in a cell. How the fuck would I know what *anyone* has been up to?"

"Then no one has reported anything to you?" I persisted.

"No. And if anyone had reported it to Mike, I would have heard it. Emergency calls get routed to both cell phones when we're out of the office." He glanced at Evin. "How do you take your coffee?"

"White and one."

Harris nodded, made the coffee, then carried over three cups, handing one to Evin and one to me before sitting on the chair I'd propped my foot on earlier. "What are you getting at, Hanna?"

"I'm not Hanna."

"Well, until you remember your name, I need to call you something. Now answer the damn question."

"While you and I were hunting your prisoners, Denny and his friends kidnapped Evin."

"What?" He glanced sharply at Evin, eyebrow raised in query.

"It's true," Evin said. "I have the bruises and rope and silver burns to prove it."

"And I have the ransom note." I took the piece of plastic out of my pocket and handed it over. He read it silently and shook his head.

"Why would the damn fool do something *this* stupid?"

It was a rhetorical question, but I answered it anyway. "It was a ploy to get me out to the whaling station alone, where dearest Denny intended to exact his revenge. Except they were expecting me to drive out there and, as it turns out, I have an alternate shape—a seagull. That ability allowed me to get there ahead of time and get the jump on them. I disabled their trucks, rescued Evin, and we both got the hell out of there."

Harris raised an eyebrow. "Did Denny and his friends survive the encounter?"

He didn't actually sound like he'd mind if they hadn't. "Of course they did."

"Good." His tone wasn't convincing. "But I'm not seeing the connection to Mike."

"When we were driving back, we saw West coming in the opposite direction. He was almost at the old whaling station, and the only way he could have gotten there so fast would be by leaving soon after I did."

"Which means someone told him what was happening."

"Or he was watching my place, saw me leave, and maybe even saw one of Denny's friends go in to try to retrieve the ransom note."

He digested this for a moment, then simply said, "No."

"Someone else—someone other than Evin—has been reporting back to the people behind all this. I can think of no better person than a cop who is dissatisfied with where he is and what he is doing."

"Mike is a *good* cop." It was stubbornly said.

"I'm not saying he isn't. I'm just saying he's a cop who may have taken on a little outside work."

"I can't believe he'd do something like that—"

"You worked your way up through the ranks in Sydney. You know that being a cop isn't always black and white, but mostly shades of gray. I'm not saying Mike's gone bad, I'm just saying he might be providing information in return for something he wants—a transfer out of here."

Hell, he'd all but said that the first time I'd met him. I took a sip of coffee and watched Harris's expression. Or, rather, the lack of it. He was a hard man to read, and I had no idea whether he believed me or not. Even his body language was giving nothing away.

I tried another angle. "Who sent the request for information about me to the Directorate?"

He hesitated fractionally, then said, "Mike."

"And do you know for certain that he sent it?"

"Why the hell *wouldn't* he send it?"

"Because I'm Directorate. I don't *just* work there. I'm a guardian."

"What?" His expression was incredulous. "You can't be. You're a werewolf."

"Exactly what I said," Evin murmured.

"I'm a dhampire—werewolf and vampire. I work in the daytime division in Melbourne."

"But how—"

"Long story," I cut in. "And it's really not important right now. The point is, if Directorate staff suddenly disappear, an alert goes out to all divisions."

"And if some cop in a godforsaken town suddenly starts asking for information about someone who matches the description of that missing personnel," Harris said heavily, "all hell should break loose."

"And it hasn't. Which to my way of thinking means the request never went through."

"Unless they're just a slack outfit over in Perth. I sent the information to them about the murders, and I haven't had a response back from those, either." He took a sip of coffee then added, "And according to you, these types of murders would have been red-flagged as a priority."

"They *should* have been." So why had no one contacted Harris? That's what I *couldn't* understand. I took another drink of coffee, then added, "It might be a good idea to actually phone them again."

"You mean, right now?"

"Why not? We have a dangerous vamp who's connected to an organization that's hiring out killers for revenge purposes. The Perth staff don't know I'm here or that I'm Directorate, so they should be getting their butts out here ASAP."

"True."

He reached sideways, pressing the speaker button on the phone before punching in a series of numbers. The phone began to ring, the sound echoing across the brief silence.

But before it could be answered, the line went dead.

"What the fuck?" Harris picked up the receiver and pressed several buttons, then glanced at me. "Nothing. It's as dead as a doornail."

Evin rose and walked across to another desk. "So's this one." He put the receiver back down. "Christ, you don't think Denny and his friends would be stupid enough to try to attack us?"

"Intelligence was never his strong suit, but even Denny and his friends aren't *that* stupid." Harris glanced at me. At that moment, the lights went out.

"Down, get down," I hissed, dropping out of the chair and hitting the floor on hands and knees. My coffee went flying, spilling across the carpet as the cup rolled even farther away from my fingertips.

Then I felt it.

An energy, a presence, that sang to my heart, wrapping me in warmth and passion and making me feel safer than I'd felt since I'd woken in the desert.

I couldn't recall his name, but I knew *him*. Loved him.

I scrambled to my feet and ran for the door. It opened, revealing only the darkness of the night. But he was there, hidden in the shadows, and I launched myself at him.

The darkness wrapped me in a hug that was fierce and joyous, pressing me against a body that was so very *real*.

"Thank *God,*" he whispered, his cheek pressing against mine as he hugged me ferociously. "I really thought I'd lost you for a while there."

"You almost did." As the shadows hiding his body began to dissipate, I kissed him, with every ounce of the love and relief that was surging through me.

Only to be practically torn out of his arms and into the arms of another. A man who wore the masculine version of my face and who was the other half of me. The brother that Evin wasn't.

"Oh, thank Christ," he said, his hug every bit as fierce as my vampire's. "I was going crazy with worry."

"I take it," Harris drawled from behind us, "that you know both of these men and that I should drop my weapon."

"If you don't," another voice said from the very back of the room, "you might just get shot yourself."

I twisted out of my brother's grip and saw another vampire standing in the cell block doorway. I knew his face, knew he was my boss, and was both relieved and surprised to see him here. But I couldn't damn well name him, and that was frustrating.

He was holding a laser aimed straight at Harris, and

the whine of the weapon firing up indicated he was very close to pressing the trigger.

"Everyone, relax. Harris is the cop here, and Evin is a friend. They're both on our side."

The whine of the laser shut down. Rich green eyes met mine. "What the hell is going on here, Riley?"

Riley. The name fit. It felt right. *Riley Jenson.* That was my name. I wanted to dance with the joy of finally *knowing* me.

But right now, there were more important things to concentrate on. Celebrations could happen later, when the mess surrounding me and Evin had been cleaned up.

"A truckload of shit is what's been happening," I replied. "But the first thing you need to know is the fact that there's whole chunks of my memories missing. I know who you all are, but I can't for the life of me remember your names. In fact, until a moment ago, I couldn't even remember my *own* name."

"What?" my brother said.

"It's all part of the plot," Evin said. He was sitting on the edge of the desk, his stance suggesting he was ready to fight. He wasn't about to trust the three men in my life—and I couldn't entirely blame him. Not with the dark and dangerous look my brother was flinging his way.

Evin added, "According to her driver's license, she's Hanna London. I'm her brother, Evin. We were supposed to be here for a week."

"So you're part of it?" My twin stepped forward, anger practically oozing from every pore. He wanted someone to blame—someone to take his frustration out on—very badly indeed.

I grabbed his arm. "Not willingly. And would you mind introducing yourselves? I can't exactly do it."

He glanced at me. "I'm Rhoan, that's Jack over near the door, and Quinn is the brooding presence behind us."

I looked over my shoulder and gave him a smile. And noticed for the first time the fading scar down the side of his face. I reached out and touched it gently. Saw again the truck hitting the black car, that car rolling over and over, and shivered inwardly. He was lucky to be alive. I guess we both were.

He caught my fingers and kissed them gently. "Do you know why your memories are so sketchy? Was it the accident, or was it deliberate?"

"Deliberate."

He touched my temple with his free hand and power washed around me, warm and familiar. "I can feel the imprint of another. We might be able to undo it."

"Good. But not right now." I turned around and looked at Jack. "We've had two murders here in Dunedan, both revenge killings very similar to the one I was investigating in Melbourne. This time, Harris and I managed to capture the killer and the helicopter pilot who was coming to pick him up."

Jack shook his head. "Even kidnapped, you still manage to find yourself in the middle of a murder investigation."

"Even when she was repeatedly told to keep her

nose out of it," Harris murmured, humor touching his lips as his gaze met mine.

"Ah, well." Jack walked across the room and helped himself to some coffee. "I've been her boss for years and, let me tell you, getting her to obey orders is impossible."

"But in this case, it was a good thing." I leaned back against Quinn. His warmth and his smell soaked through my pores, filling a void I hadn't even been aware of until now. "Because it was the similarities of the murders here to the ones I'd been investigating in Melbourne that began triggering memories."

"Probably because whoever was doing the memory rearranging didn't know enough about your life to make it stick."

With the back of my head resting against Quinn's chest, his voice seemed to rumble right through me. It was a wonderful sensation.

"That makes sense, because the stuff they didn't know about—like my seagull shape and clairvoyance skills—I could access, but my wolf shape, and the knowledge of who and what I was, I couldn't."

"So why didn't they erase your mind completely?" Harris asked. "That would have been a whole lot easier, surely?"

"It would have," Jack said, "but Riley has extremely strong shields. Most vampires wouldn't break past more than the first few layers of memories."

He could, as could Quinn, but even they were no longer able to dive deep into my subconscious. I'd grown too strong over the past year.

The thought made me smile. It was nice to actually *remember*.

"Which is why you've lost the everyday stuff and not most of the deeper, instinctive information," Rhoan said. His gaze went to my ear. "Have you been wearing a set of those nulling implants like the ones that Kye placed on you several months ago? Because I haven't been able to feel your presence, and Quinn wasn't able to sense you."

"Not until about an hour ago," Quinn added. His lips brushed the top of my head. "You have no idea just how much of a relief that was."

I smiled and placed my hands over his. "We took the implants out about then." I glanced at my brother. "When I disappeared, did you go talk to Blake?"

His thin cold smile said it all. "Yes. He claimed to know nothing."

"And you believed him?"

"No. But I couldn't kill him, either—not until we found out where you were. He's still under surveillance."

"Blake?" Evin said, sitting up a little straighter. "You mean *our* Blake? The leader of the Jenson pack?"

"The very one," Rhoan said, still eyeing Evin critically. "With that hair color, I take it you're from the Jenson pack?"

"Yes." He was staring at the two of us with an odd sort of expression. "You're Riley and Rhoan Jenson, aren't you?"

I raised an eyebrow at the edge in his voice. "I think we've already established that."

"No," he said, almost savagely, then added, "I mean, you don't understand. My father is Vernon Jenson, and he married Rayanne Jenson in a human civil ceremony some ten years ago."

I stared at him. "Your father married our mother? That means—"

"That I was right. I *am* your brother. By marriage, granted, but kin all the same." He smiled. "And you have a brother and two sisters you really need to meet."

"What?" Rhoan's gaze jumped between me and Evin. "Mum wouldn't do that."

Evin raised an eyebrow. "Why wouldn't she?"

"Because she swore never to have any more children after the way we were treated. And a civil ceremony? That means they're not soul mates—"

"But they love each other all the same. It may not be the deep, forever connection of a wolf mate, but it's still there and still real. And we have siblings to prove it."

"Fuck," Rhoan said, and thrust a hand through his short hair. But when he glanced at me, his eyes were bright and shiny. "We have brothers *and* sisters."

And underneath those words ran one joyous sentiment: *We are no longer alone.*

We had siblings. We might not know them, nor they us, but we had blood kin. We were a part of a family unit. And for wolves who had been so alone for so long, that was a powerful realization.

"But why the hell would Mom swear such a thing? And why would Blake want to kill you?" Evin asked. "Mom's never said much about your reasons for leaving, only that it was for the best. And certainly Blake's never mentioned you."

"He wouldn't, especially after what we did to him last year," Rhoan said. "But I bet he's been plotting his revenge since then."

"A revenge he denies being a part of." I squeezed Quinn's hands then pushed away from his warmth. His grip loosened reluctantly—a reluctance that echoed fiercely within me. I didn't ever want to leave this vampire's side. It was a surprising revelation given how long it had taken me to realize I even loved the damn man. I walked across the room to retrieve my coffee cup. "But we have several avenues to explore to find the link. And I think if we manage to undo whatever has been done to my memories, we'll discover he's very much behind it all. Because it's certainly *his* voice I keep hearing in my mind, telling me to enjoy my new life while I can."

"Then let's go kill the bastard," Rhoan said, voice flat and deadly.

"Hold the anger in check," Jack snapped. "Riley's safe. The rest of it can wait. We are *guardians,* and we have the people behind these revenge killings to stop. That has to be our priority."

"Then am I to gather," Harris said, his arms crossed and face as impassive as ever, "that your presence here is the reason why the Perth Directorate has not responded to our request for help?"

"Basically, yes," Jack said. "Although I have to say, there will be some ass-kicking in Perth, because they did *not* flag your request through to us as soon as they got it."

"We were wondering what was going on. Hanna—" Harris hesitated, then glanced at me with a smile, "*Riley* kept insisting it should have been a priority-one message, even if the request came from a small-town cop in the middle of nowhere."

" 'Should' being the operative word. When we did actually receive it, we accessed your system for details and saw your search for information on one Hanna London. And of course, Hanna London just happened to be the spitting image of our missing guardian. We got out here as soon as we could."

On Quinn's private jet, no doubt. The Directorate wouldn't have been able to move that fast, even if it was to recover a missing guardian. Whatever else it was, the Directorate was still a government department, and they are *always* bogged down by paperwork.

"How is the investigation actually going?" I asked. "Did you get much information out of the two shifters we caught at the brothel?"

Jack shook his head. "Several contact names—two we tracked down and one we didn't. This organization is like government—lots of different sections that don't know what the other is doing or where it is located."

"Meaning we might not have much better luck with the vamp."

"We can but try."

"We also have the pilot who'd come to pick him up in custody," Harris said. "The helicopter is privately owned by a company listed as Daskill Holdings. I was checking the validity of the licenses when the vamp gained control of my deputy's mind and sidetracked me."

"Daskill? I've heard that name before." Jack frowned. "Rhoan, contact Sal and get her to do a complete background check on that company and its owners."

Rhoan nodded and reached for his phone. As he made his call, I walked across to the machine and made three coffees, sliding one across to Rhoan before picking up the other two and returning to Quinn. After handing him a cup, I turned to face Jack.

"Are you going to interrogate the vamp?"

He raised an eyebrow. "Meaning you don't want to?"

"Well, considering I shot him twice to stop him from hitting me telepathically, I very much doubt he's going to cooperate with me."

Jack raised an eyebrow. "Why didn't you just telepathically hit him back? The vamp in the cell isn't an old one—I can tell that from here—so you'd have the mind strength to restrain him at least."

"I had a silver bullet in my leg. It was breaking my concentration and draining my strength."

"Hence all the blood," Rhoan murmured, briefly putting his hand over the phone receiver. "I did wonder."

"We got it out quickly, so there's no lasting damage." The area around the wound might still be numb, but at least the numbness that had stretched the length of my leg had faded a little.

"But that's not the reason why you don't want to interrogate the vamp, is it?" Jack said. "Give, Riley."

I hesitated. He'd already said he wanted to concentrate on solving these murders first, but I wasn't about to let a possible clue slip through my fingers. Right now there was very little chance of West knowing we suspected him. We needed to grab him—and question him—before he could warn anyone the jig was up.

"We have a possible connection to my kidnapping, but I need to talk to him *tonight,* before he realizes I've got a whole chunk of memory back."

"If you're talking about West," Harris said, voice flat, "then you're not doing *anything* without me present. I'm sorry, but I owe the man that much."

I waved a hand. "Fine."

"There is one problem," Evin said. "Like me, West probably has to report in every night. Once you talk to him, then he's going to jump straight on the phone and tell them what is going on."

"Only if he remembers it," Quinn said, amusement in his gaze as he glanced at me. "And considering the memory issues you've been having, maybe I should be the one who tackles his memory adjustment."

"It's not that I can't do it," I said mildly. "It's just that I couldn't *remember* that I could do it."

"But that still doesn't solve the overall problem," Evin said. "When you disappear, he's going to report it."

"That, too, can be fixed."

"West is a *good* cop," Harris said adamantly. "I can't—won't—believe he's aware of the true gravity of the situation. At least give him a chance to make amends before you start messing with his mind."

"That we can do," I said, and returned my gaze to Jack.

"Okay," he said heavily. "Do it. Rhoan, you can stay with me. We'll interview the vamp."

Rhoan didn't look happy, but he didn't argue, either. As the two men disappeared into the cell area, I said to Harris, "It's probably best if we confront West here. Are you able to call him in?"

"That very much depends on whether he's decided to answer his cell phone or not."

But he reached into his pocket and pulled out his phone, holding it away from his ear slightly so we could all hear it. After several rings, West answered. His gruff tones were clear over the speakers.

"Where the fuck have you been, Mike? There's been a second murder and all hell has broken loose. I want you back at headquarters ASAP."

"I'm on my way."

"From where?"

"Just passed the Old Well Road."

Harris grunted. "Floor it." He disconnected then glanced at us. "He'll be here within half an hour. I would suggest you two move away from the doorway so as not to spook him."

We did. I walked across to sit on the desk beside Evin, but Quinn merely stepped to one side of the doorway. Ready to block off any immediate escape once West saw who, exactly, was waiting for him.

We waited patiently—although in my case, that

wasn't exactly easy. I mean, after all the confusion of the last few days, I just wanted to hunt down all the clues and catch the bastards behind *both* crimes.

Lights eventually swept across the front windows as a truck rumbled into the driveway and stopped. A car door slammed, then footsteps approached.

A second later, the front door opened and West stepped in. His gaze swept the room and came to rest on me. There was a brief flash of surprise, but nothing else. He obviously had no real clue as to why we were all here.

"Denny and his friends have lodged a complaint about you," he said, walking across to the coffee machine and helping himself to a drink. "I told them they were damn fools and that if they didn't get charged with kidnap and blackmail, they'd be damn lucky."

"I'm not here to lay charges against Denny and his friends," I said calmly.

"Then you're a damn fool, too."

"She didn't say *I* wouldn't," Evin snapped. "And trust me, those bastards *will* pay."

"Good. They need to be taught a lesson." West took a sip, then turned around to face Harris. "Where do you want me to start?"

"I think a good place," Harris said, voice flat, "would be by telling us exactly what you know about the kidnapping of Riley Jenson—whom we happen to know as Hanna London."

He didn't even look at me. Just raised an eyebrow, his expression even and unfazed. "I have no idea what you're talking about."

"Lie," Quinn said impassively.

West glanced at him. "Who the hell are you?"

"Riley's lover, and a consultant to both the vampire council and the Melbourne Directorate." His sudden smile was neither warm nor friendly. In fact, it reminded me of a predator about to consume its prey. Quinn's anger and need for revenge might be less visible than my brother's, but that didn't mean it was absent. Far from it. "It is the first of those you should be worried about, because trust me, I *ache* for the chance to see justice done."

"That," West said, "sounded very much like a threat."

"Mike," Harris said heavily. "Hanna—Riley—is a guardian. Being involved with kidnapping a guardian puts you beyond our laws. I'd seriously advise you to stop the pretense and start cooperating, or they will *make* you."

"I'm an officer of the law. That gives me rights against this sort of—"

"No, it doesn't," I cut in, my voice edged with the anger roiling through me. He had no choice and nowhere to run—surely he could see that? "Whoever is behind this has not only kidnapped me and messed with my mind, but they're holding Evin's pregnant mate hostage and they attempted to kill Quinn. That means we can legally question, torture, or even kill *any* nonhumans involved in this case, and there's not one damn thing Harris or anyone else can do to stop us. So quit messing with us, West, or we really *are* going to start messing with *you*."

The threat tasted bitter on my tongue and I had to resist the urge to rub my arms. With a lot of my memories back in place, the ache *not* to do this job was coming to the fore again.

I didn't *want* to be a guardian. Didn't want to threaten people—and worse—for a living.

I had to get out. I really did.

Then you need to let me help you. Quinn's thoughts ran lightly through mine, gentle and yet filled with a strength that made me just want to step back and let him sort out the mess that my life had become.

But I'd been standing on my own two feet for too long now and, as stupid as it sounded, part of me was afraid to start leaning on someone else. At least when it came to something like this—something that was going to affect the direction of the rest of my life.

Which wasn't saying that I *wouldn't* let him help, either. That I didn't *need* his help.

Jack won't let me quit.

He doesn't want you dead, either. There are always options, Riley. Trust me.

I do. With my heart and my life. But I need to sort out one mess at a time.

Then we'll sort out your kidnapping first, followed by the Directorate. And we'll do it together.

I hesitated, then said, a touch reluctantly, *Okay.*

But with that brief, one word of acceptance, I suddenly felt a whole lot better. I *wasn't* alone. I hadn't been alone for a long, long time. And it was about time I accepted that—and let the man that I loved *in*.

West shrugged. "It's not like I know a whole lot."

"Another lie," Quinn said.

West swung around. "Damn it, keep out of my *thoughts*."

"No." Quinn crossed his arms. "Although I merely read your surface thoughts, not deeper layers. Be thankful for that."

Confusion crossed West's face, and I can't say I entirely blamed him. Even *I* wasn't sure what Quinn meant—I mean, reading deeper thoughts wasn't painful for either the reader or the readee. Though maybe it could be, if the reader wanted revenge rather than mere information.

"Harris," West said, "surely you can—"

Harris was shaking his head. "You've basically just confirmed what everyone in this room already knew, Mike. I'd given you the benefit of the doubt, but that belief was obviously misplaced. I will *try* to ensure fair treatment, but you had better start answering their questions. As they said, they can legally do what they want with you."

West slumped back onto the nearest chair. He took a sip of coffee, then said heavily, "I was only doing a favor for a friend."

"A friend who was going to return the favor by getting you transferred to a city location." It was a statement, not a question. West had told me as much earlier. "In many respects, that could be considered accepting a bribe."

"He was just going to recommend me for positions," West retorted. "I wasn't being given *anything*."

"A technicality in this day and age," Harris said

heavily. "Especially given the many corruption inquiries over recent years. Surely you understood the
risk?"

"But I needed the help, damn it!" West exploded.
"Being stuck in this goddamn piece of nowhere is
killing me. No department wants a cop whose only experience is in a backward country town where *nothing*
happens."

Two murders in twenty-four hours isn't what I'd
call nothing. But then, maybe that was simply because
I was here, and I tended to attract trouble.

"So what is the name of this friend you did the favor
for?"

West wiped a hand across his face. "His name is
Tyson Jenson. He's the pack leader from the Cona
Creek—which is in Queensland—London pack."

I frowned. "How can Tyson be the leader of the
London pack? He's a *Jenson*."

Even as I said the words, something inside me
twisted angrily. Tyson Jenson might not be from *my*
Jenson pack, but he was related. He was Blake's
brother.

Evin's hand touched mine, squeezing gently. He
might not be able to read thoughts, but he could smell
anger, and right now, his senses were probably
swamped with it.

West shrugged. "He challenged for the lead. I guess
since he was mated to the pack leader's eldest daughter,
they allowed it."

Then they were fools. "So what, exactly, did he ask
you to do?"

"He told me he needed to get a troublesome wolf out of the way for a week or so. He asked me to keep on eye on both her and her brother, and to report back anything and everything they did."

"Did he tell you why?"

West shook his head. "He just said you were causing serious trouble within the pack, and he needed you out of the way while he calmed things down." He hesitated. "I asked how the hell I was supposed to even keep you here, and he said that wouldn't be a problem."

"Because I was being drugged and I had my memory tampered with."

"He didn't tell me that. He said it was Evin's job to keep you calm."

"But surely to God you suspected something was up?" Harris said, frustration edging into his normally smooth tones. "You're a *good* cop, Mike. You had to have to have been a *little* suspicious."

"I've known Tyson for years. We went through training together—although he washed out during the last few weeks." West shrugged. "I had no reason not to trust what he was telling me. Not initially."

"And yet you didn't send through Harris's request for information about me to the Directorate. Was that at Tyson's order?"

He hesitated. "It wasn't an order."

Order or not, it wasn't right and he knew it. "Did he say why?"

West took a sip of coffee, then shrugged again. "He asked me to delay it a day or so, that's all. When I asked why, he begged off, saying it was related to the mess he was trying to sort out."

"And this didn't raise your alarms?"

"Of course it did. That's why I was keeping an even closer eye on you. And how I knew that damn fool Denny was up to something." He hesitated. "I *did* go out to the whaling station to rescue you. I wasn't involved with that idiot's plans in any way, shape, or form."

"So why did you keep driving toward the whaling station when we passed you on the road?" Evin asked.

West frowned. "I didn't see—" He hesitated, and snorted. "You were in Grant's truck. That's why he was so pissed off."

"Shame we didn't actually wreck the truck," Evin murmured. "The bastard certainly deserves it."

I smiled. Evin might not be blood kin, but he certainly *thought* like us. "How do you contact Tyson?"

"He phones me."

"Home or cell?"

"Cell. Every night at ten."

I raised my eyebrows. "Even tonight?"

"Yeah. He was furious when I told him that Denny had snatched Evin and was holding him hostage against your appearance."

"So you also went out there because he ordered you to?"

Anger flashed through his expression. "As I said, I went out there because I'm a cop and it's my duty to stop him. No one told me to do *anything*."

But the fact that his duty and Tyson's orders co-incided wouldn't have hurt.

"Is Tyson the only contact you've had?"

"Yes."

"What number does he phone from?"

"I don't know. The number is always blocked."

I gave him a disbelieving look. "You're a cop, and you're trying to tell me that didn't bother you? When this man is your friend?"

He smiled thinly and reeled off a number. "It's a Northern Territory number. Tyson's pack is in Queensland."

I glanced at Evin, who shook his head. "The number I phone is a Melbourne one."

"So we have Tyson in the Northern Territory and the people holding your mate hostage in Melbourne. Meaning Tyson's not alone in this."

"We all knew that from the beginning," Quinn commented. "Just as we all know who is behind this."

I glanced at him. "We can't move until we've rescued Evin's mate. And a little concrete proof would be nice, too." Certainly it'll make it easier for Jack to issue a retribution order.

Or a death order.

Something within me shivered. I really didn't want Blake dead, no matter what he'd done, but I might not have that choice anymore. I'd given him one chance already, and he'd thrown it back in my face.

And I had no doubt he'd keep at me until he achieved his aim: my death, and maybe even Rhoan's.

We had a pack of our own to consider—we had a

child on the way. It went beyond my and Rhoan's safety now.

"We have two choices, then." Quinn's face was still impassive, but the sense of menace brewed like a storm around him. "We go after Tyson, or we hunt down those who have Evin's mate."

"If we go after Tyson, the game is up. Besides, such a move would only endanger Lyndal—Evin's mate," I said.

"Then we do a trace on the number Evin calls, and hit them before tomorrow night."

I raised an eyebrow. "Jack wants us to solve the other case first."

"You're not the only guardian he has, Riley. Blake—and whoever else is behind this—needs to be stopped immediately. Otherwise, next time they might just settle for an assassin's bullet."

And as he'd already said, Jack didn't want me dead.

I glanced at West. "Do you know if Tyson has any other spies in this town?"

West shook his head. "Not that I know of. Besides, it'd be overkill."

If it meant their plans for my eventual end ran smoothly, I had no doubt that both Tyson *and* Blake would employ as much overkill as they thought necessary.

"Then you need to keep playing the game. Report on time, and don't give anything away."

West didn't look happy, but I was betting he was smart enough to know he had little choice in the matter. "And if I do?"

"Then maybe you get to keep your job."

As I spoke, a sliver of energy spun through the air. West blinked and his eyes went briefly lifeless— although if you weren't watching him carefully, you wouldn't even have noticed it.

What did you do? I asked, without looking at Quinn.

Just applied a little insurance. He won't be able to warn Tyson even if he wanted to.

Good. I glanced at Harris. "I need to use your computer."

He nodded and rose, walking across to a desk in the far corner of the room. I followed him across, watching as he typed in his ID and had his iris scanned.

"Okay," he said, stepping back. "You're ready to go."

"Thanks." I sat in the chair and scooted forward. A few key taps, several passwords, and an iris scan later, I was into the Directorate's database. "What was that number again, Evin?"

He repeated it. I typed it in then hit SEARCH. As I waited for the results, I glanced up at Quinn. "How soon can your plane be ready to leave?"

"Turnaround is usually an hour." He glanced at his watch. "We could be gone in twenty-five minutes, if need be."

"Want to warn them, then?"

He smiled. "Already have. The pilot is telepathic."

"Handy." I glanced down as the search results flickered up on the screen. The number was listed as belonging to a house in Mickleham, which was an outlying area of Melbourne rather than one of the recognized suburbs, and made up of small farming subdivisions rather than high-density housing estates. It also wasn't that far away from Essendon Airport, where Quinn usually landed his planes.

I rose. "Evin, you'll need to stay here—"

"No." He thrust to his feet, his expression belligerent. "I'm coming with you. I need to help—"

"The best way you can help," Quinn said gently, "is by continuing the scam here. If they get the slightest idea that something has gone awry, then your mate's life will be even more at risk. These men are dangerous, and they will do whatever they think is necessary to protect themselves."

"This is what we do," I added softly. "And we're damn good at it. We *will* get her back safely."

Which was a stupid thing to promise, given we had no idea what her situation was, but I couldn't help it. I liked Evin—stepbrother or not—and I didn't want to see him face the pain of losing a soul mate like I had.

One loss in the family was more than enough.

Evin glanced from Quinn to me then back again. His shoulders slumped. "Okay. But let me know the minute you've found her."

"We will." I took a deep breath and blew it out slowly. "And now to tell Jack."

Quinn stepped forward. "I can—"

I held up a hand. "No. This is my battle."

I spun around and walked into the cell area. The vamp's door was open and Rhoan leaned casually against the door frame. He glanced at me. "Find out anything interesting?"

"His contact was Tyson." I stopped and peered into

the cell. Jack was sitting on a chair, and the vamp was upright on the concrete bed. They looked for all the world like they were in the middle of a staring contest, but the sweat beading the younger vamp's forehead was evidence enough that something else was happening.

And that he was losing the battle.

"Meaning Blake definitely is behind it. Tyson wouldn't spit without his big brother's approval."

"Tyson's usurped the London pack in Cona Creek and made it his own."

Rhoan's expression was contemptuous. "He always was a lazy bastard. Should have guessed he'd steal a pack rather than make one of his own. We going after him?"

" 'We' are not going anywhere," Jack said, without taking his gaze from the other vamp. "Not until we finish here, anyway."

I glanced at him. "Boss, I tracked down the number Evin phoned his reports into, and it's a Melbourne number. We need to hit the address and rescue Evin's mate as soon as possible."

"Riley, the murders we're investigating occur during the day, which means we're limited in our guardian usage."

Specifically, it meant there was Iktar, Rhoan, and myself. But there wasn't anything I could do that Iktar and Rhoan couldn't—other than talk to souls, and the reality was, we weren't really getting that much information from said souls. These people were far too clever.

"What about a deal, then? Let Quinn and me go

after Evin's mate tonight, and then we'll concentrate on solving the murders."

"And Blake?" Rhoan asked.

I glanced at him. "Can wait until we have the time to work up a really *good* revenge."

"The minute you free Evin's mate, he'll know the game is up."

"Not if the guards are forced to believe she's still there."

He grimaced. "I don't know—"

I touched his shoulder, squeezing gently. "We'll deal with him. Just not yet." I glanced at Jack. "Can we go?"

He glanced at me then, and his eyes held a hint of regret. It was the sort of look I imagined a parent got when their kids finally left the nest.

Maybe he realized that's exactly what I was trying to do.

"Contact me the minute you free her. We'll probably have more information about the murders by then."

"Thanks, boss." I squeezed my brother's shoulder and turned to head back out into the main room, then hesitated and looked back at Jack. "Boss, you might want to talk to Harris before you leave."

His concentration was back on the vamp, so his reply was almost absent. "What about?"

"About his ability to bring down helicopters with kinetic force. He's also mind-blind. He could make a perfect replacement for Kade."

Or better yet, for me.

He merely grunted. The vamp was sweating even

more profusely, so Jack's constant telepathic barrage was having an effect.

I winked at Rhoan then continued outside.

"Well?" Evin said, almost anxiously.

"We're a go. We just need you two to keep relaying information and pretend everything is as it should be."

Evin scrubbed a hand across his face. "He'll expect me to be overwrought and anxious, and that certainly won't be hard to fake."

West didn't say anything and he looked no happier than before, but even with Quinn's restrictions in place, I very much doubted he'd do anything to jeopardize the operation. He might not love working in this town, but I had a suspicion he *did* love being a cop.

"I'll phone the minute we have news. And Harris?" I smiled his way. "Thanks."

A hint of amusement crinkled the corners of his bright eyes. "You're welcome. And anytime you feel the need to find trouble, please try not to find it in my town."

"Deal. But your life will quickly become boring without me."

The amusement crinkling his eyes broke out across the rest of his face. "*That* I can deal with."

I snorted in amusement and walked across to Quinn. He spun around and held out his arm. "Let's go raise some hell."

"So," I said, unbuckling the lap belt and walking over to the plane's plush, well-appointed bar. "Given we can't exactly plan our method of attack until we see what we're up against, and we have a five-hour flight ahead of us, what do you suggest we do?"

He walked up behind me and wrapped his arms around my waist. "I can think of one or two things," he said, kissing the side of my neck.

His lips were so cool against my skin that I shivered. I hadn't noticed it before—probably because I'd been so overjoyed to see him—but his body heat was decidedly down. He'd obviously been worrying more about me than feeding himself.

At least that was something easily remedied.

"Only one or two?" I said archly. "My dear vampire, I thought you had a better imagination than that."

"Oh, I have. But given this is a five-hour flight, I don't think we'll have time for the rest of them."

I laughed and turned around in his arms. "I'm so glad I mostly remember you again. So glad that damn truck didn't squish you into tiny little pieces."

"It's hard to kill an Aedh."

I raised a hand and lightly caressed the scar on the side of his beautiful face. "This suggests they came close."

"But not close enough." His lips captured mine and for a long, long time, there was very little sound.

When we finally came up for air, the rapid pounding of my heart was a cadence that filled the silence. I opened my eyes, stared into his. Saw the desire burning bright—desire that was both sexual *and* blood need. He was controlling both urges, but the second only just.

"Do you want to go into the bedroom?" he whispered,

his teeth grazing my earlobe and sending a heated shiver through my entire body.

"I don't care where we go, as long as you promise to ravish me senseless."

"Oh, I don't think that's going to be a problem." He bent, swept me up in his arms, then carried me into the plane's luxurious bedroom suite.

Once there, he stripped me. Slowly, seductively, one piece of clothing at a time, exploring and reacquainting himself with each piece of flesh as it was revealed. By the time I was naked, I was quivering with desire.

Even so, I took the time to undress him, letting my fingers roam across the strong planes of his body, remembering what I loved about it, exploring new scars.

Eventually, I kissed him. Whatever vestiges of control we had were totally and irreparably smashed by the force of that kiss, by the passion and love and sheer *need* behind it.

We fell onto the bed wrapped in each other's arms, his flesh driving deep into mine. He began to move, and all I could do was move with him, savoring and enjoying the sensations flowing through me.

But it went far beyond the physical, because our minds were joined as intimately as our bodies. That was an even more glorious sensation, filled with warmth and love and intimacy, and it made every physical move sharper, deeper, more resonant and powerful. Made our lovemaking so incredible that I just wanted to cry.

And in that moment I knew, without a shred of

doubt, that it was time to get real about our relationship. To commit, wholly and fully, to *us*.

Then his lips claimed mine again and the thought fled, lost to the pleasures new and old. His strokes became fierce, hungry thrusts that shook my entire body, and sweet pressure had begun to build low down in my body, quickly reaching boiling point.

We came together, his roar echoing across the silence, his body slamming into mine so hard the whole bed seemed to shake. His kisses became as fierce as his body, but as he poured himself into me, his mouth left mine, his teeth grazing my neck, but not taking. I'd already lost far too much blood for one day.

When I finally caught my breath again, I took his face between my palms and kissed him long and slow. "I think we both needed that."

"Hell, yeah."

He kissed me again, then rolled onto the bed beside me, and tried to gather me into his arms. I resisted, propping myself up with one hand so I could study him. In the soft light, his skin was golden and the scars down the left side of his body—the same side as his face—did little to detract from the beauty of it.

But it had been so close, no matter how blasé he was about it. And that only served to crystallize the decision I'd made.

"You have an extremely serious expression right at this moment," he commented, lightly running a finger across my lips.

I kissed his fingertips, then said, "That's because I have a very serious question for you."

"What? Wait, let me guess—do I have enough food on this tin can to satisfy a hungry werewolf?"

"Well, no," I said, amused. "Although that *is* a damn good question."

He laughed softly. "I'll always cater to your hungers," he teased. "No matter what those hungers are."

"For which I'm extremely grateful."

"So you should be. What, then, is this oh-so-serious question?"

I hesitated. Not because I was uncertain or scared, but because I really wanted to savor the moment and relish the anticipation. "It really just requires a yes-or-no answer. Nothing too difficult."

He raised an eyebrow. "So ask."

I smiled and placed my hands over his. "Will you marry me, Quinn O'Conor?"

Chapter 14

For once, his vampire expression failed him. His response was right there on his face, in full view and easily read. He went from surprise to disbelief then hope and sheer, utter joy all within a split second of each other, then he let loose a huge whoop of delight and swept me into his arms, hugging me fiercely.

"That is the one question I never, *ever* thought you'd ask." He cupped my face between his hands and kissed my nose, my lips, my chin, then moved up to my lips again. It was almost as if he were in such a state of excitement, he couldn't concentrate on one area.

I laughed softly and draped my arms around his neck. "To be honest, I never really considered it before. But if these last few days have taught me anything, then it's been crystallizing what, exactly, I want from my life. And making our relationship official is my number-one priority. Well, that and breaking free of the Directorate's leash."

"And a more perfect way of celebrating your return I could never have imagined. I will *adore* marrying you." He kissed me again, softly and sweetly. "I guess we now need decide just how soon and what type."

I grinned. "The vampire sounds anxious."

"The vampire has long considered you his, but to make it official—" He stopped and simply looked at me for a moment, and in his gaze and expression was enough love and joy to light up our solar system. "—that was a dream I'd thought impossible. So yeah, let's get this done quickly."

I laughed softly. "I'm not going to change my mind, you know."

"I know that, but fate hasn't exactly been kind to you over the years, so let's get this done before something stops us." He dropped another kiss on my lips. "As to how, I don't really care. Human mode or wolf, whichever way suits you."

"Swearing our love at dusk, on the night of the full moon, will take away the emotional desire for others, but it doesn't actually kill the ability to have sex with anyone else. But the lack of desire might prove a problem considering you can't live entirely off my blood and you prefer to take blood during sex."

"Prefer, not *must*. And if swearing to the moon brings you and me together as one, then I will top up my blood the regular way—donations via the arm or neck of willing participants—or via that revolting synth stuff."

I frowned. "I thought you didn't like the blood whore clubs?"

"I don't. But there *are* certain establishments that cater to those who prefer their donations from those who aren't hooked on the giving, or who prefer little or anonymous contact."

I raised my eyebrows. "How can a donor be anonymous when you're sucking their neck or arm?"

"By the careful placement of screens."

"How come no one knows about these establishments?"

"Because their whole purpose is to cater to the rich and/or the famous—those who don't want to be seen consuming in public, and who can afford to pay for the privilege of anonymity."

"Ah. These things always come down to money."

"Of which I have plenty," he said. "So, how swish do you want our wedding?"

I laughed. "A werewolf ceremony is a simple one. You, me, close family—because we sure as hell won't be swearing *anything* without letting Rhoan and Liander in on the action—and the moon. Clothes are optional."

"Now, why am I not surprised about that?"

"It also involves sex."

"Given it's a werewolf ceremony, I'd be surprised if it didn't." He paused, and said reflectively, "Maybe that's why the ceremony with Eryn didn't work. We said the words but didn't go through the motions."

Eryn Jones was the wolf he'd been engaged to before I'd met him. Only, she'd used an experimental "love" drug to snare him and had been after little more than his money. He'd caught her exercising her werewolf nature with several willing wolves, and he'd made her pay by snatching her memory and giving her a new life—that of a hooker.

He wasn't a man you ever wanted to betray.

"Well, all I can say is thank God, because otherwise we would not be here today."

He smiled. "So maybe I should start forgiving her?"

"Might be an idea."

He nodded, his expression somewhat distracted as he trailed his fingertip down my neck.

I licked my lips, and said, "So you're happy to go with the werewolf ceremony?"

"It's what you've always dreamed of, isn't it?"

"One of the things, yes."

"Then that's what we'll do. Although I wouldn't mind exchanging rings. I'm a big believer in those old-fashioned things."

"Something for me, something for you. It'll be perfect." I kissed his fingertips as they trailed back up and across my lips, then snuggled my body closer against his. Felt the hardness of his rising erection, the excited pounding of my pulse. "And do you know what would be the perfect way to celebrate our upcoming nuptials?"

"I think I can guess," he murmured, a heartbeat before his lips claimed mine.

From that moment on, there was little talking, only kissing and caressing and lovemaking.

And it was perfect.

* * *

*I*t was nearly four by the time we got to Mickle-ham. There was little traffic on the roads and few lights on in any of the houses. Our target was situated in the Mount Ridley estate, which was basically dozens of mini-farms ranging in size from two acres to eight. There weren't a whole lot of trees or cover to be had, but given the time, I doubted there'd be too many people up and about to notice us.

Quinn slowed the Porsche and all but crawled past the property.

"Three life-forms inside," he said softly.

I glanced at him. "You can see that from this distance?" There had to be a good acre between us and the house.

He smiled. "You may have infrared, but you don't have a vampire's blood hunger. That makes all the difference when it comes to sensing life within walls."

"I guess it does." I looked back at the house. In the darkness, it looked like a squat and ugly box, but it was two stories high and dominated the skyline. There were no lights on in the house, and there didn't seem to be any animals grazing or sleeping in the paddocks.

"I'm betting it's not as peaceful as it looks. They wouldn't be that careless."

"There will probably be alarms on the house, at least," he agreed. "And we also have the problem that, as a vampire, I can't go into the house. Not without an invite, and I very much doubt they're going to extend one."

"So, we need a distraction." I paused as we cruised

past the boundary of our house and another—slightly prettier—one came into sight. A light shone in one of the rooms on the first floor. Night owls were *not* what we needed right now—not when they were right next door to a house we needed to break into. I glanced at Quinn. "How well can you act?"

He raised an eyebrow. "Did you know I was once a very sought after actor in Elizabethan times?"

Amusement ran through me. "Weren't Elizabethan actors considered rogues and treated with suspicion?"

"Only initially. Once the queen began granting licenses to the aristocracy for the maintenance of troupes, acting became more regulated and the actors' popularity increased greatly." He smiled, almost wistfully. "That was a very enjoyable period of my life."

"Meaning there were lots of women to be had, no doubt," I said with a grin.

"Of course," he said, amusement warming his words. He swung the car into a driveway and turned around. "Although it's been a while since my stage days, so my acting skills are probably rusty. But I think I could manage a passable drunk looking for his lover's house. If I make enough noise, it'll hopefully distract their attention."

"It's extremely difficult for vamps to get drunk," I said doubtfully. "Given that the men inside that house won't be human and will sense what you are almost immediately, do you think they'll buy the drunk act?"

"Just because it's difficult doesn't mean that it doesn't happen." He shifted the gear into first and drove back past the house. "Besides, there just happen to be several bottles of Dom Perignon sitting snugly in the backseat. I'll tip a little over me for increased verisimilitude."

I gave him a look of utter horror. "And waste such fine Champagne? That's *criminal*."

He chuckled softly. "I said a *little*. The rest we can save for later."

"Well, that's all right then."

He drove back past the house and continued on to the end of the street. Once there, he pulled over to the side of the road and stopped. "How long do you think you'll need to get to the house?"

I glanced at my watch. "Five minutes should be enough. I doubt they'll have much in the way of sensors or alarms in the paddocks—the wildlife would play havoc with them. I'll just have to be more cautious near the house."

He nodded then handed me a cell phone. "Take this, because you may need to prove who you are to Lyndal. And be careful. I don't want my wife-to-be getting too messed up before our wedding night."

"Trust me, I've had more than enough excitement lately to last me a lifetime." I returned his kiss briefly, then opened the door and climbed out.

The night was crisp and cold, and the darkness somehow more intense with the absence of street lighting. I ran across the road and climbed through the wire fence. It was tempting to simply run down the road, but if someone *was* up in our target house, then a lone runner at this hour of the night was going to raise all manner of suspicion.

Not that someone jogging across paddocks *wasn't*.

Of course, I could wrap myself in shadows and run along the road that way, but there was no guarantee that both of the guards were wolves. Blake knew I was Directorate, knew the Directorate would be involved in any search for me, so he'd surely have more than wolves as backup. And he would have figured out a way to get a vamp guard past the threshold restriction—and rented houses did have restrictions, even if public places didn't. It was still somebody's home, and that was the difference.

I kept close to the tree-lined boundary fences—though the trees themselves were small and shrubby, and didn't really provide much in the way of cover. But they at least gave me deeper shadows to hide in.

Somewhere off to my right, a dog began barking, the sound more friendly and excited than one of warning. I slipped through the wire fence dividing the two properties and ran forward, once again keeping to the fence line until I was near the house. There was very little in the way of cover around it, but there were garden beds with white stones along the length of the side I could see, and a covered patio area around the back. A garage dominated the right side of it, and it had motion sensor lights attached to the front. I cursed inwardly and scanned the roofline, and saw more lights jutting out from the corners of the house. The minute I went near it, those damn things would come on.

Which left me with one option—the roof. It was a basic, red tile roof, the sort that could be seen on millions of houses all over Australia. And tiles—unlike the iron roofing often used these days—were easy to move. I called to my seagull shape and took to the sky. As I landed, a car turned into the road, tires squealing as Quinn took the corner too fast. High-beam lights turned the shadows into day, and music—heavy, thumping rock—blared so loud that I could hear it from here.

I'd wanted a distraction, I thought with a grin. Quinn was certainly giving me it.

As the car drove up the driveway and the bright lights pinned the house, I shifted back to human form and carefully began sliding tiles to one side. Given they were concrete, it was difficult *not* to make noise, but I hoped the steady thumping beat of music would cover any sound I was making. By the time Quinn had pulled to a halt outside the front entrance, I'd created a big enough hole to get through. I didn't drop into it, however, wanting to make sure the guards' attention was on Quinn rather than what else might be going on within the house.

"Hey, Emma?" The voice, though Quinn's, was loud and slurred. "Why did you leave me, baby? Come out and talk to me."

The lights came on around the house, then a booming voice said, "There's no Emma here. You've got the wrong house."

"Who the hell are you?" Quinn said, with all the belligerence of a true drunk. "And why the hell are you in Emma's house?"

I grinned and dropped down into the roof space. It was—not unexpectedly—dark, so I switched to infrared and carefully began crawling along the rafters, dodging the air-con vents and various pipes and wires that seemed to breed up in roof spaces.

Outside, the rumble of voices was getting louder—not so much on Quinn's part, but certainly that of the guard who'd answered the door. His frustration over the "drunk's" refusal to believe he was in the wrong house was increasing. He hadn't yet ventured out—his voice was still coming from the same position—but maybe if he got angry enough, he would.

He'd be Quinn's the minute he did, which would leave me with only the one. And while I'd coped with more than one assailant many times, I was still sensible enough to prefer one at a time.

Unlike my brother, who often seemed to think the more, the merrier.

The trapdoor was located in the far corner. I crawled through a final strut and grasped the latch handle. There was no sign of body heat in the room immediately below, and little in the way of noise to give away the position of the second guard. Not that much else could be heard over the racket erupting from the front.

I pried the cover up and looked down into the white-tiled bathroom. The air here smelled warm and moldy, and there was a pile of damp towels thrown into the corner near the shower. Obviously, the guards weren't into washing.

There was no one in sight. I listened for any indication of where the other guard might be, but the house was quiet—if you ignored the music and two men yelling out the front, anyway. I flared my nostrils, drawing in the more distant flavors, trying to find some hint of the other man's location. Cabbage and cooking meat were the most intense scents filling the air, but underneath that ran the foul scent of vampire.

It wasn't strong, meaning he was probably several rooms away, but that was close enough to hear me—or, rather, hear my heartbeat. So why hadn't he come running?

Maybe Quinn was doing a better job of distraction than I'd thought.

Praying that it kept that way for a few seconds more, I grabbed the sides of the manhole and dropped down lightly, my rubber-soled shoes making little noise as they hit the tiles. I stayed in that half-squatting position, my heart racing as I listened again for any hint of movement.

Again, there was nothing. I crept forward, still half crouched. My barely healed leg protested, and pain slithered through my muscles. I ignored it and continued on.

The scent of vampire was stronger near the door, and seemed to be coming from the right. I couldn't see the blur of his body heat in the immediate vicinity, though, which was odd.

I risked taking a quick look into the hall. It was empty of life *and* unlife. There were three doors to the left, two of them open, the other dead-bolted. No need to guess who lay behind *that* door, I thought grimly. The only real surprise would be her condition. I had no idea what Blake's orders would have been for Lyndal, but given that he probably had measures in place to kill us all the minute anything went wrong, he might not have cared what the men did to her as long as she remained able to talk to Evin.

A shiver ran through me. For Evin's sake, I had to hope that I was imagining the worst. That she was fine and unharmed in any way.

And tomorrow, pigs might fly.

I brushed the thought aside and slipped out into the hallway. The stench of vampire suddenly seemed stronger, and though I could hear no sound, instinct warned me he was on the move.

The stairs were to the right. I stepped across the hall and, keeping my back to the wall, crept toward them. The vampire scent was getting stronger, and my nose twitched in distaste. I still couldn't hear him, but then, Blake had the money to hire the best.

He'd hired Kye, after all.

For the first time since I'd killed him, my soul didn't ache at the mere thought of his name. The emptiness remained—would probably always remain—but the pain and the hurt were no longer knife-edged. Maybe my decision to commit to Quinn had been exactly what I'd needed—what my soul had needed.

I stopped several feet away from the corner, with a hall table between me and the stairs. I reached out and carefully picked up a vase of long-dead flowers. The vamp had to know I was here—he'd hear the beat of my heart even if he was as blind to body heat as I seemed to be—and he'd come around that corner fast. So I needed something to distract him with.

I waited, breath caught somewhere in my throat, for

his approach. When it came, it was lightning fast. One minute the hall was empty, the next minute there was a long, thin stretch of vampire hunkered down in the middle of it holding a gun.

I swung the vase and let it go. Dead flowers and foul-smelling water flew, soaking the carpet. I jumped forward, following the vase with a kick. He ducked both and pulled the trigger. I twisted out of the way, felt the bullet burn past my hip, and lashed out, my clenched fingers taking him under the chin, throwing him up and back but not knocking him out. He hit the carpeted floor hard and his gun went flying.

I leapt for it, my fingers latching onto the barrel even as he caught his balance and lunged for me. I didn't have time to shift my grip to the trigger so I simply twisted around, smashing the weapon against his face with as much force as I could muster. Flesh and bone gave way under the impact and he went down, but he was still far from out. I scrambled to my knees and hit him in his throat with the side of my hand. His eyes rolled back into his head and he went limp.

It wouldn't last long. Vampires were too tough to be immobilized for very long—even by a blow that would have killed a human.

I switched the gun's safety on, shoved it into the waistband of my jeans, then took a moment to rub at my leg. There was no blood and the wound hadn't split, but the ache was deep and relentless, despite the numbness that still ringed the actual wound.

But I guess if that was the worst aftereffect of getting

shot with silver for the umpteenth time, then I could consider myself lucky.

I grabbed the vamp's arms, lifting his head and shoulders off the floor, then dragged him down the stairs. The other guard hadn't come up to investigate the gunshot, so I had to presume Quinn had managed to grab him outside.

Indeed I have. His thoughts rolled through mine, warm and amused. *It appears my acting skills are not as rusty as I thought. Did the other one manage to wing you?*

The bullet barely even scraped my side.

Which, knowing you, probably means there's a hole the size of a fist in your body.

I laughed and hauled the vamp down the last step, then dragged him across the foyer to the open front door. Quinn was standing on the porch, his arms crossed as he watched me. The other guard was propped up against the thick white columns.

"I've dealt with the first guard already." As I stepped over the door threshold, Quinn took the vamp's arms and jerked him sideways, depositing him rather roughly beside the other guard. Not that either man deserved any form of gentle treatment after the hell they'd put Evin through. "Neither of them will remember our arrival or notice their captive is missing."

"Good." I glanced down at my side. My sweater was torn, but the wound was little more than a scratch and there wasn't even much blood. Which was probably a good thing, considering how much I'd lost before Harris had removed the silver bullet. "Has either man got a key on them? Lyndal's door is chained and padlocked."

He patted down both guards, then shook his head. "Nothing in their pockets. Check the kitchen or their sleeping quarters."

"On it." I spun around and headed back into the house. The kitchen was at the back, and it was huge. But the counters were full of crap and the sink was littered with unwashed dishes. Obviously, neither of them was worried about mice or ants, because there were crumbs all over the floor and ants were currently enjoying the leftovers on several plates.

All of which was just more evidence they didn't intend to be here long, because surely any lengthy stay would have required a bit of hygiene. The wolf, at least, would have been driven to distraction by the smell—it was bad enough already.

Although that could have just been the aroma of cabbage and boiling meat that was coming from the pot on the stove.

Nose twitching, I hunted around for keys but failed to find anything except stacks of newspapers and betting slips. I guess they had to do something to fill up the days—and they couldn't harass Lyndal twenty-four seven if they wanted to keep her alive.

I turned around and walked back up the stairs. The first room was a bedroom that had been converted into a living area. There was a TV in one corner, several lounge chairs, and a coffee table set against the side walls. To the left of the door was a bank of wires and monitors.

I stepped inside. Four monitors showed slowly panning views of the sides of the house and the immediate surrounds. One was fixed on the front gate, another swept the rear garden, a third appeared to be scanning a bathroom, and the last one was in a bedroom.

I watched the pan of the camera. Saw the bed, the TV, and the bucket, and felt fury sweep through me. The bastards hadn't even offered her decent toilet facilities. I should have smacked that vampire a little bit harder.

The camera finally panned around far enough to reveal Lyndal. She was standing near the window, her face pressed up against the barred glass, as if desperate to see around the corner of the house and figure out what was going on. She was naked, her skin bruised but otherwise clean, meaning that while they'd not given her proper toilet facilities, they'd at least allowed her to shower. It didn't ease the anger burning through me, though.

I spun around and headed into the next room. This one was set up as a bedroom, with two single beds and a battered pine coffee table squeezed in between them. On this sat wallets, coins, cash, and keys—two sets of car keys and another ring holding five other keys. I swept them up, spun around, and ran for the padlocked room.

"Lyndal," I said as I sorted through the keys trying to find the right one. "It's Riley Jenson from the Directorate. I'm here to rescue you."

One of the keys finally slipped into the lock and it snapped open. I unlatched the door and pressed it open. A bucket came flying at me, its stinking contents splattering through the air.

"Whoa," I said, jumping out of the way. "Easy, Lyndal. I really *am* here to rescue you."

"Riley Jenson is up in Dunedan, not down here in Melbourne."

So the men had told her what Evin was doing and who he was minding—which was only more evidence to the fact that they never intended for any of us to live.

She stepped into my line of sight, her fists clenched and fury etching her features. Her face was unmarked, green eyes spitting fire, but her limbs were as bruised as her back and there were ugly welts around her wrists and ankles. She'd been tied with silver more than once.

Even her gently rounded belly had bruises, and for the second time in a matter of minutes, I wished I'd hit the vampire harder.

"What fucking game are you lot playing now?" she added furiously.

"No game, I promise you." I reached into my pocket and withdrew the phone. "You can ring Evin, if you like."

I pressed the appropriate number, made sure it was ringing, then tossed her the phone. Her expression was still a mix of defiance and disbelief, but she nevertheless held the phone to her ear and waited.

Evin answered, and her face just about crumbled. "Oh god," she said, "It *is* you."

I don't know what Evin said, because it didn't exactly sound coherent from where I was standing. *Quinn, we need to get these two back together ASAP. Any chance of your plane coming to the rescue again?*

I'll have to get another pilot, but yeah, we can do it.

Fantastic. I stepped over the puddle of urine and fecal matter and into the room.

Lyndal's gaze jumped to mine and she backed away a step. "What does she look like?"

I paused, waiting. Her gaze slipped down my body, and the tension riding her eased. She closed her eyes briefly and said, "Yeah, it's her."

I held out a hand. She hesitated, then handed me the phone. "Evin—"

I didn't get any further, because he was all but crying "Thank you, thank you, thank you" over and over.

"Evin," I said sharply, even though my heart ached for him. "We've got to go. You need to listen."

He took a deep, shuddering breath. "Okay."

"We're sending Lyndal to you via Quinn's plane. She'll get there around lunch. But you need to carry on phoning every night as usual. They have to believe everything is fine."

"But the guards will know—"

"The guards won't remember a damn thing, and they'll believe she's still here safe and sound. As long as you and West keep up the charade, we should have a few days' leeway."

"But what if they *do* realize? We're sitting ducks staying here."

"I didn't say you were staying there. I just said you needed to keep phoning."

"But caller ID will tell them—"

"Caller ID can be faked. They'll think you're still there, Evin. Trust me."

"I do." He paused, then said, "When you confront

Blake, I want in. Whatever you do, I want to be a part of it. He has to pay, Riley. For you, and for Lyndal."

"He will. But I haven't yet decided what—"

"I don't care. Just factor in my help."

"And mine," Lyndal murmured. "I may be pregnant, but, by god, someone is going to pay for what these bastards did to me."

I glanced at her and saw the fire in her eyes. The need for retribution. And understood it, totally. I gave her the phone. "We need to move. Say good-bye."

I turned and led the way downstairs. She talked and walked, hanging up as we neared the front door. She paused when she saw Quinn, her nostrils flaring, then glanced at me and marched forward.

Not at Quinn, but the two men. She raised a fist, but Quinn caught it before she could land a blow.

"I can understand the need to lash out," he said softly, "but leaving a bruise they can't remember might just undo the mind washing I've done."

She glanced at him, her thin face fierce, then nodded once and stepped back. "Will the Directorate take care of them later?"

"If not the Directorate, then I will," Quinn said. And he said it with such an utter lack of emotion that it was chilling—and totally believable. "They are dead men walking."

"Good." She crossed her arms over her breasts, though it wasn't an attempt to cover her nakedness. "What next?"

"We've some clothes for you in the back of the car, if

you'd like to climb in and dress." Quinn glanced at me. "You need to put the guards back."

"Put them back how?"

"The vampire tripped on some loose carpeting going up the stairs, hit the hall stand, and knocked himself unconscious."

Meaning I'd have to ensure there was loose carpet. "And the wolf?"

"Before the vamp had his accident, he and the wolf had a minor altercation. The wolf was knocked down and smacked the back of his head on the tiles."

And given I'd neutralized my scent before we'd come here, no one would scent me. "Neither man has appropriate bumps."

He glanced at me, his smile cold. "Oh yes they have."

I snorted. "And you stopped Lyndal from hitting him."

"I built my bumps into their memories."

"You could have done it to hers."

"It's not easy to account for bruising to the front *and* back of the head. In a case like this, where you're adding memories and forcing them not to see certain things, too many complications can risk blowing the whole thing."

"Which is what happened with me."

He nodded. I grabbed the vamp's arms, dragging him back through the hall and up the stairs. I was sweating by the time I reached the landing. He might appear to be little more than a string bean, but he obviously had heavy bones.

I dumped him on the floor, knocked over the hall stand, then ripped up a little of the carpet covering the top step. Then I ran back downstairs to grab the were-wolf. Him I dragged into the kitchen.

I locked the front door as I came out. Quinn touched my back lightly, guiding me across to the car. At least the ear-splitting music had stopped. "We must find time to undo your mind restraints, too."

"As I said, that's not important right now. We need to track down our killer first then confront Blake."

He opened the passenger door and ushered me inside. "You do know that *this* time, defeating him won't be enough."

His words had something twisting inside, if only because they were forcing me to confront what I'd long known but hadn't really admitted.

Because the guards inside that house weren't the only ones who were dead men walking.

Blake and whoever else was involved in this scheme were, as well.

But not via the Directorate.

Not via a gun.

It could never be that easy.

No, I had to kill Blake the same way he'd killed my grandfather.

With my wolf.

It was the only way to keep the pack from coming after me and Rhoan and everyone we loved.

Chapter 15

Twelve hours later, with Evin and Lyndal safely tucked away in the West pack's heartland and with Harris's promise to keep them safe at all cost, Quinn and I walked into the day division's tiny conference room.

Sal was the only other person who'd arrived, and she was working at the terminal and frowning at the images flickering across the remote screen. She spun around as we entered, and her smile was wide and genuine.

"Well, well, if it isn't our lost wolf," she said, voice droll but humor crinkling her eyes. "Enjoy your holiday, did you?"

"Totally." I plunked down on the chair next to hers. "I'd love to say I missed your cheery face, but the truth is, I couldn't even remember it."

"I heard that. Shame you didn't also forget you worked for the Directorate. It's been so peaceful around here without you."

I grinned. "So you were bored shitless, huh?"

"Totally. So do try not to get kidnapped again." She glanced at Quinn, and her expression became more formal—which surprised the hell out of me. "Would you like some coffee?"

"Yes, thank you," he said, the barest hint of amusement in his voice.

I glanced at him as she rose and walked across to the coffee machine—which was sparkly new, and had obviously been installed during the time I'd been missing.

I'm an old one, he said, the amusement that had been barely evident in his words bubbling through his mental tones. *Sal's merely showing the respect we old ones are due.*

I gave a mental snort and he added, with another burst of amusement, *Of course, it also helps that she's been asked to become an official member of the Melbourne vampire council and I happen to be one of those who have the deciding vote.*

But Sal hates the council. She said that months ago.

Things change. In this case, I believe the change of heart goes by the name of Norman.

Norman? What a staid old name. I hope he's not.

Oh, trust me, Norman's not staid.

Well, good, because she deserves better.

Careful. That almost sounds like you care.

She's bringing me coffee. Of course I care. I glanced

around as said coffee was plunked in front of me and I gave her another grin. "Should I inspect it for arsenic?"

"In deference to you being returned to the fold, I left it out. But don't drink tomorrow's coffee." Her tone was amused as she handed Quinn his coffee then headed back to her computer.

I took a sip, then asked, "Why are you fiddling with the computers in here?"

"It's quieter. Jack doesn't want anything distracting me once the operation starts."

A comment that would no doubt be explained once Jack got here. As if on cue, he and Rhoan walked in, both of them looking tired and more than a little rough around the edges. Both carried large cups of coffee, although given the bags under my brother's eyes, it was going to take more than a bucket of the brown stuff to keep him awake and alert.

"Got the systems hooked up yet, Sal?" Jack asked.

"Finalizing it now," she said briskly. "Just a few minutes more."

Jack grunted and slapped several folders on the desk as he sat down opposite us. Rhoan just perched on the table's edge, his posture reflecting his tiredness. Obviously, he couldn't be bothered walking any farther.

"Remember me saying that I thought the name Daskill sounded familiar?"

I nodded, and he pushed a folder forward. Quinn stopped its slide across the desk and opened it. I'd been expecting a rundown of whoever Daskill was, but what we got instead were photographs. Vivid, bloody photographs of the remains of what I presumed were a woman and child. They'd been so torn apart it was hard to tell. Only the remnants of their nightdresses gave their sex away.

"Bobby Daskill's wife and child were murdered in their beds while he was on a business trip. The main suspect was Bobby's business partner, Henry Kattram, who had apparently been having an affair with Bobby's wife for over a year. She refused to leave Bobby and apparently broke it off. Those pictures are the result."

"Then why is Kattram still listed as a suspect?" Quinn asked. "Why was he never charged if the police are so certain he was their murderer?"

"Because Henry Kattram was found dismembered in his bed twenty-four hours later." Jack indicated the photos. "In a manner eerily similar to the way Jenny and Evie Daskill were killed."

"Daskill obviously was the main suspect, so why was he never charged?" I asked.

"Because he was one hundred miles away with friends at his country retreat. One of those friends was a high court judge."

"Convenient," Quinn murmured. "But from what I've heard about Kattram, he'd be the sort to have closed circuit TV both inside and outside. What did that reveal?"

"A shadowy figure wearing a mask, gloves, and some sort of shoe covering."

I raised my eyebrows. "Surely not a demon costume?"

Jack half smiled. "No. It was just a black mask and padded clothing, but the idea is the same. If they leave no prints, and you can't see their face or body shape, it's hard to make any sort of ID."

Quinn closed the folder and pushed it back to Jack. "If he *is* behind these murderers for hire, he surely wouldn't be stupid enough to use his own planes or helicopters."

"He might if it was an emergency and there was no obvious link back to him. Daskill owns a private jet and helicopter charter service catering to remote areas. The helicopter Harris downed was hired by one Harry Jones——who is not the vamp and who actually doesn't exist."

"Charter services these days have to have cameras and facial recognition software installed in their offices, so what did that come up with?"

"Again, nothing. We suspect he might have been a Helki wolf, because the one capture we got of his face showed their distinctive eyes."

I nodded. If you were going to use fake ID, then what better person to use than someone who could physically alter their human shape? Not so much their size or actual shape, but their physical characteristics. Hair, minor facial shifts, teeth, easy stuff like that. They could also change their eye color, but that apparently took more effort and drained their energy faster. "So what's the plan? We have no obvious connection to the man, just our suspicions."

And Jack never moved on suspicions alone. Well, rarely, anyway.

He gave me the sort of smile that a shark might have

a heartbeat before he attacked. "Every bad guy makes one mistake. In Daskill's case, he keeps records."

I raised an eyebrow. "I'd imagine such records would be *extremely* well protected."

"They are, but we have some of the world's best hackers in our employ." He glanced Sal's way. "Sal, for instance, is a genius at hacking into security-sensitive areas."

"Which I've just completed." She glanced over her shoulder. "We now control Daskill's security systems in both his house and his Melbourne office."

"Excellent. And the computer files?"

"Randy is still downloading. There's a lot of information, and it's all coded." She paused, glancing briefly at the screen and flicking a button. The screen divided into four, each one showing a different section of what looked to be a grand mansion. "Initial investigations on one of the earliest files downloaded indicate intensive records concerning the movements of a man who was found murdered three days after his release from jail. If he isn't the brains behind this scheme, he's certainly involved."

"And that is all we need to go in and get him." Jack glanced at me. "Daskill has been going home to have lunch with his new wife every day between one and two-thirty—"

"Obviously he doesn't trust the new missus *not* to take a lover," I murmured. "Which says a lot about the power of his loving. Or the lack of it."

Maybe he just fancies his new missus, Quinn commented, eyes twinkling as he glanced at me. *Hell, when the company is fully transferred to Melbourne, expect me to be breaking up a boring day by coming home for a quick bit of loving quite frequently.*

That's because you hang out with a werewolf, and the randiness has finally rubbed off.

"The reason doesn't matter, just the result," Jack said. "He has a security force of eight men who rotate on twelve-hour shifts, as well as the cameras."

"Having eight security guards on standby is a bit of overkill, isn't it?" Rhoan said, frowning. "Even for a man whose first wife was murdered."

"They work in teams of four," Jack said, "which makes the numbers more even. And given he's either in charge of, or involved with, an organization that runs a stable of some extremely well-trained hit men and women, then no, I wouldn't think his precautions are over the top."

"If we move on Daskill, that stable of killers may just melt into the woodwork."

Jack glanced at me. "He's the brains and the money behind it, so he's the one we need to take out first. The others can be found in time."

Fair enough. "Then what's the plan?" He obviously had one, because he wouldn't have called Quinn here otherwise.

"We're going in at one-thirty. Quinn will take out the guards, as neither myself nor any of the other guardians is able to venture out at that hour."

Even Quinn was pushing it.

I'll be fine, he said. *At worst, it'll give me a nice tan for our wedding night.*

You'll be naked on your wedding night. No one is going to care about your tan.

I'll be wearing trousers. I may not be quite as old-fashioned as I used to be, but Liander is not going to get the joy of a full frontal. Not when I'm getting hitched.

Amusement bubbled through me. *Who said I was talking about the ceremony?*

"Riley," Jack said heavily, "stop mind-talking to Quinn and concentrate on the business at hand."

"It takes two to talk," I commented. "And I *am* listening."

He gave me a disbelieving look, then continued. "You and Rhoan will hit the house once the guards are taken out. He does keep two rottweilers inside, so you'll have to watch out for those."

"A good stun gun will fix those quickly enough," Rhoan said dryly. "But someone this security conscious is going to have standby systems we don't know about."

"And a gun by the bed, no doubt," I said.

"No doubt, so be careful." Jack was looking at me rather than Rhoan when he said that, which wasn't exactly fair. Rhoan tended to be more reckless. The only problem was, the bad guys just didn't seem to enjoy munching on his body as much as they did mine.

Jack opened another folder and passed several sheets of paper to me and Rhoan. "These are the house plans. Memorize the layout while you're heading down to the armory."

Rhoan barely even looked at them before standing, but he was good enough at his job that he probably didn't need more than that. "Which we'd better do now if we want to get to Brighton with sufficient time to spare."

"Just weapons," Jack warned. "Don't grab body armor. If some overwatchful guard spots you before you near the property, we don't want them suspecting anything is up."

"The minute we drive up with Directorate plates, any watchful guard is going to know the jig is up," I commented. "And we have *body* armor? Why was I never told?"

"Which is why we'll be using false plates. Be down in the parking garage in—" He hesitated and glanced at his watch "—ten minutes. And you've never been given body armor because someone who can move with the speed of a vampire rarely has any use for it. It's for nonguardian personal, like the cleanup teams."

He'd obviously forgotten about all the bullet holes I had in my body. "I've never seen Cole or his team in them."

"No, but they have them in their cars." He glanced at Sal. "Keep me updated on any movements. Quinn and Riley, you'll need to be fitted with external earpieces, seeing we haven't the time to fit internals to either of you."

For which I was extremely glad—and not only because my poor ears were still recovering from the previous ones being hacked out.

Jack rose and headed out the door. I glanced at Quinn. "Do you want a gun, as well?" Jack hadn't suggested that, but I couldn't see him objecting.

"I'd rather not." He touched a hand to my back to

guide me out the door, and a warm shiver ran down my spine. But it wasn't really sexual, more a rightness. A feeling of being protected.

And that was nice.

We headed down to the armory to suit up, and ten minutes later were down in the underground parking lot climbing into unmarked Directorate cars.

The drive to Brighton was quick. Daskill's house was located in Cosham Street, which, according to those in the know—namely Quinn and Jack—was one of the area's most sought-after streets.

And that in itself had to be a pointer to the fact that he was making his money via means *other* than the aircraft-for-hire business. The current downturn in the economy meant airlines the world over were suffering from a lack of passengers. Even Quinn's business had nosedived—but he'd been around long enough to have investments in lots of different arenas. Daskill hadn't—although if he was behind the murder operation, I guess it could be said that he *had* diversified.

We pulled up several houses away, Jack in an SUV and the rest of us in a black four-door sedan that didn't look out of place in this neighborhood. The street was lined with old trees and the houses were a mix of old and new. Daskill's was the latter—a series of big white concrete and glass boxes surrounded by a huge, black concrete fence. Even from where we sat in the car, the security cameras were very noticeable. His wasn't the only house in the street that had them, either.

Most of the houses were on regular-size lots, but

Daskill had obviously bought up the residences to either side of him, because if the sheer length of the fence was anything to go by, there had to be at least an acre of land behind it.

Quinn touched his ear lightly, his expression intense as he listened to Jack speaking through the earpiece. His face held a slight sheen thanks to all the sunscreen he'd lathered on—mine probably did, too. With my skin still so sensitive to sunlight, I thought I'd better start protecting myself. I just had to hope that it didn't develop into something deadly. The one vampire condition I *didn't* want was their need to stay out of sunlight. Well, that and the need to drink blood.

I could hear Jack's voice echoing lightly, but it wasn't clear enough to understand. A second later, Quinn leaned forward and kissed me. "We're a go. Jack will contact you when I've taken down all the guards."

I ran my fingers lightly through his silky hair, taking care not to touch any skin and disturb the sunscreen. "Be careful."

"There are only four of them. Piece of cake." He smiled and winked, then climbed out of the car.

I leaned forward, watching him stroll casually toward the big black fence. The security cameras were rotating, but away rather than toward him. He glanced around, then with a leap any shifter or wolf would be proud of, disappeared over the fence.

I blew out the breath I'd been holding, and Rhoan glanced at me. "He'll be fine."

"I know. The man was a cazador, after all." And four security guards, however well trained, weren't going to present much of a problem for a man who spent hundreds of years as a hit man for the vampire council. "It doesn't stop the worry."

"Then you know what he goes through every time you walk out the door."

I raised an eyebrow. "Now, there's a case of the pot calling the kettle black."

"I was a guardian when Liander met me. He knew going in what he was getting into."

"I still worked for the Directorate. I handled the care and feeding of a boatload of vampires. That's not a risk-free job."

He raised an eyebrow. "But it doesn't exactly hold the same level of danger as being a guardian, does it?"

"No." I drew in a breath and released it slowly. "Which is why I'm talking to Jack once this job is over."

"Talking to Jack about what?" Jack said, into my ear.

I jumped. The external earpieces were so comfortable, I'd totally forgotten they were in.

"It's not important right now," I said. "Have you got any word on Quinn's progress?"

"Two guards are down, and he's just tackling the third now." He paused. "The third one is down."

"And the last?"

"Inside the main house. We can't risk trying to draw him out and alerting Daskill, so Rhoan, you slip in through the back and take care of him. Riley, your task is Daskill. He's upstairs with his wife."

Great. Just what I need to see—a bad guy having sex. "I'm gathering all security will be down by the time we get to the doors?"

"Sal's finishing it now. She reverse-coded, so it'll appear on when it's off."

"Give me a few minutes to get around the back," Rhoan said, his hand on the car door handle. "And be careful."

"If one more person says that to me," I said, an edge in my voice, "I'm going to punch them."

He merely smiled. "We just got you back. Give it a week and we'll be back to our uncaring selves."

I snorted and pushed him lightly. "Get out and go. The sooner we get this done, the sooner we can get back to the real business at hand."

The amusement fell from his eyes. He knew just what that involved. And, like me, he wasn't happy about it—even though it had become a necessity if we were ever to live free of Blake's shadow.

He touched a hand lightly to my cheek, then opened the door and climbed out. Like Quinn, he disappeared easily and quickly over the wall.

I glanced at my watch and waited a couple of minutes, then grabbed the car keys, climbed out, and locked up. This might be a posh area, but that didn't mean unlocked cars were any safer.

I shoved my hands into the pockets of my sweatshirt and strolled toward the fence. The damn thing towered over me, and, wolf or not, I had trouble just grabbing the top, let alone hauling my ass over the edge.

I *really* needed to work on my upper body strength, I thought, as I landed rather inelegantly on the other side.

The lawns were landscaped and there wasn't a blade of grass to be seen, but the shiny white rocks clashed nicely with the green and red cordylines and native wild grasses.

My skin crawled with sudden awareness, and I glanced around to see Quinn walking through the shadow provided by the towering fence. Although walking was something of a misnomer—gliding would have been more apt.

Rhoan's in the house. He stopped beside me, his gaze on the house. *Daskill and his wife are still upstairs. There is a second life-form on the ground floor.*

I cursed softly. *Besides the guard, you mean?*

Yeah. I suspect it's either the butler or the chef. I know Daskill employs both.

Lazy bastard.

Amusement played around his mouth. *The mega-rich do like their little treats. And he probably won't live long enough for them to get old.*

There was no probably about *that.*

Okay, he added, *the guard is down. Rhoan is moving to the back of the house. Time for you to go.*

I blew him a kiss, then ran across the carefully manicured garden, my steps so fast and light I didn't disturb any of the rocks.

The security box near the front door sat in the alarmed position, and I hesitated fractionally before grabbing the handle and opening the door. No alarms sounded. Sal had done her job well.

I closed the door and looked around to get my bearings. The entrance hall looked bigger in life than it had on the plans, the ceiling double height and dominated by a massive gold chandelier. Four doors led off the entrance and a glass staircase complete with a gold banister curved its way up to the first floor. The scent of unknown werewolf was coming from the living area, which was the door on my immediate right, and from the back of the house came Rhoan's familiar tang as well as the soft hint of roses. Given that it was accompanied by the mouthwatering aroma of freshly baked bread, I was betting it belong to the chef.

I headed for the stairs. Rhoan reappeared as I reached for the banister, and I raised an eyebrow in question. He raised a finger, then folded it half down. Meaning the chef was out for the count.

And if the crumbs on his shirt were anything to go by, so was whatever he was baking.

We climbed the stairs swiftly but silently. There were six doors leading off the overly large hallway, one of which was the bathroom, one a study, and the others were bedrooms. Daskill's was the last one on the left.

We crept forward, every step swallowed by the lush thickness of the carpet. Obviously, no one had told him shag pile had gone out of fashion with the Dark Ages.

There wasn't a whole lot of noise coming out of the

bedroom. Daskill and his wife were obviously quiet types. Either that, or they'd finished—although the scent of lust and desire riding the air was increasing, not fading.

I glanced over my to brother and motioned to the other side of the double door frame. He nodded and moved past me, his movements a blur as he raced across the open space.

There was still no indication that Daskill and his missus had any idea something was wrong.

Rhoan raised three fingers and began counting them down. I got my laser out but didn't fire it up. The damn things were noisy and, in the hush surrounding us, would have been too obvious.

The last finger went down. We moved as one into the room, Rhoan going to the right and me to the left. Like everything else in the house, the bedroom was white and gold. The only spot of color was Daskill's ass, and the black and silver of the guns sitting on either bedside table.

Daskill really *didn't* like to take chances.

She saw us first, and her eyes went wide. As she opened her mouth to scream, I fired up the laser and heard its echo from the other side of the room.

"Bobby Daskill," I said, slipping my free hand into my pocket and withdrawing my ID. "You're under arrest on suspicion of murder. Please move away from your wife and stand with your hands up."

For the barest of moments, he froze. Then he did the stupidest thing possible and lunged for his weapon. I

fired, as did Rhoan. The twin beams of light cut across
the room, hitting Daskill's reaching hand. The smell of
burning flesh stung the air as the lasers severed then
cauterized the first three fingers on his left hand.

His screams joined his wife's. Rhoan glanced at me,
his expression one of disgust as he shook his head and
walked forward. That's when the wife moved. One
minute she was screaming like a banshee, and the next
she had a gun in her hand and was aiming it at Rhoan's
head. There was no time for finesse. I simply shot.

I meant to get her hand, but she was moving too fast,
and the beam took off her arm instead. Her severed
limb plopped inelegantly to the bed, and the weapon—
thanks to the fact that her finger was still curled around
the trigger—fired. The bullet skimmed past Rhoan's
nose and thudded into the wall behind him.

The wife went back to screaming. High-pitched,
wailing sounds of horror, but I wasn't feeling any sympathy. Not when the bitch had just tried to kill my
brother.

He glanced at me, blinking, the tip of his nose somewhat blackened. "Damn, that was close."

"Totally." I strode forward, grabbed Daskill by the
scruff of his neck, and dragged his wobbly pink butt off
the bed. "Bobby Daskill, consider yourself under arrest. Now get your scrawny ass down those stairs."

"But I'm naked—"

"Like I care." I pushed him toward the door, my finger still on the trigger and the laser whining ominously
at his back.

Rhoan hauled the still-screaming woman up by her good arm, grabbed the sheet, and threw it roughly around her body. Then, with his hand still clamped around hers, he forced her to march forward.

We headed down the stairs, then outside. I couldn't sense Quinn near, but almost before I could form a question, his thoughts were flowing through my mind. *I'm in the car. Things were getting a little warm, even with the protection of the sunscreen and the shade of the wall.*

So do you brown or do you peel?

Brown. If a vampire burns, it usually results in the death of said vampire.

Well, I don't want you dead before I swear to you, so good move.

His laughter ran through my mind, warm and light.

Daskill had finally realized we were going out into the main street and balked as we neared the gate. But a hard nudge in the back with the laser soon put an end to that.

The two vans sat several houses away, one holding Jack and the banks of computers that were controlling Daskill's security system, and the other for the transfer of our prisoners.

The prisoner van door opened as we approached, and the stench of vampire wafted out. There were at least three guardians inside. Jack wasn't taking any chances.

We handed over our prisoners and stepped back as the door slammed shut. Even though the van was re-inforced, I could still hear the wife's screaming as the vehicle took off.

"Well, that was almost easy," Rhoan said, sounding more than a little peeved.

"And it makes a nice change," I said, rubbing my arms. The time had come to talk to Jack, and I really wasn't looking forward to it.

I can—Quinn started.

No, I said firmly. *This is for me to do.*

"Riley, Rhoan," Jack said into my ear. "Go through Daskill's house and see what you can find. Another van is on the way to take care of the guards. They'll remain neutralized until then."

Meaning Quinn had messed with their minds and told them to stay. I pressed the little earpiece and said, "I need to talk to you first, boss."

He hesitated, then said, almost reluctantly, "Come on in, then."

Rhoan gave me a smile and a quick shoulder squeeze for support, then spun around on his heel and headed back to the house. I took a deep breath that did little to calm the twisting in my belly, then strode forward determinedly.

I slid open the van door, stepping inside and shutting it quickly so there was no risk of sunlight touching Jack. Not that it would have, given he was down at the far end of the van, sitting in front of a bank of monitors.

"What is it, Riley?" he said without looking up.

"I don't want to be a guardian anymore." I said it in a rush, because any other way and the words would have stuck in my throat.

He leaned back in his chair and raised his hands,

crossing his fingers on the top of his head. There was little surprise in the green of his eyes.

"You can't leave the Directorate. The drugs are still affecting you, and we have no idea what direction the changes are likely to take."

That sick feeling in my stomach increased, rising up my throat and momentarily preventing me from breathing. It was all going to hell—all my hopes and dreams of walking away turning to ashes simply because I knew what he was saying was true. And yet, that stupid, stubborn part of me refused to give up. "But—"

"There are no buts on this," he said heavily. "We have no idea what might happen, and it's simply too dangerous for everyone around you to let you go unmonitored."

"There has to be some sort of middle ground, Jack." I said it softly, without the desperation burning through me. "I've given up so many of my hopes and dreams in the last few years that I really don't want to give up any more. I want to live long enough to see my babies grow. And we both know that isn't going to happen if I remain a guardian."

"Riley," he said, voice gentle, "you were growing weary of being my assistant when you actually were. Now that you're a trained hunter, I very much doubt you could go back so easily to office work."

Maybe. Maybe not. But he wasn't saying no outright, so there was still some degree of hope left.

"Jack, I can't continue like this. I *won't*."

"You know the choice, Riley. It's us or the military."

So much for hope. I stared at him for a moment, mouth drier than the Simpson Desert. "Is that a threat?"

He returned my stare, his green eyes showing little in the way of compassion. Not giving in, not giving up. "No. I'm merely stating your options. They haven't changed. They will never change." He paused. "The military has been keeping an eye on you."

I clenched my fists and battled to remain calm—battled *not* to show the fear clawing away at my insides. Which was useless, given that he was a vampire and would sense it regardless. He couldn't help it when my pulse was racing at a million miles an hour.

"You can't *make* me do either," I said, an edge creeping into my voice was that was part fury, part fear. "I'll fight you, I'll fight the Directorate, I'll even fight the entire Australian military if I have to."

"Riley," he said softly. "You may be a strong telepath, but so am I, and so is Director Hunter."

"And so is Quinn," I retorted. "Do not think I'll be alone in *any* battle." Because if he tried *anything* like that, he'd not only lose me, but Quinn, Rhoan, and Dia, as well.

And he knew it. The frustrated anger that just about fried my skin said as much.

"What about a compromise?" I said, desperately battling the urge to cross my fingers. To pray to the gods I didn't believe in.

"What kind of compromise?"

"You have specialist consultants on the books. Dia's one. Why can't I be another?"

"Meaning," he said slowly, "you'd be willing to come to murder scenes whenever required, to talk to souls?"

"Yes." I wouldn't like it, but I'd do it if it meant not having to risk life and limb every single day of my life as a guardian.

He studied me for a moment, as if judging my seriousness, then said, "That is a risk in itself. We both know that."

Yes, talking to souls was a risk. They could drain me to the point that I might not be strong enough to get back from their realms. But the key here was finding a solution that suited us both—and offsetting a greater risk for a smaller one was one of those.

"It's the lesser of two evils, Jack, and it gives us both something we want." And it gave me the chance of an almost normal life. It gave me the ability to raise Liander and my babies and be a steady, *regular* influence in their lives.

He studied me for several more—very long—minutes, then a small smile touched his lips. "I knew this was coming. Especially given you've found your own replacement."

Hope bubbled through me, but I stamped down on it. Hard. I knew fate well enough not to trust her so easily. "Is that a yes?"

"It's more an 'I could live with a deal like that.'" He hesitated and studied me grimly. "Which is not to say that Director Hunter *will*."

"But you'll support the idea in principle?"

"Riley, I am many things, but I am *not* stupid. And I do not want to destroy what is left of the daytime division." He smiled grimly, then added, "Nor do I wish to go to war with a man who was the finest cazador the council ever produced."

I let go a whoop they would surely have heard in Sydney, then leapt forward, throwing myself into Jack's arms. He caught me with a grunt, but his laughter ran all around me.

"Don't get your hopes too high. As I said, it'll still have to go before Director Hunter for final approval."

"I know, I know." But if Jack approved it, that was three-quarters of the battle. The Directorate might be his sister's, but the guardian division was *his*.

"Then untangle your arms from around my neck and go help your brother clean up the house. Consider it your last official duty as a guardian." He hesitated, green eyes suddenly serious. "Unless, of course, you want official status when you confront the bastard who kidnapped you."

I stepped back, my joy suddenly tempered. "We're going to do it on Jenson lands. Pack law will apply."

He half nodded. "It still won't hurt to have the Directorate behind you. After all, he kidnapped Evin and his mate, kidnapped and mind-washed you, and damn near killed Quinn. His death is slated. So, if you like, that can be your last official task."

"And it doesn't matter which way I choose to apply it?"

"I don't give a damn, as long as the bastard dies."

"He will. He has to."

Jack nodded. "Then go help your brother, and I'll get the paperwork started. For both things."

"Thanks, Jack. You're the best."

I leaned forward and kissed his cheek, and damned if he didn't blush. "Just go, and let me get some work done."

I grinned and all but bounced out of the van.

One more thing to attend to, and then my life was finally mine.

If I survived the encounter with Blake, that was.

Chapter 16

As eager as we all were to confront Blake, getting rid of him wasn't simply a matter of walking onto Jenson pack land and challenging him. We had to stop his whole damn family, because Blake was simply one poisonous head on the Medusa. Cut him off, and another would grow in his place.

And whoever replaced him would probably be even *more* hell-bent on revenge.

To end the cycle, we needed to bring down the whole lot of them. Maybe then those who didn't quite fit into the Jenson pack ideal could live free of tyranny and fear.

So we spent precious time tracking down every one of his siblings and his get. Where possible, Jack sent out vampires to read their minds and gather information. It quickly became apparent that the Jenson pack's change of fortune hadn't come from good management but rather blackmail, robbery, and even murder. And as I'd suspected some time ago, Henry Bottchelli—the man who'd hired the red Mazda driver to follow me—was one of Blake's aliases. He had several others, as did Tyson and most of his sons.

We worked practically nonstop. We gathered our evidence, we stuck our fingers into their bank accounts, and we raided their computer systems, and slowly but surely we got ready to snatch the whole damn lot of them.

When Jack wanted vengeance, he went all out. And with the force of the Directorate behind him, it was a pretty awesome sight to behold.

In the end, it took us nearly three days to get to the Northern Territory. Quinn's plane landed in Alice Springs at four forty-five, and by five, the three of us and our one bag had cleared security and we were heading out into the car park.

The air was clean and warm, and it smelled like home. I inhaled deeply, loving the crispness of it, the way the flavors and the scents suddenly seemed all that much sharper.

It would be nice to come back here occasionally. Maybe once Blake had been dealt with, we could. After all, we now had a reason. We now had family.

You always had family, Quinn commented. *It's just that it wasn't by birth and blood.*

He was right, of course.

When you hang around on this Earth as long as I have, you get to know a thing or two. He smiled, but his dark eyes were serious. *Whatever happens after today, Liander and I will always be here.*

I know. And it warmed the places deep inside that had been cold and empty for so long.

A large black SUV pulled up. Evin and Lyndal climbed out. Evin smiled when he saw us, but then surprise crossed his features.

"No guns?"

"We don't need them," Rhoan said, his voice calm. Yet an undercurrent of violence and excitement rode through every word and motion. The switch to guardian mode hadn't been flicked yet, but he wasn't far from it.

"But the minute we enter pack land, he'll know," Lyndal commented softly. "He'll have shooters in place."

"Which is why," I said, opening the SUVs back door, "we asked you to rent this type of truck rather than just a car. You know all the locations of the border guards. You, Lyndal, and Quinn are going to go to each and every one of them and take them out as we stroll onto pack land."

His frown increased. "But we don't use SUVs to move from location to location. There's no need to, when a good run is the best way to get anywhere or to finish a shift. They'll know something is up the minute they spot it."

"Blake's still doing his surprise inspections, isn't he?" Rhoan asked, resting a hip on the side of the SUV and crossing his arms.

It wasn't really a question, because we'd already gleaned the answer from the minds of his family.

"Yeah, but—"

"But," I said, "a recent car accident mangled his leg, and even though he shifted to heal it, infection has set into the bone and he's recently undergone a series of operations to fix it. He's been ordered to keep off his leg as much as possible, in either wolf or human form."

Which is why he'd been limping when he'd confronted me at the truck accident. And why he'd looked so beaten up.

Lyndal stared at us. "How do you know all that, when even we didn't?"

"We're guardians," Rhoan said blithely. "We know all sorts of shit."

Evin raised an eyebrow, amusement warring with concern. "That doesn't alter the fact that the minute we get close enough, they'll know we're not Blake and warn the pack."

"Which is where this comes in," Quinn said, and raised the bag he was carrying. "It's a jammer. The minute I switch it on, all phones and radios will cease to work. And as we drive up, they *will* see Blake, not us."

Evin stared at him. "You can do that?"

"Easily."

"Wow." He swallowed. Obviously, no one had ever told him just how powerful old vampires could be.

"Besides," I added, "Rhoan and I walking onto the pack land will catch their attention and give you time. Blake won't order us to be shot immediately. He'll want the whole pack to witness our defeat."

"But—"

"It'll be fine. *We'll* be fine. And you and Lyndal will be safe—Quinn will make sure of it." I glanced at my watch. We were cutting it fine. Jack had his end of the whole show—arresting all various siblings and off-spring who weren't currently on pack land—set to go at six, and it'd take us nearly an hour to get onto Jenson lands. "Now stop worrying, get in the car, and get us there."

"I'm not worried about me and Lyndal," he said, but climbed into the car and started it up.

It was a quiet journey out. I sat in the back between Lyndal and Quinn, with Quinn's arm draped loosely around my shoulders and his fingers gently caressing my arm. It was comforting, that touch, and yet it gave me strength.

I'd spent most of my life avoiding the confrontation I was now driving toward, and it was damned good to know that I wasn't doing it alone.

Was I scared?

Hell, yeah.

I'd seen wolf fights. I was well aware of how bloody they could get. How deadly. And while I had faith in both my fighting skills and Rhoan's, I wasn't trusting fate. I wasn't blithely walking in there thinking every-thing would go our way.

We would both get hurt doing this, I knew that.

But deep inside me, there also burned a hunger to be done with it.

This was the last step in washing my hands of my old life. From now on, I could focus on me, Quinn,

Rhoan and Liander, and the pack and the life we were creating for ourselves.

And more than anything else, that's what drove me past the fear.

The flat red landscape soon gave way to red outcrops of rocks and the soaring hills that filled pack land. The twisting anxiety in my stomach grew the closer we got, and by the time Evin pulled over to the side of the road, I really thought I was going to be sick.

"This is it," Evin said, looking back at me through the rearview mirror. "We're five minutes away from our border. We need to cut inland here if we're to get to the first outpost."

I took a deep breath and released it slowly. "Then let's do this."

Quinn opened the back door and climbed out. The evening air swirled around me, thick with the rawness of nature. I took another deep, steadying breath, then climbed out.

"Good luck," he whispered, his arms going around my waist as he gently kissed me. "I won't tell you to be careful because, given what's about to happen, that's a pretty useless sentiment. But do try to not get too slashed up. The full moon is in a couple of days, and we have a sunset wedding."

"I have no intention of either missing our wedding or being too messed up to enjoy our first night as a mated couple." I kissed him again. "Although you do realize that, since I'll be a wolf once the moon rises, it's not going to be the usual human type of night."

He smiled and ran a finger lightly down my cheek.

"We have the rest of our lives to celebrate sexually. That night will be a celebration of an event I never thought would happen."

"Riley," Rhoan said softly behind me.

I kissed Quinn quickly one more time, then spun around and looked back at Evin. "Quinn will tell you when it's safe to approach the compound."

He nodded. "I'll see you then."

I glanced at Lyndal, who was looking decidedly nervous, then caught Rhoan's hand and walked away without looking back. When we crossed the invisible line that marked the beginnings of pack land, something within me stirred—an eagerness, a hunger that, until now, had remained in the background.

The wolf within me wanted this.

Wanted it *bad*.

We let go of each other and broke into a run. We didn't run at top speed, simply because we actually wanted to be spotted. Blake needed to know we were coming—and give the all clear—before Quinn, Evin, and Lyndal got to the scouts and put them out of action.

The sensation of being watched soon began to grow, until my whole neck itched with it. The tension emanating from Rhoan suggested he felt it, too.

I kept running, but my gaze swept the barren landscape, looking for watchers that Evin mightn't have known about. After all, Blake would more than likely have introduced stricter security measures once his plot against me had started. He was smart enough to realize the Directorate would retaliate the minute they found any connection.

It's just a shame he wasn't intelligent enough to keep his anger and need for revenge to himself, rather than actually acting upon it.

We started up the long slope that was the final division between us and the place we'd grown up. My stomach was still in knots, and my heart was beating nine to the dozen. We reached the top and, as one, slowed.

Below us lay the valley of our childhood. In many respects, it looked more like a large ranch with lots of outbuildings than a city like Dunedan. The old, wood-shingled buildings blended in with the red of the surrounding countryside and contrasted sharply against the bright pockets of green—the football oval, the cemetery, and the few acres surrounding the dam that had always been the swimming hole for every kid who grew up here.

There were people out and about but, as yet, it didn't appear that we'd been noticed. My gaze went almost with a will of its own to the ramshackle but beautiful old house that sat one behind—and slightly to the side—of the main gathering house. That's where we'd grown up. It had been our grandfather's place, but never really our home, as much as our mom had tried to make it seem otherwise. Our grandfather had tolerated us, he'd fed us, and he'd educated us, but he'd never really loved us. We were half-breeds and, in his eyes, a tarnish on the Jenson name.

Maybe that was why he'd turned a blind eye to so

much of what Blake and his family had done to us over the years. He'd always stopped it from going too far, but I think that had been more for Mom's sake than from any real need to protect us.

Mom.

For the first time since all this had begun, I actually began to think about her. Neither of us had seen her for well over ten years. We didn't communicate, didn't share birthdays or Christmas or Easter.

And yet I knew she'd loved us.

How was she going to react when she saw us? When she realized what we were going to do?

How the hell were we going to react when we saw her?

I shivered and rubbed my arms. Rhoan hugged me fiercely. Then, without saying a word, he wrapped his fingers around mine and started off down the hill.

We were spotted about halfway down. Initially it was nothing more than people briefly pausing for a look, then getting on with whatever they were doing, but word of who we were must have gotten around fairly quickly. By the time we'd hit the valley bottom, we'd drawn quite a crowd.

But it was a silent one, and that was weird.

Rhoan released my fingers as we neared the first of the outbuildings, but he kept close, our arms brushing each other as we walked. The tension that had been riding him earlier had gone, and he walked with the loose-limbed ease of a predator who knows his prey cannot get away.

I wished I could imitate him, but it simply wasn't possible.

Scents swirled around us, rich with familiarity and memories. I closed my mind to them, concentrating on the silent figures watching us, wondering what they were thinking but not daring to find out. Their expressions were closed, unreadable, and for one uneasy moment, I wondered if we'd misjudged the pack. Wondered if we'd bitten off more than we could chew.

We continued up a slight incline, heading toward the main gathering hall. Blake could have been anywhere, but the hall was the seat of power for the pack. It's where business was handled, where justice was meted out, and where major events were celebrated.

If he knew we were coming—and he surely did by now—then this is where he'd be.

Of course, our confrontation would not happen in the hall itself, but rather in the arena behind it. It was here where the blood disputes were handled and where the challengers to leadership were heard and decided.

Blake had killed my grandfather and taken over the leadership there, and now it was where he would meet his own death.

Behind us, the crowd continued to grow, sweeping in behind us and effectively cutting off our exit. The scent of wolf and home and anticipation swirled around me, filling my lungs and twisting my stomach. I flexed my fingers, but it didn't do much to help me relax.

Then two figures appeared out of the building above

us. Both were males, broad of shoulders and strong of build. Both wore contemptuous expressions.

Blake and his brother Tyson.

I glanced at my watch. It was after six. Jack's half of the operation had already swung into action. If Blake had any suspicion that his empire was crumbling around his ears, he wouldn't be standing there so calmly.

We stopped when there were still ten feet or so between us, with Rhoan slightly behind me. This was my gig, my revenge. He was here as my second and my backup, though in truth he was a better fighter than me. And he'd need to be to take out Tyson, who was almost half his width again.

"You trespass, wolf," Blake said, his voice booming out across the windswept silence.

"And you, Blake Jenson, stand accused of fraud, kidnap, and murder." I took a piece of paper out of my pocket and threw it at his feet. "You may read the charges if you wish."

He didn't bother looking at the paper, just left it fluttering at his feet. "So you're here to arrest me?" His expression was mocking. Contemptuous. "You and I both know that pack land rights give you no such power."

"Pack land rights give the *police* no power," I corrected. "But we're not police. And we're not here to arrest you."

"Then what are you here for?"

"To carry out the sentence."

A murmur went through the crowd, rising and

falling like a tide. Neither Blake nor Tyson seemed concerned.

"As I said, pack law gives me protection. Kill me, and my family will see to it that you, the Directorate, and everyone in your family pays for it—legally and monetarily."

I smiled thinly, my expression no doubt as contemptuous as his. "Right now, both your family and Tyson's—every son, daughter, brother, and sister—are being rounded up by Directorate personnel. Their fate very much depends on just how deeply they've been involved in your schemes. Personally, I wouldn't care if they wiped out every last trace of your DNA from this earth."

That wiped the smiles off their faces. Blake clenched his fists and took a step forward. "You wouldn't dare."

I stepped forward, meeting him glare for glare. "I warned you what would happen if you came after us again. And this is just the beginning."

"What do you mean?" Tyson said, and just for a moment, there was doubt and uncertainty in his expression. But Tyson, for all his size, had never been half the powerhouse that his brother was.

"I mean," I said softly, my gaze not wavering from Blake's, "that I challenge you to *ad vitam aeternam*." Which was an old Latin phrase that meant *to eternal life*.

In other words, a fight to the death.

His eyes widened ever so briefly, then he threw his head back and laughed.

Laughed.

The man was a bigger fool than I'd thought.

No one else seemed to find it funny. Not even his brother, whose expression now wavered between uncertainty and fear. Tyson obviously had some sense of the trouble they were in. Blake didn't.

"Riley, Riley, Riley," Blake said, wiping at his eyes as if there were tears of mirth there. "I couldn't have asked for a better solution to our problem."

I raised an eyebrow. "How so?"

"Because I've been going out of my way not to kill you, and here you hand me the perfect opportunity with no chance of repercussion from the Directorate." He shook his head, as if he couldn't quite believe his luck. "I shall enjoy ripping your throat out, in much the same way as I enjoyed ripping out your grandfather's."

"If you last that long, you're welcome to try," I said softly, and stepped back.

Rhoan took my place. "Tyson Jenson, I challenge you to *ad vitam aeternam*."

Blake frowned. "You can't. He now no longer lives on these lands—"

"No, he runs his own pack in Queensland," Rhoan said smoothly. "But he is here, and therefore falls under the rules and regulations of this pack. We checked."

Blake's expression darkened. "I know the rules—"

"Where is your son Lodden?" Rhoan cut in.

Blake's fists clenched. "He played no part in my vengeance. He has no role in the arena."

"The jury is out as to whether he was involved in what happened to Riley, but we have evidence of him being fully immersed in your other schemes." Rhoan paused, but Blake didn't waste breath denying it. "So he has the choice. He can take his chances in the arena with me, or he can be arrested and risk pleading his case to the Directorate."

And if the Directorate—in the guise of Jack—thought his crimes were bad enough, then Lodden *would* die regardless. No ifs, buts, or maybes.

"Where is he, Blake?"

There was a flicker in his eyes, but it was too fast to identify. It could have been fear, it could have been cunning. Maybe even both.

"He isn't here. He's checking the boundaries."

Rhoan glanced at me, one eyebrow raised. He didn't believe Blake any more than I did. But it didn't matter. Lodden could hide for now. We'd find him easily enough later.

"What is your answer, Tyson?" Rhoan said.

He had no choice, we both knew that. Once a challenge was issued, there was no walking away from it.

"Yes. The answer is yes." Tyson shook his head and gave his brother an almost bitter look. "You've killed us all with your need for vengeance."

Blake swung around to face him. "We will *win* this. Have no doubt of that." He glanced back at us, and spat. The globule landed at Rhoan's feet. "We've beaten this trash before. We'll do it again."

Rhoan merely smiled. There was nothing warm or pleasant about it. "Then let's get to it."

"Yes, let's," Blake said, all arrogance. "I have somewhere to be later this evening."

He spun around, presenting his back to us, showing

his contempt. I shared another glance with my brother, saw the slight twitch of his fingers as temptation called, saw the deeper hunger and anticipation in his eyes. But he didn't say anything, and neither did I. We simply followed our nemesis around the meeting hall to the arena at the back.

There was already a crowd gathered there. My gaze swept the sea of faces, but I couldn't see anyone familiar. If our mom was there, she'd changed beyond recognition.

But I very much suspected she wasn't there. She'd no doubt been forced to watch Blake rip her father apart, and she probably had little faith that we could win this one. No one in their right mind would want to see such violence again.

The arena was just over an acre in size, and positioned on a slight incline. The ground was strewn with boulders and broken trees, and no grass ever grew in the soil. It was if the blood of all those who had fought and died in this place had made the earth barren.

The gate slid open as we approached.

"Left corner," Blake said, as the four of us walked through.

The left corner was prime position. It was close to water and situated at the top of the incline. We'd known Blake would claim it, even though as challengers, the call was legally ours.

We trudged down the hill, watched by the silent crowd, surrounded by their anticipation and tension. I flexed my shoulders, trying to not let it get to me.

"We need to end this fast," Rhoan said softly. "There

can be no chances, no mistakes, and definitely no doubt in anyone's mind of the consequences should anything like this ever happen again."

"Blake's ruled for years, and he knows this arena well." I shook free of my jacket as we neared the other end of the arena. "And he packs more weight than me. That'll tell in this fight."

"He may be bigger, but you're faster and stronger." He gripped my arm. "You'll be fine."

"I know." I also knew that it wasn't going to be as easy as Rhoan believed.

I rolled my shoulders, flexed my legs. Prepared, as much as anyone could prepare for the brutality that was a wolf fight.

Halfway up the arena, a green flag went up. A horn sounded immediately—its note haunting and poignant—informing all those not already aware that *ad vitam aeternam* was about to start. As the final notes drifted away on the breeze, the flag dropped.

Rhoan and I jumped forward as one, flowing from one shape to another as we raced up the hill. Blake and Tyson were already halfway down, suggesting they'd jumped the flag, their growls and fury staining the crisp air.

I swerved to the left, getting out of Rhoan's way, running at an angle across the hill. Blake moved to intercept me, taking several gigantic strides before he leapt. I met him in the air, our chests crashing together, the sound cracking across the arena like a whip. I bared my teeth and lunged at his face, snapping and snarling. His teeth slid across my nose, tearing into flesh as we dropped to the ground. I dove away, twisted around, rearing up on my back legs as he came at me. Again our chests met as my paws clawed his side and my teeth sank into the ruff of his neck. He pulled away, but I hung on, twisting and shaking my head, trying to tear flesh. He snarled and slashed with his jaws, his canines ripping into my ear. I released him, jumped back. Felt the blood coursing down my neck, thick and warm.

Saw, out of the corner of my eye, the glint of silver on a distant rooftop.

A rifle.

Aimed at Rhoan, not me.

Fury swept me. I should have *known* the bastard wasn't going to play by the rules.

Blake lunged. I twisted around, rolling under his leap, then ran, with every ounce of strength I had, toward Rhoan. Heard the crack of a gunshot, and dove, shifting shape as I did so, straight at my brother. I hit him just as he was leaping at Tyson, heard his grunt of surprise as I grabbed him with both arms and rolled us both out of the way. Tyson flew over the top of us, but Blake was right behind.

The bullet that had been aimed at Rhoan's head went through my leg instead. It was silver, and it burned like a bitch, but it also went in one side and came right out the other without appearing to do any serious damage. For once, fate was giving me a break.

"Sniper on the rooftop," I said, releasing his midriff and rolling to my feet. He scrambled to his, meeting Blake's charge chest first as the big red wolf leapt, knocking him to one side before twisting around to meet Tyson's charge.

I kept in human form and ran, every sense I had focused on the sniper. He was aiming again. There was only one way to stop him. I threw open my shields and hit him with every ounce of telepathic power I had. I felt the brief resistance of a nanowire before it shattered under the force of my attack and I plunged into his mind. This was no gentle attack. It was hard and fast and brutal, and his mind snapped as easily as the nanowire.

Lodden Jenson wasn't dead, but his mind was.

I bent, scooped up a rock, then twisted around and threw it at Blake. I moved so fast he didn't even see it coming, and the rock smashed into his face full force, shattering his nose and jaw. His furious growls turned to a high sound of pain and he stuttered to a halt, shaking his head to clear the blood that was spurting into his eyes.

"We gave you the chance to play fair, Blake. We were obeying the rules of the arena when, by law, we could have just walked in here and killed you both. You chose to fight dirty, so that's exactly how I'll kill you."

And with that, I shifted shape and lunged at him. He saw me at the last minute and jumped away, but anger fueled my movements now and he was far too slow. I hit his side and sent him tumbling. He rolled, desperately trying to regain his feet and get away, but I hit him again, knocking him back down.

And then I repeated the process, again and again,

driving home the point that he couldn't get up and couldn't beat me.

He kept trying, I'll give him that.

I hit him one more time, then shifted shape, crossing my arms as I watched him slowly climb to his feet. Across the arena I was aware of low growling, then there was a godawful howl that cut off abruptly.

Rhoan, finishing off Tyson. It was just me and Blake now.

He climbed to his paws, his head snaking low and broken teeth bared. There was anger in his eyes and tension in his body. He was waiting for the final blow.

"As I said, you started this dirty, so I intend to finish it that same way. Blake Jenson, shift shape." The words were barely out of my mouth when I hit him with every ounce of psychic strength I had left. It crashed through the barriers of his nanowire and swept into his mind. His eyes widened a fraction before the fist of my thoughts wrapped around his. *Change shape,* I whispered into his mind. *Become human.*

He had no choice. His fury lashed around me, useless, impotent, as his body shifted from one form to another. In human form, his face looked more battered, and his gray eyes gleamed with maliciousness and fury. But he couldn't move. My grip on his mind was too strong.

I walked forward until I was nose-to-nose with the man.

"This is for our childhood," I said softly. "For the innocence you snatched away."

I raised a hand and chopped it across his neck. Felt

muscle and flesh give away as his throat collapsed inward. He made a low sound of pain, but he still couldn't move. Couldn't fight.

Part of me wanted to end it swiftly, to just break his neck and walk away from him and everything bad he represented. But I couldn't.

I needed this vengeance. Hated it, but needed it.

"And for my mother, who had no recourse against your treatment of us; for my grandfather, who was an old man when you slaughtered him in this arena; and for my stepbrother, whose mate you kidnapped and tortured. For all of them, I give you the inglorious justice of being killed in the arena in human form." I paused, letting my words sink in. Watching the hatred and fury and finally fear roll through his eyes and his mind. "Maybe you will find the hell in afterlife that you gave us in life, Blake."

And with that, I hit him a final time, crushing his larynx and breaking his neck. He dropped like a stone, dead before he actually hit the ground.

I took a deep breath and released it slowly, then looked up.

Straight into my mother's eyes.

She was standing at the fence, her face serene and her gray eyes giving little away. I might have been a stranger for all the emotion she was showing, and I guess in many respects I was. After all, I was still a teenager when I'd left. Now I was an adult, and a trained killer besides.

But she hadn't changed all that much—there were a

few more lines around her eyes and mouth, and perhaps a little gray in the red of her hair, but otherwise she was still very much as I remembered her.

I continued to stare at her, unsure what to do, what to say. Unsure if I even wanted to say or do anything. Awareness prickled across my skin, and I knew without looking that Rhoan was approaching. He stopped beside me, his fingers weaving through mine, then he, too, stared at the woman who had given us life.

After a moment, she smiled—a short, warm smile that said more in the few seconds it appeared than any words ever could.

I took another shuddering breath and felt like the weight of the world had lifted off my shoulders.

The horn rang out again, haunting, mournful. As the last notes died away, I said, not raising my voice, "By this death, and by right of *ad vitam aeternam,* I now lead this pack."

My gaze swept around them. No one looked away. No one countered or objected. They were all tense, waiting. It made me wonder just what Blake had told them about us.

I continued on in the same soft tone. "And my first order of business is this: The Jenson pack will no longer suffer the rule of one man, or one wolf. By my right of leadership, I declare that from now on, the Jenson pack will be ruled by a council of three."

A murmur ran through the crowd, a sound that was excitement and satisfaction and surprise all mixed together. For a pack that had been ruled for so long by tyranny, being given the right to have a say had to come as a complete shock.

"I hereby declare that Evin and Rayanne Jenson will rule in my stead until formal elections can be organized and held. These *will* happen within two months." I paused, my gaze sweeping the arena, searching for my stepbrother. He and Lyndal were standing near the gate, and there were tears in Evin's eyes. We hadn't told him this part of the plan. "Evin Jenson, do you accept the duty?"

He stood up a little straighter, his eyes shining. "I do."

My gaze returned to my mother's. "And Rayanne? Do you accept the position?"

"In honor of my father, who would be so proud of what his grandchildren have done here today in this arena, I most certainly do."

Tears stung my eyes and I had to blink them back. *Proud* was a word I'd never thought to hear when it came to our grandfather and us.

Rhoan squeezed my hand lightly, and I cleared my throat. "Then I formally step down from the leadership and hand over control to you both."

A roar erupted, the sound almost deafening. Rhoan tugged me into his arms and hugged me fiercely. "It's done," he said. "We made it."

I didn't reply immediately, just held on to him as reaction set in and my body shook. After a while, the awareness that someone was near grew and I pulled away, turning to see Evin and Lyndal.

"Come and meet your brother and sisters," he said softly, then spun around and walked away.

"Brother and sisters," Rhoan said, a silly grin on his face as he glanced at me. "How damn good does it feel to say that?"

"Brilliant," I said, as we followed Evin.

And it *was* brilliant. This place might not be home anymore, but we had *family*.

Finally, after all those years in the wilderness, we belonged somewhere.

Epilogue

The wind meandered through the treetops, filling the dusk with the whisper of leaves. The mountain air was cool, fresh with the recent rain and rich with the humus of the forest.

I walked through the trees, my bare feet sinking into the grass and leaving a trail of wet prints behind me.

In a couple of hours, the full moon would rise and I would become a wolf.

But before then, before the sun had fully set, there was the time of promises.

Soon Quinn would become mine, and I would become his.

It was all I could do not race up the remainder of this hill, to where he and Rhoan and Liander waited, to say the words that would bind us as one forever.

The only thing that could have made this night

more perfect would have been for Rhoan and Liander to perform the ceremony alongside us. But Rhoan was still refusing, and Liander wouldn't push. He understood Rhoan's reasons. We all did, even if we didn't agree with them.

But I wasn't about to spoil this night by dwelling on such matters.

Not when I was about to commit to the man of my dreams.

My pulse was racing and my heart was light, and every now and again the sheer force of it all had my feet breaking into a happy little dance.

High above the treetops, the sky was a blaze of color, and though the moon had yet to crest the horizon, the heat of her was in the air. Her music sang through my veins—a richness that was sweet and intoxicating. The change would come with darkness, but before it did, our promises would be made.

I walked up the rest of the hill. The last of the day's sunlight broke through the trees as I did, warming the clearing ahead and spotlighting the three men who waited there.

Rhoan and Liander stood to one side, their arms entwined and grins as silly as my own on their faces. Quinn stood in the middle, as naked as I was despite what he'd said earlier. And oh, he was beautiful. Simply beautiful.

He smiled as I stopped in front of him, and briefly reached out to caress my cheek. I pressed into his touch and silently said, *Do you know all the words?*

They have been very firmly drummed into my brain by

your brother and his lover, he replied. *They made sure no mistakes would be made.*

They'd made sure I would make no mistakes, as well, hammering the words into my still somewhat faulty memory banks. Despite Quinn's best efforts, not all the past had been recovered. Some of it would remain forever gone. But the past no longer mattered. The here, the now, and the future did.

Good, I replied softly. *I did threaten to cook for them for the next year if things went awry.*

His laughter was like quicksilver through my thoughts, bright and shiny. Then he dropped his hand and bowed formally.

I watched him, struggling to contain my joy, struggling to reach the seriousness this ceremony required.

"Does my lover know what night this is?" I said softly.

His eyes shone like black jewels in the dusk, filled with such warmth and love that it threatened to steal my breath and words away.

"It is the night of the full moon," he returned solemnly. "The night of promises."

I stepped forward, pressing my body against his. Feeling in the no-longer-slow beat of his heart an echo of my excitement. Feeling in the rigid heat of his erection the equal of my desire. "The night of destiny."

The air stirred around us, running with slivers of energy that raised the hairs at the nape of my neck.

"You are my heart, my soul," he said, his arms going around my waist and holding me tightly.

"As you are mine," I repeated. The magic in the air

got stronger, thrumming through the forest, matching the rhythm of our breathing, matching the beating of our hearts.

"Dance with me, this night and for the rest of our nights," he said. "For as long as the moon shines in the sky and for as long as we live underneath her."

I shifted my stance slightly, readying myself for the more intimate requirements of the ceremony. "In her name, I offer you my body."

Desire and something else—something more ethereal and powerful—swirled around us, warming my heart, tugging at my soul. The heat of him slid inside of me, so deeply that it felt like he was claiming every single inch of me. And lord, it felt *good*.

"In her power," he said, as he slowly began to rock inside of me, "I offer you my heart."

The energy in the air was becoming fiercer, burning across my skin, making all the little hairs stand up on end.

"In her shadow, I offer you my soul." My words were breathless, almost inaudible, lost to the pleasurable assault on my senses and the thrumming in the air. It didn't matter. The magic in the night heard and acknowledged it.

His hands slid down to my rear, gripping my butt fiercely, holding my body tightly against his as his movements became more urgent.

"Do you accept the gift of my seed?" he growled.

His thrusting was deep and hard and urgent, and the world was spinning, burning, with power, until it felt like there was no separation between any of us, that our flesh, the magic, the moon, and the night were all one being.

"Yes," I gasped. "Do you accept the binding of the moon and the promises we have made on the night?"

"Yes," he cried. "Yes!"

The words were barely said when he came, his body going rigid against mine, the force of his release tearing my name from his throat. Heat and power and magic exploded around us, through us, and my climax came in that moment, stealing all thought and plunging me into an abyss that was sheer and unadulterated bliss.

I rested my forehead against his, desperately trying to catch my breath, desperately trying to ignore the rising heat of the oncoming night. I would change soon, but there were still words to be said.

So I took a deep breath and raised my head, staring into the beautiful dark pools that were his eyes. "May the moon bless this union and grant us a long life together."

He smiled and gently brushed the sweaty strands of hair away from my forehead. "And what the moon has bound, let no man or woman sunder."

He leaned forward and kissed me. Gently, sweetly. Then he bent and gathered a small, silk-wrapped package by his feet. "And now, for the human part of the ceremony." He opened the silk, revealing two identical, black onyx rings. He plucked the smaller of the two free and slid it onto my finger. "With this ring, I thee wed."

I smiled and repeated the process. Then I flung myself

into his arms and said, "You can't get away from me now, vampire. You're mine until eternity ends."

"And a better place to live and die I couldn't think of."

"Run with us tonight."

"Oh, I intend to. No bride of mine is spending her wedding night with her brother and his lover."

I laughed and kissed him, with all the fierce joy in my heart.

From behind us came a whoop of delight, then suddenly Rhoan and Liander were all over us, hugging and kissing and crying.

It was the perfect way to start our new lives together. As a family, as a pack.

But as the call of the moon got fiercer and fiercer, and the thrum of the change began to tingle across our skins, Liander made the night just that little bit more perfect.

"Here," he said, and handed me a small photo.

I took it and looked at it, but wasn't really able to make sense of the odd black-and-white image. "What is it?" I asked, looking up.

"Those," he said with a grin that lit up his entire face, "are our babies. Riley Jenson, you and I are having twins."

At long last, Keri Arthur's riveting
Myth and Magic series
continues with

Mercy Burns

Coming soon from Piatkus

Read on for a special preview . . .

Mercy Burns

"We'll have you out in a minute, ma'am. Just keep still a while longer."

The voice rolled across the gray mist enshrouding my mind—a soothing sound that brought no comfort, only confusion. Why would he say I shouldn't move?

And why was he saying it just to me? Why wasn't he saying anything to Rainey, who'd been driving the car?

Ignoring the advice, I shifted, trying to get more comfortable, trying to *feel*. Pain shot through my side, spreading out in heated waves across my body and reverberating through my brain. The sensation was oddly comforting even as it tore a scream from my throat.

If I could feel, then I wasn't dead.

Should I be?

Yes, something inside me whispered. *Yes.*

I swallowed heavily, trying to ease the dryness in my

throat. What the hell had happened to us? And why did it suddenly feel like I was missing hours of my life?

The thing that was digging into my side felt jagged and fat, like a serrated knife with a thicker, heavier edge, yet there were no knives in the car. People like me and Rainey didn't need knives or guns or any other sort of human weapon, because we were born with our own. And it was just as dangerous, just as accurate, as any gun or knife.

So why did it feel like I had a knife in my side?

I tried to open my eyes, suddenly desperate to see where I was, to find Rainey, to understand what was going on. But I couldn't force them open and I had no idea why.

Alarm snaked through the haze, fueling my growing sense that something was *very* wrong.

I sucked in a deep breath, trying to keep calm, trying to keep still as the stranger had advised. The air was cool, yet sunshine ran through it, hinting that dawn had passed and that the day was already here. But that *couldn't* be right. Rainey and I had been driving through sunset, not sunrise, enjoying the last rays before the night stole the heat from us.

Moisture rolled down the side of my cheek. Not a tear; it was too warm to be a tear.

Blood.

There was blood on my face, blood running through my hair. My stomach clenched and the fear surged to new heights, making it difficult to breathe. What the hell had happened? And where the hell was Rainey?

Had we been in some sort of accident?

No, came the answer from the foggy depths of my mind. *This was no accident.*

Memories surged at the thought, though the resulting images were little more than fractured flashes mixed with snatches of sound, as if there were bits my memory couldn't—or wouldn't—recall. There was the deep, oddly familiar voice on the phone who'd given us our first decent clue in weeks. And Rainey's excitement over the possible lead—our chance to discover not only what had happened to her sister, but also to everyone else who had once lived in the town of Stillwater. Our mad, off-key singing as we'd sped through the mountains, heading back to San Francisco and our meeting with the man who just might hold some answers.

Then the truck lights that had appeared out of nowhere and raced toward us. The realization that the driver wasn't keeping to his own side of the road, that he was heading directly for us. Rainey's desperate, useless attempts to avoid him. The screeching, crumpling sound of metal as the truck smashed into us, sending us spinning. The screaming of tires as Rainey stomped on the brakes, trying to stop us from being shunted through the guard rail. The roar of the truck's engine being gunned and a second, more crushing, sideways blow that buckled the doors and forced us through the very railing we'd been so desperate to avoid. The fear and the panic and the realization that we couldn't get out, couldn't get free, as the car dropped over the ledge and smashed into the rocks below, rolling over, and over, and over . . .

The sound of sobbing shattered the reeling images—deep, sobbing gasps that spoke of pain and fear. Mine. I sought desperately to gain some control, to quiet the sobs and suck down some air. Hysteria wouldn't help. Hysteria *never* helped.

Something pricked my arm. A needle. I wanted to tell them that whatever they were giving me probably wouldn't work because human medicine almost never did on us, but the words stuck somewhere in my throat. Not because I couldn't speak, but because I'd learned the hard way never to say anything that might hint to the humans that they were not alone in this world.

And yet, despite my certainty that the drug wouldn't work, my awareness seemed to strengthen. I became conscious of the hiss of air and of the screech and groan of metal being forced apart. Close by, someone breathed heavily; I could smell his sweat and fear. Further away was the murmur of conversation, the rattle of chains, and the forlorn sighing of the wind. It had an echo, making it sound as if we were on the edge of a precipice.

What was absent was Rainey's sweet, summery scent. I should have been able to smell her. In the little hatchback there wasn't much distance between the passenger seat and the driver's, yet I had no sense of her.

Fear surged anew and I raised a hand, ignoring the sharp, angry stabbing in my side as I swiped at my eyes. Something flaked away and a crack of warm light penetrated. I swiped again, then a hand grabbed mine, the fingers cool and strong. I struggled against the grip but couldn't break free, and that scared me even more. He was human, and I wasn't. Not entirely. There was no way on this earth he should have been able to restrain me so easily.

"Don't," he said, gravelly voice calm and soothing, showing no trace of the fear I could smell on him. "There's a cut above your eye and you'll only make the bleeding worse."

It couldn't get worse, I wanted to say. And I meant the situation, not the wound. Yet that little voice inside me whispered that the pain wasn't over yet, that there was a whole lot more to come.

I clenched my fingers against the stranger's, suddenly needing the security of his touch. At least it was something real in a world that had seemingly gone mad.

The screeching of metal stopped, and the thick silence was almost as frightening. Yet welcome. If only the pounding in my head would stop. . . .

"Almost there, ma'am. Just keep calm a little longer."

"Where . . . " My voice came out little more than a harsh whisper and my throat burned in protest. I swallowed heavily and tried again. "Where is Rainey?"

He hesitated. "Your friend?"

"Yes."

His hesitation lasted longer. "Let's just concentrate on getting you out and safe."

There was something in his voice that had alarm

bells ringing. An edge that spoke of sorrow and death and all those things I didn't want to contemplate or believe.

"Where is she?" I said, almost desperately. "I need to know she's okay."

"She's being taken care of by someone else," he said, and I sensed the lie in his words.

No, I thought. *No!*

Rainey had to be alive. *Had* to be. She wasn't just my friend, she was my strength, my courage, and my confidante. She'd hauled me out of more scrapes than I could remember. She *couldn't* be gone.

Fear and disbelief surged. I tore my hand from his and scrubbed urgently at my eyes. Warmth began to flow anew, but I was finally able to see.

And what I saw was the crumpled steering wheel, the smashed remains of the window, the smears of blood on the jagged, twisted front end of the car.

No, no, NO!

She couldn't be dead. She *couldn't*. I'd survived, and she was stronger—tougher—than me. How could she die? How could that be possible?

And then I saw something else.

Bright sunlight.

Dawn had well and truly passed.

That's why my rescuer had been so vague about Rainey. They couldn't find her. And no matter how much they looked, they never would. The flesh of a dead dragon incinerated at the first touch of sunrise.

I began to scream then, and there was nothing anyone could do to make me stop. Because they didn't understand what a dragon dying unaccompanied at dawn meant.

I did. And it tore me apart.

Though in the end, I *did* stop—but only because the pain of being wrenched free of the twisted, broken wreck finally swept me into unconsciousness.

I left the hospital as soon as I was physically able.

The staff had tried to make me stay. They'd tried to convince me that one day after an operation to remove a six-inch piece of steel from my side, I should be flat on my back and recovering, not strolling around like there was nothing wrong with me.

But they didn't understand what I was. I couldn't have stayed there even if I'd wanted to, and not just because they would have noticed how fast I healed and started asking questions.

No, the real reason was Rainey.

Her soul still had a chance to move on.

The souls of dragons who died without someone to pray for them at sunrise were destined to roam this earth forever—ghosts who could never move on, never feel, and never experience life again. But those who had died *before* their time had one small lifeline. If I caught and killed those responsible for Rainey's demise within seven days of her death, I could then pray for her soul on the rise of the eighth day and she would be able to move on.

I had five of those seven days left, and there was no

way on this Earth I was going to waste them lying in a hospital bed. No matter how much it still hurt to walk around.

Which was why I was sitting here, in this dark and dingy bar, waiting for the man we'd arranged to meet before that truck had barreled into us.

I reached for my Coke and did a quick scan of the bar. It wasn't a place I would have chosen, though I could see the appeal to a sea dragon. Situated in the Marina district of San Francisco, the bar was dark and smoky, and the air thick with the scent of beer, sweaty men, and secrets. Tables hid in dim corners, those sitting at them barely visible in the nebulous light.

There was no one human in those shadows.

A long wooden bar dominated one side of the venue, and the gleaming brass foot railing and old-style stools reminded me of something out of the old West—although the decor of the rest of the place was more ship-related than Western-themed, with old rope ladders, furled sails, and a ship's wheel taking pride of place on the various walls.

I'd attracted plenty of attention when I'd first walked in, and I wasn't entirely sure whether it was due to the fact that I was the only female in the place, or the rather prominent scar on my forehead. Most of the men had quickly lost interest once I'd sent a few scowls their way, but the bartender—a big, swarthy man of indiscriminate age—seemed to be keeping an eye on me. While some part of me figured he simply didn't want trouble, something about it bothered me nonetheless.

Then the door to my right opened, briefly silhouetting the figure of a man. He was thick-set but tall, and his hair was a wild mix of black, blue, and green, as if some artist had spilled a palette of sea-colored paints over his head.

When my gaze met his, he nodded once, then stepped into the room.

I took another sip of Coke and waited. He weaved his way through the mess of tables and chairs, his movements deft and sure, exhibiting a fluid grace so rare in most people.

Of course, he *wasn't* most people. He was one of the other ones. One of the monsters.

"Angus Dougall, at your service," he said, his deep, somewhat gruff voice holding only the barest hint of a Scottish brogue. "Sorry I was so late, but there were protestors up on Mission Street and the traffic was hell. You want another drink?"

"Not at the moment, thanks. And why meet here if it was so far out of your way?"

"Because I know these parts well enough."

Implying that he felt safer here than anywhere else, I guessed. He took off a blue woolen peacoat that had seen better years and tossed it over the back of the chair opposite, then walked to the bar. He was, I thought with amusement, very much the image of a sea captain of old, complete with jaunty cap and a pipe shoved in his back pocket. His multicolored hair was wild and scraggly, his skin burned nut-brown by the sun, and his beard as unkempt as his hair. All that was missing was the parrot on his shoulder. And the wrinkles—because despite looking like an old-style sea captain, he couldn't have been any older than his mid-forties.

Only I doubt he'd ever been near a boat in his life. Sea dragons had no need for that mode of transport. Not according to Leith—a friend who was currently running a background check on Dougall. And he should know, because he was a sea dragon himself.

Angus came back with a beer in his hand and sat down. His gaze swept my face, lingering on the half-healed wound that snuck out from my hair to create a jagged line across half my forehead. Once it was fully healed, it would be barely visible, but right now it was fucking ugly.

Which was a small price to pay, considering the other option. Tears touched my eyes and I blinked them away rapidly. Now was *not* the time to grieve. I had far too much to do before I could give in to the pain and hurt and loss.

Angus took a sip of his beer then said, "I wasn't actually expecting you to make it today. I thought you'd been in an accident?"

Fear prickled my spine. I took a drink to ease the sudden dryness in my throat and wondered if he'd been behind the wheel of that truck. Wondered just how safe I was in this bar, even with the dozen or so strangers around us.

"I was."

"You look okay."

"I am." My fingers tightened around the glass. "Who told you about the accident?"

Certainly *I* hadn't mentioned it when I'd finally received my possessions from the mangled car and had given him another call. In fact, I hadn't told anyone—although that hadn't stopped Leith from ringing the hospital frantically to see if I was all right. But then, he had other methods of finding these things out.

Angus shrugged. "I saw it mentioned in the *Chronicle*."

If the *Chronicle* had run an article on the accident, why hadn't they contacted me? I was, after all, one of their reporters. But I could sense no lie in his words or in his expression, and reading a newspaper had been the last thing on my mind when I'd awoken in hospital. For all I knew, he *was* telling the truth. Yet there was a strange tension emanating from him, and that made me uneasy. I eased my grip a little on the glass and took a sip.

"I was also told you're draman," he continued.

Meaning someone *had* been checking up on me. And given the accident, that couldn't be a good thing—especially considering I wasn't exactly popular at home. I knew for a fact that many in my clique hoarded a grudge as avidly as they collected all things shiny—which was the reason behind my original move to San Francisco.

It was entirely possible that one of those long-hoarded grudges was the reason behind Rainey's death. After all, someone had given that deep-voiced man my cell phone number, and Mom still lived within the clique's compound. She was extraordinarily trusting when it came to the dragons that she lived with and loved.

And just because I was presuming it was linked to our quest to discover the reason behind the death of Rainey's sister didn't mean that it actually was.

And if I was wrong, then Rainey would pay.

But I wasn't wrong. I felt that with every inch of my being.

"What does it matter to you what I am?" I asked, wondering if he, like many full dragons, held a grudge against those of us who weren't.

It was a sad fact that most full-bloods considered us a blight on the dragon name. In times past, it had been common practice amongst the dragon cliques to regularly cull the draman ranks. These days, such practices were outlawed by the dragon council, but I very much doubted it was done to protect us. The fact was, humans were encroaching on dragon land more and more, and mass cleansings—as they were called—were bound to attract notice sooner or later. It said something about the council's desperation to avoid human notice that they were allowing our numbers to increase.

But if Angus was one of *those* dragons, then I wasn't entirely sure what my next step would be. I desperately needed the information he apparently had, but he was a sea dragon and a man besides. He had me bested in both strength *and* skill.

He took a sip of beer, his face giving little away. White froth briefly decorated his wiry beard before he wiped it away. "You're a member of the Jamieson clique, aren't you?"

Again that sliver of fear ran down my spine. Maybe I'd stepped out of the frying pan and into the fire—and this wasn't the sort of heat I could control. Not if things went wrong. "How do you know that?"

"Because I'm not stupid enough to meet anyone without checking up on them first."

"And if you're inferring that I am, then you're mistaken." Although he wasn't. Not entirely.

A smile briefly touched his mouth before disappearing. "Jamieson's one of the oldest ones, isn't it?"

I raised an eyebrow. "They're all old, simply because there are no new cliques. There haven't been, for hundreds of years."

The rogue towns certainly didn't count. Not yet, anyway—although I had no doubt that the council would move on them sooner or later. They seemed to think the only way to stop the humans from discovering us was to rule us all with the iron fist of fear and retribution.

Which is why Rainey and I had thought that the council might be behind the cleansings of both Stillwater and Desert Springs. But the clues weren't really adding any support to that.

Angus took another sip of beer, then leaned forward, blue eyes wary as he said, "Prove you are who you say."

"What? Why?"

"Because I need to be sure it's not a trap."

"Why would you agree to meet me if you think it's a

trap?" And why would he even *think* I was trying to trap him?

Hell, even Rainey wouldn't have tried something like that, and she'd had the full spectrum of dragon powers. But she'd also had a lot more respect for full-bloods, despite what we'd gone through growing up.

Angus's smile had a bitter edge. "You ask that, two days after a serious accident that landed you in hospital and left your best friend dead?" He shook his head. "You'd be better off walking away right now, little draman."

He was probably right. I knew that, even if I had no intention of ever doing it. "I can't."

"Even knowing you could be risking your life? These people aren't the type to let anyone off easily. We both bear the scars to prove that."

"What they've done has only strengthened my determination to track them down." Tears welled and I blinked them away quickly, internally repeating the mantra that had become a theme for me this last day and a bit. *Don't think, don't feel.* Not until it was all over, one way or another. "And if you've got scars, where the hell are they?"

Angus shoved an arm across the table and pushed up the sleeve of his shirt. His leathery skin was criss-crossed with a myriad of thickly healed wounds. "My whole body bears the evidence of their attack. They're not going to get a second shot."

My gaze jumped from the scars to his eyes, and I saw the glint of determination and fury there. And suddenly, I knew *why* he'd chosen this bar. Not because it was a refuge for would-be sea dogs, but because it was close to the sea. Which was his to call, like fire was for dragons. He'd drown everyone if he thought I was in any way here to trap him.

I blew out a breath, then said, "What do you want me to do?"

"If you are who you say you are, show me your stain and prove it."

The stain was a leathery, luminescent strip of skin that swirled around the spines of all dragons, whether they were of the air, sea, or a half-breed like myself. The colors varied depending on clique and parentage, but usually involved a myriad of iridescent colors. I'd never been able to shift shape and attain dragon form so, unlike most stains, mine was just a boring brown.

But there were only a few people who could know that—past lovers, my mom, and my brother.

Neither my mom nor my brother would give out personal information like that, so that left past lovers. And while I could name a couple of those who'd delight in not only telling all but in getting back at me in any way possible, both of them had left the clique a couple of years before Rainey and I had and, as far as I knew, had disappeared.

"I'm not stripping in public just to prove who I am." Especially *not* in a bar filled with shadowy men who maybe weren't less-than-savory types, but who were still unknowns all the same.

And you never trusted an unknown. It was a motto that had saved my skin many a time growing up, and I wasn't about to abandon it now, no matter how badly I wanted information.

Angus studied me for a moment, then said, voice still flat, "Then dance fire across your fingertips. I'm told you have extraordinary control."

I frowned. I didn't like using dragon skills in public— in fact, not using them *anywhere* humans were likely to see them had been hammered into my brain since birth. There might be no humans currently in this bar, but there was nothing stopping them from walking in at the wrong moment. "Why is this so important to you?"

"It's important because I've been caught unaware before and have paid the price for it." Bleakness flared in his eyes, and his somewhat fierce expression was touched fleetingly with sadness. A sadness that tore at my heart, and made the reporter in me want to ask what was wrong. But I very much doubted he'd answer that question when he didn't even trust me with the information I was going to pay him for.

Then the sadness was gone and he took another sip of beer before adding, in a voice that was edgy and sharp, "And I've discovered the hard way that lies and entrapments fall from the prettiest tongue as easily as the ugliest."

"Well, I hope I fall into the former group rather than the latter," I said, a little alarmed by the sudden fierceness in his tone. Something was very off, but I wasn't sure what. Then my gaze flicked to his arm. Maybe his fierceness *was* understandable. With scars like those, survival must have been touch and go, even for a dragon who could heal far better than any human.

"Do it," he said, "or I walk out of here now and you'll never get your answers."

I looked around the room, seeing no one looking our way or showing any undue interest. That might change given what I was about to do, but there wasn't much I could do about that. Not if I wanted my answers.

If this guy *could* provide answers and wasn't just yanking my chain.

I mean, the voice on the phone that had given us this lead had been oddly familiar, and that alone had raised questions. But Rainey had convinced me that we needed to take the chance if we were ever to get some answers. And now Rainey was dead and I was here talking to a stranger who might not only be connected to her death, but who might well be here to trap me— the one who had escaped from their little "accident."

And while Leith and his people *were* doing the background check on Angus, I simply didn't have the time to sit back and wait for the answers. Hence the reason I was here, taking this godawful chance.

I had no other choice if I wanted to save Rainey.

I pushed the Coke back then held up a hand, keeping it close to my chest so that there was less likelihood of everyone else noticing.

Then I reached deep down into that place in my soul where the dragon resided. She came roaring forward in answer, heating my skin and making it tingle. But she was all flame and no substance, as usual. I focused on the energy burning through my body, controlling and restricting it, until it was little more than flickers of fire that danced joyfully across my fingertips.

Few dragons could do that with their fire. Most had full flame or nothing.

I met Angus's gaze. "Satisfied?"

He nodded, but oddly he didn't seem to relax. In fact, the tension that was knotting his shoulders and arms seemed worse than ever.

"So tell me," I added, "what you know about the cleansings."

He laced his fingers together, then leaned forward. "I know where the bodies are."

Watch out for Keri Arthur's Damask Circle Trilogy –
full of passion, danger and intrigue…
Available now from Piatkus:

CIRCLE OF FIRE

Sixteen teenagers taken from their homes. Eleven bodies
recovered, each completely drained of blood. Some believe
vampires are responsible. Jon Barnett knows it's something
far worse and, while trying to stop the killers, he soon
becomes enmeshed in a web of black magic and realises he
needs help. But fate gives him only one choice.

Recluse Madeline Smith is afraid of the abilities she cannot
control. But when she is brought a warning of danger and
her nephew goes missing, Maddie must learn to overcome
this fear – and place her trust in Jon. But as the search for
the teenagers becomes a race against time, the greatest
danger to them both could be the feelings they refuse to
acknowledge.

978-0-7499-0919-2

CIRCLE OF DEATH

In one vicious night, Kirby Brown's world is torn apart. Her best friend is dead – killed by a madman who is now after Kirby – and she has no idea why. Doyle Fitzgerald has been sent to Melbourne to hunt down the killer but what he doesn't expect to find is a circle of witches, and a sorceress determined to take that power for herself. And he certainly isn't expecting to play bodyguard to a woman who is more than she seems.

But while inexplicably drawn to Doyle, Kirby fears trusting him because of the magic that lies in his soul. Because Doyle isn't the only one with power – Kirby's magic is capable of destroying the world.

978-0-7499-0917-8

CIRCLE OF DESIRE

In ten years of working for the Damask Circle, shapeshifter Katherine Tanner has never come across anything that goes after kids the way this monster does. It's not something she wants to confront but with the Circle's resources stretched to the limit, she's given very little choice. And the last thing she needs is interference from a cop who has no idea what he's up against.

Ethan Morgan's niece is missing and he's determined to bring her back alive, even if he has to break every law in the land to do it. He will use anyone to achieve his aims – even a woman who claims to be a witch. Yet time is ticking away and the monster rarely keeps victims alive for more than seven days, and four of those days have already passed.

978-0-7499-0918-5

Other bestselling titles available by mail: